Varangian

Varangian

Stuart G. Yates

Copyright (C) 2018 Stuart G. Yates
Layout design and Copyright (C) 2021 by Next Chapter
Published 2021 by Next Chapter
Cover art by Cover Mint
This book is a work of fiction. Names, characters, places, and incidents are the product of the author's imagination or are used fictitiously. Any resemblance to actual events, locales, or persons, living or dead, is purely coincidental.
All rights reserved. No part of this book may be reproduced or transmitted in any form or by any means, electronic or mechanical, including photocopying, recording, or by any information storage and retrieval system, without the author's permission.

Author's Note

The great luxury of the novelist is that they can create and invent as much as they wish. This is sometimes called 'artistic license'. I would simply call it 'fiction'. Although based on historical events, it should be remembered that this story, above all, is such a work: one of imagination. The tale is set in and around Byzantium in the mid eleventh-century, when the Byzantines referred to themselves as Romans and their city as Rome, sometimes Constantinople. Harald Hardrada, a real person, is at the centre of what happens. He did fight for the Byzantines, in the famous Varangian guard. Other characters are also real. But the story is not. It is not history. So, my apologies to students of the period, who will no doubt find mistakes, and the inventions are here to enhance the narrative. To everyone else: I hope it might stir your interest and so lead you to discover for yourself the wonders of this magnificent, lost Empire.

1066, Early September... aftermath

The bodies lay in great heaps upon the sodden ground, distorted clumps of mangled flesh and bone, the stench of death everywhere. Over on the far side rooks had already settled upon the carcasses, beaks pulling at open wounds, gorging themselves on this unexpected bounty.

From his position at the top of the rise, hidden behind an outcrop of gorse and rock, Hereward was able to see across the entire area, a flat plain which stretched out in all directions. It was a large, uninspiring field, hyphenated by the silver streak of a river that wound its way along, untroubled by the catastrophe that had befallen the men of England that day. As if to emphasize the fact, Hereward saw grinning Vikings wandering about, the occasional flash of a blade cutting through the air as the wounded were dispatched. The cries of those others nearby who awaited the same fate filled his ears and he turned away, dragging his hand over his face.

"Dear Christ," said Hereward.

Morcar, some distance away, growled. He lay propped up against another boulder, breath rasping in his chest. A long, vicious looking cut ran across his chest. In his hand, itself streaked with blood, he still held onto his battle-axe and Hereward eyed it, impressed. He had stood beside the Earl, in the boggy ground next to river, seen him cleave the skulls of many of the Norse. The outcome may well have been different if there had been more like him that day. Hereward closed his eyes, the sight too much. If only there had been more...

"I think perhaps we should go," said one of the others, a gigantic housecarle, blood spattered, wounded, but still, by the look of him, fully prepared to fight if need be.

"I cannot," said Morcar in a tired voice. "Here is where I stand, here is where I die."

"No," said Hereward, eyes open now, sitting forward. "It is best if you live. That we all live. There is no shame in this. We fought, we lost. Now we must lick our wounds and send word to Lord Harold. If we are to prevail, we must survive to fight another day."

Morcar trembled, his face reddening. "God's teeth, I'll fight them now!"

"Aye, and die." Hereward looked over to the other men, housecarles, thegns, fyrd, and mercenaries. "What good is that?"

"None," answered the big man, and shook his head. "If we stand, we die. As you have said, best to live, get word to King Harold in the south. Then we can avenge this day."

Morcar muttered something, gathered himself and sat up. His eyes screwed up and Hereward could see the pain etched into the lines of his old friend's face. A Viking sword had cut into Morcar's flesh, and the blood ran in thick, black rivulets down his arm. His mail had managed to prevent more serious damage; nevertheless, he had lost blood and that meant he was weak. Hereward knew as much, having lost blood himself many times in the past. Not this day, however. This day he had fought like one possessed and the Vikings had flinched, pulled back as those who came up against him already, had died. Few could live against Hereward, few except perhaps Lord Harold. And the devil himself, of course, the leader of the Viking army – Hardrada.

The big housecarle grunted as he helped Morcar to his feet.

"We must go."

A few feet away, a swarthy foreigner, whose speech was sometimes unrecognizable, set his jaw and glared down to the field. "I believed

I would kill him this day." He looked at Hereward. "Hardrada. I want him dead."

Hereward sneered. "So do we all," he said, voice cold, distant.

"But for me it is ... personal." He looked again at the field, the dead, and the Vikings who strutted so arrogantly, awash with victory. "I have waited so long, so very long."

"Your day will come," said Morcar. "Unless others get to him first."

"No," snarled the foreigner, "he is mine. I will kill him, make no mistake."

"Well, not this day," said the big housecarle. "Today we need to lick our wounds."

"Aye," said Hereward, and took one more look across the shattered plain and the bodies of Saxons strewn across the grass. The men had died along the banks of the Ouse, fighting for their lives, their homesteads, their loved ones. The Vikings had been as plentiful as the grass itself, perhaps twice the number of the English set to stand before them. Many of the Vikings lay dead on the ground, for the Saxons had acquitted themselves well, but not well enough. Numbers had won the day, not the lack of bravery or skill in arms. The Army of the North, destroyed. The whole of England open to the Norsemen once again, just as it had been years before. Part of Hereward wanted to stay, do as Morcar and the foreigner had said. Fight and die. That was the way of the housecarles. He knew, however, that the sensible thing was to withdraw, prepare defences, rebuild. And, above all else, get word to Lord Harold, King of England. To do that, they had to live. He hefted his axe and motioned for the others to follow.

They kept low and moved away from that dreadful, fearful place known as Gate Fulford.

One

In the court of the Byzantine Emperors
Some Years Before, 1042, in Byzantium.

Inside the dark, damp cell, Harald Sigurdsson, soon to be known to the whole world as Hardrada, sat slumped in the corner, staring at his fingers, wondering how he had managed to allow himself to fall so low. A matter of days ago, he and his men had been celebrated across Byzantium as great warriors, fearless, prestigious, without equal. Privileges abounded and, amongst them, the chance to acquire booty, a mere percentage of which had been declared. Hardrada had assembled a sizeable personal fortune, one which would help him to become a leader of repute. His ambition was simple. To become king of Norway. The riches he had accumulated would help in that endeavour, pay for the recruitment of mercenaries. Seize the throne of the Norse by force. That was the plan.

Until a few days ago.

Everything had collapsed, for him and the Varangian bodyguard in which he served, in spectacular fashion. Coming across them at night, the newly formed Scythian Guard overwhelmed the Varangians whilst they slept, slitting throats, splitting skulls. Those Varangian Norse who managed to rise and resist had been too slow; they were bundled onto the ground and pinned down. The Scythians castrated them, one by one, then left them to bleed to death, writhing in agony, their screams filling the night. Hardrada and his lieutenants, blades to their throats, were frog-marched to the cells. Now, some days later, incarcerated in that place, Hardrada could still hear those screams burning through his brain. His men. All dead. Not given to showing emotion, locking it all away deep within him, this time he struggled to maintain an even keel. He gritted his teeth and stood up.

"I cannot sit in this place and rot – we have to do something," he said. It was an empty phrase, said because he felt he had to say something, and had no real idea what. Someone stirred in the corner. One of the others, his companions, Haldor or Ulf, taken with him to that cell, to wait. Hardrada himself now waited, for someone to speak, to lighten the oppressive atmosphere, give some hope to what was, when all was said and done, a hopeless situation.

"What would you suggest, My Lord? Dig a tunnel?" In the murkiness of the farthest corner, the man's fist pounded against the wall. "This is Byzantine masonry. Thicker and stronger than anything in the known world. We'd never manage it, even if we had the tools."

"I didn't say anything about tunnelling."

"What then?" The owner of the voice sniggered and stepped forward. Haldor Snorresson, one of Hardrada's most faithful companions, and a man not afraid to voice his opinions. "We're in a tower, high up above the street. Perhaps we could fly out of the window, jump from roof top to roof top..." He laughed again, a harsh rasp, and went over to the solid door and hammered against it with his fists, shouting out, "Come on and finish us, you heathen swine!"

"Heathen?" The other man, Ulf Ospaksson, took his turn to scoff. "How long have you been a Christian, Hal?"

"All my life."

"*All your life*? And all your life have you believed in any of it?"

"Pah, don't patronise me, Ulf! We're in a heap of shit right now, and anyone who can come to our aid, be it a Christian angel, or an old Norse god, I'll not turn away either." Haldor turned to Hardrada, "What of the Empress?" He spread out his hands. "She will come to our aid, for certain. We have never done anything that would make her doubt our loyalty."

"Nothing *you've* ever done, at least," added Ulf, his eyes never moving from Hardrada's.

"For all we know," said Hardrada, ignoring the barbed comment, "she has been thrown inside some rotting cell herself. If not, she would come to our aid, if she could."

"The one thing that will come to our aid," said Ulf, not bothering to get up, "is a Varangian blade."

"They're all dead." Hardrada blew out his cheeks, "All of them, butchered by those bastards."

"Not *all*," said Ulf. "Only our own detachment. When news gets round, the others, those posted in the north, they will get us out of this, don't fear."

"And how will news get round, Ulf, with us stuck in this God-forsaken cesspit?"

"I'll make a note," said Ulf and he reached inside his coat and pulled out a small, sheepskin satchel which he opened. He took out some pieces of what looked like vellum, together with a stub of charcoal. "My schooling will come to our aid, as I always knew it would! I shall write a short message, attach it to a stone, and send it down to anyone who happens to be passing."

"And if it's a Scythian?"

Haldor piped up, "Or one of that eunuch Orphano's guards? What then?"

"What are the chances of anyone being able to read it anyway?"

A cloud fell over the Norseman's face and Ulf grunted, "Ah ... I didn't think of any of that to be honest..." He looked down at the vellum and slipped it back inside the satchel.

"As I said," muttered Hardrada, "what are we to do?"

* * *

In her private apartment, the Empress Zoe sat just inside her balcony whilst her maid, Leoni, combed her long, blonde hair. She hadn't spoken since rising, the news having reached her late the night before. Hardrada, arrested, thrown into prison, awaiting conviction. Treason, they had said. But what he had done, or had planned to do, no one had bothered to inform her. The huge, black guard Crethus, Captain of the new Scythian bodyguard, had looked askance after he had burst in to tell her the news and she had demanded details.

He had stood, without speaking. As cold and as immovable as a column of granite. A surly, brutish man, nothing like Hardrada in manner, but everything like him in physical form. Barrel chest, arms like slabs of marble, hands so big they could have crushed her like an insect. How many times had she fantasised over Hardrada pressing himself against her, ripping away her dress, plunging into her soft, yielding flesh. The thought of it now almost made her swoon.

Crethus was like that, assured of his manhood, relishing the fact that people's eyes dropped to his crotch as he stood there, imperious, aloof. He was like that now, after delivering the news of Hardrada's arrest. He seemed to relish what had happened, and did she detect a slight upturning of the mouth? It couldn't be termed a smile, more a tiny fluttering of something brushing across his lips. His eyes crackled, the flecks of gold within those black orbs signalling something, arrogance mixed with … victory? Zoe gazed down the length of his body, drinking him in, and as she did so she felt her heart begin to palpitate. The man drew her in, the sheen from his bare arms, those muscles rippling just beneath the ebony flesh, his thighs, like great pillars, and that inescapable bulge beneath his breeches. Her eyes settled on the spot for a moment too long and she felt the heat rush to her cheeks.

She had coupled with Hardrada many times, his mouth clamped on hers to stifle her cries of passion. This man could be like that. Pulsating, strong, as good a lover as Hardrada ever was. However, that was where the similarities ended. Where Hardrada was learned, intelligent, found humour in the slightest aside, Crethus had the face of a hawk, intent on one thing – conquest. A man who expected subservience and, if it were not forthcoming, then his anger would boil and his great, gnarled fist would fold around the hilt of his blade and violence would soon follow. Serious, hard, unremitting: not her usual choice. Nevertheless, the man might still prove useful, if merely to satisfy her needs. Married to the former Emperor Michael IV, her bed had been kept warm by the Viking. As things had transpired her lover, Harald Hardrada, an officer of the Varangian guard, had been dismissed on the orders of the new emperor, another Michael. Michael the Fifth. Since ascending to the throne, Michael had gone through a number of metamorphoses. At first quiet, submissive almost, listening to her, doing as she bid, learning from her how to be a ruler, a true emperor of Rome. They spent the twilight hours studying the history of the great Empire, the ways of past rulers, their successes and mistakes. Michael was an enthusiastic student, both in and out of the royal palace. He learned much about diplomacy, tact and good grace.. Soon, however, the worms began to bore into him, and he changed, deciding to move against everyone he deemed a threat. Hadn't Caligula done the same, a thousand years before?

So, those surly Scythians with their black eyes and black hearts, replaced Hardrada and his Varangian Guard. Zoe despised the new men, even Crethus, despite his allure. She hated their arrogance, and she didn't trust them either. Why had Michael rushed to enlist them, almost as soon as he had surmounted the throne on his father's death? What was it he feared from the Norsemen? A secret, perhaps, something that could topple him? Something that Hardrada knew, something that might cause an already disheartened people to rise up and rebel?

"You seem tense, my lady."

Leoni's voice came floating out of the air like an angel's, so soft, so relaxing, returning Zoe from her dreams.

The empress forced a single laugh, "No. Not tense. Upset."

"Ah."

Zoe turned a little, considering the maid with a slight, sneering smile. "From that utterance, Leoni, I take it you have reached some hasty understanding of my feelings?" The empress felt the knot in her stomach tighten. She hated being judged, or presumed upon, at the best of times by whoever they might be and servants most of all. Leoni had been with her for just over two years, a good girl, kind, courteous, always there when needed. One of the few servants entrusted to enter the inner sanctum of the empress's private apartments. A privilege which, of course, gave the girl access to some of the more extreme Royal practices. Gossip abounded, the most notable snippet being Zoe's relationship with her bodyguard, Hardrada.

There were those in Court who whispered that they were having an affair of such passion that the very icons in all the city's churches blushed. Their love, so it was said, knew no bounds. The high-born Empress of Byzantium, beloved of her people, renowned as one of the most desired women in all the world. A stunning beauty still, despite the years advancing relentlessly, as they do, taking their toll for over 50 years. When she entered a room, mouths hung open in shock, hearts missed a beat, men's stomachs turned to water. A woman to dream about, to worship. And Hardrada had indeed shared many moments of intimacy with her, moments that most dreamed about. Envy and jealousy seeped out of every glance, every muttered comment.

"I am sorry for any offence I may have given you, my lady."

"No offence, Leoni. But do not assume to know, or even understand, the depths of my heart."

"I would never do that, my lady."

"Then why the utterance?"

Leoni allowed her hand to close around the head of the brush. Gold surround, encrusted with rubies, the brush was worth more than Leoni could hope to accumulate in a lifetime. She pulled in a breath, "Because I feel some of your pain, my lady. With the Lord Harald taken away…"

Zoe measured her servant with an unblinking stare. "What of it?"

"It must be as cutting as any blade."

"And just as painful." Leoni's eyes sprang wide, and the empress dropped her voice, "Can I trust you?"

Leoni made a face, mouth hardening, "My lady, I have been with you for more than two years, and never have I given you so much as the slightest cause to doubt me—"

Zoe held up her hand, settled back in her chair, and signalled for the girl to restart her efforts with the brush. "I know that, Leoni." She pursed her lips, breath slipping out, quiet and controlled. "Forgive me. I shouldn't have snapped at you like that. I am not myself. Harald's arrest has unsettled me. I am at a loss as to why it has happened." She closed her eyes as the brush ran through her hair, feeling the tension leaving her shoulders. Leoni was a good girl, trustworthy, a real companion in a cold and empty world. It was churlish to round on her so. None of it was her fault. "Please, tell me what is on your mind."

"The rumour is that he has kept gold, my lady, gold that he had collected from taxes and secreted away to aid him in his desire to be a king, in the far north."

"Is that what they are saying?"

"So I have heard."

A short laugh again. "Well, the truth is a little different."

As the strokes of the brush soothed her, Empress Zoe revealed the true story of Harald Hardrada's amassed fortune. "The riches he has are mine, Leoni. True, some of it came from his official duties, when he would extract debts and the like from outlying regions, but most of it is gifts. I have never asked him what his intentions are … or were. He is free to come and go as he pleases, and if that means he wishes to leave, then so be it. I would never stand in his way."

"And this treasure, he still has it?"

"Oh, yes." She smiled, motioned her closer, and whispered in her ear.

Leoni stepped back, a puzzled frown on her lovely features. "So, forgive me my lady, you allow him to keep all of this, even though he is … I have to ask, do you not love him?"

"Love?" Zoe gave a small laugh. "I am not sure if I know what love is."

"Majesty." Leoni stopped the brush and her voice became soft, thick with emotion. "Love is that stirring in the stomach, that thrill in the heart. Waking up in the morning with the picture of your lover in your mind, the same picture that you went to sleep with. Smiling and laugh-

ing without knowing why, surprising people with your outbursts, always singing and—" She stopped. "I am sorry, my lady."
"So, you are in love then Leoni?"
"I ... I'm not sure, but I am happy. Perhaps that is the same thing."
"Well, if I have learned anything in my life it is that you must seize the moment, for the years flitter by and, before you know it, life draws to its end and regrets have the most meaning."
"Lady, that is so sad."
"Is it?" Zoe shrugged, moved her hand to touch Leoni's own. "Perhaps that is what my life has become, Leoni. A long stream of regret." The empress squeezed the girl's hand. "Seize the chance for happiness, my sweet child, before it too becomes nothing more than a distant memory. Now," her voice became sharp and focused again and her hand fell to her side. "Help me get dressed. I must look my very best and become an empress once more, and address myself to his Royal Highness, Michael!"

* * *

The general Maniakes caught her by the arm and pulled her behind one of the massive marble pillars that lined the approach corridor to the empress's private rooms.
"You have it?" he rasped, eyes darting this way and that, anxious that no one was close.
Leoni smiled, pulled herself free from his grip, and encircled his waist with her other arm. "I have it all, My Lord General." She pressed herself against him and purred as she felt his manhood stiffen. "All and more."
His voice sounded thick with desire, "By Christ, we will rule the world you and I."
She tipped her face back, ready to receive his lips, "But first, I wish you to rule my bed."
"Of that," he said as he brought his lips to her, "you can have no doubt."

Two

"The reality of the situation is simple, my liege." The eunuch sidled up to the new emperor's shoulder. "We have to move now, strike whilst everyone least expects it. Hardrada laments in his cell, her royal highness dithers, the people are thirsty for change."

From his throne, Michael looked down at the small, bloated figure of Orphano, the architect of everything that had occurred during the last few, momentous days. It was he who had come to Michael's royal apartments in secret to voice his scheme for regime change. Zoe was weak, ineffective, he had said. With the sudden death of the Emperor Michael IV, what the Empire required was strong government. Pressures on the borders were growing. To the east, the Saracens were mustering. To the west, the Normans, and the north Russians. If Byzantium were to prevail, it would have to have at its head someone ambitious, resourceful and, above all else, courageous. Orphano had been the one to convince Michael that it was his destiny to become emperor. Michael V. A heady proposal, and the royal eunuch had worked wonders in persuading Zoe, the royal blood coursing through her veins, to support Michael. So this latest plan was received with open arms, and very few doubts.

They had moved, with alarming speed, using the Scythian Guard to neutralise the threat, real or otherwise, of Hardrada and his Varangians. The one obstacle that remained was Zoe, together with her patriarch and confidant, the bishop Alexius. A man of colossal intellect, the empress's chief advisor and most loyal friend. If Zoe were to be removed, then the holy man too would have to go. Michael knew this, but the problem being how to achieve success without raising too many alarm bells throughout the senate.

He considered the rotund eunuch, forcing himself to lock eyes with the half-man. The very thought of him almost turned Michael's stomach; that flaccid skin, rotund belly, pasty and puckered. He shuddered, despite his best efforts, turned away from the eunuch's bald pate and stared out across the sleeping city. "And Alexius? When do we do it?"

Orphano wrung his weak, wet hands together, slinked further forward, breathed in the night air. "If my liege permits—"

"Just give me your council, man, for pity's sake!"

The eunuch spread out his hands. "Night would be best. The early morning." He nodded towards one of the standing candelabra, flames flickering in their gold holders. "When the largest of these candles has died, my liege – that is when we strike." He smiled. A sickening leer to Michael's mind. The new emperor drew his purple robe closer about him. Orphano inclined his bald head, "With my liege's command, of course."

"Make it so."

Orphano bowed lower, right hand sweeping around in a dramatic salutation. "As my liege so orders." And with that, still keeping himself bowed low, the eunuch backed out of Michael's presence and slipped through the great double-doors.

Michael let out his breath long and slow. He moved across the room to the open balcony, took in the view and pressed himself against the edge, taking in great gulps of air, managing to settle the rising nausea from within. He promised himself there and then that once this business was out of the way, the throne ensured, he would move against the detestable Orphano, liquidate him and his repulsive retinue of obsequious supporters.

A footfall behind him caused him to whirl around.

He gasped.

Varangian

Leoni, the empress Zoe's personal maid stood there, an image of complete and total beauty, her thin white robe accentuating every curve of her perfect body. The swell of her breasts protruded through the soft silk, her nipples erect. His eyes locked on them, tongue running along his bottom lips. As she floated closer to him, his erection grew and his throat became dry.

Her perfume invaded his nostrils, fresh jasmine and honeysuckle. He closed his eyes, breathed in her aroma . She drew close, her body melting into his as her arms wrapped around him. "My lord," she breathed.

Michael forced his eyes open. He felt he was being carried away by the wings of angels, lifted up into a state of heavenly bliss. His whole body ached for her, her hand already over his crotch, fingers tracing the outline of his hardness. He swallowed hard, trying to lubricate his voice box, find the strength to speak.

"You spoke to him," he asked at last.

"Yes." Slowly her fingers came up to his chest, pulling open the robe. Her head rubbed against his chin, her long hair falling against his chest. The sensation caused him to moan.

"You coupled with him?" he asked, tongue so thick in his mouth.

"Repeatedly," she said, her voice low, soft. Her lips pressed against his throat, the tongue tracing a thin line across his flesh.

Michael almost cried out. He longed for her to rip away the folds of his robe, bring out his cock, work it between her soft, nimble and expert fingers. Then the mouth … Oh dear God, the mouth!

"He had you," he continued, heart thumping against his chest, so loud, so fast he thought it might burst. She moaned again, her fingers returning to their initial resting place, running over his bulge. "Where did he have you?"

"Outside my mistress's room." She lowered herself to her knees, pressing her mouth over the area where the robes covered Michael's throbbing erection. "He threw me to the floor, plunged into me … he's so big."

"Big?"

"Huge." She looked up at him from where she knelt. "I screamed as he drove into me, splitting me. So strong." Her hands dipped in between the folds of the material, searching him out. "He made me come before he had slid the whole length into me. Just rested the thick, soft head against me, pressing it there, waiting for me to come beneath him."

"Oh, dear God." Michael was in delirium, her voice, those fingers, the pictures conjured up of Maniakes expertly fucking her.

"Then," she licked her lips, "when I had come, and begged him to fuck me, he did. Little by little, sliding that monster into me, pausing every so often, allowing me to regain my breath before—"

"Yes?"

With a violent jerk of her hands, she pulled away his robes, allowing the blood-engorged length to at last spring free. Michael roared like a rutting elk as she gripped the shaft with one hand, whilst she ran her tongue over her lips. "He drove it in, right up to his big, fat balls, fucking me, over and over, in my mouth, my arse, everywhere, until I was completely satisfied."

Her mouth engulfed him, the tongue rolling as the new-emperor ejaculated almost at once, yelping out a string of profanities as he did so.

Leoni held him in her mouth, sucking him dry, trying to keep her eyes open. God, how she hated this. Hated him, with his pathetic little penis, sticking up like a baby's index finger! The humiliation of it. Maniakes knew what he was doing, of course he did. He had to, placing her in this awful predicament, humiliating herself in order to do these sickening things. Lure him in, Maniakes had told her. Do whatever it takes. Capture his heart, soul and his cock with that body of yours. Do that, and we will have him.

Well, she had done all that and more, belittled herself to pleasure this pathetic man. It had taken her some time to discover Michael's weaknesses, his particular penchants, but when she had she had capitalised on it, turning the man into a quivering wreck as she brought him to the peak of sexual gratification. Her imagination knew no bounds, which was a good thing as she could escape into her dreams as the vile little man heaved and sweated above her. Thoughts of Maniakes sometimes came to her, sometimes Crethus, the giant Scythian, sometimes an officer of the guard who had caught her eye, but mostly it was Hardrada.

Almost always, it was Hardrada.

Three

The sound of her shoes tapping across the marble-floored corridor reverberated around the massive, soaring vaulted ceiling. She was alone, no bodyguard to overhear conversations, or alert the eunuch Orphano of her intentions. Flitting between the pillars, glancing behind her every now and then, Empress Zoe of Byzantium moved quickly. Alexius would know what to do.

After Leoni had left her, she had gone to her bed, waited a moment, then fell to her knees to pray. Sometimes, in the dead of night, she would lie awake, conjuring up fearful images of her death. Cold, alone, nothing more than a waxen shell, her spirit gone. Would God embrace her, accept her into his kingdom? She tried to live a good life, baulked at violence, deceit. Being part of the royal family had given her every opportunity to become sinful, but she liked to think she resisted such cravings. Unfortunately, that was a lie. She often succumbed to the needs of her flesh, sometimes with strangers, sometimes with men like Hardrada. She always sought forgivingness afterwards, knowing she was weak. Faith had been her guide.

Was it enough? This was her fear. Because, of course, there had been Hardrada so many times ... God reached into her heart, pulled apart the intrigue, the deceit. He looked deep inside to reveal the truth. Did He truly forgive her?

She pressed her forehead against her clasped hands, squeezing her eyes shut, bringing images of the Holy Mother into her mind. Such images had always been her comfort. The Holy Mother understood the mind of a woman, a woman who was at once all powerful, but desperate and so alone.

When the door eased open, her heart froze. She remained deathly still. Had it been her imagination, or was there someone? Then came the softest of footfalls and thoughts of the assassin's dagger reared up inside her head. She flung herself backwards, already bringing up her hand in a vain effort to defend herself, eyes wide with terror.

"Mistress!"

The voice, low and urgent. A male's.

From out of the gloom stepped Clitus, the young manservant, Leoni's lover. A crown of tightly curled hair, set in the old Roman style, a finely chiseled face, high cheek bones. Some called him beautiful. Youthful, kind. An assassin? Dear God, was there no one on this good earth who could be trusted.

He stooped down to her. "Mistress, forgive me. I have little time."

Her mouth trembled as she formed the single word, "Yes?" Not an assassin then, but what? A new sensation, one of anger at being so abused, so insulted by this unwarranted intrusion upon her privacy. As her heartbeat lessened, and her cheeks burned with rising fury, the boy held up his hand.

He said, as if sensing her changing mood, "*Please,* forgive my bursting in like this, Highness. You must listen to me. There is a plot against you. You must leave the palace at once, before they come for you."

Zoe, Empress of Byzantium, rose to her feet, mouth agog at this affrontery. Had she heard him correctly? How could he know this, who had told him? A manservant, nothing more. Whose ear did he have in order to gain such preposterous news?

Clitus moved his head around, eyes wide, anxious, fearful, as if he believed that someone might be close. He stood up, bowing low. "Forgive me," he said again and was gone before she could give a reply.

Stunned, she sat staring into space, her nightgown crumpled around her, unable to believe the audacity of it all. This boy had broken into her apartments, a disgraceful act, and one that she considered serious.

An assassin he may not have been, but such ... she stopped herself, a sudden thought turning her skin cold. What if he were an assassin? He had come into her royal apartments without any form of announcement, had marched into her private room with no one to confront him. Her bodyguards would pay for their neglect.

Anger mounting, she strode over to the door, tore it open and peered outside.

Clitus had gone. The guards were nowhere to be seen.

A chill ran through her. The guards should have been at their station, preventing anyone from coming in without her consent. She had not ordered their dismissal, so where were they? Pin-pricks of sweat broke out across her forehead. Clitus had spoken of a plot; a plot would first need the guards to be neutralized... ice coursed through her veins. She took her robe, gathered it around her shoulders and rushed outside.

She half-ran through the huge, cavernous corridors of the royal palace. No one was about, an eerie silence, a pall of sheer terror hanging over everything, a precursor to doom. She shook her head, trying to rid of herself of such thoughts. But the feeling of dread refused to go away. Something was terribly wrong.

Nearing the apartments of Alexius, and having gone through Clitus's indiscretion over and over in her mind, she knew what he had spoken of was the truth. Why else would the guards be missing, the palace as silent as the grave? She was unprotected and alone. That thought brought tears to her eyes. Someone was plotting to overthrow her, to bring her down, replace her as empress. But who? Orphano perhaps, the eunuch, confidant and brother of the deceased emperor, Michael IV? Maniakes, the ambitious general with the power of the army behind him, or...

She pulled up short.

Michael.

Could it really be that her own stepson, Michael, the former emperor's namesake, coveted the throne of Byzantium so much that he would be prepared to murder one of his own family, to leave the path clear for absolute rule? True, they were related through marriage, and bound by promises and agreements made to the former emperor, but even so, without her there would be no blood-tie to the ancient line of Byzantine emperors. Such a scheme that would see her removed, or even sidestepped, would be an abomination.

She shivered. The old Roman propensity for treachery and violence still simmered away in the blood of her family. There could be little doubt of that.

For a moment she considered seeking out the giant Scythian, Crethus, perhaps woo him as a sort of ally. The man fascinated her, the way his eyes followed her everywhere, the desire so apparent. They had never been alone, and he had never so much as spoken a single word in friendship, but there was something in his manner that left no doubt in her mind. Men had always been her weakness, she couldn't deny it. She had used her body to good effect, securing husbands and lovers of immense power and riches. If they chided her, belittled her, or left her unsatisfied the way that idiot, Romanos, had, she never hesitated in removing the problem. She was, after all, the Empress Zoe, a direct descendant of the emperors of Byzantium. No man could deny her. And yet, the Scythian was low-born. If she promised him anything, it would all have to be lies, and he would see through the deception with ease. No, the only thing she could ever give him was her body. The way he undressed her with those eyes, she knew he would not refuse, but would it be safe to pursue such a cause? Could such a man be trusted to come to her aid, to help her in this, her most desperate hour of need? It was a stupid idea, and she dismissed it, with some disappointment. Perhaps, however, there were other considerations. To sample his physical charms, that would be something.

With images of his firm body pressed against hers, Zoe had to struggle to bring her thoughts back to the present. She needed help, advice, and she needed it right now. There really was no one else she could turn to.

Alexius would know what to do. With renewed vigour, she pressed on, breaking into a trot, as the doors to the old patriarch's inner apartments came into view before her.

Four

Something Ulf said troubled Hardrada greatly. The giant Norwegian stood, head resting against the bars of the tiny window, the pictures swirling around inside his head, refusing to budge. The Empress Zoe, her lithe body that caused his heart to beat as fast as a racer at the Hippodrome, eyes that smouldered, hands that roamed. Lips that brought moans to his throat, like no other woman had ever been able to do. Why had she not come to his rescue?

He squeezed his fist tight, pounded the wall once and turned around.

The others slept. He envied them, minds untroubled by gut-wrenching thoughts and visions. Women. Damn them, they broke into your heart, ripped it apart, then left it to quiver, destroyed. Why had he allowed himself to surrender to her charms? He should have known it could never be. What had begun as a mere physical attraction soon grew to consume his whole being. And now, she had abandoned him, as he knew she always would. He pressed his fingertips into his eyes. What an idiot he was. The great survivor, the masterful warrior, champion of any number of contests. Damn her hide, he would never allow himself to succumb to a woman's wiles again.

Haldor stirred, turned in his sleep, mumbled then lay still. Ulf breathed deeply, his sleep total. Hardrada allowed himself a smile. He didn't blame either of them. Together they had fought through every battle, crossed every sea. To end up like this, dogs, lying in stinking straw awaiting whatever fate these foul ,effete Byzantines had in store for them. It wasn't right that it should end this way. A Viking should fall in battle. That was the way it had always been, and always would be until the Viking World died.

Not like this.

He closed his eyes, letting the memories return. Together they had gone east, the three of them, searching out profit and fame in the court of the Byzantine emperors. They had become part of the renowned Varangian Guard, trusted, handpicked fighting men, the bulk of whom were Norse. Viking adventurers, like themselves.

"My God," Haldor had said, reflecting his brush with the Christian religion, "this is better than we could have imagined!" They had donned their new uniforms, caressed the glimmering blades of the axes, practiced moves, getting used to their bright, shining hauberks. This coat of mail was like their own *byrnies*, but longer, providing more protection to the groin and thighs. They preferred it and as they honed their skills, so they came to the attention of the captain of the guard, a man known as Umthar. A Saxon of indeterminate age, he had signaled Hardrada to close with him, and they parried and probed for a few moments before the giant Norwegian grew tired, spun, moved like no one had ever seen anyone move before, and unceremoniously dumped Umthar onto the ground, sword point to his throat. The onlookers laughed, Umthar's face blackened.

Two nights later Hardrada, lying in the barrack room, felt rather than heard the movement next to him. He came up, his dagger already in his hand. Fortune was with him that night, for the darkness in the room was as much a friend to him as it was a hindrance to his assailant. They grappled and fell back across the bunks, Hardrada jarring his back against the hard and heavy wooden frame. Cursing, he turned his foe, his hands gripping the man's wrists, forced him backwards.

The dagger found its mark and Hardrada experienced that rush of exhilaration that always enveloped him during combat. The sheer thrill of victory, as the blade sank home. He held it there, feeling his assailant weakening as the life drained from his limbs and he collapsed, deflated, the satisfying death-rattle bubbling in the throat.

Hardrada, drunk with the ecstasy of killing, stumbled to the door and ripped it open. It was not yet dawn, but the many stars sprinkled across the sky gave enough light for him to find the water barrel. He plunged his head into the freezing water, tossed his great mane of hair from side to side, and stepped back, breathing hard, waiting for normality to return.

When the dawn finally did rise, they found Hardrada outside, asleep against the barrel. They took him in for questioning and the Byzantine officer, resplendent in his golden armour, sat behind an enormous, oak desk and scowled. The man listened to Hardrada's story without a word, steepled his fingers and seemed to slip into a sort of daydream. Hardrada wondered if the man had drifted off the sleep and was about to speak when the officer at last brought his face up.

The officer said, "You expect me to believe that the Captain of the Varangian Guard crept into your room at night and attempted to murder you?"

"That is what happened. Why else would I kill him?"

"Why else indeed. Seems you had already bettered him once. Was it your intention to make it a more permanent victory?"

"Not at all. As I said, he came to kill me."

"Mmm..." The officer sat back, studying the giant Norwegian carefully. "You're quite a celebrity, Hardrada. Already your name is spoken of in high circles."

Hardrada frowned. "Oh?"

"Don't tell me this wasn't all part of your plan."

"Part of my plan for what?"

"Sir. Address your commanding officer as 'sir'. You're not in the wilds of Denmark now."

"Sorry. *Sir*." Hardrada forced a grin, "I'm from Norway, to be precise. Sir."

"You're all Vikings though, are you not? And we all know what the Vikings covet more than anything else. Fame. To be a hero. Isn't that right?"

"Some still hanker over the old ways, yes. But I am not one of them."

"So why kill Umthar?"

Hardrada pulled in a breath, working hard to keep his voice even as the anger threatened to overtake him. Anger had always been his downfall in the past. At the age of twelve he had slain his neighbour over an argument about a girl. They had banished him that day, the village elders, and the regret still lived within him, deep in his bones. "I've already told you why, sir."

"Well, I don't believe it. I can't prove it, but I believe you somehow conjured up this whole episode. You deliberately belittled the man in front of his troops, knowing full well that honour would force him to seek redress. You engineered it all, didn't you. So you could bring more attention to yourself, perhaps even step into Umthar's shoes, take up command of the Guard. Isn't that right?"

"None of it is right, sir. I swear."

"You swear? Would that be a holy oath, Hardrada? Sworn on the Bible?"

"It could be, yes sir. I would be willing to swear an oath to it."

The officer considered the notion for a long time, then stood up, reached over for his helmet with its black feather plume and settled it over his head. "I haven't got the time to be debating this with you. When I have gathered the evidence against you, I'll bring you down, Hardrada. Have no doubts about that. In the meantime," he adjusted his chin-strap, "you will begin your duties as commander without delay."

Hardrada blinked, turned his face to the officer as he began to move away. "I'm sorry, sir. What did you say?"

The man smiled. "I'm going to give you what you want, Viking. The chance to become a hero, have epic poems written about you, songs sung in your honour. You, Harald Hardrada, are now *king* of His Imperial Majesty's Varangian Guard." He tapped the giant lightly on the chest. "Fuck up, and the next time I see you you'll be swinging from the barrack room entrance by your neck."

"Yes sir!" Hardrada brought his hand up to his chest in salute and held his breath until the officer had gone. He then slowly let the air out from his lungs and looked across at one of the guards standing in the corner. "Did he just say what I thought he said?"

"Yes, sir, indeed he did sir."

"Holy mother."

"Begging your pardon, sir." The man averted his eyes from his new commander's gaze. "We are not allowed to blaspheme in the Guard, sir."

Hardrada ran his hand through his hair and laughed.

And so it was that he had become commander of the Varangian Guard, and inevitably came to the attention of the Empress Zoe.

That first meeting...

He opened his eyes. The cell still stank, his companions continued to sleep. They had become lovers, Zoe and he. So why, he wondered, had she not come?

Five

Looking up from his studies, Alexius smiled as Zoe stepped through his door. Of all the people in the palace, she alone was allowed to enter unannounced. That might soon change, of course, now that Michael had begun to assert his authority. A new emperor, a new regime, perhaps a new set of rules. The patriarch stood up.

"My child," he said and opened his arms to embrace her.

Zoe, however, hesitated. "Where are your guards?"

The old patriarch frowned, somewhat taken aback by her unexpected question. "My guards? I don't understand..."

The empress swept forward, taking him by the elbow and steering him back into the room. It was a huge space, dominated by an enormous writing desk. Lined with shelves, heaving with ancient rolls and other texts, the light diffused from a dozen or more sputtering candles, it was a quiet, inner sanctum where learning could flourish. Alexius, the most educated man in all of Byzantium, kept this area for himself, allowing no one to peruse his collection of tracts. He guarded it jealously, and his guards kept him – and the room – safe. Or, at least, that is what he assumed.

"My guards have disappeared, yours too, by the look of it."

His frown deepened. "What are you saying?"

"Listen. I received a visitor, bearing news. We are to be arrested, my old teacher."

"By whom?"

"Who do you think? Michael, of course."

"He wouldn't dare. My bodyguards—"

"Your bodyguards are either dead, or have been bribed to leave their posts. I should have known this would happen, as soon as Michael moved against Hardrada."

"The Varangian Norse? This is connected with what happened to them?"

Zoe brought her knuckles up to her mouth and bit down hard into the flesh, "God's teeth, I should have expected this. By removing us, Michael will become the absolute power in Byzantium. He has moved without hesitation, his plans well worked out in advance. We've been out-flanked, and there is nothing we can do about it!"

"Don't be so sure," said the old man. "Your popularity knows no bounds. If he is so stupid as to think he could overthrow you ... the people would rise up against him."

"Without leaders, they would be helpless against Michael's troops."

"So, we will lead them!"

Even in that dim light, she could see how flushed his face had become. "We cannot do that if we are dead."

Her words hung in the air like lead weights. Alexius thought for a moment, then gathered his robes about him. "I have a secret passageway that leads out beyond the city walls. We will make good our escape, move to the outer reaches of the Empire, gather supporters..." He stopped, catching something. Her mood perhaps, which remained stoic. "What is it?"

"I cannot leave."

He gaped at her. "If what you say is true, that Michael has moved against you, then your life could well be in danger – you cannot stay here."

"I have no choice. This is my home and the people would never forgive me if I abandoned them." The old man went to speak, but she silenced him with a raised hand. "You, my teacher, you must go. Do what you say, travel to the north, muster support and return."

"But child," Alexius reached out, took her face in his hands. "He may kill you."

"He would not dare." Her hands closed over his whilst he still held her face. "Trust me. Go, gather forces. The Varangian mercenaries who fight in the north will be easily bought and then, march on the city. The people will rise up and we will reclaim the throne."

"You are sure of all of this."

"I am not sure of anything anymore." She smiled, gently pushing his hands away. "Go, before they discover what has happened."

He hesitated for a moment, nodded and went over to his desk. He gathered up some papers and then moved into the far corner which lay deep in shadow. Zoe heard the wheezing sound of something being opened, a secret door perhaps set in the wooden panels of the wall. Alexius's voice, as kind and concerned as it ever was, came to her out of the darkness, "I love you, my child. Stay safe. And stay alive."

The panel closed again and Zoe was left alone.

As she stood there, in the murky half-light of that enormous chamber, she thought she could make out the sound of approaching feet. She cocked her head and listened.

What she feared most was about to happen. Michael's Scythian guards were coming, perhaps to murder her.

She turned and stood facing the door of the chamber and waited, all of her years of training making her appear strong and resolute, back straight, chin up. Inside, she felt none of these things.

Six

Feeling ashamed and dirty, Michael plunged his hands into the gold basin and swilled his face, patting his cheeks and neck. With hands gripping either side of the bowl, he stood, bent over, staring into the water. Why was he so weak, allowing the demon to take hold of him so easily. Why couldn't he find the strength to fight, to push back the black tentacles of desire that enfolded him every time his mind slipped into thoughts of sex. Perversion. That was what it was. His bishops would flay him alive if they knew. If God knew.

Of course, God *did* know. God knew everything, could look deep inside his very soul and eke out his darkest, blackest secrets. Michael squeezed his eyes shut. Dear God, forgive me my sins, for I know not what I do. A weak, detestable sinner am I ... forgive me.

Michael opened his eyes, pushed these thoughts to one side, took another handful of water and splashed his face, then turned.

He gasped. Crethus, the giant Scythian stood there, silent as stone, massive arms folded across his chest. The black eyes seemed to pierce Michael's soul and the newly-established emperor palled under the stare and had to look away for a moment. This was not something he thought he should do, showing weakness in this way. The Scythian had that effect.

Michael coughed, dragged a sleeve across his mouth and waited. When it was obvious that the Scythian was not going to speak, Michael became angry, "Well? What is it that is so important that you barge into my apartment?"

The Scythian bowed, ever so slightly. "Pardon, My Lord. We have arrested the Empress and escorted her to—"

"You mean the *former* Empress."

"My Lord?"

"Damn it man, don't pretend you don't know! The former empress is now stripped of all her royal patronage, titles and powers."

Crethus dipped his head again. "My Lord."

"And Alexius?" Michael brushed past the guard, moving across the room towards his exquisitely carved bed, the gold alabaster pillars around it coiled by serpents' eyes inset with precious jewels. Thick heavily woven drapes of the deepest purple fell down on either side. Michael took up the heavy material and dried his hands. He turned, an eyebrow arching. "Well? Did the old goat protest?"

"No, My Lord."

Michael clicked his tongue, a little disappointed. He would have liked Zoe's patriarch to have resisted, perhaps receiving a sword thrust through the heart for his efforts. A public hanging, although the best of all possible outcomes, would perhaps allow some dissident voices to be raised. No, a private killing would have suited him, well away from the public glare. Michael sighed. Unfortunately, such a simple outcome was not to be, so it seemed. He would have to learn to accept the will of God, now that he was emperor.

He took the giant Scythian by the arm and walked with him towards the doors, "I don't want him treated too badly. He is to die, Crethus. In public view. I want him to be untainted, unbruised. You understand me." They stopped by the great doors. Michael tapped the man on the chest. "As soon as he is dead, Zoe will crumble. He has supported her for years, advising her, filling her head with nonsense. Once he is dead, she will then have no choice but to support me, and with that, the people will come to me as well." He smiled. He noted that the guard's face remained impassive. "Well, get on with it! Take him to the palace dungeons."

"I cannot, My Lord."

"You *cannot*?" Michael stepped back. "What is this?"

"My Lord," Crethus let his massive shoulders sag. "The Patriarch has gone."

"Gone?"

"Fled. Escaped. We were too late, he had already been warned of our approach. By the lady Zoe."

"By the lady..." Michael's words died on his lips. Bands of iron began to press around his chest, squeezing him in a vice and he felt his legs give way. Reaching out, he stopped himself from falling by holding onto the nearby wall. Crethus moved, reaching out to lend support, but Michael, quick to recover, pushed him away.

"We have to find him," he managed.

"But, My Lord, how? We know not where he has gone, nor for how long. It would be an impossible task to—"

"I don't care!" Michael, his strength returning, gripped the giant's blouse front. "Find him, damn you, and bring him back here. Dead if you have to, but find him!"

Seven

The overpowering smell of rotting straw and hay filled the cold air as Stracco swept the stable. He was about to swap the rake for a pitchfork when a shadow filled the doorway. He flinched, and swung himself around, bringing up the fork, ready to confront the intruder. It was far too early for anyone to be wandering around at such an hour. "Who's there?"

Pulling back the hood of his robe, Alexius stepped out of the shadow and revealed his face. "Good day to you, my old friend."

Stracco gasped, dropped to one knee and lowered his head. "My Lord."

Stepping forward, the patriarch gently placed his hand on the man's head. "The time we have long spoken about has come. The hawks have gathered and they hover, preparing for death. I have to leave the city."

Without a word, Stracco rose to his feet, placing the rake in a corner before moving to the rear of the stable. "I shall collect some food and water for you, My Lord. Then I shall saddle a horse." He bowed before moving over to the other corner. He pulled open the twin doors of a small cupboard and rummaged inside. He gave a little cry of triumph, and turned around, holding up a rough, hessian sack. He handed it over to the patriarch. "I have some clothes for you, My Lord. Simple peasant's garb. Dressed as you are, you would soon attract undue attention."

Alexius smiled, took the proffered sack and peered inside. The clothes were indeed simple and rustic. Ideal. The faithful Stracco had done everything he had been asked, and more. A true friend, despite his low social standing. "God bless you, Stracco. I'll change at once."

Stracco bowed again and slipped out through the back door.

Alexius looked around. There were no animals here, but the smell of recent occupation was everywhere. An oil lamp suspended from the ceiling, gave off an eerie light. He wondered, not for the first time, how ordinary people could live such mundane lives, eking out an existence amongst such poverty. It all seemed so pointless, so laborious. He knew, as everyone did, that reward would come in Heaven, but was it necessary to live out one's days in such a shallow, unfulfilling way to achieve reward in Heaven? Clearing out stables...

He rubbed his hands together. A cold morning, sharp and fresh. Soon the sun would peak out over the mountaintops and a new day would begin. A new day like no other. One full of fear and danger. Alexius had to reach the city outskirts before the alarm was raised, otherwise he would find it virtually impossible to outrun his pursuers. And he knew, if he knew nothing else, that there would be pursuers.

Giving a heavy sigh, the patriarch took off his heavy robes of office and was soon dressing himself in the peasant garb. As he tightened the thick leather belt around his waist, the rear door creaked open and Stracco returned, carrying a bundle and an old cloth bag. He smiled at the patriarch, and motioned towards the great man. "Your rings, My Lord."

"Eh?" Alexius looked down at his fingers. Three on the right hand and two on the left, massive great gaudy things, designed to advertise his position of authority within the hierarchy of Byzantine power. Up until this moment, Alexius had never given them much thought, he had worn them for so long. "The rings of my office?"

"They identify your high rank like beacons, My Lord." He gave a grim smile. "I am sorry."

"Not your fault," said Alexius, and he began to work at the huge chunks of jewellery, twisting and pulling them until at last they jangled together in his hand. "I would never have thought of it." He brought up his fist, full of the rings. "I could use them, I suppose. As bribes, perhaps?"

Again that grim smile. "My Lord, if anyone was to find such items in the pockets of a peasant ... " Stracco shook his head. "Besides, as soon as you handed them over, you'd end up in a ditch with your throat cut."

Nodding, Alexius dropped the rings into Stracco's open hand, who looked at them with something like awe on his face. "You know much about the ways of this cruel world, Stracco." He paused and smiled. "Keep them. Think of them as a payment, for your help."

"I have never asked for any payment, My Lord."

Alexius rested his hand on the man's shoulder. "I meant no insult by it, Stracco. Nevertheless ... "

Stracco slipped the rings inside his jerkin, then motioned to the things he had brought in from outside. "These few things, some fruit, cheese, bread, they will keep you going." He shrugged. "Not much, I'm afraid. I will saddle you a horse, it won't take long." He turned to leave again.

"I am in your debt for this, Stracco. You're a good man."

Stracco paused at the door and smiled across at the patriarch, who stood there, as a peasant, but who bore all the stature of someone far greater. "I do what is best for the Empire, My Lord. Those in authority seem to think that we peasants know nothing of the intrigues that are played out in court. But we do. We hear much. For too long we have seen how the leadership of our once great Empire has dithered and stumbled about without focus or aim, whilst our enemies grow stronger. We have faith in our lady Zoe. We love her. But, if what I suspect has happened has indeed happened," he shook his head. "I can see great trouble ahead."

"Well, it *has* happened. Michael has moved against us. Even now, the lady Zoe is probably being taken to some stinking cell, to await whatever fate is planned for her. She told me of the conspiracy. How she came by such news, I know not. All I do know is that I have to flee, gather what support I can, and prepare for the coming struggle to regain the throne for the empress."

"We know what lies at the heart of the throne, My Lord. In the empress we see someone kind, passionate, caring. She loves us, and the Empire. We know that, and because of that, we love her. The people will rise up against the usurpers, My Lord, have no fear."

Alexius squeezed the man's shoulder. "God bless you, Stracco. You must be careful during the coming days. Watch your back. Spies are everywhere."

"I know as much, My Lord. That eunuch Orphano has everything wrapped up ... but not our hearts, My Lord. He may keep us in fear, but he cannot subdue our feelings."

The patriarch pressed his lips together. A man like this, a humble man, loyal, righteous, how could he know so much, living in a place such as this, away from palace intrigue? Not for the first time, Alexius reminded himself of the power of rumour and gossip and how much of it was true, how talk could run like wild fire through a population. Michael and his new regime would do best not to underestimate the strength of feeling amongst the people.

"Nevertheless," Alexius said at last, "you must take care. Protect yourself, and your family. Michael's guard may well seek you out, if they suspect you have been in any way involved. Almost certainly they will come after *me*, Stracco. And they will stop at nothing to find me."

"Then you had best be quick, My Lord." He gave the great patriarch a meaningful look. "God is with us, My Lord. And you. With that knowledge, how can we fail?"

Alexius smiled as the man disappeared into the grey dawn and he offered up a silent prayer that the man's words would, indeed, come to pass. In order for them to do so, Alexius would have to stay alive, and that meant travelling in the shadows, keeping himself quiet, not attracting too much attention. No one could be trusted, except for men like Stracco. With men like that, the future of the Empire would be assured. Against him, the insidious, all-pervading ruthlessness of the eunuch Orphano, the real power behind the throne. He had, after-all, stage-managed the previous emperor's affair with the Empress Zoe. The rewards had been great. Orphano now languished in the most superb private apartments in all of Byzantium. Cutting off the head of this particular serpent was the only certain way to success.

The cold morning called and Alexius gathered his new, somewhat coarse clothes about him, took up the bundle of food, stuffed it into the cloth bag and went outside to where Stracco was busy adjusting the straps of a horse's saddle. The man smiled, and jutted his chin towards the north. "Don't stop until you are well outside the city boundaries."

"I won't. And thank you. I shall not forget you, or your kindness, Stracco."

"And we will not forget how much you care, My Lord. God be with you."

"And you."

The patriarch eased himself up into the saddle, took up the reins and made his way out of the yard.

Stracco watched the old man disappear into the morning and wondered if he would live long enough to lay eyes on him again.

Eight

It was true what Alexius had said. Spies were everywhere.

The one who lurked behind the large pillar noted how long the meeting had lasted, then slipped through the darkness to his master's room. He moved with amazing stealth and no one noticed his passing.

Standing outside the main room were two guards. Large men, barechested, their bodies oiled and gleaming in the half light. In one hand, they clutched a long spear, the other held a shield, animal skin stretched tight across the whicker frame. Both men brought these shields together, blocking the spy's entrance. He glared at them. "I have news for my master. Urgent news."

The guards exchanged glances, slowly opened up the barrier and the spy went through the door.

Orphano, chief eunuch to the court of the Empress Zoe, reclined on an ivory framed couch, a mattress of studded leather supporting his back. A silken robe, open at the chest, fell down at the sides as he moved, a ponderous belly revealing itself, smooth and perfectly round. Kneeling beside him, a young boy, no more than sixteen, polishing the eunuch's fingernails. At the man's feet, another youth, attending to Orphano's toes. A third stood behind, wafting a large, peacock-feather fan with almost hypnotic slowness. The room oozed with opulence and decadence, the inner sanctum of a man confident in his own power. No one spoke; no one looked up. Only Orphano, who seemed to be expecting the intrusion. He held out his right hand, already manicured, for the spy to take and kiss.

"Be brief."

The spy bent down on one knee, head lowered. "I watched Clitus enter Her Royal Highness's room. Listened to him tell her of the plan to arrest her and the Lord Alexius."

Orphano bristled. A chill fell over the room and the youth behind the couch stopped moving the fan. The others glanced at one another. The eunuch stared into nothingness, chewed at his lip, then got to his feet, pushing the boy at his hand away. He glared at them, "Get out!" Without a word, they did as bidden. When alone with the spy, Orphano breathed out audibly. "You are certain?"

The spy gave a single nod.

"And how did this Clitus come by this news?"

"Through his lover, Leoni. Who is also the lover of General Maniakes."

Orphano stood, his eyes clouding over. He seemed to be wrestling with something inside his mind. Abruptly, he gathered his robes about him and hurried off into a corner of the room, his bare feet slapping over the marble-tiled floor. He returned almost at once with a long, curved dagger in his hand. The spy gaped, made to turn, but the eunuch was too fast and struck home with the blade, burying it deep into the man's back.

Orphano stepped away, and watched the spy crumple. A good man, trustworthy, loyal. Much of the news he had given over the past few months had been of the utmost reliability. He would be difficult to replace. However, things were moving fast. Soon, the Empress Zoe would be sent away, Alexius executed. Risks could no longer be taken. A single word out of place could bring everything tumbling down, and his dream to have his family set upon the throne destroyed, possibly forever.

Sometimes, to achieve success, death was the only way.

Nine

There was shouting in the streets. Hardrada pulled himself up and went over to the barred window and peered out. The early morning sun, a burnished orb peeking out through bands of purple cloud, was barely over the horizon. Dawn. And already the mob was about.

"What the hell is that infernal racket?" Ulf came up to his big friend's side, tried to look out himself, but was not tall enough and stepped back. "What are they saying?"

Hardrada strained to hear. There were high up in a tower, at the far end of one of the streets that branched off from the main boulevard, close to the Varangian church of St Mary's. They had been there for so long they had lost count of how many times the sun had filtered through the barred window. The only thing that punctuated the day was when the bolts were drawn back and the guards came in with the food. Always the same guards. Black as night, bristling with muscles and weapons, and always the same food. Peas and beans. Never any meat. Rarely any bread. The guards brought in a large jug of small-beer and that was what the captives washed the food down with. Tasteless and mundane, they consumed it anyway. There was no real choice.

Now, with the commotion on the streets, the mundane had been replaced by a tiny hope that something, however distant, might be happening that would raise the level of boredom slightly above wishing they were dead. Hardrada listened, and then looked first at Ulf, then Haldor, who still sat against the wall, legs splayed out in front of him. He looked like death, eyes mere slits in a face pasty and drawn. "They are shouting something about Zoe."

"What about her?" Ulf stood on his tiptoes, but he still couldn't manage a view.

Hardrada listened again. "They are making chants, 'Death to traitors, death to traitors ...' Over and over. And ..." He closed his eyes, turning his head so that his left ear pointed towards the window, "Some are shouting, 'Restore the Empress ...' " He stepped down, right hand clamped around his chin, working through his beard. The words unsettled him a little. Empress Zoe was their patron, their reason for being. They had served her for years, fighting across Europe and Asia Minor, keeping back the wolves from the door of Byzantium. Suddenly, within a blink, all of it had changed. Manacled and frog-marched to this stinking cell, without a word. His own men, his own loyal, unquestioning men, slaughtered. And now this. Crowds in the street, angry, raising voices of criticism, seeking justice, perhaps even revenge. "Restore the Empress, Death to traitors".

"What has happened, do you think?"

Hardrada looked at Ulf and shook his head. "I don't know. But if the mob is in the street, it must be serious. I can only guess that Zoe, in some vile way, has been overthrown."

"Overthrown?" Ulf staggered away, looked down at Haldor. "Could that be possible?"

"It would make everything fall into place," said Hardrada. "The reason we were attacked, imprisoned here. There has been a coup of some sort, Empress Zoe overthrown, the crown seized by—"

"Maniakes."

The others looked down at Haldor, who spoke for the first time that day. He sounded weak, his voice mirroring the pallor on his face.

"That vermin wouldn't have the balls," muttered Ulf. He paced up and down the cell, his feet kicking through the damp, stinking straw that covered the floor.

"Nor the intelligence," added Haldor. He looked up, "Although he is a sneaky bastard. Good in a fight, best general the Byzants have had for over a generation. Maybe more."

"Then it has to be Orphano," said Hardrada.

"That bastard?" Ulf stopped, rubbed his face with both hands. "He would never be able to muster the Scythians. They hate him as much as we do. It has to be Maniakes."

"No," said Hardrada. "I think I know. Something I've always known. I've watched them, talking in little huddles, sending their spies to watch us, the Empress, the patriarch Alexius, everyone."

"Who then?"

"It's simple. They are in it together. A power-bloc of three, led by the only man who could possibly seize the throne for himself."

"Michael."

Hardrada and Ulf both looked at Haldor and nodded their heads. Hardrada said, "No one else. He is a legitimate claimant, the others are not. Royal blood courses through his veins, and that would make him eligible in the eyes of the Church, the only real validation needed."

"But they couldn't move against the Empress without reason," said Haldor.

"They've concocted some lie about her. Probably something to do with money, or…"

"Infidelity?"

The silence yawned around them. Hardrada looked away from his old friends. Haldor's single word had cut deep, striking into his heart. The rumours had always been there, but never spoken in Hardrada's presence. Everyone feared the giant Norwegian. It was there, nevertheless, the insinuation. Hardrada and Zoe. Lovers. In the depths of the night, it was said, he would slink to her room, slide under her bedclothes, ravage her body. That is what they all believed, and Hardrada knew it. Their small minds fastened on the belief that it was purely a physical need, a drug that had to be taken and taken regularly to quell the burning. If only they knew. If only they understood.

"It's all lies," said Hardrada, his voice small. It wasn't lies, just distortion. He had no desire to enlighten anyone of the truth at that moment.

Ulf said, "So why the angry mob?"

Hardrada shrugged. "Isn't it obvious? Zoe. The people love her, always have done. She has no airs and graces, showers them with gifts, festivals, entertainments. When they are hungry, she opens up the grain stores, when they are hot she turns on water sprinklers, when they are bored, she organizes games. They respond with affection. And loyalty." He grinned, "By God, if those three believed they could oust her without causing massive unrest, then they have seriously underestimated the depth of feeling that runs through the streets."

"It could be something we could use to our advantage," said Ulf, pacing again. "If there was some way we could support her, show the people, everyone, that we remain loyal."

"Help restore her," said Hardrada, almost to himself. "That is what the people seem to be saying. Already word has leaked out to the masses…I think you're right, Ulf. If we could be seen to be supporting the empress, as we always have, our rewards could be great."

"You two seem to be forgetting one tiny factor in all of this," Haldor adjusted his position against the wall, stretching out his legs even more. "We are locked up in this godforsaken place. How do you propose we get out?"

Hardrada grinned, "I thought you might ask that."

"It is quite a pressing problem."

"Yes. And the solution is simple. Now that we know what is happening, we can break out and help. Our future would be guaranteed if Zoe were returned to the throne."

"Not wanting to labour the point," said Haldor without any enthusiasm, "how?"

Hardrada's grin widened. "Bribery."

Ten

Ranulph 'Strongbeard' sat at his table, playfully jabbing at the wooden surface with the point of his knife. He was absently carving runes, having listened to what the old man had said. Now, with the silence, he had to think.

"All of them dead."

"So I am told. Hardrada and his immediate comrades lie awaiting their fate in a cell. No doubt they will face the executioner as soon as Her Royal Highness, the Empress Zoe has been taken elsewhere."

"They will not kill her?"

"That would be suicide, and they know it."

Ranulph finished the runes, brushed away the slivers of wood left behind after his carving, and sat back to consider his handiwork. He had yet to look into the old priest's eyes, judge the authenticity of his words. That would come. What mattered now was how to respond to the news that Hardrada's Varangian guard had been slaughtered by those stinking Scythians.

"You are certain the Empress has not been harmed?"

"I am fairly confident that this is the case but the longer we prevaricate, the more uncertain that conclusion becomes." He spread out his hands. "I have been on the road for two days and nights, keeping myself to myself, sleeping rough, always conscious that danger lay behind every copse, every rock. Nowhere is safe, but I knew I had to reach you, the only man I could trust. Time is of the essence. We must *act*."

Ranulph at last brought his eyes up and met those of the priest. He held his gaze, staring deeply, gauging him, and saw that his words were truthful. Here was someone who cared, someone who put their own personal safety second to that of the rightful ruler of the Empire. He nodded, reaching his decision, and stood up, moving around the desk. "I will muster my men. It has been hard here, the fighting difficult. You need to know that. If we desert this outpost, the Russians, perhaps even the Normans will take their chance, surge forward unopposed. Who knows when or where they will stop. Perhaps only at the gates of Byzantium itself."

"If our Empire is led by Michael and his cohort of evil miscreants, disaster will engulf us all. The whole Empire will disintegrate and not only the Normans will feast on our bones."

The Viking stroked his beard. "I believe you are right." He brushed passed the priest and stepped outside.

Alexius watched the man go. For years Ranulph had led the mercenary Varangian forces on the borders of the Empire, holding back the Russians. Normans were only the latest threat. Byzantine troops may well swell the ranks, but it was the Varangians who were at the core. Mercenaries they may be, soldiers of fortune, fighting for the highest bidder, but their hackles would rise when they heard of the treachery that had befallen their brothers back in the great capital. Hardrada was like a god to these men, already his life passing into mythology. Alexius had no doubts that they would march and come to the great Norwegian's aid, and that of Zoe's too.

Taking the opportunity, Alexius reached out for the flagon of wine that sat on the table top and quaffed his thirst. Then he took up a few crusts of bread and the cheese that Ranulph had left behind and crammed them into his mouth. He closed his eyes and moaned. The simple food was like a feast. He had not eaten for well over twenty-four hours, the food provided by Stracco having long since been consumed.

Raised voices caused him to turn. Wiping his mouth the back of his hand, he dipped through the tent's entrance and went to find out what was happening.

All around him was a surge of men, rushing this way and that, gathering up weapons and supplies. The camp was being struck and the soldiers were anxious to get moving, the atmosphere charged with tension and excitement. Alexius spotted Ranulph striding towards him, flanked by two other men, fully clad in chain mail and helmets. They appeared grim.

"Normans are close," said Ranulph, breathless. "Scouts have only just returned, reporting that Norman cavalry are approaching. At least five hundred of them."

"That sounds like damned lucky timing."

"Luck has got nothing to do with it," spat one of the other men. "Those damned Normans have caught wind of what is happening in Byzantium. News travels fast when disaster strikes."

"Then we have to stand?"

Ranulph nodded. "Aye. Stand we do, defeat the bastards, then we can march south. I told you they would come."

"I didn't realize it would be so quickly."

"Damned bloody Normans are nothing if not opportunists! They know when to strike. We have to stand."

Ranulph barked some orders and the two men ran off in opposite directions to prepare their men. Then he turned and lowered his brows, "You will stay well inside the camp. Stay safe."

Alexius reached out a hand, took Ranulph by the arm. It felt like solid marble, so hard and bulging were the muscles there. "I could help. Give your men a blessing, carry a banner, anything."

"I need you alive, Lord priest. You can stay here and I'll leave some men behind to guard you. Besides, most of my men have turned their back on your Christian god, returning to the promise of greater glory with Odin. They prefer sword blades to crucifixes."

"And what do you prefer, Ranulph? Salvation, or the drinking halls of Valhalla?"

"I prefer," said the Viking, pulling himself away from the old priest's grip, "to win this coming fight. If I fall, you will have to take my men back with you. You can't do that if you're dead." He smiled, clapped Alexius on the back, and strode off to his tent.

Alexius closed his eyes. Imperfect timing. Bad luck was his constant companion since this sorry business had begun. The Normans were formidable. If they managed to break through … he shook his head, putting such thoughts to the back of his mind. He had to remain positive. Ranulph had spoken wisely. Displays of courage by him would be misplaced at this moment; the important thing was to stay alive, for Zoe's sake.

He offered up some silent prayers. One for victory in the coming clash with the Normans, and a second for the life of Zoe. Three days he had been away. Time enough for Michael, Maniakes or that creature Orphano to move against Her Royal Highness. Dear God, protect her. He glanced up towards the iron-grey sky and crossed himself, hoping that God was indeed listening that day.

Eleven

They made love as the sun crept in through the drapes that hung down across the open balcony. He was his usual attentive self, his warm, gentle hands seeking out her sex, bringing her to the point of no return before he entered her. She clamped her hands over his firm, young buttocks as they moved up and down. She loved the feel of his taut flesh, such a welcome change to the slack, roughly hewed skin of Maniakes. The general may well be large, but he was selfish, impatient, always anxious to relieve his own needs. Clitus was different. He loved her, and she could tell. The way his lips nuzzled against her breasts, the tongue lapping at her nipples, cooing as he did so, telling her how much her body pleased him. "I love you," he said huskily, bringing himself close to orgasm, his thrusting becoming more urgent, "Oh dear God, Leoni! Oh dear God!" His cries of passion drowned her own as his hips became a blur, ramming into her as he became lost in the throes. She held onto him, gripping his buttocks, allowing him to take her with him, the orgasm building as his hot seed pumped into her.

He subsided, breathless, spent. She held him, listening to him as he began to whimper. He always cried after they made love, the beauty of it too much for his gentle soul to take. She kissed the top of his head, "There, there," she said. Clitus was a good lover, knew how to please her, but he was stupid. He had allowed ambition to get the better of him, had believed that he knew which way the wind was blowing. He had made the calculations, reached his decision, and had chosen the wrong path.

She kept one eye on the door, knowing what was to come. She had always known it, of course. One day Clitus would overstep the mark. When the boy had given her the news, she had not been surprised. Clitus had been to see the Empress Zoe, to warn her of some news he had overheard. Because of his actions, the plans of the General Maniakes had been thwarted, and now revenge, or retribution was sought. Leoni had listened to Clitus, then rewarded the young man by taking his firm, solid cock in her mouth. It didn't take long, a few moments only. She had heard it said that all of Orphano's slaves were homosexual, and Leoni was pleased to dispel that rumour in the most gratuitous way she could think of. The boy pleased her, and she was pleased to school him, give him instructions on how to best please a woman. She filed him away in the back of her mind for future reference. Unfortunately, his time with her was only a fleeting moment. Someone would have to replace Clitus, now that Clitus was to die. The General had made it quite clear that there could be no other route.

The door opened at that moment and the soldiers slipped inside the room, swords drawn. Clitus flinched, turned and gave out a cry of alarm. Leoni let her arms stretch out as the huge guards took hold of the boy, pulling him away from her. She glanced at him fleetingly, as he struggled in their grip. For a moment, a tiny tingle of regret stirred within her. The sight of him like that, so good and pure. His young body, well muscled, the cock hanging limp between his legs, a cock she would never sample again. Regrets or not, there was nothing she could do, not now. She closed her eyes and turned away as he screamed, "Leoni! For the love of Christ, *help me!*"

The door closed with a resounding crash and the only sound that came now was the retreating cry of his voice. She pulled up her pillow and wrapped it around her head.

Twelve

They came thundering over the rise, spread out in a wide crescent formation. The ground rumbled with the pounding of a thousand and more hooves and Alexius, although far from the frontal barricade, felt the tingling fear spread through his body like a virus. He had never known such terror. His hands trembled as they raked through his hair. He didn't know what to do, or where to go. The tent out of which he had stepped would offer little protection if the Normans broke through. He whirled, looked at his guards. "Will we hold?"

The bodyguard, a wiry individual, with long hair falling to his shoulders, and beard almost touching his chain-mailed chest, shrugged. He turned and spat into the dirt. "We will hold."

If the man's quiet confidence was in any way meant to convince Alexius, it failed. The pounding of hooves was by now very close and he looked across the encampment and saw that already battle was being joined. He saw those first few, tentative probing of the Viking defences at the barricade and calculated the odds. Alexius didn't like the result.

The mounted soldiers, encased in surcoats of mail, and iron helmets with nasal bars that distorted their features, raced to the barricade, veering away at the last moment, delivering showers of javelins against the defenders. The Varangians, shields interlocked, were barely tested, but as the fight continued, and the waves of Norman showed no sign of diminishing, the occasional man fell back and slowly cracks began to appear.

Behind the barricade, the Varangians had little opportunity to inflict any answering casualties and, no doubt because of that, frustration grew. One or two broke ranks, clambering over the barricade to engage with the enemy. Soon individual contests spread out across the whole line, as Varangian foot soldiers wielded their two-headed axes and men and beasts alike fell and died, limbs, torsos and heads littering the ground, a ghastly cascade of red, shredded human flesh and bone.

Alexius had never seen such violence, such endeavour to destroy life. He felt his stomach heave, battled against it, but then something else made him forget about how nauseated he felt.

Nothing else mattered anymore except the sheer terror of what he saw moving straight towards him.

A Norman cavalryman, spear down, had broken through the barricade. Alexius froze, limbs solid with total, debilitating fear. He knew he should run, or dodge, or anything at all, but logical thought had flown, leaving him exposed and unable to defend himself. Nothing worked, all of his senses locked in on the glint of the spearhead as it drew closer and closer. Ears, head, mouth became filled with the pounding of hooves, and the rumbling of the earth as it trembled beneath the huge, solid mass of the warhorse.

And then – more terrifying than either horse or weapon – he saw the face of the warrior, eyes set, teeth clenched, concentration complete, every fibre of his body tensed, unerring, intent on killing.

Alexius closed his eyes, opened his mouth, and screamed.

Something solid and hard slammed into his side, knocking the breath out of him, sending him reeling to the ground. He rolled over, hands coming up, lashing out widely, not knowing how close death was, only aware that he didn't want his life to end like this, in this place, all of his plans unaccomplished. He scurried backwards, hardly registering what was happening. By the time he realized that nothing was, the two men had become locked into a desperate struggle. Alexius's bodyguard was the one who had pushed him out of the way, to save him from certain death. Alexius lay there, propped up on his elbows and watched. The Varangian moved nimbly from side to side as the Norman reined in his steed, bringing it around for a second charge. But he moved too late, and the Varangian was on him, ducking under the spear, grabbing a handful of hauberk to unhorse his foe. The Norman hit the ground with a tremendous, dull thud, the wind audibly knocked out of his lungs. He managed to scramble out of the way, well trained in how to react in such circumstances, and already his sword was singing, free from its scabbard, the blade cutting through the air in a blur. The bodyguard threw up his shield and the dreadful crash of metal against wood reverberated all around.

Alexius got to his feet, breathing hard, unable to tear his eyes away from the furious fight that continued before him. He had never seen such ferocity in human beings as weapon smashed against weapon. Grunts and groans rang out as the men flexed muscle and sinew, spat fury and vile oaths and tried, with every fibre of their bodies, to end the life of the other.

The Norman was a large man, and soon the exertions of the combat began to takes its toll. The Varangian, no doubt sensing this, increased his efforts, and soon the blows from his axe, a blur of solid strikes, drove his adversary back until the man lost his balance and stumbled. The end came swiftly then and Alexius turned away as a great gout of blood spurted out in a wide arc from the Norman's body.

The patriarch jumped as a heavy hand fell on his shoulder. He spun round, only to see the Varangian standing there, face awash with sweat, his mouth gaping open, sucking in great gulps of air. "Damn bloody Normans," he spat. "Come on, we need to get you—"

From nowhere an arrow struck his neck, penetrating deep within the flesh. He floundered, gagging loudly, tried to rip away the offending dart, but already he was falling, eyes rolling into the back of his head.

Alexius screamed again, turned and ran. He made for the tent in which he was supposed to have remained. He wished he had never ventured out, kept his head down, buried himself in the corner. Anything but wander out here, in this wild, unpredictable hell of carnage and noise. He pulled back the canvas entrance and chanced a look behind him.

The Varangian bodyguard was dead all right, splayed out in the dirt, the axe, still dripping with blood, lying next to him, the arrow still protruding from his throat. Alexius felt the bile rising, burning the back of his throat, but he couldn't tear his eyes away from what was happening throughout the camp. All around, mayhem had erupted. The Normans had broken through the barricade and horses and men were pouring through the gaps. Alexius saw the furious struggle as the Varangians struggled to close with the wildly circling horses. Swords and axes flashed through the air as the fight became more and more desperate. Groups of men, surrounded by cavalrymen, were hacked down mercilessly. It didn't seem to Alexius that the Varangians had any real chance of overturning what was – as far as he could see – imminent defeat.

Over to his left came a wild scream, so close that it brought him out of his half-dazed state. A man in a long mail surcoat was charging him, mouth wide, teeth bared, sword raised high above his head. In his left arm, a long kite-shield. It was a Norman and Alexius froze, unable to move a single muscle. It was all happening again, but this time there was no bodyguard to come to his aid. Although his mind demanded his body break into some sort of flight, nothing responded and his felt all of his lower body beginning to melt, no feeling, no strength, just a horrible sense of drowning overcoming him.

From somewhere, he managed to drag up some vestiges of strength and he rapidly backtracked, stumbled, tripped, and fell into the tent, landing painfully on his back. Stunned, he lay there, looking up towards the canvas roof of the tent. Would this be the last thing he would see, he wondered, and closed his eyes as he felt the attacker enter into the confines of that canvas tomb. He pulled himself up and the Norman stood there, advancing slowly, a dreadful smile splitting his face. The man did not speak, just came on, one step at a time, relishing the moment, confident and determined. Alexius could see every crease of the man's face, the wild fury in his eyes, the barely controlled hatred etched within his very flesh. He wore no helmet, only the mail coif affording him protection.

If it was designed to turn a sword blow, it may have had some use, but there was no protection against the spear that erupted through his midriff, meeting no barrier. The weapon's journey through the man's vital organs continued, the leaf-shaped point sliding through muscle and sinew with quite frightening ease. Alexius stared, open-mouthed, as his would-be nemesis fell forward onto his knees, then slumped sideways, felled like any tree.

"Damn your eyes," said a voice, cruel sounding and rough. A gnarled hand pulled Alexius to his feet and he looked into the blond, savage face of a Norse warrior. "Ranulph said to keep you alive, but you're making it fucking difficult, you arse! Now stay here!" He whirled around and returned to the bloody fray outside.

Alexius slumped down on the truckle bed that lay there, and stared at the still body of the dead Norman, the man who would have gladly cut his throat. How could men do this, with such fervour, such wanton abandon? Killing and being killed, with no thought, conscience or mercy. Alexius knew he was in the minority, his humanity an oddity in a world where savagery and violence were the accepted norm. The Scriptures gave the guidance, but no one heeded the words. Those in power appeared to listen, but Alexius knew that they were no different from the people they governed. He had believed that Zoe and her husband could have done something, awakened a new spiritualism, a new world based purely on love and compassion. But even her ideas changed as she turned to a younger man and allowed lust to rule her heart. Alexius knew that he was alone in his hopes that humanity would change, could change. Perhaps one day, but not in his lifetime.

He got to his feet, shuffled to the entrance and chanced a look outside. The fighting continued. Varangians cleaved skulls and Normans speared torsos. Everywhere was the cry of battle, the noise from metal weapons, the screams of wounded and dying. He caught sight of Ranulph, standing on top of the barricade, swinging his great battleaxe like someone possessed. His blond hair whipped around his face, obscuring his features, but Alexius knew somehow, without being able to see it clearly, that the man was smiling. Bloodlust was up, the ecstasy of killing that seemed to run through the blood of the Norse, making them so feared, so indomitable in battle. It had taken hold of them all now, and Norman soldiers fell like so many sheaves of wheat, scythed for the harvest.

It returned then, the nausea overtaking him, and Alexius bent double and retched loudly. More than anything, the numbing fear brought the vomit into his mouth. How could he be sure that the Normans would not prevail, and then what would his fate be? A patriarch of the true faith? Castration, crucifixion … or perhaps even both … he heaved again, unable to keep down the rising, overwhelming dread that turned his stomach to mush, and he became weak, unable to stand and he fell head first into the tent and lay there, on the ground, praying that soon it would all pass.

Thirteen

"If what you say is true," said Haldor who squatted down next to his two companions, "you will still have enough money remaining to ensure your place on the throne of Norway."

"Almost certainly."

"Almost?"

Hardrada tugged at his beard, "All right then – *definitely*! I have amassed enough gold and jewels to buy an entire kingdom."

Ulf grunted. "And how much of it will you promise the guards?"

Hardrada smiled at Ulf. "As much as it takes. I'll give them a sweetener, as proof of my sincerity, and then direct them to more as soon as we are free."

Haldor and Ulf exchanged glances. "You reckon it'll work?" asked Haldor.

"Of course it will! Nothing works better than the thought of riches. I'll have them eating out of our hands in next to no time, you see if I don't."

"But they are Scythians. Perhaps they don't put the same value on gold as we do?"

"He's right," said Ulf. "They have all kinds of strange beliefs. They don't drink for a start. Never trust a man who doesn't drink, I've always said."

"And for once, that philosophy of yours is glaringly true." Haldor sat back. "We can but try, I suppose."

Hardrada said in a voice full of resignation, "Have we any choice?"

The two other men both looked at Hardrada for a long time before answering, in unison, "No!"

* * *

When the bolt was drawn back, with its usual accompanying clang, the three Vikings remained in nonchalant attitudes around the cell. They were half-expecting the guards to enter, as they always did, the first carrying the tray of food, the other two hanging back, scimitars drawn, ready. This time was somewhat different, however, and Hardrada cast a look towards his companions, who had picked up on the changed atmosphere and appeared concerned, their faces clouded over.

"On your feet, Norseman!" The leading Scythian jabbed his sword towards Hardrada, face set in a snarl. "Jump to it!"

Frowning, Hardrada climbed to his feet, making great play of brushing bits of sodden straw from his breeches, taking his time, not wanting the man to see how troubled he had become. "What is it you want, Scythian?"

"The Emperor would speak with you, so get yourself moving. You two, wait here!"

Haldor went to speak, but Hardrada silenced him with an outstretched palm. "If they wanted me dead, they would have done it before now."

"Don't be so sure, Norseman."

Hardrada merely smiled, not wishing to create a situation. He was intrigued, more than alarmed and he allowed himself to be taken by the guards to be marched out of the cell. He managed to look back at his friends and give them a wink before the door banged shut behind him. He eyed the guards, all with their swords drawn, teeth clenched, and Hardrada wondered if his usual unerring confidence was this time just a little misplaced.

The giant Crethus stood leaning against the wall, arms folded across his chest, staring at the former empress with thinly disguised amusement on his chiseled face. She felt uncomfortable under his gaze, his black eyes boring into her as if they were searching out her innermost secrets. She shuffled on the couch, crossed her legs and turn away slightly. The man was an animal: wild and magnificent, but an animal nevertheless.

She wondered, not for the first time, what it would be like to couple with such a man. The muscles in his arms bulged like huge, marble stones, his stomach flat, chest thrust out. The features on his face, the thin nose, the broad mouth, unblemished skin of deepest brown ... if she thought about it long enough, she would have to ask him if it was true what all the servants said. That his member was as long as a donkey's, and as thick as a man's wrist. If she did, he would probably offer to show it to her, and then she wasn't at all sure what she would do. She glanced towards him, and his eyes hadn't moved.

"What are you staring at?" she demanded.

He neither shifted his gaze, nor his attitude. "At your beauty, my lady."

"You are insolent."

"Perhaps. But I know a rare jewel when I see one, and you are one of the rarest of all. Perhaps you should consider being my concubine, now that you have lost your position of power?" She gasped at his audacity, but he continued without a pause. "I would satisfy you, my lady, as no man could ever do. You would be content, live a life of comfort and safety. I am the new commander of the Varangian Guard, my position is secure. In a few years, I will be rewarded with my own villa, on the coast. You could share in that luxury, and become enraptured by my prowess."

"You think very highly of yourself!"

He shrugged. "I speak the truth. Why don't you allow me to show you what I can do? You will not be disappointed, I can assure you."

Sweat broke out on her upper lip, but she daren't wipe it away. Any sign of weakness, and this animal would pounce. It may be quite a delightful pounce, but... She crossed and re-crossed her legs, lowered her head a little. Her heart pounded in her chest, and she found it difficult to speak, her throat having become thick, tight. His words, so confident and assured, they sent her into a whirl. How could a man be so aware of his skills? He must have loved so many, satisfying them as he had said, and knowing it. And now he was offering to make her his. "I, I," her mind spun and when her hand came up at last to dab at her lip, her fingers trembled. She looked at them, terrified.

In a moment he was beside her, kneeling down, his huge hands engulfing hers. She went to move away, but then felt the most delicious sensation flooding through her, one of total surrender. Why not give herself up to this man, sample the delights of his finely honed body? She had had many men before, some good, many not. Hardrada was a supreme lover, bringing her to a height of ecstasy she could never have believed possible. But there never was any love there, no affection. This man, this Scythian, reminded her of the Viking. Apart from his skin, of course. The way it shone, so soft, and yet so strong,

"Madam. Let me take you to my bed. All of your dreams will become reality. Just give me a sign, a simple sign, that you will not reject me."

Her face burned. She wanted so much to run away, to retreat from his eyes, those probing, unblinking eyes of his, burrowing into her very soul. An invisible force pulled her face around towards him, and there he was, a hand span away from her. She felt as if something unseen and irresistible was urging her on, and her mouth opened slightly, the lips readying themselves to close with his. Her eyes became moist and she felt herself slipping into the most gorgeous, warm and soft place that she had ever been to before. His hand encircled her waist and pulled her closer, so close she could smell the heady musk aroma of his body. A tiny whimper emanated from her throat as all resistance melted away.

The door burst open and Michael stood there, purple robes voluminous, giving even his slight frame an imposing look. "What is this?"

Crethus scrambled to his feet, bowing low, "Pardon, Highness. I was helping the lady with—"

"Silence! I'll not have you helping her in anything at all, do you understand me?"

"Yes, Highness."

"Now get out, before I have you publicly flogged."

Zoe felt the giant Scythian tense, but the man remained quiet and strode out of the room, keeping his head low, gaze averted.

Michael watched the man depart, then turned to his stepmother. "A sly one, that Scythian. Not to be trusted."

Zoe still felt her heart beating in her chest, making her a little light-headed. She wiped away a lock of hair from her face, to give herself a little moment to regain her equilibrium. "He seems kind enough."

"*Kind?* Dear Christ, don't tell me you actually believe that!" He stepped inside and closed the door behind him and leaned against it. He studied her. "You seem ... troubled."

She smoothed out the creases in her long dress, more for something to do than anything else. The Scythian had affected her, in a way that not many men had done before. No, she modified that thought almost at once. Only *one* other. Hardrada. But Hardrada was in a cell. Defeated. He would soon be forgotten, his usefulness spent. "Not at all, My Lord. I am merely tired. Tired, confused and," she brought her face around to his, "angry."

He sneered, "Isn't that just like you, Zoe. To be angry over things you have no control over. You don't think ahead, that's your problem. Too trusting, that's another. Combine the two and you might have foreseen the inevitable."

"And what is that? You, seizing the throne for yourself? Illegally."

He dismissed her words with a wave of his hand. "The throne is as much mine by right as it is yours. I am my uncle's successor! You adopted me, My Lady."

"He was only emperor because he married me. And adopting you was the greatest mistake I ever made! Look what you have become, a scheming, conniving little liar!"

"Tut, tut. I have always been gracious towards you, My Lady. But...The thing is, I *hate* the way everyone proclaims you as some sort of goddess." His eyes narrowed. "Everywhere you go, they shower you with cries of 'Empress, majesty', when towards me all they hurl are insults. Have you any idea how that makes me feel?"

"So you turn against me, because the people love me?" She shook her head. "You are making a dreadful mistake, Michael. Without me you are nothing."

"You made me Emperor, My Lady! Don't forget that. You supported me on the death of my uncle."

"I can just as soon withdraw my support."

"Do what you will, it won't be any use – I am Emperor now."

"There are only two, *true* claimants to the throne. Myself, and my sister, Theodora."

"Ah yes, the lovely Lady Theordora! Still enjoying the luxuries of Macedonia is she?"

"When she receives news of what you have done, My Lord, she will wipe that impudent grin from your treacherous face!"

Michael folded his arms. "Zoe, it is for us to decide who is best suited to lead the Empire. You have already spoken for me, publicly recommending me as the lawful successor. Any attempt to repeal that would fall on deaf ears. I have the support of Orphano, with all of his administrative machinery of government behind him, and Maniakes, with his army. What have *you* got, my lady?"

"The people."

"*The people*?" He gave a short laugh. "The people will do as they are told. If they don't," he ground a fist into the palm of his other hand, "they will be crushed, forced into submission. I will have no dissenters. There is only one person whom concerns me – Alexius. What will Alexius do?"

Zoe held her breath. She dare not let Michael see any hint of doubt or hesitation in her expression. He must already know about the patriarch, how he had got away, and no doubt Michael suspected that Zoe had warned him. Spies were everywhere, sifting out information, scraps of news. No doubt they had discovered something about the servant, Clitus? Loyal to the Empress Zoe, he had risked his life to tell her what he had overheard. If Michael had discovered the truth, even suspected it...

Michael was grinning, and Zoe didn't like that. He seemed too sure of himself, as if he had news, or knowledge of some sort. Could it be that he had already captured the Patriarch, brought him back to the capital in chains?

The Emperor came around the back of her chair and stood there, his hands resting on her shoulders. Gently he began to knead the bunched muscles, his fingers working away at her tension with surprising expertise. She tried to flinch away, but his fingers felt good and her eyes slowly began to close, allowing herself to relax.

"The thing is," he said, his voice sounding far away, as soft as a gentle cloud floating across a summer sky. Soft, slow, comforting. "I know that you warned Alexius about what was about to happen. You mustn't think that these things simply pass me by. I know everything about what goes on in these vaulted halls. The palace does not hold its secrets from me. I know, because that little shit Clitus told me." Her eyes snapped open, body jerking upright. His fingers responded, working with more urgency at her muscles. She grew more relaxed almost at once. "Don't be afraid, my sweet. What you have to understand is, I have won. As soon as you embrace that fact, then you can begin to live some sort of a life, perhaps not the life you have been used to, but a life nevertheless. I'm not a fool, despite the fact that you think I am. I know what the people want, regardless of my feelings towards them, that they adore you, love you. If you were to stand beside me, support me, then surely you can see that the Empire would profit."

"Support you?" She had not wanted to speak. She was drifting, his expert fingers working their magic, the way her late husband's used to. She longed for the sensations that travelled through her to continue, to not cease for hours. "I wish you would call me *Mother*."

"I've never been comfortable calling you *Mother*." He laughed, pressed his lips close to her ear. "Especially with the rumours."

"Which were never proven. They were all nonsense." She fought to open her eyes, bring herself out of the wonderful place his gentle massage had taken her. She reluctantly pulled herself free and stood up. Turning, she studied him for a moment. Small, thin, always a sickly teenager he hadn't really changed very much over the years. The pasty complexion, the oil black hair, eyes red-rimmed with either tiredness or some sort of malady, Zoe could never work out which. Now, emperor of the Byzantine Empire? How ludicrous did that sound? It was clear to her that the power behind the throne were the two others, Maniakes and Orphano, both of them schemers and plotters. She hated them both, especially that vile slug of a man, Orphano. Brother to the last emperor, he believed that royal blood ran through him, making his treachery all the more painful to bear. "You have always blamed me for your uncle's death … the truth is, Michael, he died from fever."

"Convenient. For you."

"For me? How so? I am of true royal blood! It was your uncle who made overtures to me, not the other way round."

"You expect me to believe that? The richest, most powerful man in Byzantium? He controlled the trade routes to Egypt in the south, and Rome in the West. Married to him, your position became invincible. But you poisoned even that relationship, didn't you."

Zoe turned away at the mention of that word. Poison. How many times had it been used in connection with her, mentioned almost in the same breath? Zoe, the poisoner. The rumours abounded that she had poisoned her previous husband, Constantine Romanos, had watched him flounder in his bath, and drown beneath the soap-covered water. Her decision to immediately run to her lover's apartments and pronounce him as the new leader of the Byzantine Empire seemed to surprise no one. Her lover, the youthful, vigorous Michael who had swept her off her feet even whilst she was married to the old emperor. The one she had made so many promises to, and now had made emperor. At first, it had proved a good decision. The people accepted him with great rejoicing. They had hated Romanos, his false piety, his gluttony, avarice. The new lover, Michael, seemed to offer a new, youthful vigour to the Empire. Zoe had manipulated it all, had everything ready so that as soon as the old emperor was gone, snuffed out, she could embrace the next. Crowned together, clad in state robes woven with gold thread, a hundred pounds of gold offered over to the Church to sanctify their union. Married and crowned within three days of the late emperor's death. No one asked, no one dared cast aspersions on the unseemly haste. The Patriarch Alexius had smiled his thanks and Zoe had kissed her husband. The new emperor, Michael IV.

"He died of natural causes," she said softly. It was true. She had been told whilst she sat in her private apartments, locked away by the very same husband that had been so loving and attentive towards her. He had turned against her, jealous. And now his nephew, the new emperor, another Michael, was about to do exactly the same. Dear God, why was she so accursed?

"I am to become sole ruler," said Michael, ignoring her words. "And you will support me, or I will banish you."

She glared at him. "*Banish me*? Why not simply murder me, and have done with it?"

"Don't tempt me."

"You pathetic little worm," she scoffed. "How did I ever think that you could rule as emperor?"

He pulled in a deep breath. "Will you support me?"

Her eyes never left his. "Not whilst I am capable of taking a single breath."

He winced, as if struck, and for a moment she thought that he might relent. Was there still a flicker of humanity hiding somewhere, deep within him?

"So be it," he said, his voice curiously flat and he turned and left the empress alone with her thoughts of miscalculations and machinations all turned sour.

Fourteen

They led Hardrada into what seemed to be some sort of ante-chamber, a side office to a much larger room beyond. A clerk sat at a small table, scribbling away on a collection of parchments, and barely looked up when the guards came through the door with the Viking between them.

"Harald Hardrada, as requested," said the third guard, squeezing passed the others.

The clerk didn't seem to notice and Hardrada couldn't help but smirk, sensing the Scythian commander's irritation. "Did you hear what I said?"

Putting down his quill, the clerk looked up, a bored expression on his face and said something in a language no one seemed to understand, then moved over to the large, double-door against the opposite wall. He pressed his ear against the solid oak whilst rapping it with his knuckles. A muffled grunt came from within and the clerk opened one of the doors, put his head inside and spoke again. Another grunt and the clerk returned to his desk, motioning to the still open door.

"Ignorant little ponce," said the commander and pushed Hardrada hard in the back. "Move in there, you bastard!"

Still smirking, Hardrada allowed himself to be shoved into the room. The owner of the grunt, seated behind his own desk, scribbled frantically across a massive roll before him. He did not acknowledge his visitors for a few moments. No one spoke and Hardrada took the opportunity to look around him. Marble pillars soared up towards the ornately decorated ceiling, inlaid with strands of silver. The walls, large, sweeping and majestic, were dotted with religious icons, some of them larger than any Hardrada had seen before. An air of solemnity pervaded everything. Here, time moved very slowly.

At last the man put down his quill with exaggerated care and looked up. An expressionless mask, meaty, a sheen of sweat lay across the sallow skin. His shaven head gleamed in the half-light of the many candles that gave off a sickly, oily light. He said, "Close the door behind you."

Exchanging looks, the guards hesitated.

John Orphano, chief eunuch to the Emperors of Byzantium and one of the most powerful men to have ever graced that position, sighed loudly and scowled at the soldiers. "In other words, *get out.*"

The Scythian commander spread out his hands, "But sir, this man is dangerous!"

"Your concern is noted, commander. Now piss off!"

This time Hardrada laughed out loud, watching the Scythians seethe with barely contained fury. The commander's eyes flashed towards the Norwegian, "I'll talk to you later."

Hardrada shrugged, then waited, manacled hands clasped in front of him, until the guards had gone. Then he walked over to a padded couch that ran along the far wall and sat down. Orphano didn't say a word and returned to his scribbling.

Stretching out his legs, Hardrada took another look around him, taking in the subdued opulence. In a room like this, a man could grow fat, slack. A tempting proposition, to live out one's days in such an idle manner. It was comfortably warm, heated by an under-floor system that kept the temperature constant. Dotted around were candelabra, with candles burning, sending out their sickly glow to every corner. There were no windows, but on the opposite wall hung, not icons, but a massive tapestry, with scenes of rolling hills, a river, and doves filling the air. In the river, a man, pouring water over another's head. "The Baptist," he said. "Anointing Christ."

Orphano looked up. "I'm pleased to see you have some knowledge of Scripture, Viking."

"Only what I've been told. I've never read the book myself."

"The *book*?" The eunuch sat back, hands dropping over his impressive paunch. "Be careful not to become blasphemous, Viking. That would never do."

"I thought blasphemy was to do with God, not his words."

"Then you thought wrongly. Blasphemy can be anything the Church deems it to be."

"But, as you have so indelicately pointed out, I am a Viking. Not a Christian."

Orphano frowned, "You still hanker over your old beliefs? Interesting. Even now, with your world turned upside down, don't you stop to question any of it?"

"You think my situation might be better if I believed in your God?" He shook his head. "The Scythians are not Christian, yet they now strut around pretending to be Varangians. There is more than the simple choice of belief in what has happened to me and my men. Treachery and deceit are beyond religion."

"You're quite the philosopher, Hardrada. I'm impressed."

The Viking sat forward, resting his manacled arms on his knees and measured Orphano with an icy stare. "Why don't you just get to the reason why you have brought me here?"

Orphano picked up the quill, studied it for a moment, then threw it across the desk and stood up. He stretched, exhaling in something like ecstasy. "I work too many hours at this damned job," he said. "The machinery of government is in constant need of supervision." He came around the desk and examined Hardrada for many seconds, as if considering him for the first time. "Diplomacy, Hardrada. Do you know anything about it?"

"Not a thing."

"You should. It is the most important aspect of government. Without it, we would not survive. The Empire is pressed on all sides. Arabs to the south, Saracens and Persians to the East, Bulgars and Russians to the north, and to the west ... Normans. It is a constant tangle of intrigue that I have to work with – promises, bribery, gifts and acquiescence. It is what keeps us all alive. The great days of Rome are long gone. We can no longer maintain all our frontiers, and protect our capital from these many pressures, we have neither the resources nor the manpower. And now, with a change of emperor, the pressure mounts. We must maintain our security whilst those around us probe for weaknesses. Michael must prove himself strong, intelligent and beyond reproach. Not only for those outside our Empire who might seek to profit from any instability, but from those within, who may not – for whatever reason – consider Michael as the true, and proper emperor."

"You've got your work cut out, that much is very clear."

"To this end, Hardrada, it would be politic to enlist the support of the Patriarch Alexius. If the Church is seen to support Michael, then the people will unite behind him. With that, we become so much safer against our enemies. It is simple."

Hardrada shifted position on the couch, beginning to feel somewhat uncomfortable under the man's unblinking stare. "Something tells me that none of this is going to be simple." He pushed out his manacled hands. "Why don't you release me from these damnable things?"

"Yes, you'd like that. How long before you had me by the throat, squeezing out my existence? The blink of an eye, that's how long." Orphano smiled. "But the question is purely academic. I haven't got the key!"

Hardrada blew out his cheeks and fell back into the couch. "Then just get on with whatever it is you've brought me here for."

"I'm there already, Hardrada. I want you to fetch Alexius, and bring him back. Not only bring him back, but impress upon him the importance of convincing the people of this great city, that Michael is the real choice for emperor."

"You must be mad to think I'd do that for you."

Orphano smiled that sickly sweet smile, a mere slit across the flaccid face. "Oh, I think you will."

"Really?" Hardrada arched a single eyebrow. "Then you certainly don't know me very well. I would do nothing for that little shit you now deem to call Emperor – and why indeed would you? Didn't the man try and poison you once, before your brother died?"

Orphano coloured slightly. Hardrada pressed on, knowing he had struck a nerve. "So, the rumours *are* true! You see, this is where all you bloody diplomats fall down. You can't remain true to yourselves. You do whatever is expedient for the moment. If it doesn't suit, change it, ditch it, reverse it. Yours is a world not of honour and honesty, but one of subterfuge, half-truths and downright lies. You make me sick, the whole pathetic lot of you!"

"And you, what would you do, eh? Use force, blunder your way through, not caring a fig for anyone in the process. Your answer would be to smash anything and everything that gets in your way, Hardrada. But your way hasn't worked, and it never will. Rome tried it, to assert its might, and we all know what happened as a consequence. We live in a changing world. You have to understand that. The old ways of conquest, they are gone."

"I don't accept that. Strength is the only thing anyone understands and respects. Strength, resilience, prowess in war. They are the unchangeable truths of nature. Of mankind."

Orphano shook his head, "I feel sorry for you, Hardrada. You're trapped in your own myths, your past. If you refuse to adapt, you will perish. Eventually." He spread out his hands. "That is how it is. I can foresee nothing but disaster for you and your kind. So, simply put, you have to try, Hardrada. Try to do things my way. My differences with Michael were buried long ago. What matters now is Byzantium and I will do everything in my power to guarantee its continuance. So, you will go north and find Alexius. You will bring him back, unharmed. And you will convince him, on the way, that his support is vital if our glorious Empire is to continue to flourish."

"I won't do it."

"You will," Orphano leaned forward, his mouth close to Hardrada's ear, " or the Empress Zoe dies."

The Scythian stepped back, allowing the manacles to fall away from Hardrada's wrists. The Viking sat there, rubbing the flesh. How long had it been? Three days, four? Or possibly more. He eyed the angry, red welts and cursed softly. When the door closed, he looked up to see Orphano leaning against the desk, arms folded.

"I'm trusting you, Viking. I know your reputation, so if you wish to attack me, do it now. You won't have a better opportunity."

Oh, but I would love to… Hardrada forced a smile, but inside his stomach was in knots. The eunuch was clever, trussing up Hardrada like a bird ready for the dinner table. There was no choice. It had all been made abundantly clear for him. He either went north to find the patriarch, or he remained here, serving Zoe with a death sentence. The eunuch had always commanded great respect, and everyone knew of his intelligence, his ability to seek out various alternative solutions to the many problems facing the Empire. Now this. The ultimate act. The death of an empress. Hardrada had few doubts that the man would carry out his threat. He blew out his cheeks, "It seems that there is little I can do but agree to do as you ask."

Orphano's face split into a wide grin, "Excellent decision, Viking! I'm glad to see that you can still think sensibly." He went around the desk, rummaged through some papers and picked up a small piece of parchment. His eyes narrowed as he scanned it. "Too much reading is damaging my eyes. Ah, yes, here it is. I sent out an order, to the local commanders of the various regions." He beamed, glancing across to Hardrada, sitting there on the couch, no longer so relaxed. "I am not a fool, Viking. I'm not going to trust you completely. One of the most trusted lieutenants in all of Byzantium will accompany you. His name is Andreas and he will collect you from your cell tomorrow morning. From there you will ride to the north where, as I understand it, Alexius will be found."

"Why not just send him? I don't see what you need me for."

"Well, there is a *slight* problem. You see, my enquiries as to the Patriarch's whereabouts have revealed he has made his way towards the Varangian outpost on our borders to the north."

"*Varangian*? You mean Ranulph's mercenaries?"

"The very same. And they would hardly likely entrust Alexius to a Byzantine officer, would they? Certainly not after the story he has told them about what has happened here."

Hardrada pulled at his beard. "How do you know all this, eunuch?"

The man winced at Hardrada's use of the euphemism. He slowly put the parchment he had been reading from down on his desk. "All you need to know is that if you fail in this quest, Hardrada, the Empress dies. If you cannot persuade Alexius to return here and bring his support to our cause, Zoe will be put to death. Your affection for her is well known. I have every faith in you."

"You're an evil bastard, Orphano." Hardrada stood up to his full height, his impressive frame seeming to fill the room. He saw the eunuch flinch and it pleased him. "I hope that when all of this is over, and your schemes lay shattered upon the ground, I will have the chance to face you again."

"Well, I doubt if it will come to that. My plans are foolproof, but, just as an added touch of security, a guarantee of your acquiescence knowing how fickle men like you can be … your friends – Haldor and Ulf – will also be put to death if you fail in this endeavour."

Hardrada felt the heat swell up into his chest. He flexed his muscles, preparing to launch himself at the sniveling little man, wrap his hands around his throat and crush him. Almost at once, he consoled himself with some loud breaths. He had to maintain control, be patient. For now. The time would soon come when his hands would indeed close around the eunuch's throat. But right now, there was little Hardrada could do. The life of Zoe, the lives of his friends, these things were too precious to gamble on, even if the ecstasy of killing Orphano was something to be relished. He let his shoulders slump, the fire quietening.

"I hate you," he said quietly.

"Good," said the eunuch. "I wouldn't want you to lose focus! Now, get back to your friends and await the morning." Orphano picked up a small, golden bell and jingled it. The door opened and the Scythian guards returned. Without a word they moved across the room to escort Hardrada back to the cell.

"Think of this as an opportunity to begin again," said Orphano. "You have always sought adventure in your life, but sometimes the paths you have chosen have been somewhat uncertain. You have a chance here, Viking, to reinvest yourself in your duty towards the Empire, without being shackled by ambition, or even love."

"You haven't got a clue about me, or what I want from life."

"Oh, but I do," said the eunuch with a smile, and lifted up yet another piece of parchment. "And here I have the exact location of all the treasure you have stolen from us."

Hardrada moved then, all of his previous self-control vanishing, his great fists preparing to strike, to smash the vile man into pulp. The Scythians reacted just in time, each one of them taking an arm to pull him back, whilst the commander swiftly came around to Hardrada's front and landed the flat of his sword across his stomach with a powerful slap. Hardrada, the wind knocked out of him, dropped to his knees, and began to cough.

"Silly thing to do, Hardrada."

Harald Hardrada looked up through blurred eyes and scowled at the eunuch with as much venom as he could muster.

Orphano merely smiled. "This really has to be an opportunity for you to start again, not one to throw everything away. Now, captain – take him away!"

They pinned him against the wall next to the door whilst the guard commander picked out the correct key. "You shouldn't argue with His Lordship, Hardrada," he said. "A wise man would listen, not answer back."

"Answer back?" Hardrada's head was still ringing. They had dragged him along the winding corridors, his feet trailing across the cold cobbles, and they had laughed and joked about what had happened. Now, they were still grinning and Hardrada made yet another promise to exact retribution when all of this was over. "How did he know where my money is?"

"How should I know? He has spies everywhere." The commander tipped his head towards the other two guards. "Some are probably within earshot right at this very moment."

Neither of the guards spoke. Hardrada grunted. "Is that how he knew where Alexius had gone?"

"No, not for that. We found a man, a saddle-maker, name of Stracco. Ah, here it is!" He pushed the chosen key into the lock and turned it, the tumblers making a loud clunk. "It didn't take us long. The idiot had left Alexius's robes in his stable! He told us everything." He winked, and motioned for his men to take another grip of Hardrada's arms. "Eventually."

Hardrada didn't want to think about the poor man's fate. The Scythians were capable of anything, as the testament of what had happened to the Varangian Vikings proved. The door was pushed open and the guards shoved him inside.

When the door clanged shut he saw his two old companions standing there, anxious looks on his face.

Hardrada didn't yet have the heart to tell them what had transpired.

Fifteen

In the middle of a piece of scrubland, away from the numerous scenes of death, Alexius built a small altar from various smooth stone that lay about. It wasn't a large undertaking, but it would suit the purpose. He had decided to hold a mass, to give thanks for the victory. He hadn't thought to inform Ranulph, not yet. Best get the stones laid down first. A few Viking warriors stood a little way off, curiosity bringing them to within earshot. They muttered things in their guttural tongue, things that Alexius had no way of understanding, but he sensed he knew what they spoke about. When they laughed, his suspicions were confirmed. These men were not Christians. Their pagan gods still held sway. Perhaps this was what gave them such strength in battle. The belief that only through battle, to die a hero's death, would they gain the immortality they all craved. No wonder so many of them rejected the holy scripture, with its emphasis on forgiveness and non-violence. Alexius had always strived to interpret the Bible's words, to suit them for whatever audience he had at any given moment. But these men, they dismissed the message of Christ, scoffed at the idea of turning the other cheek. To them, this was nothing but weakness and submission, things so alien to their hearts that Alexius could never see them being converted. He knew Alfred the Great of England had done it some two hundred years before, but with little real, lasting success. The Viking man was a killer, hard, simple and unforgiving. The Mass would be held, but Alexius doubted if many would attend. He actually suspected that none would.

He still built the altar, and stood back to survey his work. Satisfied, he made the sign of the cross and slowly fell to his knees, hands clasped in front of his face, eyes closed.

"Your words mean little here, priest."

Alexius heard the Viking's voice as if he were standing some way off, and cared not for the sneering tone that he heard. He continued with his prayer, crossed himself several times, then looked up, his eyes refocusing on his surroundings. "They mean a great deal to God," he said quietly and got to his feet. Ranulph stood and watched him, a deep frown creasing his hard face. He leaned on his great battle-axe, legs slightly apart. Alexius took note of the man's haggard look, the dark shadows under the eyes, and then glanced over the rest of him. A trail of blood, like a tiny rivulet, ran down his left arm. It had long since congealed, but it was clear that the wound was serious. The patriarch nodded his head towards the warrior. "You're wounded. I will get someone to tend to you."

"No need," growled Ranulph. "There are men worse off than me, and many are dead. I will be healed within a day."

"Still, it would be sensible to have it looked at, cleaned."

"Don't fuss. We have more pressing matters." His breathing rattled in his chest as he spoke, another clue that his wounds were far more serious than he cared to mention. "We have lost many men, and they will need to be buried, in case of plague. We also need to replace them, so I have sent out scouts to our other outposts, giving them news of what has happened here."

"How long do you think it will take?"

He shrugged. "The Normans were heavily defeated. We have some prisoners and we will question them, but my thinking is that they were merely a vanguard, that the main forces lies somewhere in the mountains. They have never ventured this far south before, so they must be brim-full of confidence. This day will set them back somewhat." He grinned, but then was suddenly racked by a bout of coughing which seemed to shake through his entire frame. His skin took on a sickly sheen and Alexius was in two minds as to whether he should go to his aid or not. Then, as soon as it had begun, it subsided, and Ranulph spat out a great gob of blood and mucus, shook his head and grinned at the patriarch. Alexius could see the blood laced across the man's teeth. "They may decide to go back, all the way to Italy."

Alexius kept staring at the man, troubled by the blood and the rattling in the man's chest. "How long before you have gathered enough men to travel to Byzantium?"

"God knows." His grin broadened when Alexius turned away from the man's use of the word. "There is no room for piety here, priest. We may be Varangians, but we are still Vikings at heart. Even those of us, from Sweden – those Rus amongst us."

Alexius sighed. It was true, and he knew it. Many of these warriors, free-booters and mercenaries all, paid merely lip-service to the Christian religion. Their job was to fight, not to pray. It still rankled him, however, that the holy Byzantine Empire should use such men. Its own army, standing at just over one hundred thousand men, was not what it once was. Not so very long ago, during the reign of Zoe's grandfather, the Byzantine Empire was flourishing, as powerful and as respected as in the days of the great Constantine. Now, it was a shadow of its former self, nothing more than a brittle, paper thin façade of magnificence concealing its empty heart. Push it hard enough and the skin would break, and then everything beneath would be revealed. Alexius knew that without strong leadership, and a deep faith in Christ, the Empire would rupture and die. Already its many borders were haemorrhaging. This northerly one was one of the weakest. The Varangians here, well paid, were merely interlopers. As soon as the money ran out, they would be gone. Then what would happen.

"A week."

Alexius blinked. "What did you say?"

"You asked me how long before we were ready. A week. Then we will have sufficient men to march to the city and do whatever it is you want us to do." He grinned, reached over and placed his hand on the patriarch's shoulder. "What you told us when you first arrived. The reward we would get? That will spur us on, so don't be unduly worried."

"I fear for the Empress, what might befall her if we tarry too long."

"It's all in the laps of the gods." Ranulph stopped, bit down on his lip, and grinned again. "Sorry. I meant *God*." Then he patted the patriarch's shoulder, turned and hobbled off towards where his men were working to put their dead comrades into heaps.

Alexius knew that what the man had said was true. There was nothing more to do than wait.

A week? He put his fingers in his eyes and tried to shut out the anxiety that was threatening to send him into panic. The Lord would provide; the Lord would guide; the Lord would do what was right. Alexius sighed, gathered his cloak about him and moved over towards his tent. A week. Please God, let it go quickly!

Crethus moved along the broad corridor as silently as a panther, his huge form like that of an avenging angel. If anyone passed him, they tended to cower away, averting their eyes. He paid them little heed, but he had to admit that their reaction pleased him. Only a few days ago he had been a mere lieutenant, an unknown. He had done his duty, carried out his orders, watched the Lady Zoe whenever he could, but as far as advancement and ambition were concerned, they were things he rarely considered. Then, within the space of a few days, it had all changed. Orphano sending for him, sitting him down, explaining the situation. The promises. A villa, money, women. Crethus had listened and taken it all in, and his chest swelled with the thought that at last his life might have some meaning.

As for the women, he only really thought of one. The Lady Zoe. Her slim waist, the swell of her arse, the way her huge golden eyes would drink him in. Just the thought of her sent the fire burning through his loins. What would it be like to possess her, to run his hands over her soft, yielding flesh, to bury his rampant member deep within her, spearing her. God, how she would scream at that, how she would surrender, give in to his peerless lovemaking. Allah had blessed him with all the right equipment, and the knowledge of how to use it well. Indeed, expertly. The women he had conquered were as plentiful as wheat from Egypt. Young, old, married, single. He cared not. This one, however, the empress, she was different. Her physical beauty was matched by her intelligence, her divine power. To possess such a woman, now that would be the ultimate prize. To have her in his lair, to take her whenever he wished. The pinnacle of his life's ambitions.

His mouth was salivating as he turned the last corner and padded down the marble floor that led to the empress's door. The thought of being close to her again made his heart hammer in his chest. He would have to stop, collect himself before he entered her apartments. If she so much as guessed at the effect she had on him, then she would have the upper hand, and that would never do. So he paused, put a hand out against a nearby pillar, and took in a few deep breaths. He would have to put thoughts of her luscious body to one side for the moment, no matter how difficult that might prove to be!

Crethus grinned at his own weakness, for it was a pleasurable weakness. No other woman had done this to him before, filled his mind with pictures of fervent lovemaking. Images of her naked body reared up in his mind's eye again, the soft, undulating curves of her waist, the downy hummocks of her breasts, milk-white, gloriously soft. Lying on a bed, arms above her head, she smiled up at him, squirming in anticipation as she hungrily eyed his erect cock, then licked her bottom lip in anticipation of rolling her moist lips over his swollen glans.

"Dear God!" he said aloud, then instantly regretted it, and looked around quickly. He relaxed. No one was within earshot. He put his hand over his face and squeezed his eyes shut, trying to dispel the images. He had to overcome these thoughts, or he would be lost. He breathed in again, settled himself, looked around to check just once more that no one had noticed, then strode on.

He was ready.

Somewhere in the darkness, deep within the shadows of the great columns that reached up towards the vaulted ceiling, the spy waited until the huge Scythian commander had continued on his way towards the empress's rooms. He wondered why the massive man had stopped, called out 'Dear God' with such venom, then seemed to wrestle with something. The spy had seen much in his years, knew how to interpret actions and innocent sounding words. The man was captivated, consumed even. That much was certain. The bulge in the man's groin proved it. His lust was up, and all of it directed towards the empress. He smiled to himself. Dear Lord, Orphano would relish hearing this!

The tentative knock at the door brought Zoe out of her mid-afternoon nap. She stretched out on her bed and for one, brief and glorious moment, everything was as she had experienced in her dream. She was still married to Michael, basking in his beauty, both of them wildly in love and enjoying every moment.

She lay there, staring up at the ceiling, the brightly painted fresco filling her vision. If only life were that simple, she mused. Bright, unchanging, secure. She had believed it would be, married to the Emperor, Michael IV, the adulation of the people, the wealth and prestige. It was everything she had ever wanted. And then it changed, as if overnight. Michael had changed. He had shut her away, taken everything from her. She had spent months hidden from the adoration of her people and slowly, bit by bit, she had shriveled up inside. Of course, her maids attended to her, her skin was maintained, her beauty still as captivating as ever, but taken from the love of her people, that damaged her more than anything. She had become bitter, angry, impatient. Her maids often ran out crying as her whiplash tongue admonished them for the slightest mistake. Michael, her lover, he had used her.

Shortly afterwards, he died.

She hadn't shed a single tear, a fact that made her realize just how much her heart had hardened towards him. The first time she had laid eyes on him, she almost screamed with desire. His lithe, gloriously muscled body, his finely chiseled face, eyes that smouldered with barely controlled passion. a mouth as full and soft as any maidens. The individual parts combined as if created by a master artist, each feature as close to perfection as anyone could imagine. When he had disrobed in front of her, she had to fight against swooning. She had never seen anyone so beautiful. The muscles swelled hard beneath the velvet skin, rippling along his thighs. The hands, soft yet strong, clasping her to him, pressing her close so she could feel his manhood. Divine. He had spent hours on her body, exploring every inch with tongue and fingers, soft lips fluttering across her skin, sending her into ecstasy. A man whose only thought was to pleasure her, unselfishly, and totally. Somewhat guiltily, she had lain back and allowed him full reign over her. How could she not do anything less, the man was a marvel.

Then, she killed him.

A smile spread across her face. Yes, it would have been wonderful, if only their love had lasted. But only God knew the vagaries of the human heart. Michael had been seduced by power and jealousy. He hated the way Zoe captured the hearts of the people. It was her name that they shouted whenever they paraded through the streets of the city. During the many festivals, Michael would blanch beside her, slumping down in his chair as she stood there, waving to them, their cries filling the air.

And now, another Michael, her husband's namesake. The usurper, her adopted nephew. Young, ambitious and as malleable as a piece of newly dug clay. However, it had not been Zoe who had shaped him, but that serpent Orphano. Orphano had always had one eye firmly fixed on the throne, but had never openly attempted to make himself Emperor. He had always worked in the background, biding his time, oiling his machine of power. Now, he controlled Michael, the new emperor, and his ultimate goal was close to realization. Michael was going to send Zoe away, but not as her husband had done. Not for her the lavish apartments of private apartments set within the palace confines this time. No, not that. Zoe was to be sent far, far away, to a lonely island and a nunnery. The only query remaining – when.

Another knock, more insistent this time. Zoe sighed, rolled over and stood up. She ran her fingers through the tumble of her hair and said, "Enter."

The doors whispered open and the guard, head lowered, stepped aside.

"What is it, for God's sake?" She turned, her impatience already surging, mixed with the annoyance of being disturbed.

Then she saw him. Crethus. Instantly, all those feelings disappeared and she felt a warm glow bursting inside her, filling her bosom. Her previous dreams were as nothing to what this man promised her. The sight of him, his size, his hard, angular face, and that bulge … oh my, that bulge!

Sixteen

They were given a good meal. Haldor and Ulf ate without comment whilst Hardrada sat, slumped in the corner, playing with the prime cuts of meat with his finger, not having tasted a single morsel. They had him, the bastards, and there was nothing he could do. He had no doubt that Orphano would carry out his threats.

He had been close to death many times, fighting alongside his good friends. If they had died in battle, then that was all to the good, because that was how a Viking should die. Hardrada knew, if he knew nothing else, that the manner of death that Orphano would choose for his old friends would be ignominious and inglorious, offering them no chance to enter the hallowed Halls of Valhalla. This fact alone would force him to agree, but there was more. His treasure. They had it. Without it, what about the future, his plans to return to Norway, reclaim the throne of his ancestral lands, become a great warrior and conqueror, to lead his people once more into greatness? That, more than anything, was his wish.

To do it, he would need that treasure, and the money it would bring. Money to buy soldiers, build great halls, lavish gifts upon his friends, his people... Orphano had found it. Damn him, and damn his network of spies. Damn them all to their Christian hell.

Of course, there was that other complication – the Lady Zoe. Her face loomed up in his mind. What of her? Her life too rested on the success of his mission to find Alexius. However, he had to admit to himself that his ardour was waning. Zoe, however beautiful, tantalizing and irresistible, had done nothing to help him. Whilst he rotted away in this cell, what was she doing? He had thought that perhaps she too was captured, but now he wasn't so sure. She had the power and the means to get word to him, but there had been nothing. Perhaps her affections had cooled. He had no basis for thinking this. The last time they had coupled, she had been just as responsive as ever, and yet this seeming indifference of his plight caused him to question the depth of her feeling.

He put his head back against the wall and closed his eyes. In the final analysis, did it bother him? He wasn't so sure. She was merely a woman, after all, and in this world, women were of no importance. He knew he didn't love her, that it was only physical. The thought of her execution, however, did disturb him. They had shared moments of tenderness, surely she deserved something more, some consideration.

He put his face in his hands. This place, and him trapped inside the confines of this damp, squalid cell, was churning up his thoughts, distorting everything. Of course she cared for him, of course he cared for her! Something must have prevented her from getting a message to him. Orphano must have had her locked away, far away perhaps. The eunuch knew of her influence, the devotion of the people towards her. What was going on in the streets, the exhortations of her name, proved it. So of course, it had to be that they had her secreted away, in a place so remote, so inaccessible that she would have no chance to get word to him. The Orphano faction caused all of this, not her. They were the ones who would pay. In the end.

"Harald. Are you well, my old friend?"

Hadrada lowered his hands and looked up. Haldor was close by, his mouth still glistening with grease, a few scraps of meat tangled in his beard. Hardrada smiled. "Don't concern yourself, all is well. Too many thoughts, that is all."

"What did they do to you?"

"Nothing. Orphano spoke to me of his plan. A deal, probably conjured up by their devil. What is his name?"

"Satan."

"Yes, that's it. Satan. He must be at the heart of it, for the deal is foul with little chance of success. If I accept, I will almost certainly die. If I refuse, they will execute us all." He grinned. "If I fail … it all ends in the same way."

Haldor pursed his lips. "Execute. For what reason?"

"Treason." Hardrada shrugged. "Does it matter? They will think of something, make it all legal. We are trussed up, my old friend. I have no choice but to accept."

"But you said there was little chance of success."

"Better that than watching them hack off both your heads."

Haldor paled and he glanced back at Ulf, who was still finishing the last of his meal. "What say you to this?"

Ulf shook his head, munching down a final piece of meat. "They are all bastards. We knew that when we signed on. This was only ever a temporary posting. Perhaps we didn't know just how temporary it was to be."

"Well, I think we should continue with our plan," said Haldor. "Bribe the guards, get them to help us escape."

Hardrada grunted and said, "They have the treasure."

There was a shocked silence. Haldor fell backwards on his haunches and Ulf spluttered on the last of his dinner. He quickly took a drink of water from a goblet, and gasped, "What, all of it?"

"Everything."

"Fuck!"

"So, like I say, they have us exactly where they want us." Hadrada spread out his right hand, palm upwards. "Right there." He closed his hand into a fist.

"What do we do?" asked Haldor.

"*We* don't do anything. It is all down to me. I have to accept the proposal, I have no choice. All I have to do is wait. We leave sometime soon, myself and one of their trusted men. A Byzantine officer. They said this morning, but we will see."

"You do know, don't you, that they will never keep their word. As soon as you have succeeded in whatever it is they have asked you to do, they will kill all of us."

"Aye. I know that." Hadrada smiled. "I'm hoping they don't realize I know that!"

"Don't underestimate them," said Ulf, running his finger around the rim of his plate, to mop up the last vestiges of his meal. "Orphano has everything wrapped up tighter than a Cistercian monk's arse."

"You would know," commented Haldor, the smile broad on his face.

"Not for the want of trying!"

Hardrada groaned. How like his friends to make light of any situation. He recalled years ago, a run in with some Bulgars. How, when the arrows were skimming over their heads, Ulf had piped up, "I wonder what it's like to rut with a Bulgar maid? As dangerous as these bastards, I shouldn't wonder." To which Haldor had replied, "Aye, but not half as satisfying!" And then they had both rushed forward, axes swinging, to cleave heads, laughing as they doled out death.

"Can't you two ever be serious?"

Both of his friends looked at him. Hardrada shook his head and closed his eyes again. It was up to him, as always, to be the serious one, to make the painful decisions. Well, he had made them, and would continue to do so. There really was no other course open to him.

* * *

Crethus kept his eyes lowered as he stepped forward. Zoe studied him as he drew closer. He was wearing a scarlet jerkin, tied loosely at the throat, a broad belt and calf-length breeches. On his feet were leather sandals. For self-protection, all he wore was a small dagger sheathed at his hip. The last time she had seen him, he was clad in the full armour of a Varangian warrior. Beneath the panoply, his physical secrets were well hidden, even though she knew what they were. Here, with everything so much closer, a mere a finger's breadth away, all she would have to do was reach out, pull away the cord that held the jerkin together, and the body would be exposed.

She ran her eyes over his torso, then lower still, and fastened them on his crotch. She noted how the material of his breeches stretch and strained, barely able to contain what lurked beneath. It was with difficultly that she brought her face up to his.

He was looking at her now. His eyes, black as olives, boring into her, the way they had the last time they met. She felt that familiar and delicious pain surge through her heart, thrilling her with the anticipation of what might happen, if only she had the nerve, the courage to open her arms and allow him to move into her.

She could smell him, the heady musk smell of a man in his prime. She took in the gleaming flesh, the bare arms, the sweat glistening across his upper lip, the sinews in his neck rigid, hard as iron rods.

"My Lady."

She blinked, caught her breath. She had been almost as far away as she had been when she was dreaming. This, however, was no dream, no recollection even. This was happening right now: unimagined, immediate and so utterly strong. Conquered. She closed her eyes as her hand drifted forward as if of its own volition. As her fingers fell upon the cord fastening, Crethus's own hand folded over hers.

"My Lady." Soft, his voice floated to her, melting any resistance and her mouth opened to accept his.

The sonorous chanting wafted up into the huge, arched expense of the church ceiling, iridescent, shimmering sound, inspired by the divine, created to lift the hearts and souls of men. With his eyes closed, Michael drifted as if in a state of bliss. He had no awareness of anything else other than the sumptuous voices, the repeated chant filling him with a kind of ecstasy. The more he listened, the more he wanted it to never end. If he were indeed still on Earth, then these voices promised him a heaven beyond his imagining. If this was heaven, then he was content.

He stood at the great altar, and opened his eyes. The light from a thousand candles caused him to blink repeatedly, eyes watering a little. He dared not flinch, however. The assembly were all focused in on him, the gathering of the great and the good. Senators and priests, resplendent in their finery, all waiting for the merest gesture, the faintest flicker of indecision. Then they would pounce, the groans of derision, the muttered criticisms. He had to remain aloof, strong, every inch the Emperor.

The patriarch Alexius bowed before him, motioned for him to kneel and receive the flesh and blood of Christ. This was Michael's inaugural communion, a public display of his obedience to God, with all eyes fixed on him: the social elite, generals, judges, senators, men of God. As the voices of the choir filled the great church with their mystical serenade to the Holy Mother, Michael dropped to his knees and received first the bread, and then the wine. The patriarch made the sign of the cross, bowed his head and stepped away.

Every inch of that blessed place rang out as the Emperor raised himself up, crossed himself, and moved backwards. The singing of the assembled masses joined with the choir, voices declaring their joy, their adoration. At least, this is what Michael hoped. He longed to turn and grin, but resisted the urge to do so. He kept his head lowered, humble and submissive, just as Orphano had instructed him. 'Resist your natural urge to smile, and respond to those around you. Have eyes only for the icons of the Holy Mother. Her image should be burned into your mind, and no other thought should invade your senses except to give Her reverence. This is your first test, and you must pass.'

Michael believed he had done well. No crude arrogance on display, just a simple man accepting his powers with grace and humility. Adorned he may be in golden robes, but a mere man nevertheless, filled with faith. It was how it should be.

A change came over the assembly. The choral chant drew to a close, and everyone began to relax as the ceremony reached its climax. Michael turned and slowly made his way down the central aisle, head still lowered. At the end, he stopped and looked up, took in the huge, gold framed icon of the Holy Mother, bent his knee, made a final sign of the cross, and turned.

The choir burst into a new choral affirmation of their new emperor, voices soaring up into the vast expanse of the vaulted roof.

No one knew what happened then, but something caused the Emperor to stumble. Was it an accident, or had a handsomely-bribed priestly attendant rucked up the scarlet carpet that had been rolled down the aisle? Michael caught his foot on the edge of the heavy material and when he stepped towards the massive doors that led outside, and the adoration of the waiting people, he tripped, staggered forward, cursed in full voice, and fell.

A loud gasp rang throughout the enormous church. The choir petered out, all of the singers having watched their Emperor gliding towards the doors, so serene, so gracious, now a floundering idiot, robes billowing around him, arms waving around, warding off the attendants who rushed to his sides.

"Leave me alone, you damned bloody buggers!"

He stopped, his mouth falling open. A new dread assailed him, a great slab of ice growing in his stomach, chilling the very fibre of his soul. *Dear God, did I really say those words, in this most holy of places, the majestic Church of St Mary?*

The stunned attendants and huddle of priests who had rushed to his aid all took a collective step back, faces aghast. No one else spoke, no one else moved. Even the stones, the marble columns, the gold and silver fitments, all of them seemed to be waiting. All Michael could do was sway slightly, from side to side, hand clamped to his mouth. He couldn't continue, not now. He couldn't step out into the Forum of Theodosius, accept the adoration of the people, knowing that he had uttered such profanities within the house of God.

Outside, however, the tumult grew in volume, the crowd restless. The ceremony, intended to be brief was nothing more than a curtain raiser for the main event – the coronation. That would be a sight to see, all the lords and ladies decked out in their finery. So Michael had thought, at his predecessor's coronation. So majestic, so wonderful. Stepping out into the sunlight, with his bride of only three days, the recently widowed Empress Zoe. How marvellous they looked, glowing almost. The crowd had gone wild that day, singing their hearts out as Zoe beamed at them, waving, letting them know that they, above everything else, was what made Byzantium so glorious.

"Fuck."

Michael grabbed hold of the closest attendant, hissing in his ear, "Take me out the back way."

"Majesty?"

"You heard me, you little shit. Take me out through the workmen's entrance. I don't want the crowd to see me."

"But Majesty, I can't just—"

"Is there a problem, Your Highness?"

Michael started at the sound of the all-too familiar voice of the eunuch, Orphano. He glared as the man stepped up to him. "I thought you said you weren't going to attend."

Orphano smiled, dipped down and smoothed the carpet with the flat of his hand. "Mmm ... seems as if the nails have come away." He stood up, gestured to the attendant to move away, and smiled at the others milling around. "We will step outside together, Your Highness." He raised his hand, snapping his fingers twice. Soon, a group of well large, brooding and well-armed Varangians closed up around the new Emperor, their faces set hard, muscles rippling.

"I don't need these men to—"

"Oh, but you do, your Highness. We wouldn't want you to take a tumble on the steps, would we?"

Michael scanned the Church, took in the faces of all those senators and lords. How their eyes bulged, how they whispered to one another, how the patriarch in all his fine robes stood like a statue, that look of sneering contempt written all over his face. Even from this distance, Michael could see that look. Disapproving, like his old schoolteachers. So what if he had accidentally let his tongue slip, what the hell did it matter?

"The emperor is the human representation of God on earth," his uncle had told him many years before. "The Patriarch embodies the spirit of Christ, but the emperor is the physical entity. The aspect the people relate to. Remember this, Michael. Revere it."

Michael swallowed hard. Yes, he remembered it all right. He'd made an ass of himself, and now the eunuch wanted to subject him to further ridicule. He spread out his hands, pleading with Orphano. "Please, can't we delay this? I don't feel..." He saw the man's unblinking scowl and knew there was no choice. He let his shoulders slump. Head full of conflicting thoughts, he turned, resigned, and took the first step towards the sunlight.

Not so very far away, standing on the balcony of his city residence, just off the Forum of Constantine, the mighty general, George Maniakes couldn't help but smile as he heard the great roars of derision emanating from the Forum of Theodosius. He already felt warm and satisfied after a rather hectic mid-morning lovemaking session with his servant girl, Leoni, but this, the sound of the people baying for Michael's blood, this eclipsed everything.

"My Lord seems happy."

Leoni came up behind him, wrapping her arms around his waist, pressing her head between his shoulders.

"I am," he said, closing his eyes. The heat from her slim, nubile body thrilled him. He was constantly amazed at her ability to bring him to erection, even after a prolonged fucking had drained him of almost all his strength. Her slim, strong limbs, those fine, pert breasts, and the way her arse stuck out, so big, so round. He groaned. Dear God, she was everything he had ever wanted physically, but he could never publicly reveal such feelings. A servant girl, a virtual slave. Too low-born for one such as he, part of the ruling elite. Instead, he had to hide her away, creep around in the middle of night, or grab any opportunity to have her, like now, whilst everyone was at the church, watching Michael being humiliated. Orphano's plan had worked beautifully. The catcalls proved it.

He turned in her arms, and put his own around her, holding her close. He kissed the top of her head. "I am happy, my sweet," he repeated. "Are you?"

"More than anything, My Lord."

"You are well satisfied?"

She giggled. "My Lord, you are the most perfect lover."

He kissed her head again, as her hand dropped to his crotch. It immediately sprung into life and he gasped as a surge of desire rushed through him. "God, woman!" He pulled back her head and kissed her, driving his tongue deep into her mouth. She tasted of strawberries, the sweet remnants of the wine they had drunk. When he drew back, he looked into her eyes. "I want you to visit Michael again, later this afternoon."

Maniakes sensed her reaction, the way the colour drained from her face revealing more than words ever could about how she felt. These liaisons with the emperor, they were taking their toll. He smiled, tipped up her head with a finger under the chin. "My sweet, do not think that I do not desire you more than any other. I know this is purgatory for you—"

"My Lord," she interjected, eyes filling up, the voice trembling. "I know that My Lord is wise and considerate, but I fail to see how ... " She turned her face from his and the sobs became more powerful.

Something like concern touched Maniakes. He soon put it to one side. He loved the body of this girl, but her soul would never be something he would be unduly drawn to. She was merely a vehicle for his own orgasms. He enjoyed her, even had feelings for her, but once her usefulness came to an end, he would discard her, like the peelings of a fruit. Still delicious, but not as satisfying as the flesh. And flesh was something he could always find more of, if need be.

"Child," he said. "You are a servant to the Holy Empire. A true Roman. Loyal, dutiful, unquestioning." Her face came up. "Trust me that everything you do is for the good of the Empire, and for the people. I am not asking you to enjoy it, but just make it appear so. Then, when he is totally infatuated, we shall have him."

"I shall have him, My Lord. At least, I shall have him this afternoon."

She smiled, but he could see the pain in her eyes and again, and that pressure in his chest swelled up. Perhaps he did have true feelings for her, feelings that went beyond what she could offer him in the bedroom. She was young, innocent of so many of life's pitfalls. Like a child, with so much to learn. Intrigues and deceptions were not things that came naturally to her, or so she liked to think. When all of this was over, perhaps he could find for her a place in his heart.

He shook his head. Well, if that were to happen, it was for the future, not now. Now, he had plots to ferment. The Emperor Michael was inept, naive, boorish and uncouth: no different from any previous emperor of Byzantium. However, the man was something more. He was dangerous. And that would be his undoing.

"Leoni," he said, and held her face in his hands. "I understand your revulsion. The man is a snake, but it will soon be over. Trust me."

"I do, My Lord. But it is not easy to couple with him, I want you to know this. He is *nothing* beside you." He sucked in the air as her hand once again clasped his member. It swelled beneath her fingers. "Nothing compared with you at all."

He moaned, bent down, lifted her into his arms and carried her towards his bed. Michael would have to wait because right now, Maniakes needed to vent his own passion.

* * *

Orphano caught sight of the man standing a little way off. Michael stood on the top step, arms spread outwards, but the crowd was in no mood to reward him with exultations. They jeered, loudly and with distinct hostility. Orphano could barely contain his joy and had to pretend to cough in order to mask the smirk developing on his face. He looked to the man and motioned for him to come closer.

"News?"

"My Lord." The man looked around him, outwardly relaxed. The members of the Senate filed past, all of them looking serious, almost as if they were in shock. The crowd was becoming ugly.

"Out with it, man!"

"Lord. Pardon. He has gone to Her Highness's chamber."

Orphano frowned. "Has he indeed. And to ask her what, I wonder?"

The man leaned his head towards the emperor. "To tell her of the plan, I understand."

"And what makes you think he went there for something else?"

"His attire, Lord."

"What the devil does that mean?"

"He was not dressed as a guard, My Lord. No armour. A shirt and breeches only."

"Brazen."

"The palace is virtually empty, My Lord."

Orphano chewed his lip. "We could use this." He smiled, clapped the man on the shoulder. "You have done well. Go back, find out if anything has *happened*. Then, return to me this evening. Tomorrow Hardrada goes north. A day late, but it matters not. I may need this snippet of news to keep him in check … if he survives."

The man bowed and turned away. Orphano rubbed his hands together. The jeering of the crowd was so loud now it filled the entire Forum. Michael appeared agitated, his face crumbling, eyes darting from side to side. Already the members of the Senate were disappearing, making their way back to their various villas and houses. Not one gave as much as a glance towards the Emperor.

Orphano exhaled slowly. What a wonderful day it had been: Michael thoroughly humiliated, Zoe engaged in some rather questionable activities with a bodyguard, and Hardrada neatly trussed up. All that remained was to find Alexius, return him to the capital and then the whole, creaking edifice would come tumbling down. The lot of them would fall, shown to be the scurrilous, unfit bunch that they really were. Yes, a thoroughly successful day. Now, all he had to think about was how to get away from the crowd unscathed.

Empress Zoe nestled her head on the barrel chest of the Scythian Crethus and let out a long sigh of contentment. The man had proved himself better than she could ever have believed possible. He had taken her in every way imaginable, his huge cock ramming into her repeatedly, bringing her to orgasm again and again. A supreme lover in every way, he had mastered her body like no one else she had ever known.

Not even Hardrada could compare with this.

Crethus. She formed his name with her lips and snuggled in closer. His great arm held her, protecting her, and she felt such a glow inside her stomach, creating a warmth that spread throughout her entire body. Safe. That's how she felt in this man's arms, and it was a feeling that she had been without for far too long.

From a long way off came the sound of voices. Distant, but extremely loud. Voices that sounded angry. She sat up. Crethus stirred next to her.

"You should leave," she said, regarding him with such longing, knowing that if she had the power, she would never leave this bed. To stay like this forever more: what a glorious thought that was. She struggled with her newfound weakness for him, knowing that he had to go.

He took her hand in his. "My Lady …"

She leaned towards him and kissed him once, then slipped out from beneath the sheets and picked up her robes. "It sounds as if Michael's inaugural mass didn't go quite as expected."

"Does that please you?"

She stopped in the process of pulling on her thin, satin robe and thought about the question. It did please her but it also worried her that the crowd's reaction, their response, might become something even more dangerous. A revolt. Enemies surrounded Byzantium, any internal strife could topple everything, bring the pagan hordes surging through the city walls and destroy two thousand years of civilisation. As long as she breathed, she could not allow that to happen. And now she had just the means to overcome the machinations of those around her.

Zoe smiled at Crethus as the man swung over and sat on the edge of the bed, looking at her, his body glistening with the exertions of his lovemaking. "It pleases me, Crethus, that you and I are together. I will have many uses for you, not least in this bed!"

"My Lady can use me in any way she deems fit."

Zoe nodded her head, "That is *exactly* what I was hoping you would say." She pulled on the rest of her clothing and tied a cord around her slim waist. "You have to go. I don't want anyone to suspect what has gone on here today. We must bide our time. The next few days, perhaps weeks, will prove extremely dangerous. I must play the part, appear suppliant, beaten even. It will not be easy for me, but I must convince my enemies that they have won."

"If you can't?"

"Then, I will truly have lost. And so too will Byzantium."

Crethus nodded his head, took up his jerkin and put it on. He stood up and smiled at Zoe as she let her eyes roam over his physique once again.

"You are a wonderful man," she said softly, about to move closer when something made her stop. Above the baying of the crowd, a muffled din being all that it was, she heard something else. The tiniest of footfalls. She froze, fear gripping her. At once, Crethus was next to her. "What is it?" She pressed a finger against his lips, and nodded her head towards the door to her room.

A dark look settled over Crethus's features and, without a word, he drew out his dagger and went over to the door, moving like a cat, padding across the floor on the balls of his feet. Zoe watched him, mesmerized, hardly daring to breathe. He stood by the doors, one ear pressed against the oak. Then he moved, quicker than anyone she had ever seen, ripping open the door. Beyond, the man yelped, tried to dart away. But Crethus was quicker, much quicker. Years of fighting had honed his body into a perfect machine, reactions finely tuned. Zoe saw the Scythian's great arm gripping the man around the throat, saw the flash of the blade as it cut through the air. The scream, the blood, the body falling like a heavy piece of sacking to the ground.

She ran over, hand held over her mouth as Crethus rolled the man over with his foot. Lifeless eyes gazed upwards, the mouth a black, gaping hole. The attitude of death.

"You know him?"

She nodded. "One of Orphano's men. He must have been sent to spy on me."

"So the eunuch knows."

"He knows everything anyway."

Crethus wiped his dagger on the dead man's tunic, and slipped the blade back into its sheath. "I will get rid of the body. You will be all right?"

Zoe let her hand fall from her mouth, every part of her trembling. "It was so quick. One moment he was alive, the next …" She felt fear then. "What will Orphano do?"

"Do? What can he do?" The Scythian shook his head. "The man disappeared, that is all."

"You are well suited to this type of intrigue, Crethus."

"Seems you have made a good choice, My Lady."

"I believe I have." She moved back to her apartment entrance, and paused at the door. "In every way," she said and went inside.

Seventeen

The evening grew cold and Michael found solace in wine. A lot of wine. By the time Orphano arrived, the Emperor was quite drunk. Sprawled out on a couch, his tunic open at the chest, a dishevelled wreck, lips trembling, eyes roaming, one hand draped across his stomach, the other resting on the rim of a heavy, bronze goblet, he barely looked up when the eunuch approached.

There were others there, in similar attitudes, in various degrees of intoxication. Men and women or, more correctly, boys and girls. Some of them partially dressed, many of them naked, bodies entwined, littering the floor as if sprinkled there like so much confetti. Orphano sighed as he looked around him. The decadence of Rome, come back to haunt the sacred corridors of Byzantium. How long had he strived to maintain the lustre of this Empire, to find it so tarnished and in such a short space of time?

The eunuch picked his way through the bodies, some of them writhing in ecstasy as they vented their lust upon each other. Lithe, young bodies, peerless, superbly defined. Scenes of the most luscious debauchery. Orphano, however, felt no stirring within him. Such feelings had long since departed from his body. No longer a slave to passion, he could keep his mind clear. Sometimes a young boy, well-hung, pretty, virile and lustful, could give him some semblance of pleasure, but it was nothing compared to what others experienced. That sweet release, the spilling of the seed … all of that, gone.

He was not envious. Gelded at twelve years of age, it was the one thing about his emasculation for which he felt thankful: the curtailing of his sexual urges. An honour they told his parents, to serve in the court of Her Royal Highness, to provide her with everything she would ever need. Well, it was long ago, and his cock only served to relieve his bladder. He could not miss something he had never had. So he watched the youngsters grunting and groaning in their passion as he might a passing flock of goats. With no emotion whatsoever.

Not so the emotions that sprang when he cast his eyes upon the sickening sight of his emperor, saliva drooling from the side of his mouth, hair in disarray, body stained with wine, food scraps, and spots of something else that Orphano didn't dare think about. He took in a few breaths, to keep down the rising nausea, then reached out to shake Michael's shoulder. "Highness," he hissed. "Highness, I must speak with you."

The Emperor's eyes flickered with something like recognition, but then his head drooped to the side and he retched loudly, the vomit gushing out in long, stinking stream.

"Holy Mother!" Orphano stepped away in disgust, holding his mouth and nose as the stench hit his nostrils. He gagged, moving back still farther, and stumbled over a couple who squealed as he stepped over them. "*Highness!*"

Michael, however, too far gone to register anything that Orphano might have to say, leaned over again and brought up another gush of stinking vomit.

"Damn it all," Orphano said and whirled about, marching out of the room without any more thought for who or what he stepped on. Damn the man. The mob had taken to the streets, gangs roaming down every alleyway, and violence threatened to erupt. The palace guard called out, and the Varangians placed on high alert. If the Emperor wished to loll away his time in alcohol and sex whilst the masses consumed his Empire's citadel, then so be it. He had tried to warn him, and he could do no more.

Orphano stood outside the room, back pressed against the wall, and looked at Crethus who stood some feet away, flanked by a good half dozen Scythians, bristling with weaponry. "The Emperor is somewhat indisposed. Post your men here, Captain, and let no one pass, either in or out. You understand?"

"No one, My Lord?"

Orphano ran a hand right over his face and across the top of his bald head. "Save myself and the General, no one is to enter or leave this room. Not even the Emperor."

The men started, exchanged glances. Crethus frowned. "We cannot deny His Royal Highness, My Lord."

"If he comes out, one of your men must run to me as fast as they can. I need to know the moment the Emperor is back on his feet. But tell him anything to keep him inside."

"Like what, My Lord?"

"Damn it man, use your fucking imagination! Tell him the palace is under attack…which, of course, it may very well soon be!"

"There are torches glowing in the streets," said Haldor. He had managed to stack up some old bits of broken furniture and bedding and was now peering out through the iron bars of the single cell window. "Lots of people, men, women, the whole lot. They seem angry."

"They sound angry." Hardrada said, but with little enthusiasm. He was worried. Orphano had told him he was to go north, but as yet no one had come to fetch him. Now, it was late. And with the mob running wild through the streets, he doubted he would be going anywhere that night. He put his head back against the wall and closed his eyes. "The whole fucking lot is falling down around our ears."

"What do you propose we do?" Ulf stood next to Haldor, straining his neck to see out. Of course, he couldn't.

"What else can we do but wait?"

"Well," said Haldor, stepping down. "Let's hope that by the morning, the Empire will have been overthrown, and we can make good our escape."

"Fat chance," spat Hardrada, his eyes still closed. "Without my treasure, there isn't much point. No, we'll just have to hang around here, see what rich pickings we can come across."

"What about the Empress?"

Hardrada opened his eyes at the mention of her. Zoe, the Empress Zoe. The times they had shared, the kindness she had shown, the fondness. He had believed she had cared for him, but now it was clear it had all been an act. No other woman had affected him in such a way and that fact, perhaps more than her betrayal, angered him. It boiled away now, the redness coming over his vision, and he squeezed his hand into a fist, crushing the dregs of his feelings by the force of his rage. "The Empress can go to Hell for all I care. She doesn't give a fig for me so why the fuck should I care about her? Eh? Answer me that."

"We can't," said Haldor.

"And wouldn't dare to do so," added Ulf.

Hardrada looked across at his two friends, and the anger slipped away, replaced by a growing sense of guilt. He climbed to his feet, opening wide his arms, "Oh, my good boys! What an idiot I've been, selling my soul for a few moments of sexual gratification, when all the time my only true and lasting friends have been here right beside me!"

The others stepped forward and all three fell into an embrace. Outside, the mob rampaged through the streets, shouting out their rejection of the new emperor, but that was no concern to any of those men right now. All that mattered was that they were together.

* * *

In her bed, the Empress Zoe lay huddled up in a tight ball, shivering with fear whilst the crowd outside chanted their vitriol. She had tried to leave her room, but guards had been posted and despite her furious insistence, they had refused to let her leave. Crethus was nowhere to be found. She hadn't seen him since earlier that afternoon and now she began to imagine all sorts of terrible scenarios involving Orphano, flashing blades, and death. Despite the cold, sweat broke out across her face. All she could do was wait, she tried to tell herself, wait until the morning brought some relief from the dreadful, suffocating terror besetting her, causing her breathing to become laboured, and her heartbeat to race. Sleep was impossible; she had little choice but to lie there and pray that the dawn would break and find her still alive.

Leoni stirred herself and padded across to the Emperor. Her eyes darted around the room. Orphano had gone and no one seemed in the least bit interested in her. Bodies were either copulating or asleep. She took a breath, pulled her thin dress over her head, and straddled the slumbering emperor.

Her hand delved in beneath the folds of his robes and found his tiny prick. She hesitated for a moment. Maniakes had given his orders, but Leoni doubted if anything would work on the Emperor that night. He was far too gone with drink for him to even think about sex, let alone engage in it.

"Leoni, my darling!"

She almost sighed aloud, but managed to hide her disappointment as Michael reached out his hands to cup her breasts. She forced a little giggle, "Majesty. I thought you were asleep."

"I was only pretending. Has that idiot Orphano gone?"

"Yes." Her fingers rolled over his manhood. He moaned, arched his back. "Are you sure you are awake, My Lord?"

"Mmm ... I am awakening, my love."

She could feel it as he slowly hardened. "My lover had me again today," she said in a teasing tone. He grew harder still in her hand.

"Oh, my God, really? When?"

"Whilst you were away, My Lord."

Michael's eyes sprang open and for a moment she thought she had made a miscalculation. Perhaps the idea of her being fucked hard by the good General whilst he himself suffered the humiliation of his subjects in the church was too much even for the perverted tastes of the Emperor? But it was too late to turn back. "He had wanted so much to be with you," she hurried on, "but I insisted he fuck me. I needed him, you see." Her fingers told her it was all going to be well. The member continued to harden.

"Really?" His voice sounded thick, his words barely able to form as he became lost in the delicious torment of the moment.

"Oh. God. yes," she said, moving down his body, her moist lips replacing her fingers.

The Emperor cried out, gripped the girl's head firmly with both hands. "Holy Christ!"

She drew her head back, "He really is supreme, you know." She smiled. "Three times he had me."

His mouth fell open. "Three ... no, that's not possible."

"Oh, but it is. Believe me!" Her tongue flicked in and out like a snake. "He came every time. I don't know where it all comes from."

"Oh, Jesus."

"Then, after he had drunk some wine, he rolled me over onto my back, pushed my legs back, and drove into me, right up to the hilt."

He was past it now, his head moving from side to side as if he were going into some sort of fit. She watched him, knowing he was completely at her mercy. In a strange way, this brought her pleasure. Nothing like the General of course, who had indeed used her, but not in the way she had described. The gift of the concubine is to embellish, invent. She gripped the Emperor's member, moved her hand backwards and forwards. "You know, when I do this to him, I can't get my hand around it."

"Jesus ... Jesus, is that true?"

She gave a tiny laugh. Indeed, this much was true. The General was quite amazingly huge, but he was a considerate lover, always took his time, made sure that she felt as little pain as possible. As the memory of him came to her, she let her fingers fall to her sex, seeking out her own pleasure as she continued to roll her other hand over the Emperor enflamed organ. She moved her fingers around the nub of her sex, picturing Maniakes loving her. She moaned in abandonment. "He doesn't have to move, all he has to do keep it in me and ... " She gasped as the Emperor cried out and ejaculated all over her hand. The orgasm had come unexpectedly, so lost had she become in her own story. She smiled, continued for a moment or two, bringing on her own orgasm as the Emperor grew slack in her fist. A great shudder ran through her, like a wave that began between her legs, then rippled through her stomach and upwards over her breasts. She cried out as the orgasm overtook her, images of the General's body melding with her own.

Spent, she fell across the Emperor's chest.

His hand gently stroked her flaxen hair. "I think I love you, Leoni."

The girl held her breath. Dear God, where did that come from? Could he possibly be serious, or was he still drunk? Her mind raced, not knowing what to think. Trapped, pushed back in a corner, she went through a number of different responses, but none of them could mask the enormous sense of panic that now gripped her.

"Did you hear me, my sweet?"

She at last found the strength to lift her head up, to meet his gaze. "Yes, My Lord."

"And what have you got to say?" He sat up and she repositioned herself, allowing her legs to undrape themselves from his body, and she slid down next to him. The couch was narrow and she had to snuggle up to him very tightly to avoid falling off. He seemed to respond positively, taking her closeness as a sign that she was pleased. He held her close and kissed her head. "You are happy?"

Her eyes glazed over with a mist of total, complete terror. The Emperor, in love with her? "Oh yes, My Lord."

Michael squeezed her shoulders. "I have never known anything like what I feel right now for you. What you do to me, what you say … I cannot imagine finding anyone to come even close."

"My Lord, I am a simple serving girl. Nothing more."

"Nonsense. You are my lover, Leoni. You fulfill all of my needs. I want you to move into my royal apartments, so I can have you whenever I wish."

Leoni squeezed her eyes shut and swallowed hard. "And the General, My Lord?"

"Ah yes, the General." He stretched out his legs. "Naturally, you can continue to see him."

She had to check herself, to stop herself crying out. "My Lord?"

"Well, we can't have you being denied that cock, can we?" He turned his head and smiled at her. "Besides, it will give me the opportunity to watch you two in action."

Her eyes held his in total disbelief and for suspended seconds it was as if she had lost the power to breathe. Then, he leaned forward and kissed her.

"You think he will agree?"

Her lips parted, but no sound came out. It was as if the very core of her being had petrified.

Michael grinned. "Oh, my sweet little girl," he kissed her again. "What fun we will have!" He let his head fall back. "Fetch me some wine would you."

Leoni needed no second invitation. She stood up, gathered her dress and looked around. Various jugs and bowls lay strewn all over the floor. None appeared to hold any wine, however. Those few couples still conscious looked as if they were in no condition to engage in anything like intelligent speech, and when she turned to inform the Emperor that she would have to go down to kitchens to find some more wine, she saw that his eyes had closed. His chest rose and fell in the gentle rhythm of sleep. Leoni gave up a little prayer of thanks, and made her way nimbly across the room to the door.

The Scythian at the entrance held up the palm of his hand, "Sorry miss. Orders. No one is to leave."

She gaped at the man. "But I have an important message to deliver."

"Sorry. No exceptions."

She bristled with indignation. "The Emperor has given me express commands to let—"

"Not tonight, miss." And with that, the guard gently pushed her back inside and closed the door.

Leoni stood for a moment, staring unblinking at the wooden surface of the door. She felt her stomach churn, as the panic mounted once more. She had to get out; she had to let the General know. Everything had gone hopelessly wrong. To be the Emperor's concubine? That was never part of the plan. To be ready for him, night and day, the very thought of it brought the bile into her throat. No, this could never be, there had to be another way. But no matter how hard she tried, she could think of nothing that would work. When she recalled the Emperor's words, loathing and revulsion invaded her mind. 'Oh, my sweet child, what fun we will have!' Fun? Holy Mother, fun would have very little to do with anything that transpired between them. The thought of him, grunting and groaning on top of her … Leoni pressed her head against the door and cried.

Eighteen

The morning was icy cold, cutting deep into Hardrada's very bones as he stood in the courtyard, waiting for the young soldier, Andreas, to make an appearance.

The guards had come early, taking him from the cell without ceremony, not even allowing him time to give a farewell to his comrades. As soon as they had deposited him in the courtyard, they had slinked back to their duties, leaving the Viking to breathe in the sharp air, and wrap his arms about his chest, trying to make himself as small as possible. His breath steamed and he cursed all and sundry for not giving him the chance to pick up his cloak.

Struck by how quiet everywhere was, the atmosphere of threat and intimidation gone, he mused on the crowds who had vented their anger in the streets, all dispersed. It was just like them. Byzantium Greeks. So fickle, meek, accepting of authority. Certainly they could shout when things didn't go well, but the promise of more bread, or the chance of a horse race and the whole pathetic lot of them would go back to their homes, contented. Hardrada hawked and spat into the dirt. Damn them all, effete bunch that they were. Conquerors of the known world? God preserve us from such weaklings!

An approaching footfall made him turn, and he tensed when he saw who it was. If he had had a weapon, he may have drawn it.

George Maniakes, General of the northern armies, a man he had fought against and alongside. Considerably talented, clever and ruthless in his dealings with defeated enemies, Maniakes had earned the Viking's grudging respect. Nevertheless, Hardrada didn't trust the man as far as he could throw him, and as he approached, Hardrada bristled.

"Morning, Hardrada. Fit and well, I see."

Hardrada dipped his head slightly, but never let his eyes leave the General's face. He knew his reputation for treachery and deceit all too well. "General."

Maniakes took in a breath, "By God, it's cold. Are you cold, Hardrada? You look it."

"I'll be fine once I'm on my horse and away from this place."

"Mmm ... Well, the grooms will be here shortly with your mounts. No doubt they will have supplies, perhaps a coat. You'll need it for where you're going. The northern frontiers can be freezing this time of year."

"You know a lot about where I'm going."

Maniakes shrugged. "I also know that you must succeed, my old friend." He looked around. Checking perhaps that no one was in earshot? Hardrada didn't know, but he suspected that another piece of deception was about to be served up. "You have to come back, *alive*. The mob was wild last night, broke into the city armoury at one point. We had to call out the palace guard. That hasn't happened for years. No one was killed, fortunately, but we pacified them, gave them the promise of a festival – to mark the inaugural mass of the Emperor. Funny," he gave a short laugh, "that was the thing that sparked them off in the first place. You know the Emperor stumbled? Then he blasphemed ... *in church*." He shook his head. "The people don't like that. They respect virtue, honour and fealty. I think they believe that Michael possesses none of those traits."

"What do you believe, General?"

"Me? What I believe has no bearing on any of it. I'm merely a soldier, old friend. The commander of the swords and spears that protect this great Empire. In this triumvirate, that now rules Byzantium, I am the least of the three."

"I doubt that."

"Well, that's gracious of you, but I'm afraid it is true. Orphano is the real power, with Michael the figurehead. Soldiers, as well you know, have only one purpose. Once that purpose has been met, they are cast aside."

"The people know you for who you are, General. A great warrior. I've fought you, don't forget."

"How can I? Sicily – that damnable place. My god, I kicked your Varangian arse that day."

"I'm Norse, General. Not Rus. You may have kicked *their* arse, but you didn't kick mine."

"No." Maniakes smiled. "No, I didn't. Sorry, old friend."

"And then you let those bastard Scythians kill my men."

Maniakes held up his hand, face ashen. "Hold fast, Hardrada! Those bastards don't work for me. They are the eunuch's men, paid handsomely and promised even more."

"All of them? Haven't you just a few who will do your bidding?"

"You're too suspicious."

"No, I've lived here, amongst you. I know the ways of the Byzantine mind. Treachery comes as easy to you as bees to a honey pot. Or should that be, as flies to shit?"

The General blew out his cheeks, then rubbed his own arms briskly. "Damn, it is cold." He smiled again. "I'll not fence with you, old friend. But I'll tell you this … when you return, be on your guard. Success may well leave you open. Your usefulness will have been spent, so make yourself *invaluable*."

More noise. Hardrada looked around and saw the grooms approaching, leading two saddled horses and a pack mule. Behind them, a safe distance from the mule, strode a Byzantine officer, resplendent in bronze-banded lamellar armour, dressed as a *Scutatoi*, a heavy infantryman, a fact that Hardrada found interesting. Not a cavalryman, then. A lowly foot soldier. Perhaps this would make him even more dangerous, as his ambition must be great for him to be chosen for this task, over all the great and worthy nobility.

"General." The man saluted stiffly as he came up beside the other two. "It is an honour to have you here, sir, to bid us farewell on our mission."

Maniakes smirked, shared a meaningful look with Hardrada, and strode away.

"He seemed friendly towards you, Viking."

Hardrada turned and regarded the youth with a searching gaze. "Who my friends are," he said softly, "and who are not is my own concern."

"No offence intended."

"None taken."

The youth nodded once, pointed towards the mule. "There is a fur coat there for you, sir. Supplied by His Illustrious One, John the Orphano."

"Bless him."

If the youth noted the sarcasm, he gave no indication. Instead, he took the initiative, went to the mule and pulled the coat free. He hefted it in his arms and brought it over. "It is of a most wonderful quality."

Hardrada took it and instinctively brought it to his face, pressed his cheek on the sumptuous collar. What the youth said was true. The fur was warm, soft, perfect for such cold weather. With it still crushed against his face, he stared over the rim at the Byzantine. "What about you?"

The youth smiled. "I do not need such accoutrements, sir. I'm a soldier of Rome."

Hardrada had to laugh. Playing such games with this lad was going to prove very interesting indeed.

A few moments later, they slipped away in the quiet of the morning, with no one to wish them well. Meandering through the empty streets, they reached the main gate and found it open, the guards standing like stone statues, still and silent. The great city of Byzantium, seat of the eastern Roman Empire, slept. Hardrada, face half-buried in the thick fur of his robe, kept his eyes glued straight ahead. He had no time for farewells anyway. The city had been his home for a handful of years, but home was a word he was not particularly partial too. It meant nothing to him, having as much substance as a snowball in a cooking pot. He had never thought himself to be sentimental. Indeed, such thoughts betrayed weakness, and weakness was not an emotion he allowed himself. The empress had almost made him forget who he was, but her indifference had brought him back. Nevertheless... As the great door boomed shut behind him, he reigned in his mount and twisted himself in the saddle to take one last look.

Only a few feet from the entrance, he had to strain to look upwards. The mighty walls of Constantinople soared, thirty feet high, the colour of burnished gold, great towers standing there, eternal, mighty, secure. When he had first laid eyes on them, he had felt almost crushed by their sheer enormity. Now, they held nothing for him but regret. He should have left years ago, as soon as he had enough money. Instead, he had allowed greed to overtake him and now Orphano had seized that money. He may never see it again.

"It is beautiful, is it not?"

Hardrada started at his companion's voice. He had momentarily forgotten that he was not alone.

"Like a woman, it draws you in. Then, when she has you, she turns her back and leaves you out in the cold."

Andreas shifted in his saddle, made a face. "I've only been on this thing less than two minutes and already my arse feels like it's been split by a Nubian's cock!"

Hardrada winced, "Holy Mother, boy! Do you have to?"

Andreas laughed. "Don't worry – it's not something I've ever participated in! Just using some friendly barrack-room banter." His face hardened. "And please don't call me 'boy'. Sir."

"Fair enough. But only if you stop calling me 'sir'. I'm not your commander. I'm a Varangian guardsmen. You are...?"

"An infantryman." He pulled at the reins, turned his mount around and kicked its flanks. The horse blew out a great steaming breath and moved forwards. "Why they picked me for this mission I'll never know. I've never ridden more than a street's width before in my life."

Hardrada spurred his own horse to follow. "I'm such a great expert myself. I don't trust horses, never have done. It's the Viking in me. We ride ponies to battle, then dismount to fight on foot."

"At least you have ridden."

"Well, we've got a lot ahead of us. All the way through Thracia, up towards Nicopolis. It'll be long and cold."

"And dangerous."

Hardrada looked across at his companion. Wise words for one so young. "Indeed it will," and he spurred his mount into a steady trot leaving the magnificent walls of the capital city of Byzantium behind.

Michael strode into the great hall, adjacent to the Imperial Palace, where desks were laid out, row on row. Behind each one a bald-headed scribe worked away at various documents. The only sound, other than the occasional cough, the scratching of pens upon velum. The most ordered Empire on earth was at work, keeping the cogs well oiled. As he made his way down one of the aisles, Michael wondered if this was really what he wanted. The trappings of being emperor held many advantages, being rich the greatest. This maelstrom of bureaucracy, however, was not something he had either thought of, or even knew existed. By the time he reached the back of the hall, he was seriously beginning to doubt his suitability to continue. Then Orphano came up next to him, that oily smile oozing across his face. "Highness. Are you ill?"

Michael blinked. "Ill? No, I'm not ill, just … " He let the sentence hang, unfinished, in the air. He gave another look down the serried ranks of desks. "What is it they do, Orphano?"

"Do, Highness? They administer. Without this army of scribes and clerks, the Empire would not function. We are the greatest Empire in the world, Highness, with our territories stretching across the Mediterranean basin, as far East as India, and as far West as Italy. Imagine the complexity of such a venture, the languages, customs, beliefs of all the various people over whom you, Majesty, have dominion. It has to be maintained, cared for, *loved*. Like a captive tiger, we must make sure it has everything it needs to live a full and contented life. If we do not do these things, like the tiger, it will turn on us, perhaps even devour us."

The Emperor shook his head. He was deeply worried. "I had no idea about this, Orphano. The complexity, as you have described, is overwhelming!"

"Majesty," Orphano's smile became more fatherly, and Michael actually believed the man really did have a heart after all. "You have working for you all of these men. Scholars. Dedicated, trusted. Many of them hand chosen by me. They are experts at what they do, and, what you have to remember is that they all work for you, Majesty. You do not have to worry."

"But the responsibility, Orphano ... I'm not sure if I can—"

"If I may be so bold, Majesty." Orphano took the young emperor by the shoulder and walked him away, out of earshot of any curious listeners. "I am here, to help you in whatever way is required. George Maniakes controls your army, I control the machinery of government. We are your friends. We are here to help you and the Empire to thrive. Relax, Majesty. You are in the most privileged office in the known world – you are Emperor of Rome! Think of your heritage, all of those great men who have gone before you. Do you not think that they too had doubts, worries, even fears? Of course they did. They found the solution and surrounded themselves with men of calibre who aided them in the offices of government. It is the same with you, Majesty. Trust me."

"Rome had all this?" His hand waved across the army of scribes.

"In a similar way but perhaps not quite so sophisticated. Rome was mighty, grand and powerful, but so vast that overseeing the many problems that befell it became an impossible task. We do things in a much more organized way, Majesty. Our communication system is the finest that exists, and our many trade links keep the Empire rich and resourceful. We have eclipsed even Rome, Majesty. And now you are at its head."

Michael chewed at his bottom lip as he considered Orphano's words. Words meant to reassure him but only served to heighten his sense of anxiety. He believed it was all going to be so simple, and that all he would have to do was sit back, smile and allow himself to be showered with riches. He was God's representative on earth, so why did he feel so inadequate? He let out a heavy sigh. "I thank for your words, but there is one thing, one person missing from your list, Orphano. The Patriarch, Alexius. I need his blessing, to confirm me as supreme head in God's eyes. I need that more than anything else."

"And you shall, Majesty. Just as soon as Hardrada returns with him."

Michael shook his head, "I don't trust him, that Varangian. I've never met him, but everything I've heard, everything others have told me leads to only one conclusion. The man is out for one person, and one alone – himself."

"That is as maybe, but he will bring the Patriarch back, have no concern. I have him exactly where I want him. The Lady Zoe is my trump card in that regard."

"Yes. I have heard the rumours." Michael had indeed heard the rumours, had often felt he should confront his adopted aunt about them. Not so long ago, she was the empress, married to Michael's predecessor and namesake, Michael IV. The idea that Hardrada and her were lovers seemed to be an open secret, to everyone that is except the former Emperor himself. What would his reaction have been, Michael wondered.

Perhaps it would be a little like his own reaction to his lover's liaisons with Maniakes. He pulled the top of his robe around his throat, the heat rising from his neck as he had a sudden image of Leoni, her body naked, spread out before him, waiting. He struggled to put the image away; no point thinking about that, certainly not at this time of day. The morning air was chill, and it helped to keep him sharp, and not dwell on the weakness of his flesh. He brought the conversation back to the problem in hand. "This soldier you have ordered to accompany Hardrada, you can trust him?"

"One of the most ablest men in your service, Majesty."

"They must have started out early."

"Yes. Before prying eyes could put two and two together – and make five!"

"How long will it take them?"

"Difficult to say. Perhaps four days to reach the frontier post, a day to arrange their return ... just over a week, if everything goes according to plan."

"And what if it doesn't? I hear there are still Thracian bands running around in the mountains to the north. It would not be wise to cross their path."

Orphano frowned. "Your Majesty is well informed. But, as long as they keep to the more well-trodden pathways, they should not encounter any tribesmen."

Michael nodded. "And Hardrada's companion? An officer in the army, but not one I know. One of the very ablest you said."

Orphano slowed himself down, as if considering his words carefully. "Yes, Majesty, just as I said. A young lieutenant, loyal and well skilled."

"Who knows the main highways?" Michael turned to go. "One of *your* men is he, Orphano?"

"Highness?"

"Never mind. Actually, come to think of it," again, he waved his hand over the assembled ranks of clerks who continued to toil away, "it would be difficult to find a man who *isn't* yours."

"Majesty, everything I do, I do for you."

"Orphano," Michael tapped the eunuch lightly on the chest, "the only person you think about is yourself. You and Hardrada have much in common." He paused before moving away and allowed himself a broad smile when he saw the look of horror on Orphano's face. "One last thing. The Lady Zoe. I am sending her away."

"Away?" Orphano took a step towards his Emperor, all efforts to remain calm, in control, slipping away. "Your Majesty, we need to talk about this, before you—"

"Before I what, Orphano? Do something rash, make a mistake?"

"Majesty, the Lady Zoe is an integral part of our plan. We need her, to rally the support of the people."

"The *people*, Orphano, will do as they are told. I am arranging a week of games for them. Horse races, plays, festivals. I am providing all the wine and food."

"The Patriarch, Majesty, will not be pleased that Zoe is not here."

"Well, he won't know, will he? All I need is his blessing – everything else will then fall into place, mark my words."

"Majesty, I have to beg to differ. The Lady Zo—"

"Is no longer your concern, Orphano! The arrangements have been made. You're very good at bureaucracy, Orphano. At *administration*. For action, foresight … look no further than your Emperor." With a great flourish of his robe, Michael whirled around and strode across the great hall, disappearing through the exit at the far end without another glance.

After he closed the door behind him, Michael leaned against it, eyes closed. He breathed hard, taking time to bring his hammering heart under control. He had confronted Orphano and triumphed! All of his fears, anxieties, all of it defeated at last. He felt incredibly proud of himself and couldn't help but laugh, as happy as a little boy who had just discovered everything he had ever wanted under his pillow on his birthday morning. Victory. How sweet it was.

He hadn't been sure he would be able to pull it off. He had rehearsed his words over and over, standing in front of a steel mirror, going through possible replies and reactions. Orphano had been stunned at the news of the Lady Zoë's exile. What a master stroke, sewing such confusion inside the usually unflappable Orphano, something which would grow to consume him. The idea itself was delicious! The trump card. Sending Zoë away, out of the limelight, to while away her last few, miserable years, well out of the public eye, exactly what he needed to secure the throne for himself. No lingering vestiges of the past. A new start. The people would forget, they always did. A fickle lot, the mob. The Romans knew how to deal with them. Games and bread. Well, he may not have the old gladiatorial games, but he had the next best thing – horse races. The people loved them, loved to gamble on their favourite teams, their star riders. They would be so drunk on it all, the food, the fine wines, the atmosphere of abandonment, that soon Zoë would be nothing to them. A memory. That was all. Pleased with how everything had gone, Michael almost skipped his way down the corridor towards one of his many offices of state.

Orphano, furious, stood chewing away at the inside of his cheek. Damn his impertinence, the miserable whelp! Didn't Michael know that by sending Zoe away, he could jeopardize the entire plan? Alexius would no sooner support Michael after that than he would an Ostrogoth becoming emperor. And then what would happen? More riots, perhaps even an uprising. With Hardrada back in the city, with his Varangians and Zoe not here, it would be virtual revolution.

He stopped, and quite suddenly all the gloom lifted from his mind, his shoulders straightened, and he grinned.

Of course, that was it!

The idiot had created the ideal scenario! Why hadn't he thought about it before now? His own plan was, in fact, full of danger and uncertainty. Through a sheer accident of fate, Michael had provided the perfect solution to the whole, miserable problem. Orphano clapped his hands together and rubbed them in glee. Some of the nearby clerks looked up from their work and frowned. "It's not break-time yet, lads! Keep at it! We have an Empire to run!"

Slowly something else began to stir inside him. Michael's plan would only work if Orphano could get word to Andreas. That would prove difficult. They had been gone, Hardrada and the Byzantine officer, for almost half the morning. A man on a fast horse might catch them. It was a chance, but it might just work. He snapped his fingers at a nearby clerk, who shuffled over to him. "Fetch the Varangian commander. Crethus. Tell him to saddle a horse, with provisions for two days, and meet me at the city gate within the hour."

The man bowed his head and trotted off. Orphano felt his heart pounding. It might work. It just might.

Nineteen

The hammering on her door caused Zoe to run across the room in some alarm. Her handmaids all stopped and stared, exchanged glances. It was unusual for their mistress to show such haste. When the empress pulled the door open, everyone understood.

Crethus bowed his head, took a quick look around, and pulled her outside into the corridor.

"What are you doing? I've been waiting for you for—"

He pressed his mouth against hers. Completely taken aback, she melted in his arms as his lips rolled around her own. She let out a little moan, as her stomach simply turned to water.

Then, just as unexpectedly, he pulled back. She gasped, blinked a few times, and managed to mutter, "What is going on?"

"I haven't long," he said, his voice low. "I have been ordered to go away, just for a few days."

"Where?"

"I don't know yet. Orphano is meeting me at the gates. But listen," he took her away from the door, just in case someone might have their ear pressed against it on the other side. "Something is going on. I don't know what. I see it in the way people rush through the corridors, their eyes wild, as if they were on fire. I want you to stay in your rooms. Trust *no one*." She went to speak, but he pressed his index finger against her lips. "When I return...I don't know how, but I will take you away from all of this."

"Crethus, please... I will be safe, don't be concerned. Just make sure you return safely."

"I will, have no fear of that. In the meantime ... " He leaned forward and kissed her again, then held her eyes with a look of such longing she almost swooned. He gripped her around the waist. "I know this isn't the perfect time, or place ... but, you have to know ... " She held his gaze, hardly daring to breathe, wondering what was to happen next. "I love you," he said, and then he turned and ran off, disappearing before she had any chance to respond.

Her knees buckled first, and she had to hold out a hand against the wall to stop herself from falling.

Love? She brought her hand up to brush away a lock of hair, her fingers trembling. How could he...? It was nonsense to even suppose that a man such as he could have allowed his heart to melt. And yet, he had spoken the words. Could it really be true that she had conquered him so completely? So many times in the past, so many men, Hardrada amongst them. She had feelings for the Viking, but this ... Hardrada had never given her any reason to suppose that he felt anything more for her than that brewed up by their physical coupling. He *needed* her, yearned for her, wanted her but love? No, that was something as alien to the Viking as air is to a fish. Crethus, on the other hand, had shown himself to be so much more of a man. Passionate and kind. Loving, in the truest sense of the word.

Zoe smiled, pressed her back against the wall and looked up to the ceiling. A wonderful warm glow spread out from inside her tummy, over-taking her entire being. It all felt so incredibly delicious!

The door opened and she started, turned her head around to find three anxious faces peering out from inside the room. Her three hand-maidens.

"Mistress?" they said in unison.

"Fret not, my little ones," said Zoe and stepped over to them, holding out her arms to receive all three as they fell into her and snuggled in close.

One of them asked, "You are well, mistress?"

"I am better than I have felt before."

Another giggled, and turned to the third. "Did you hear that, Leoni? Our mistress feels better than she has ever felt before!"

Leoni smiled and pressed her face deeper into the empress's bosom. "That makes me so happy, Majesty ... so very happy."

The General was pulling his sword belt tight around his waist when the door to his office opened and Leoni slipped inside. He gaped at her, furious that she should barge in unannounced. Before he could speak, however, she had rushed up to him, face flushed with excitement, her words tumbling out of her mouth at a frenetic pace. "Forgive me for the intrusion, My Lord, but the Empress ... Please, I have but a moment. She is besotted."

"What?" Maniakes did a double take, his anger subsiding as curiosity got the better of him. "What the hell are you talking about?"

"It is the giant Scythian. Crethus. He has captured My Lady's heart. I know it – she told us!"

"The giant ...?" Maniakes let his thoughts wander for a moment. This was news indeed. He ran a hand through his hair. "Tell me exactly what she said."

"He came to her room and she seemed to be expecting him. So excited she was. She rushed over, her face all red and full of happiness. Then, she went outside with him. We couldn't hear what was said, but after a moment she returned. She smiled so broadly and was so full of joy, she just brought us together and told us all – that he had sworn his love for her, that he was going away but, when he returned, they would be together."

"She said that? As Empress of a system that is full of serpents lurking in every shadow, it surprises me she should be so persuaded. So ... I want you to be absolutely sure, Leoni. She said those very words, 'they would be together'?"

"Yes, my Lord, I swear it. Then she went over to her bed and threw herself down upon it, giggling like a little girl, in love for the first time."

"Well, I'll be damned." He squeezed the girl's cheeks between his fingers and kissed her. "Good girl, Leoni. Good girl!"

It was gone noon by the time Crethus climbed up into the saddle of his steed. Orphano stood next to him, holding the reins, patting the horse's neck every so often. "You will have to ride hard," he said, his gaze more on the horse than Crethus. "Do not tarry, or stop more than just a few moments. You must overtake them, give the officer my note." He thrust out his hand, which held a small roll of parchment, the seal intact. "This. To no one else, do you understand me?"

"Yes, Lord." Crethus took the parchment and leaned back to put it into one of his saddlebags. Orphano's mood surprised him. The man was always curt, but this day he seemed almost afraid. Certainly the urgency of this mission was something that gave it a degree of importance that Crethus had not come across before. The man's agitated state lent more strength to this idea. Not since the night he had been summoned to the General's private apartments, to be given the secret orders to attack the Varangian Norse in the night, overpower them, castrate and leave them for dead, had Crethus experienced this type of urgency. All the Varangians had died, save Hardrada and his immediate lieutenants. Crethus remembered it now, sitting there on that horse, his mind relieving the way it all happened, that night something out of his worst nightmare. The horror of it, the blood. He had fought many times, seen many terrible things, but that night ... to see warriors such as those, emasculated, the screams, the agony ... He shuddered.

"If you are cold," said Orphano, gritting his teeth, "best for you to get on your way – ride fast, and don't look back."

"My Lord." Crethus pulled his mind back to the present, took up the reins and spurred his mount, already breaking into a gallop before he had cleared the city gates.

The road from the city gates snaked out before him, bisecting the outlying plain, running up through the hills and on into the distance. Well maintained, the road was another of those great Roman legacies, a testament to the ancient engineers who had given the world so much. The Byzantines strived to continue in the same vein, preserving the glory of Rome for all generations. Crethus knew, however, that those ancient wonders were just that – old. There was nothing new now. Except Greek Fire. The Roman's had had incendiary pigs, but Greek fire, that was the thing that would keep the wolves from the door. Until, that is, the wolves became so plentiful that even their endless ingenuity could not save the Byzantines. Crethus had no idea what Orphano's plan was, and he had no intention of breaking the seal to read the words on the parchment, despite the fact that he could. He could read, a secret he kept very much to himself. Better to appear ignorant, it was safer that way. And better to remain ignorant of what Orphano had written for Andreas. Whatever it was, Crethus knew, more than anything, that it meant trouble for Hardrada. Why he was still alive was a mystery, but perhaps this letter would speed his end. At least, that was the hope. For he knew, although nothing had been spoken, that Zoe still had feelings for the Viking. To have him removed, taken out of the picture altogether – Crethus could wish for nothing more.

Setting his gaze to the distant horizon, he bunched his shoulders, and spurred his horse onwards.

The messenger met the General as he descended the steps from his headquarters. Maniakes could see by the man's agitated state that he was the bearer of important news. "What is it?"

"His Excellency John Orphano requests your presence, sir."

"Does he now?"

"Yes, sir."

"Immediately, I shouldn't wonder."

"He politely requests that you attend him within his private apartments, at your greatest haste, sir."

Maniakes blew out his cheeks. He sometimes wondered if Orphano ever actually realized just how ponderous his position would be without the support of the army. He looked at the messenger's bowed head, "Well, in that case, you'd better take me to him."

They crossed the great square and slipped into one of the main arteries that led across the inner city towards the Zeuxippus baths and the Senate House. He nodded towards several Senators who mingled about in the cold air, all of whom had the good grace to acknowledge him. This gave Maniakes a little stir of good humour. His reputation was secure, since he had bettered the Bulgars a few years back. His social betters, no doubt begrudgingly, knew to remain in his favour, and Maniakes grinned as he went through the gates and strode into the palace complex.

The vastness of the place always struck him. The majestic buildings of state, shimmering even that grey day, standing as eternal reminders that this was the centre of the greatest empire on earth. All around was a sea of green, cinnamon groves and olive trees, amongst which sat dozens of mansions, chapels and gardens. Orphano, who had rooms in the cluster of private apartments to the west of the Royal Bodyguard complex, should really have worked in the Grand Chamberlain's palace, but he had always been fearful of assassination attempts and preferred to keep as low a profile as was possible. So, his rooms were small, private, unassuming. Not that what went on inside was in any way ordinary. Far from it. As Maniakes walked through the main entrance, the smell of decadence invaded his nostrils almost instantly and he instinctively pulled away his neckerchief and held it against his nose.

"What is that infernal stench?"

"I believe it is merely jasmine, sir."

"Well, it fucking stinks. Which room is he in?"

The messenger, aghast at the General's harsh words, pointed a trembling finger to a set of large double doors to the left. Maniakes grunted and moved on, waving the man away.

"Barbarian," the man muttered and slipped away as quickly as he could.

Orphano was in the rear room, soaking in a huge, square bath. All around, incense of varying different types, burned in their large, black metal holders, plumes of perfumed smoke spiralling towards the ceiling. A thick dusting of jasmine lay strewn around the bath, a perfumed carpet upon which Orphano could tread. Two youths, probably no more than eighteen or nineteen, sat next to the eunuch in the milky white water, gently massaging him with large, soap-filled sponges. Orphano, arms stretched out along the top of the far wall of the bath, had his eyes closed, a look of undoubted ecstasy on his florid face.

Maniakes stood watching for some moments, arms crossed, foot tapping. At last, unable to wait any longer, he coughed loudly.

"Ah, my good friend the General," cried Orphano, eyes springing open. "Good of you to come."

"Your messenger said it was urgent."

"Did he? Well, yes, I suppose it is." He waved the youths away, and watched them as their lithe, muscular bodies climbed out of the bath. Both of them were naked, their large members dangling between their legs. Orphano licked his lips as he drank them in. "Boys, don't go far."

They both sniggered, exchanged wide-eyed looks, and then ran off. One of them glanced across to the General, who scowled back.

"You must forgive my little wants and needs, General." Orphano stood up. The contrast between his corpulent, pot-bellied frame and the slim hard bodies of the youths was marked. Orphano seemed unfazed by it as he pulled himself free from the bath, letting the water drip from his bulk, stretching out his arms and letting out a long, luxurious sigh of total contentment. He seemed to enjoy exposing himself, although why that would be, Maniakes could not begin to understand. Orphano's puny member was barely visible amongst the rolls of fat around his groin. Maniakes doubted if the man could ever achieve an erection. He knew nothing about the reasons for his castration, all he knew was that a man without balls found it impossible to couple with a woman. But boys? Perhaps that gave Orphano some pleasure, but he didn't wish to dwell on the idea. It repulsed him and the sight of this bloated creature brought the bile to his throat, forcing him to look away, pretending to search for a chair upon which to sit.

Having found one, he took his time lowering himself down upon the cold marble of a two-seater bench. When he looked up he found that

Orphano had, fortunately, wrapped himself in a towelling robe and Maniakes found he could now look upon the man once more without feeling sick. "Are you going to tell me what you want?"

Orphano grinned, "Of course, General. Michael came to see me with the germ of an idea I found rather … how can I phrase it? *Ingenious.*"

"Michael had an ingenious idea? That hardly sounds plausible."

"Well, by accident or design, it really was the most wonderful, inspirational thought." Still smiling, he padded over towards Maniakes and plonked himself next to him. "Our original plan, of sending Andreas with the Viking, of taking him up towards the Varangian outpost of the north-western border, of allowing Hardrada to convince the patriarch to return, seemed good at first. At the head of those Varangians, the Viking would give us the security that we need to wrestle control from Michael." He rubbed his hands together. "The Lady Zoe would be there beside him, showing herself to the people, who would rise up and send that dithering idiot of an Emperor we have to the hell in which he belongs."

"I know all this, Orphano. What has changed?"

"Michael is sending Zoe away."

"What the hell does that mean, '*away*'?"

"To a monastery. Within the next day or so."

"You can't be serious! The people will—"

"Exactly, my friend. So, I've decided to change the plan. Instead of taking Hardrada to the Varangians, he is going to meet his death in the mountains of Thrace. They will be set upon by those wild tribesmen, and he will die a hero's death." Orphano giggled. "Then Andreas, who miraculously manages to escape, will continue north, bring back the Patriarch, *alone,* and deliver the news to the people in the Forum of Constantine. Then, we shall appear as the saviours. You will use the Royal Guard to rescue Zoe from her banishment and we will depose Michael once and for all."

"So, what is the difference between that and our original plan? They will both have the same result. Zoe will be Empress, Michael will be removed, and you and I will bask in the glory. The Empire will continue."

"But with those damned Varangians milling around, asking questions, Hardrada is too dangerous! We can deal with him and his men in the field, not in the city. We can't even pay them off, because Hardrada will do so . Either way, they won't return without Hardrada. With him gone, we are free to do what we want. Zoe will be distraught, of course she will. No doubt it won't be long before she finds someone else to keep her bed warm."

"She already has."

"Eh? What do you mean?"

"What I say. Look, all of this is very well, but how do you propose to tell Andreas of the change of plan? As far as he is aware, his mission is to make sure Hardrada does as he is told, to get him to Alexius. Nothing more."

"I've sent a messenger. Crethus, the commander of the Scythian Guard, and a man I can utterly trust. He will overtake the others within the day, deliver to Andreas the change of plan. Hardrada is as good as dead, so we will have no more worries on that score. The Varangians can stay in the north. It is all taken care of, my dear General, with all my usual meticulous attention to detail!" He grinned again. "Now then, please tell me what you know about Zoe's. I am intrigued, if not a little concerned."

"Concerned you should be. Because, if what I know is true, then you might find that your plans have become somewhat unstuck before they have even begun. All things being equal, I think that perhaps keeping Hardrada alive would prove the most profitable."

"I don't understand your reasoning. Explain."

It was Maniakes's turn to grin. "The problem is, you may know a lot, but you don't know everything. Your messenger and the Empress's lover are one and the same."

Orphano's eyes grew wide. "Crethus?"

Maniakes nodded. "The very same. Complicated, isn't it?"

Twenty

They stopped in a glade, just a few feet from where the river ran by. The sun had shown its face and the afternoon had become pleasantly warm. Hardrada hobbled the horses whilst Andreas prepared the camp stove. For centuries beyond imagining, the Roman legionary had carried everything he needed on his back. There had seemed little point in changing something so good, so now Andreas, the Byzantine soldier, inheritor of much from the Roman army, prepared the mess tins for a meal. He poured out some dried peas and mixed in an assortment of herbs, brought the tin up to his nose and sniffed. He grunted his satisfaction and stood up. "I will go and fetch some water." He delved inside one of his knapsacks and tossed over a little bundle towards Hardrada, who caught it in mid-flight. "Flint and steel," Andreas explained. "Set a fire, would you. Please."

Hardrada grunted and gathered some small twigs, together with some dried grass, both in plentiful abundance as it had not rained for weeks, perhaps even months, and the coarse undergrowth was tinder-dry. Without glancing upwards, Hardrada worked at making a spark whilst Andreas tramped off to the river.

It took a few attempts, but at last the dried grass took hold, and the Viking bent down to gently blow on the crackling flames until it was burning. He fed the fire with more sticks, then more until he could warm his hands in front of the blaze. Happy with his handiwork, he rocked back on his heels and gazed into the flames, loving the feel of the heat on his face. He closed his eyes and sighed. If only it could stay like this, simple and unrefined, he would be a happy man. All this intrigue, desire, sex ... He shook his head and rubbed at his beard. It itched in the heat. He could do without all the complications in his life, but right now he could do without the heat from the fire. He stood up and stretched, peered down at the mess tins, filled up with the dried peas. Curious fellow, that Andreas. Quiet, determined, just like a soldier of Rome should be. What was the word they used to describe a man such as he? Uncomplaining, strong, brave probably... *stoic*, that was it. Stoic. He just got on with it, didn't seem troubled by thoughts. Unlike himself. Zoe. Now there was someone to think about. Those slim, strong legs, fine arse, the way he could mould his hands around each plump and juicy...

Hardrada opened his eyes and stared back towards the river. Where the hell had that damned Andreas got to? How long did it take to fill one tin of water? He was about to call out when something stopped him. A thought, tiny at first, just niggling at the edge of his consciousness. It grew, and with it came the tendrils of icy fear, crawling slowly up his back, playing at the nape of his neck. He went into a crouch and carefully drew his sword.

This was not right; he could sense it, tuned as he was to danger. Hardrada moved forward, careful where he planted his feet. He opened his mouth in order to hear better and when he came out of the thick undergrowth that marked the edge of the river bank, he flattened himself to the ground, and inched his way forward.

From the slight rise, he could look right across the river, and all along the sides. Andreas was nowhere to be seen. The sun was sinking lower in the sky, but it still cast its face upon the surface of the river, silver streaks playing across the slow meander. Somewhere close by a heron, or a crane, flew from across the other bank, searching for its next meal. The only sound the playful trickle of the water as it rippled by. Hardrada peered at the water. It seemed tranquil enough, and yet the more he looked, the more he could pick out eddies and whirls, indicating that every now and then powerful, hidden currents lay in wait for the unwary. There were no voices, no wind rustling through the trees, just the gentle gurgle of the passing river. A perfect, autumn evening. And yet…

He spotted it just a little way off from the edge of the river. The other mess tin, the one Andreas was going to fill with water. It lay there, on its side, abandoned. Hardrada gripped the hilt of his sword very tightly, looked left, then right, seeking out any signs that would point to Andreas having been ambushed and taken away. Nothing. If someone had attacked the young soldier, they must have been experts. There had been no warning sound, and now there was no evidence. He scolded himself. There might well have been a sound, of course, but he was so lost in his thoughts that he would not have heard a ballista bolt as it shot through the air. Hardrada allowed himself an exhalation of breath, cursing Andreas for needing to fill up the tin, and the whole world in general for getting him into this situation in the first place! He took another look along the river bank. It had happened, he thought philosophically. Not much he could do about it now – what had happened, had happened. The problem now, how the hell to resolve the situation? There wasn't much he could do, except perhaps to show himself and hope that the damned bastards who had kidnapped Andreas would try the same trick a second time.

Throwing back his head, he roared a wild battle-cry and rose to his feet, swinging his sword high above his head, and raced over the rise towards the river edge.

He pulled up, breath coming in great blasts, and readied himself, prepared to meet the attack. The seconds stretched out into painfully slow minutes. Where were they, damn their eyes? Body rigid, he forced himself to wait, just a little while longer. They could be watching him, even now, perhaps even levelling their bows on his body. Instinctively he crouched down, eyes scanning the tree line, then across the river to the far side. There was nothing and no one. At the crack of a branch from the undergrowth, he swung around, half expecting a bunch of fiendish warriors to come charging out of the trees, swords raised, but again, nothing.

He caught a movement and held his breath.

A small deer appeared, its nose twitching, testing the air. It saw him and for a second locked gazes with him. Then, it bolted, disappearing like a phantom amongst the greenery.

Hardrada allowed himself to relax and straightened himself to his full, imposing height. This was beyond strange, it was uncanny. He had heard stories of sprites and evil spirits lurking in these sparse, remote lands, but he had always dismissed them as tales for children. Could there be some truth in them? Did beings beyond the understanding of men, things that feasted on souls, really exist? His own people believed in them, ancient legends of monsters, demons. Who was to say that they weren't real? Could this be what had happened to Andreas? A mystical beast, invisible, had sprung out and snatched him away? Hardrada's eyes, filling up with tears of dread, roamed once more across the surface of the water. A demon from the deep, lurking in the dark, icy depths, waiting hungry, desperate... He knew such things existed. Not a phantom, a real creature. The Egyptians spoke of gigantic monsters that lived in the Nile, ones that consumed people whole, without warning. As quick as a blink, huge mouths with an array of protruding sharp teeth, they would seize some poor unfortunate, drag them to the bottom of the murky water, and devour them.

He trembled.

A single, plaintive cry, almost a whimper. He stood motionless, holding his breath, head tipped to one side. It came again, like a whisper on the wind, "Hardra-a-daaa!"

He bounded towards the river's edge, brought his hand up to shield his eyes from the dipping sun. Squinting, he slowly surveyed across the water, until his eyes came to an outcrop of large rocks, huge boulders smoothed by the constant play of the river as it swirled and eddied around them. A tiny barrier amongst the fast current.

He was there, lodged in between two enormous pinnacles of rock. Andreas, his arm waving pathetically, his voice like that of a tiny child's, "Hadra-a-daa ..."

Immediately the Viking summed up what had happened. The youth had slipped, fallen into the depths and had been taken down stream, his armour pulling him under as easily as the sea-demon Hardrada had conjured up in his imagination. The youth more than likely couldn't swim either. Who the hell could in such a place as this? A Byzantine soldier, trained in all aspects of fighting – on land! But Hardrada was a Viking, born to sail, and had lived half of his life on board longboats, visiting distant shores. He had been shipwrecked more than once, and was a strong swimmer. He tore off his sword and belt, threw away his boots and plunged into the river without another thought.

It took him by surprise; the strength of the current, the sharp, painful coldness of the water snatching his breath away. For a moment he floundered as he fought to recover himself. Then his strong arms cut through the water and he allowed the current to take him towards his stricken companion.

Luckily for them both the river was not in flood. The lack of rain was their ally that day, and Hardrada found that he could easily negotiate a pathway towards Andreas. As he drew closer, he could see the blue haze on the young man's skin, and he knew that Andreas was more likely to die from cold as he was from drowning. The thought caused him to strike out even more strongly, and within a few seconds he was next to the soldier, pressing his palm against his cheek, realizing that time was running out.

"You have to hold onto me." He had to shout here, the river around the rocks, although not powerful, created enough noise to muffle his voice. "Damn it, do you understand?"

The youth managed a nod and Hardrada smiled in relief. He took hold of one of the lad's arms and draped it around his own neck.

"Listen, I want you to hold on tight. Imagine you are strangling me." He grinned, and added wryly, "You'll enjoy that, I reckon." Andreas merely groaned. "We will go to the other bank. That is our only chance." He knew that if he tried to make it back across to their camp, the burden of the youth would be too great against the current, and both would be washed downstream. Their only chance was to get across to the opposite side. Taking in a breath, Hardrada screamed, "*Now*," then plunged headfirst back into the icy water.

Twenty-One

Crethus took his horse up the steep incline and tethered it whilst he stretched himself out in a sort of cave on the side of the mountain he had just scaled. From this vantage point he would have a good view of the surrounding plane, but right now he needed rest. His horse was blown and he knew that if he pushed it much harder, it would give out completely. So he lay down, closed his eyes, tried to calm himself and find his second wind.

When he opened his eyes, he knew he had been asleep for too long. The afternoon had stretched on and it was now evening. The air had grown much colder. He sat up, frantic, disorientated for a few, horrible seconds. How long had he slept? Desperately, he gathered his few belongings and went over to the horse, which seemed much happier now that it had rested. He fed it some oats from the saddlebags. As the animal munched through the grain, Crethus stared out across the flat plain below. It was dusk. Really, if he had any sense, he would stay where he was. It was well sheltered, this slit in the ground he cared to call a cave, was as good a place as any to rest for a few more hours. But then, he caught the red glow in the far off distance and knew it was a camp fire. Beyond it, the silver thread of a river, flowing through the land like an artery of hope. He made the calculations and decided he could still make the camp before night fell completely. Quickly he put away the oats, took hold of the reins and began the slow, cautious descent.

Hardrada took off Andreas's body armour. His hands were numb with cold and he found it difficult in the extreme to undo the buckles and clasps. All feeling had left his fingers, but he gritted his teeth, continuing as best he could whilst Andreas lay there, shivering, skin tinged with blue.

Hefting off the armour, and discarding it with a satisfied grunt, Hardrada looked around. Light was failing fast by now, and he knew the temperature would continue to drop. If he wasn't kept warm, Andreas would die, of that, there could be no doubt. Hardrada had seen it before; men washed ashore, convulsed with cold, dying, their bodies turning hard, muscles unable to work. It had terrified him then and it did the same now. If only he had a dry blanket, he could wrap the Byzantine in it, huddle up close, warm one another. Survive.

Across the river, he could see that the camp fire burned. He had made a good job of that, he mused. Much good it would do them now. If he were to save Andreas's life, he would have to swim across the river with him, get him next to that fire, warm his body through to bring the life back to his limbs. He looked down at the youth and he knew, in that single look, that it wasn't going to happen. He sighed and sat back in the coarse gravel of the river edge. He trembled terribly with the cold and wrapped his arms around himself, trying to create some warmth. Perhaps together, they might be able to generate enough heat. If he could move Andreas up the bank, into the surrounding scrub, find some shelter, perhaps a ditch in the earth, anything to give them some fragment of shelter. Sitting here, like this, exposed to the elements, he would probably not see the morning himself. Gripped by this realization, he took a few deep breaths and stood up. His legs were already seizing up and it frightened him to think he might die like this, on a lonely river bank, with no one to sing of his great endeavours, becoming merely food for the crows. He gritted his teeth. This would not be the manner of his passing. He girded himself, clenched his fists and felt the rage burn through his body, spirits rising. He reached over to Andreas and hauled the youth to his feet, then swung him over his shoulder. Hardrada had to force his legs to move, brain screaming out its commands. First the right, then the left. One step at a time, driving himself on. There was no sensation in his muscles, his legs numb. He knew they could do the job, had always done the job, but the cold was conquering him. It had invaded his sinews and tendons, but he knew he couldn't succumb. Once he stopped, it would be over. He would lie down and die. Onwards then, nothing else for it. He gave full vent to his fury, screamed out his trademark battle-cry, and pushed on, working his way over the river bank, making the rise, and continued into the undergrowth skirting the area. Grunting like a pig, he dipped in amongst the overhanging trees. Only when he was amongst the rough scrub did he fall down, not caring if Andreas was dead, or injured. All he knew was that he had made it, and the relief overwhelmed him. Rolling over onto his back, he lay there, staring up at the blackening sky, searched out the first star he could find between the branches, and he gave thanks to his gods that they had given him the strength to survive.

He managed to dig out a shallow hole in the soft earth, gathered some bracken and leaves, made a primitive type of pillow for them both. Then he rolled Andreas into the makeshift shelter and lay down beside him. The youth breathed very slowly now and despite all of his efforts, Hardrada had been unable to revive him fully. The fact that he still breathed was some small victory, Hardrada surmised. At least it gave him hope that if the gods continued to smile, then the morning would find them both alive. Pressing himself as close as he could, he put his arms around the shockingly cold Byzantine, pulled more leaves over them both, and closed his eyes and tried to calm the chattering of his teeth.

Sleep didn't come. The cold gnawed away at him, and the sounds of the forest seemed amplified somehow. Animals rustled through the undergrowth. Rodents, lizards, the occasional fox, or boar. Boars worried him. Angered they could be dangerous, and he had no weapons to help defend himself. And he had left Andreas's armour and sword down by the river edge. He cursed his stupidity, didn't understand why common sense had deserted him. Was that also something to do with the cold? Did it attack thinking as well as muscle? He didn't know, he didn't care. Andreas slept, but for him, there was no such relief.

The noises became louder.

And nearer.

He sat up, alert. Boar it might be, but it sounded bigger. Much, much bigger. Something large was coming through the scrub, and was making little effort to conceal its progress. He looked about, but could see nothing. The night had fully enveloped them now. With his senses focused, Hardrada waited, hardly daring to breathe.

Whatever it was that was making its way through the undergrowth was coming straight towards them. The Viking bunched his fists, the only weapons he now had, and got to his feet. Some of the feeling had returned. He hardly dared hope that it would be enough.

Crethus left his horse some way off and drew his sword. He could be moving into the camp of the Viking, then again he may not. Other people moved around this land, some of them dangerous. Thracian tribesmen were renowned for their ferocity, and their stubborn resistance to Byzantine rule. Many stories filtered back to the city, of kidnapping, enslavement, brutal death. He had never heard of them encroaching this far east, but he wasn't about to take any chances. , Furtively, he moved furtively from tree stump to rocky outcrop,. Although the night was his shield, the sounds of the outlying land seemed so much louder than during the day, as if everything was conspiring against him. Alert, eyes wide, peering through the darkness, the camp fire the focus of his entire being, he moved like a mouse, scurrying, but quiet.

Abandoned. He saw that as he came closer, thanks to the fire. Mess tins, still filled with food, illuminated by the crackling fire that was struggling bravely to continue. It hadn't been fed for a while. He squatted on his haunches, stirred the embers with the point of his sword and looked out towards the nearby river. This was strange indeed. Almost as if some huge bird had plucked whoever had camped here from the earth.

A rustle to his right caused him to spring to his feet, sword ready to strike. A horse neighed. Pounding of hooves upon the earth. Not his mount, that was for sure. He crept towards the sound.

Two horses, hobbled, stood amongst the few sparse trees. He patted their flanks, calmed them. Nervously, they shied away, but he brought them closer, tethered their reins to a nearby branch. He rummaged through the saddlebags but he could only find some clothes and bits of food. Nothing that would lead him to the identity of the riders. Until, that is, he moved closer to the second horse. Its saddle was unmistakably that of a Byzantine officer. At that moment, Crethus realized he had found them.

He went rigid as an unearthly screech broke the encroaching silence, a sound unlike anything he had heard before. Animal, wild, unknown. He stood and waited, knowing an attack would surely come.

The figure, a shadow against the black of the trees, stood, its breath coming slowly, and it waited, waited for Hardrada to move. Well versed in the art of killing, Hardrada knew better than to rush into attack. So he too waited.

Both of them stood there, as if turned to stone. Hardrada experienced no anxiety, no fear. The figure did not appear to have a weapon, and a great cowl hid its features. But it was slight, not at all what Hardrada was expecting. In truth, he had been somewhat surprised to discover that the thing making the noise had revealed itself as human. What type of human remained to be seen. Witch, magician, some strange, alien forest dweller… He couldn't begin to tell, but the longer it stood there, as still as the air, surveying him, the more Hardrada's nervousness increased. It was measuring him, gauging his strength. It would soon determine that his strength had ebbed, sucked from him by the cold. Then, would it launch its attack? He decided to act, but perhaps not in the way the figure expected. He slowly brought up his hands, open, palm outwards, and said, "I am unarmed and wish you no harm."

It tilted its head. Perhaps his tongue was unknown to it. Or perhaps – much more likely, as far as Hardrada was concerned – it was merely biding its time, knowing that the Viking was weak, and weaponless.

"Your companion is hurt?"

Hardrada almost fell over with shock. It was a woman.

She stepped closer, an arm's length away, pulling back the cowl to reveal a face of quite startling loveliness. A wide, full smile and round eyes drew him in. Hair tumbled down to her shoulders and even in the darkness, he could see that it shimmered with gold. An elfin face, the chin slightly pointed, the cheekbones high. Hardrada felt his mouth drop open and then, without any warning whatsoever, the strength drained from his legs and he fell to the hard earth, the last thing registered her plaintive cry, a loud shriek, cutting through the still night.

From this distance it was impossible to gauge the direction of the cry. Crethus stood by the river's edge, tensed, ready to fight. It had sounded like a woman, but why would a woman be out here, all on her own? And what would cause her to cry out like that. It had echoed out across the plain, and had no doubt penetrated the trees on the opposite bank. It was hopeless to try to see anything, so he backtracked to the fire which, by this time, was barely spluttering. He quickly threw a few pieces of kindling on top of the remaining embers and, thankfully, they caught fire. Before very long, he had piled on a few more twigs, rubbing his hands in front of the blaze.

It was a damnable situation. He had no real idea what to do, but one thing was certain – the morning would bring answers. Until then, he would curl up here beside the warmth of the fire, get whatever sleep he could, and then investigate as soon as the first light came over the horizon. With this in mind, he went to his own horse, tethered it with others, and took out his blanket from his saddlebags. Wrapped up, with his sword beside him, he did his best to gain what rest he could in that strange and slightly menacing place.

He was warm. The feeling had returned to his fingers, toes, and most importantly, his arms and legs. A heavy fur lay over him. For a long time he allowed himself to wallow in the luxury of snuggling deep into the fur; he had been cold before, but never had it bitten so deep.

Hardrada opened his eyes and had to snap them shut almost instantly. Morning had returned, the sun bright and welcoming. He flexed his joints, took a deep breath and sat up.

He was in the hollow that he had managed to dig out with his hands the night before. At least, he assumed it was the night before. He had no real terms of reference since his collapse. Had he been asleep for only one night, or many? He certainly felt refreshed, ready to face the challenges that a new day would bring. As he looked around, the only things he could see were the trees, the scrub, and rocks. Over to his right, he could hear the gurgle of the river. So, he hadn't been taken elsewhere. It must have been the woman who had covered him over with the fur, and perhaps she had merely rolled him into the ditch. It would be difficult for her to carry him, if she were alone.

If she were alone.

He looked around more anxiously now. Andreas had gone. There was no sign of him at all. With his heart pounding in his ears, Hardrada scrambled to his feet, brushed off the dried leaves from his breeches, and scurried off towards the river.

It was deserted, and looked much the same as he remembered it. Even Andreas's panoply still lay where he'd thrown it. He looked across the water, water which seemed so much less dangerous now that the sunlight played with the gentle ripples on the surface. However, he remembered how strong the current had been. That much would not have changed, whether he had slept for one day, or an entire month. He gritted his teeth. On the opposite shore were the horses, all of their equipment, supplies and weapons. He had to find some way of getting across that would not endanger his life.

"There is a ford."

He whirled around, and saw her, as before, silent, staring. For the second time, the woman had come upon him unheard. It was a thought that made him uneasy. Was he losing his renowned sixth sense, that ability to act upon his unerring intuition, and be ready to defend himself when others were still wondering what all the fuss was about?

Or was she a skilled hunter, able to move through the undergrowth unheard, unseen? This scenario was even more chilling, because with it came the almost certain knowledge that at any time she could have slit his throat.

He found a grain of comfort in the fact that she hadn't. She posed no threat, but who exactly was she? She had saved him, kept him warm, protected him from the cold. Andreas too. Andreas. Hardrada put his head on one side, "Where is the Byzantine?"

She frowned, deeply. "Byzantine? Is that what he is?"

"So, he's still alive then?"

"Of course. He is strong like you."

She stepped towards him then, and he held his breath, to prevent himself from letting out a whimper. She was beautiful. He had never a face so perfect; clear, milky skin, which seemed to shimmer in the early morning light. The light which filtered through the trees gave a strange, dappled effect to the patina of her flesh and he watched her with unblinking eyes, thinking that at any moment the spell would be broken and he would find himself once more alone in that ditch, all of it a dream.

She touched his arm and he started, realizing at once that this was indeed reality. She was here, very close, that face peerless, hypnotic in its loveliness.

"I'll take you to him," she said, her features expressing no emotion. A flat voice, almost bored in its timbre. "If you wish to cross the river, to your horses, I can show you the ford also. But," her fingers brushed over his arm, "you need to know something. On the far side, in your camp, there is another man."

Hardrada immediately whirled round, crouching low, half expecting an arrow or javelin to come hurtling through the air, as if her words would signal an attack. She giggled, clutched his arm again, pulling him to her. "He has gone."

So close now he could smell her perfume. He closed his eyes, allowed himself to be lifted by the scent. A woman of the forest. Is that what she was? So clean, so beautiful? Living out here, all alone, how was that possible? He opened his eyes again and found her staring up at him, those smouldering eyes searching his face, looking for a sign, anything that might tell her what he was thinking. He remained neutral, not daring to let his guard slip. She's a vixen, that's what she is. He could tell. That intuition was beginning to work again.

"You saw this man?"

She nodded. "I watched him. Huge he was with skin like charcoal dust. He slept in your camp, looked after your horses, fed and watered them, then, at first light, made through the undergrowth along the bank of the river." She pointed her finger away into the distance, the opposite way from where she had indicated the ford to be. "He is searching for you, knowing that you must be close."

Hardrada chewed at his bottom lip. Crethus, the Scythian commander of the new Varangian guard. What in all that was holy was he doing here? Trailing them, but for what reason?

"He wishes you harm?"

"He might do." He saw a questioning look flash over her features, a trace of fear flitting through her eyes. "He has been sent to follow us, for what reason I cannot say because I do not know."

"If he continues that way, he will die."

"*What?*"

"Oh yes. I am not the only one who has been shadowing you. You make more noise than a wild beast. A war band is abroad, and they have your measure. They mean to rob and kill you, if they find you still alive after your adventure in the river."

"How the hell do you know all this?"

She smiled, and began to pull him further into the trees, "I am one of them."

Twenty-Two

They came for her early. Two guards, voices gruff, hammering on the door to her chamber. The handmaidens had done their best, shouting, demanding that they leave. How dare they burst in like this?

The men paid them no heed and strode through the outer-apartment, ignoring the girls' attempts at delay. Zoe, already woken by the shouting, sat up in her bed. This would never have happened in her husband's day. Not like this. Such impertinences, such effrontery.

"Madam," said the first, his teeth flashing in his hard, black face, "You are to dress yourself and accompany us to His Royal Highness's throne room."

She seethed with rage. "Get out!"

The man glanced over to his companion who stood, impassive, eyes glaring ahead. "Madam. You are *commanded* to accompany us."

She threw back her bedclothes, swung her legs over the bed and stood up. "I said get out, whilst I dress myself you ignorant cur!"

The two men both grunted, turned and went out into the antechamber.

"She's a fucking firebrand," said the main speaker.

"Yeah. Did you see her tits under her nightdress? She is bloody gorgeous!"

The other winced. "Keep your fucking voice down! They'd cut off your balls for talking about the royal family like that."

"No wonder Crethus fancies the knickers off her!"

"Well, that's another thing you want to shut up about. He'll take your head off if you ever say that within his earshot." The man looked around, and took his companion's elbow and steered him towards the main door. The maids had all dispersed, some of them going in to attend to their mistress. "Listen. I reckon something big is happening. Her Ladyship," he jerked his thumb towards the bedchamber door, "won't need all these lovely maids, so I think there'll be rich pickings for us."

"You really think so?" The man licked his lips. The girls were all very slim and very tasty and he had been a long time away from his homeland. "Now *that* is worth considering."

"Too right. Anyway, keep your mouth shut, yeah? We'll just have to wait and see what happens. In the meantime, we do our job, no questions asked."

The other man winked and allowed his imagination to flow with pictures of nubile, naked girls bouncing all over his rampant body.

Michael was anxious. Zoe was a formidable adversary, so, to minimize problems, he had run through what he would say a thousand times. Best to be fully prepared when dealing with such a viper as she. As long as everything was done quickly and quietly, there shouldn't be any problems. Spirit her away, disguised, with very little fuss and no one would become suspicious. By the time it became common knowledge, no one would care. He had already coached his heralds, who would begin to take up stations in all the major parts of the city. Once the announcements of a full week of festivals had been made, no one would give a moment's thought for the empress. The mob would be so drunk with wine, feasting and merriment, that none of them would care. No, it was a good plan and all that it really depended on was the timing. To get her away within the hour, that was the key. Michael knew it could happen, as long as he didn't allow her free reign to make some sort of a scene.

The throne room was empty, save for himself. He stared down the long approach to his dais. Large marble columns rose upwards, where they arched across the stunningly decorated ceiling. Scenes from the lives of past emperors, all of them safely ensconced in the glory that was Heaven. Green, rolling hills, azure rivers, brilliant suns beating down. Michael gazed over its beauty. Was it really like that? And if it was, how did the artists know? Would he, Michael V of Byzantium, already have a place set aside for him, to share with those great men from ages gone by? And could he ever scale to their heights? Constantine, Vespasian? What could do to make him remembered, to carve his name in the annals of history? It was a thought that gnawed away at him, had become his constant companion. The need for fame, for glory. To take his place amongst those greats. When he had stood and watched the tiers of clerks scribbling away at the mountain of administration that engulfed them, he had doubts, but now, after having had time to think, he knew where his destiny lay. He was the master of all, but he didn't need to *know* all. His trusted advisors could handle all that nonsense. Men such as Orphano.

The problem, of course, lay in the fact that he despised Orphano. He grinned to himself. The man made his skin creep, and the thought of bringing him down, destroying him, was a delicious one. Rumours about the man's sexual excesses had circled the palace for many years, but nothing had ever been proven. How could it, when Orphano dealt so effectively with anyone who dared so much as hint at any impropriety. Michael promised himself that as soon as this trifling matter of secreting Zoe far away was successfully concluded, he would turn his attentions to the Royal eunuch. To do that, he would need an ally, and Michael knew exactly whom he could recruit.

An urgent rapping on the door brought him out of his reverie. "Enter," he said automatically, still relishing the thought of how he could destroy Orphano.

His grin broadened as he saw the two Scythian guards escorting a silent and serious Zoe.

"Ah, my dear Aunt, how lovely to see you." She stood, unperturbed and his grin instantly vanished. He waved the guards away.

When they had gone, his gaze returned to Zoe. For a moment, Michael believed she would not speak, that his poor attempt at wit would not proffer the result he wished – flash of anger, a glimmer of annoyance. He knew that what he was about to do was the right course, the only way to solve the dilemma he was in, but that knowledge didn't make it any easier. The woman had supported him, brought him to the dizzy heights of becoming emperor. She had to go, but it wasn't easy.

Zoe slowly approached the dais, and the throne. Michael watched her and she moved as if she floated, making no sound, her progress like a regal swan gliding over the glassy surface of a tranquil lake. He could not look away, and he hated that. Hated her beauty, her supreme majesty. Hated the way she mounted the steps towards the throne as if it were hers.

Michael had been standing just to the left. Now, he ran across towards the throne, grabbing hold of the sleeve of her robe, preventing her from going any further.

She let her head drop, and then she sighed. She looked at him over her shoulder. "Take your hand off me, Michael."

Her words hit him like slaps across the face, stinging him, forcing him to blink away the tears. "I am your Emperor, Madam! You call me Majesty, or Highness—"

"I call you what the hell I please, you impudent upstart." She tore her arm free from his grip, swung round and settled herself on the throne. She sat there, whilst he seethed, and ran her tongue over her top lip. Savouring the taste of her impending meal, like a mantis, poised, ready to strike. "What do you want, Michael?"

Damn the bitch. She could always do this; reduce him to his lowest, like he was some naughty child. He wanted to hurt her, with his fist, not words. Wipe that grin off her gorgeous face. Then, it came to him, the answer, and he pulled himself up, smirking. "How old are you now, Auntie?"

"What?"

"First sign, that. Hearing going." He grinned, deliberately raised his voice, "I said, *how old are you?*"

She half-rose from the chair, a wild tiger, preparing to strike. She glared at him but then she sat back down, smiling herself now. Michael knew his victory had been short-lived. Not even a victory really, just a glancing blow across her supreme self-confidence. Not enough to fell a mouse.

"You have so much to learn, Michael – about the subtleties of being a ruler."

"You would know all about subtleties, of course."

"Royal blood runs through me, you would be well advised to remember that."

"Royal blood? Well, that may be so, but you officially adopted me, don't forget! So, the Royal lineage is mine as well."

"But what can be given can so easily be taken away."

He felt his hackles rise, and leaned towards her, the spittle flying from his mouth as he shrieked, "Don't you threaten me! I am Emperor of the Byzantine Empire, chosen by God as His supreme representative on earth! You have no *right* to talk to me in that way! No right."

"Put away your tantrums, Michael, and grow up! You have about as much religious fervour coursing through you as a piece of lead! Look at what you have done since choosing to become sole ruler – murder. Do you think God looks kindly on such acts?"

"Murder? You talk to me of murder, when your last husband died so young, and the previous one drowned in his own bath?"

"Neither had anything to do with me."

"Well, God will be the judge of that."

She leaned back in the throne, a single fingernail tapping at her teeth. "How many deaths have you been responsible for, in the short time you have sat here? Fifty, a hundred? All those Varangians, murdered on your command ... I think when God tallies up the numbers, your sins will far outweigh mine."

"All I did was cleanse the palace of undesirables, heathens!"

"And replace them with Infidels?" She smirked. "Don't try and fence with me, Michael. You'll lose."

He squeezed his temples with finger and thumb and let out a long, rattling breath. "Fine. We'll stop, then." She was right, of course. She'd lived her entire life in this place, breathing in the power. The guiding force behind three emperors – two of whom sent her away, but not as far as he was about to. She would remember him for that, every waking moment. He let his hand drop down to his side. "You are to leave, Auntie."

She stopped, arched an eyebrow. "Leave? Leave when? Where?"

He spread out his hands. "It's all organized, so no need to be concerned."

This time she came fully off the throne, moved right up to him, so close he could feel her breath on his face. "*Concerned?*" Low, in control, but the anger teetering around the edge of the words. "There are times Michael when I almost admire you. The things you say, the way you say them, it's almost … it's almost as if you've rehearsed it all."

He stepped back. What was she, a soothsayer? "You're going away."

"You've said that. I want to know where."

"*Principus.*"

Her face told it all. Ashen, unable to utter a single word. The look of defeat, and his victory.

Later, in the quiet of her room, Zoe sat on the chair, the tears streaming down her face as her maid, Leoni, very carefully cut off the empress's hair. Leoni too was sobbing and she had to concentrate hard on her task, in case her trembling hand slipped and she gouged Zoe's scalp with the secateurs she used. The other maids busied themselves with packing away Zoe's things; personal items and a few clothes. Nothing extravagant, that was what Michael had said. After all, she was going to be a nun from now on, locked away on the island of *Principus,* in the Sea of Marmara. The monastery there awaited her, but would accept her in the same way they would accept any other novice. There she would be anonymous, no fawning and kowtowing for her. To live a life in the service of God, a pure life, innocent. All past sins forgiven. The abbotess had agreed as much with Michael when the arrangements to accept Zoe into the nunnery were made. Simple obedience would be all that was required in return.

Zoe sniffed loudly. She dared not look into a steel mirror, to see her beautiful locks hacked away, a shorn pate, crude and ugly with little tufts of hair punctuating her scalp. A curse on Michael for doing this. No other man had ever treated her this way. True, her other lovers, emperors, had locked her away, but in her own apartments, surrounded by her servants and all the trappings that went with her royal personage. This, this was beyond anything. Michael had become a monster and she rued the day she had ever answered her husband's call, stood over him as he lay on his deathbed, body swollen like a pumpkin, all of his beauty gone and yet still so young, the pain etched in his face, and agreed to the plan – arranged, as always, by John Orphano – to announce Michael as the new emperor. She had already adopted him as her son, although she preferred to think of him as a nephew. Now, he would be ruler. Zoe had believed she could control him; he was, after all, a mere boy with no experience in the machinations of government. Unfortunately, she had underestimated Orphano, and his vile trickery. It was he who had manipulated the entire scheme to favour Michael, so that he would be the power behind the throne. Emperor in everything but name.

This had not been the first time Orphano had promoted another to the seat of Emperor. He had been the one who had put the former emperor, Michael IV on the throne; such a wonderful man in those early days , Zoe recalled with sadness. Breathtakingly beautiful, she had wanted him as soon as she had set eyes on him, and when Romanus, her husband, died, they had married and been crowned. However, as soon as he had become emperor, it began. The undermining of her position. Excluding her from the royal bed, locking her away in her rooms. Orphano had at first been delirious with joy, but soon he too realized that the new emperor was not so malleable as he first expected. He worked so hard, became pious, and *responsible*. Then, he had become ill, dangerously ill. He would have fits, so terrible that they had to close the drapes around his throne so no one could see. Everyone knew, of course. So, the plans had been mad and Zoe had gone along with them, to replace her husband and install Michael *Calaphates* as the next emperor.

She had underestimated Michael right from the start, but so too had Orphano. It had only taken a few months for Michael to manoeuver himself into position, removing all the obstacles to his sole control over Byzantium. Everyone had been duped and now, there was nothing left but to resign herself to the inevitable.

A life, as a nun. What a cruel and ignominious end to a life of luxury and privilege. If only Alexius had been here, to prevent all of this from happening. But he wasn't, and neither was Crethus. No one to come to her aid and stop this villainous and unjust act!

Leoni stepped back from her mistress, looked down at her handiwork and was engulfed by a new wave of tears. Without a sound, Zoe ran her hand over the top of her head and stood up, letting the cloth that had been wrapped around her shoulders fall to the ground to join the chunks of hair that lay all around. The empress turned to Leoni and, with extreme tenderness, reached out and stroked the young girl's cheek. "I will miss you, Leoni."

The handmaid wept openly, pressing her face into her hands, her whole body shaking.

"I must go on this journey alone," the empress continued, brushing away a few fallen strands of hair from her simple gown. "No doubt you will find service with someone else."

"But I don't want to be with anyone else!"

"Nonsense." Zoe gently took hold of the girl's wrists and pulled her hands away from her face. "You're a good, girl, Leoni. A hard worker, diligent, loyal, even if you do report back to your lover, the General, with all the news and gossip that you hear."

Leoni gaped and had to swallow hard before she could speak. "My Lady, I—"

"Please." Zoe's voice was subdued. "It doesn't matter now, none of it. The General was probably privy to it anyway."

"I don't believe he was, My Lady."

"Well, that's as maybe. I don't really care anymore. The rest of my life has been mapped out for me and there isn't a great deal I can do about any of it."

Leoni bit her lip, "My Lady, I could speak with the General, tell him how wrong this is, ask him to—"

"No. Enough is enough. I had hoped that the Patriarch would come, but I fear that it is too late for him to help. Messages were sent to him, I understand. But I doubt if he will be able to save me, not now."

She went over to her bed and looked down at the few remaining articles that still had to be packed away. This was it, the last sight she would have of this room, this place. How long had she been here? A year, two possibly. She never once thought, not for a moment, that any of it would ever come to an end. Why should she? Michael was in his position because of her. She had supported him, convinced the Senate, the Church, everyone. And now, he had cast her adrift.

"I won't let him see me cry," she said, more to herself than anyone else.

Leoni came over to her, tentatively placed her hand on her shoulder. "Mistress. There must be something we can do."

"We?" She shook her head, resigned to it all now. "No, Leoni. See to it that my things are brought down to the port." She lifted her head and smiled. "I have a boat to catch."

Twenty-Three

Andreas slept in the tiny hut, wrapped in furs. He had woken once or twice, and each time the girl had tended to him, feeding him hot soup, or washing his brow. The young Byzantine fluctuated between burning fever, and extreme shivering.

Each time Hardrada poked his head through the door to catch a glimpse, the girl ushered him out again. But he had seen the deathly pallor on the young man's skin and didn't like what he saw. It was the mask of death, a thing encountered many times on the faces of wounded men after battle. As they lay in the dank earth, the cuts from axe blows or sword thrusts, the way the wounds sucked and oozed, as if they themselves were living things. The way the flesh turned to pale stone, then became a sickly wax. He had seen it, and he did not know of any man who had lived after that cast came over their flesh.

Save one.

Himself.

He sensed the girl at his shoulder and he turned. She was drying her hands on an old cloth. "He is very sick," she said, not looking into the Viking's eyes. "If you hadn't helped him he would already be dead."

"He was cold, I warmed him. That is all."

"Well, without you he would be in their Christian heaven right now." She tossed the cloth away. "I'm going to make us something to eat."

"Why?"

She frowned, then a slight, bemused smile. "Because we are hungry! We need to—"

"I *meant*, why did you help us? You tell me I kept Andreas alive, but without you, both of us would be dead."

"Is that his name, Andreas? That's really quite beautiful, don't you think?"

It was Hardrada's turn to frown, "Oh, yes, like an angel's."

"That's exactly what I was thinking," she gave a little skip, then clapped her hands together. For a moment she looked like a little girl and Hardrada had to laugh. His biting sarcasm had been completely lost on her. A curious mix of innocent young girl, naive in her dealings with others, yet supremely confident in her environment. She eked out some sort of life amongst the woods, far from prying eyes, and she thrived on it.

"I have to ask you," he said quickly, changing the subject. "You mentioned a war band. And that you are one of them..." He swept his hand over the small encampment, with its leather-sided tent, the pots and pans strewn here and there, an animal skin pegged out to dry. "This is their camp too?"

She bit her lip, looked back to the tent for a moment, then shook her head. "They sometimes pass this way, but not often."

He didn't understand that. A woman, as beautiful as she, living out here in the wilds, left all alone? Who were these men that they did not come and visit her? And who was she that was able to keep them away? Warriors, men skilled in death, why would they choose to leave her alone. There was something not quite right in any of this.

"I married a Roman," she said, by way of explanation, possibly sensing his unasked questions. "He left me riches, a fine house, servants. I gave it all away, to live my life here, as my mother had."

"Your mother? I don't understand."

"Why should you?" She shrugged, stooped down to pick up a pot. He watched her as she went to fetch an animal skin, filled with water. She poured most of it into the pot, and settled it down on the makeshift brazier above the flames of the camp-fire. She threw in some herbs. "My mother was a soothsayer."

A tiny chill ran down his spine. "A sorceress?"

She gave a small laugh, gathered up some vegetables and began to slice them into crude chunks, plopping each one into the water. "That is what the war band believe. Who am I to tell them otherwise? Such knowledge keeps me safe from them."

"Because they believe you to be one also, a sorceress?" Hardrada blew out his cheeks. "We must give thanks for their stupidity. Or blindness."

"They are not stupid, and certainly not blind. Simply mistaken. My mother was renowned for her knowledge of herbal lore. Everyone came to her when they were ill, or had some malady that they could not shift. Then, one day, a young soldier was brought to her, dying from his wounds. And no matter how hard she tried, she could not save him. He died, right there." She pointed to a small clearing of bare earth a few steps away. "Nothing ever grows there, not since his life blood seeped out and soaked into the soil."

"Men die all the time from their wounds. I should know, I've seen it often enough."

She shook her head. "No, this was like no other death. He was a nobleman's son, high-ranking, and they don't die like that. Alone, in the cold, damp earth. So, they killed her. My mother. His companions ran her through with their swords. I watched them, tried to stop them. But what could I do, a mere girl against such brutes. The commander, he was the cruellest of all. He seemed to enjoy my suffering." Her slicing of the vegetables became much more violent, the heavy knife in her hand chopping through the various ingredients for the soup, like they were the skulls of the men who had killed her mother. "It was only after she lay there, dead on the ground, that it happened."

Hardrada held his breath. Something about her, the way she had changed, made her seem suddenly capable of violence. Looking back to the dreadful deed, her eyes narrowed and glazed over, it was almost as if she had returned to that moment. Her voice was hard, controlled, but with an edge to it that had not been there before. It made his heart freeze. "What happened?" he managed.

"The soldier, the boy. He sat up, completely healed."

It took him a moment to react. He heard the words, but not the meaning behind them. The way she spoke, her face, it all made him feel very uneasy. "What do you mean? You said he was dead."

"So he was. My mother placed the herbs into his wounds, said the words, lay her hands upon his body, then he died. At least, I thought he had died. Everyone else too. But he hadn't. He sat up, blinked a few times and grinned." She looked at the Viking with eyes filled with tears. "Now, you understand why they don't come?" Her eyes, now as black as coals, bore into him. "My mother had brought him back from the dead."

The day had already turned cold by the time Hardrada stood on the opposite side of the ford. The girl had given him a packed satchel bag, some concoction of herbs which she said would heal any wound, and a map. He had studied it before his departure and it seemed clear enough. A path through the treacherous mountains would cut down his travel time to the northern border by at least a day. With good weather he should make the camp of the Varangians this time tomorrow. Andreas, still not fit to travel, would stay there and Hardrada could pick him up on the return. At first he had been reluctant, but images of Zoe, and his two friends' death at the hands of the detestable Orphano loomed large in his mind, and he acquiesced.

She watched him from a little way off and he raised his hand slightly as he took the first step into the icy water. He sucked in his breath sharply. It was even colder than he remembered. It must be snowing up in the mountains, a thought that did not improve his mood, but he gritted his teeth and made his way across the river to the opposite bank, the water rarely reaching above his knees.

He turned again as he stepped up onto the bank. The girl had gone, disappearing amongst the trees like a ghost. For some reason he shivered and instinctively pulled the fur around his shoulders. All that talk of sorcery and raising the dead, it didn't sit well with him. Never a superstitious man, Hardrada had nevertheless met witches in his own country. Usually old and misshapen, he had dismissed their arts as the stuff of nonsense, although he was always wary of them, never asked them questions or sought out their help in any way. Perhaps there was something in what they did; he simply did not want to think about it.

Along the river edge, he came across his sword and scabbard, exactly where he had left them. Quickly, he buckled the belt around his waist, hefted the blade in his hand. It was good to have it back; it reassured him, made him feel safe. Then, he turned and scrambled over the bank and into the broken ground and sparse tree line that had been their camp. The ashes from the fire were grey, cold and dead. The pot with the peas was also there, most of the peas now gone. Someone had been here, cooked by this fire, made themselves comfortable.

Sure enough, as he investigated further, he came across the unmistakable signs of habitation. The slight impression in the earth, footprints, and, over by the trees, defecation.

A horse whinnied.

Whoever had made themselves at home in this place was no thief. The horses were tethered in a little glade and, once again, he saw the remains of oats on the ground. The visitor had fed the animals, cared for them. Not the actions of someone selfish and unconcerned. A friend? But who? Hardrada chewed at his lip, suspicions growing, but kept his mind busy with other things. He saddled up his horse, attached the saddlebags and blanket, tied the reins of the other to his own, then lifted himself onto his horse's back. Andreas's mount snorted loudly and Hardrada led them out of the glade and set his course on the pathway that ran alongside the river.

He glanced over to where the girl had her own encampment, but he could see no signs of either her or her tent. It was as if the whole lot had been swallowed up the forest over there. If he did not already know it existed, he would certainly not know now. No wonder she could eke out her life undisturbed. Perhaps it had nothing to do with sorcery after all. She was simply unknown to anyone. That must be the logical explanation.

Surely.

Twenty-Four

In his offices of state, Orphano was sat at his desk going through some papers when the door burst open and two huge guards strode in. He looked up from his work and gave them a steely stare. "What is the meaning of this?"

"By His Royal command," the first brute said, keeping his eyes away from the eunuch's face, "His Majesty summons you to his presence."

"Does he by God?" Orphano leaned back in his chair, hands clasped over his ample stomach. "And what does he wish to summon me about?"

"I can't say, sir, because I don't know."

"Very well." Orphano threw his pen down, some of the ink splashing out over the paper. "Marcus!"

Instantly a short, squat man appeared from the darkened corner. He shuffled over to the desk, head held low. "Master?"

"Get these papers done and then go and tell the General that I have been … *summoned*."

Marcus bowed. "Sir."

Orphano stood up, pulled on a short coat over his usual monk's habit and gestured for the soldiers to lead the way. He tried to remain outwardly calm, but inside his heart was racing. The manner of these soldiers, their abruptness, it was not something that had happened before, not in all of his years of service to the Imperial court. Not only were they surly, but they were obviously in a rush. Orphano had worked diligently and tirelessly for them all, even Michael. He had offered what advice he could and, up until recently and the breakdown of relationships with Zoe, he had always had the Emperor's best intentions uppermost in his mind. It couldn't be that Michael had figured out what was really in Orphano's heart. Unless the General … but no, he dismissed that thought immediately. The General was of the same mind.

They crossed the main courtyard, the three of them. A few people gave them questioning glances, and the occasional senator bowed, but no one stopped to speak. Even the few Scythian bodyguards, who lazed around, gave him nothing but a passing glance. It was as if everything was as it should be, a fact that made Orphano increasingly nervous. It seemed as if the whole of the city of Constantinople knew what was happening. Everyone, save himself.

The palace was filled with the usual throng of courtiers, high nobility, hangers-on. The mumbling and occasional outburst of laughter ceased almost as soon as Orphano came into the large antechamber. Again, he puzzled at this. Obviously word had got round. Curious that he should not have been informed.

Then, near to the huge entrance doors to the Emperor's throne room, he saw why. The youth who he had entrusted with almost everything, the one who had even shared his bath, stood there, bare arms folded across his chest, a spiteful look on his smooth face and at that moment Orphano experienced a tightening across his chest, like steel bands contracting. He had to stop, catch his breath, and when he brought his hand up to wipe his sweating brow, he saw that it trembled. One of the soldiers insolently nudged him in the back.

"Move on," he snarled. "His Highness awaits."

Orphano was about to say something, but he bit his tongue. The man, dangerous looking, barrel-chested, was not the reason. It was the collected throng. Every eye was on him. The vultures, waiting for their pickings, he mused. So, he turned and walked up to the great doors and pushed them open without so much as a rap on the wooden surface.

"Leave us!"

Michael glided from behind his throne and peered towards his visitors. The soldiers bowed and did as they were bid, closing the door with a resounding crash. The sound echoed around the vast room, something which served merely to exaggerate Orphano's growing feeling of isolation.

Orphano bowed. "Majesty."

"My dear friend." Michael smiled and took the few steps on the dais and settled himself down on his throne. He spread out his hands. "I trust you are well."

Orphano, with his head still bowed, had to suppress the impatience in his voice. What was going on? "Majesty. Very well, thank you."

"Good. Come closer, dear friend. I wish to speak to you in a more, how should I put it … *fatherly* tone."

Orphano looked at his emperor from beneath his brows. That use of the term 'dear friend', how that aggravated him! Michael only used such slavish language when he had some ingenious scheme to reveal, something he believed would be the most wonderful thing in all creation. He had hinted as much at their last meeting, when he had come up with the plan to intercept Hardrada. Orphano stood up straight and padded closer to the dais. He looked around. There were no other chairs so he stood there and waited.

Michael had a humourless grin plastered across his face, like a permanent fixture. "I have something to show you in a moment, dear friend. But first, I have this." He reached into his robe and pulled out a thin piece of parchment, neatly rolled up. Slowly, Michael opened it out, gave it a cursory scan, then passed it across to the eunuch.

Orphano read it and felt his whole world begin to crumble. Everything, all of his power, his influence, none of that mattered now. The words seared into his very soul. He read them again, just to check, then took a breath. He would have to be careful, remain calm, bring all of his intelligence to bear and try and extract himself as best he could. "It is obviously a lie, Majesty." Michael pursed his lips, then held out his hand for the roll. Orphano hesitated for a moment. "You don't believe this, surely?"

Michael gestured impatiently with his hand and Orphano put the roll into the emperor's palm and sighed.

"There are witnesses, Orphano."

"You know it's a lie."

"Do I? So why would they all lie, these people who have come to me – of their own volition, Orphano. No one was forced to do any of this. This statement," he held up the roll, "is your death warrant. You understand that, don't you? …Uncle, and dear, dear friend."

"Majesty!" Orphano could feel the panic rising, but there was nothing he could do to prevent it. "Obviously, enemies have concocted this whole affair. You can't think that I would plan to poison you?"

Michael sat back, tapping his chin with the end of the roll. For a long time he sat there, as if weighing up his actions, considering how best to proceed. He stopped the tapping abruptly, suddenly shouted out, "*Guard!*"

Orphano whirled around, not knowing what to expect as the doors swung open and the same brutish soldier who had escorted him to palace strode in. He bowed. "Sire?"

"Bring him in. And the other one."

The guard bowed then went out. Orphano watched, transfixed. A few barking commands were made and then two more soldiers came in with the youth who had stood so brazenly by the door. Another young lad also stood there, one that Orphano remembered as the youth who had often fanned him during the hot, sultry evenings. Both of them stood in relaxed attitudes, surly sneers on their beautiful faces.

Michael's voice was matter-of-fact, "Tell me what you told my guards, exactly. Word for word."

The first youth bowed. "Majesty. We both observed our master, Orphano, preparing a concoction one evening. We did not know what it was and we stayed in the corner, out of sight, to watch him. Then," he looked at his companion, who coughed nervously and stepped forward. He too bowed.

"Sire. We saw the Lady Zoe coming into our master's chamber. They greeted one another as old friends. Then, our master handed over the phial, into which he had placed some of his concoction and said these words, 'Put this into … forgive me, sire…'"

The boy suddenly grew very red and looked around in a desperate manner, as if his words were to spell his own doom, not someone else's.

Michael roared, "Continue, damn it!"

The boy bowed even lower, "Sire, he said, 'Put this into … *Michael's* wine before he sleeps tonight, and everything will be as it should be.' Then, she took it, kissed him on the cheek and left."

"This is nonsense," interjected Orphano, taking a step towards the youth. Instantly, the brutish soldier moved between them, hand on the hilt of his sword. Orphano swung around to face his Emperor. "This is a tissue of lies, Majesty! Why would I do such a thing? I have supported you every step of the way, given you my unbroken service from the moment you ascended the throne!"

"Aye, And waited for your moment to strike," hissed Michael. "Like the viper you are!"

"Majesty, never have I so much as—"

"Silence!" Michael leaned forward in his chair. "You did the same with my uncle, the Emperor Michael IV! Damn your eyes, you put him on the throne, your own brother, after having murdered Romanus! The whole City knows of your lies and intrigues, Orphano! You have manipulated and schemed for too long. Well, now you have met your match. In bringing me to the throne, you have hastened your own death knell!" He snapped his finger towards the brute. "Send Her Lady in."

The soldier bowed and marched across the room to the far corner, where a small door led to one of the many adjacent offices and dressing rooms. A few moments later and Zoe appeared.

It was unmistakably her. The face, high cheekbones and oval eyes that drank you in. The fine figure, discernible even beneath the simple, plain gown she wore, corded around the waist. Bare-footed and, most shocking of all, a bald head, cropped to the skin. Orphano gasped, both hands clamped to his mouth. "Dear Christ!" he managed.

"Dear Christ indeed," said Michael, enjoying the spectacle. "The Lady Zoe is off to a monastery, Orphano. I won't tell you where. Suffice for you to know that she is going there to sit out her days in quiet contemplation and service to Christ Our Lord. She leaves this very night. And you," he came down the steps, "will not be able to utter a single, damnable word about any of it!"

Orphano shook his head, struck dumb by what had transpired. He knew of the plans to send Zoe into exile, but he had always believed it would be as before, under house arrest. To put her away in a monastery, how could the Emperor even contemplate such a thing? Orphano had completely underestimated Michael, had never believed he could be capable of such duplicity, such barefaced subterfuge.

"You see, dear friend," Michael reached inside his robe again, and held up a small, stone bottle. He held it up and peered at it, tilting it slightly. "This is the poison, Orphano. I tested it, on one of the dogs. It dropped dead within a few moments. Quite horrible really." He looked across at Zoe. "She hasn't denied it. How could she – she had it in her possession."

"No," Orphano managed to utter and moved towards the dais, "No, that isn't right! None of it! Majesty, this is not going to solve anything! Your killing me, banishing the Lady Zoe, none of it will work! The people, Majesty, the people will *know*!"

"Will they? I doubt if they will even care. I am addressing the Senate this evening, and tomorrow I will open a week of games and festivities for the people. I very much believe that by the end of their drunken, fornicating seven days they won't give a damn about you, the Lady Zoe, or anything else that might enter into their small, pathetic minds! And besides," he nodded at the soldiers, "I'm not going to kill you, Orphano. I'm going to send you away too. You are my uncle, after all. What would Mummy and Daddy say?"

"Jesus, you are a sinful, insolent little cur. What would your *Mummy* say? She'd put you over her fucking knee and spank the living daylights out of you, that's what she'd do."

Before anyone knew what was happening, Michael had ascended the dais at speed and struck Orphano across the face. The blow staggered the eunuch, and he took couple of teetering steps backwards, clutching his cheek, eyes watering from shock more than pain.

Michael stood, breathing hard, his face flushed. He snarled, "Well, Mummy's not here, is she! You still think of me as a baby, Orphano. The way you strut around, head up, nose in the air, as if *you* are the real power. I'm not a child, and I am the one who makes the decisions – not you. Not anymore. Guards!"

Orphano tensed himself, ready for the strong arms to grab him and drag him out to whatever fate Michael had in store. But, as he closed his eyes and waited, nothing happened. The cries to his right forced him to turn, and he saw that it was the two youths who were being manhandled. He watched in utter astonishment and increasing horror as the soldiers held onto each youth in turn, and the brutish one drew out his sword, turned to the Emperor and waited. Orphano saw it, the slight nod, then the curled back lips. "Kill them," said Michael softly.

Before anyone could move, or cry out, or even set up some sort of struggle, the brute ran his sword right through the first youth, the cruel blade cutting upwards to his breast bone. The second youth screamed, and attempted to break free, but it was useless. The soldier holding him was too strong and as he kicked and writhed around in the man's enormous hands, the youth could see that his end was near. The brute pulled out his sword from the other's torso, a great gout of blood and a jumble of grey, red-veined intestines tumbling to the floor, which he ignored, stepped towards the other, and slashed him clean across the throat. Both young men were on the ground, a few gurgling sounds coming from deep within their bodies as their life drained from them.

The brutish soldier cleaned his blade on the shorts of one of the dead victims. He sheathed the blade and stood to attention and waited.

Orphano closed his mouth, tried to swallow but found that all of his saliva had gone. His throat dry with terror, he turned his eyes to the Emperor, tried to speak, but could not.

"Dear God," said Michael, falling back into his throne. "Did you have to make such a mess? Get it cleaned away before I throw up."

"Tut, tut, Michael." It was the Lady Zoe, speaking for the first time since she had come into the room. She had watched the whole ghastly episode without uttering a single word. She seemed completely unaffected by what had occurred, and even smiled as she slowly shook her head in a gesture of what looked like disappointment. "What's the matter, haven't you the stomach for it."

"Shut up, you bitch!" Michael gave a short bark of a laugh. "I know you have the stomach for it, plenty of it. How many husbands did you see off? Two? Watched them die, as you did the rounds? No doubt you were being screwed whilst they writhed in agony."

"You've improved your vocabulary," she said, "as well as your ability to murder."

"Don't lecture me, damn you!" He wiped his mouth. "It had to be done, imbeciles that they were."

"Naturally. We wouldn't want the fact that they were paid stooges to come out, would we?"

Michael glared at her, then pointed at Orphano, who still stood completely non-plussed. "You are to be taken away, Orphano. Placed under house arrest, until I can decide what to do with you. Those two bastards have sealed your fate, and don't think I won't use this," he held up the roll again, "if you so much as mention a word of what you've seen here today to anyone. Do you understand me, dearest friend?"

Orphano nodded, then looked at Zoe who did not meet his gaze, but turned, clasping her hands in front of her in a practiced attitude of prayer, saying as she did so, "I shall go and prepare myself, Michael. I doubt if I shall see you again."

"Not in this life," sniggered the Emperor.

"No. Nor perhaps the next."

Michael shot her a look that would have withered most, but Zoe merely moved away, as quietly as she had entered, and glided into the anteroom, closing the door softly behind her.

"Damn her," Michael spat. "I'll be glad to see the back of her with her airs and graces." He turned to consider Orphano. "You look ill, dear friend. I know you had feelings for those boys, but even you must have known that they could not live."

"I expect not. I just wasn't … Majesty, what you are doing—"

Michael held up his hand, palm outwards. "I don't want to hear it, Orphano. Your counselling days are over. My men will escort you to your chambers, where you can gather your things. Not too many, mind. I want you to travel light. Besides, where you're going, you won't need for very much."

"You won't get away with it."

"Won't I?" Michael smiled, and looked around him smugly, "It seems like I already have."

Twenty-Five

As the distant skyline became tinged with purplish hues, Hardrada felt the heavy weariness begin to crush him. Surrendering to it, he leaned forward across the horse's neck, allowing his eyes to close. He had been tramping along the chosen path now for hours, the stillness of his surroundings lulling him towards sleep. He had fought against it, successfully too, but now it was becoming too much. Then the horse whinnied and he snapped his eyes open and sat up. He cursed himself for being so weak. No sleep, not until the darkness fell and he could settle himself somewhere easily defendable.

The pathway arched upwards at long last, giving him a moment to rein in his mount, and he looked around before slipping down from the saddle. He patted the horse's flank, tethered it up to a nearby tree and then scrambled down the short incline to the river.

All the way along the path, the river had been his constant companion, always just a few steps away, its gentle meandering bringing him a sense of comfort. A lifeline, which would lead him back to the girl and Andreas. What need had he of a map when he had this great silver finger, forever pointing to the way home?

He got down on his knees and scooped up handfuls of icy water and splashed his face. He rubbed his eyes and hair, shaking himself like a great cat, revitalizing himself. He felt instantly better, the weariness fading as cold needles of water pricked his flesh.

The footfall might have surprised someone less experienced than he. He made as if he was continuing with his washing, but readied himself. The second step made him move, rising and turning in one flowing movement, hand already bringing out the sword, parrying away the attack. He put his shoulder into the assailant, knocking him back into the dirt as a second assailant came on. Hardrada swept round, keeping low, the sword slicing through the man's shins. The attacker screamed as he went down. Over to the other side, the horses whinnied and stamped and Hardrada saw them, out of the corner of his eyes, rearing up. Other men were closing, trying to take the horses. Squat men, wrapped in furs. The war band.

A sword strike came like a blur. Hardrada took it, ran his blade down the other's, twisted it away then kicked out, catching the man in the groin. He grunted, pitched forward, and Hardrada brought his blade down across the back of the man's neck. With no time to admire his handiwork, Hardrada was dipping and dodging another blow. This one was much stronger. A big man, wild eyes, chipped teeth in a mouth open and cavernous. He wielded an axe above his head, whooping in a strange, grotesque manner. Others took up the battle-cry. How many, Hardrada couldn't tell, he had no time to think. Three were down, a fourth pressing forward. Others were closing and he knew, in that instant, that there were too many. He could perhaps kill three more, but not this many. No matter, he would fight, end it all here and now, falling in the glory of battle. A true Viking. He roared, parried and cut.

From out of the trees erupted a terrible sight. A huge man, black skinned, massive arms sweeping an evil, curved scimitar which sliced through flesh and bone with horrible ease. The Viking saw two, then three of the wild war band falling, bodies split open, blood gushing out.

Hardrada lifted his voice in his own great battle-cry, and smote his attacker with the axe, the man falling with a deep, guttural groan. By now, the first attacker was getting back to his feet and, without turning, Hardrada thrust backwards, felt the satisfying impact of heavy metal sinking into soft flesh. He jerked the blade free and the man crumpled to the ground. Suddenly, everything became quiet, the receding sound of fleeing warriors the only thing to interrupt the lull, but soon that also was gone. Hardrada came up ready, sword before him, and there stood the great swarthy Scythian, grinning, drunk with the ecstasy of killing, the blood and brains of his victims sprayed across his chest.

"Crethus," breathed Hardrada. He remained tense, not knowing what the massive Scythian would do next. Then, he saw the great warrior sheath his scimitar and he allowed himself to relax a little. However, he held on to his own sword, and waited.

Stepping between the fallen assailants, Crethus came up to the Viking, bowed his head slightly, and smiled. "You haven't lost your touch, I see."

"Nor you yours." Hardrada slowly slid his sword into its scabbard. "Except that this day you didn't castrate anybody – whilst they slept."

The smile froze on the Scythian's face and for a long time they both held one another's gaze, until at last Crethus looked away, and counted up the fallen. He shook his head. "Two got away. They were a scouting party, and soon the others will be upon us." He looked up. "We must go."

"Go? Go where?"

"I have orders to accompany you to the Patriarch." A frown came. "Where is the Byzantine who accompanied you?"

"He is safe."

"Not dead then?"

"No. Not yet. Why do you ask? Is he part of your orders also?"

Another frown. Hardrada knew he had touched a nerve, made an inroad. Who would send the Scythian all this way, and for what reason? Something must have changed, the plan needed altering, perhaps even abandoning altogether. Had the mighty Crethus been sent to assassinate them? And the Patriarch too?

"My orders are to escort you to the camp of the Varangian mercenaries under Rufus Wolfberdbrüder, and ensure that you return to Byzantium post-haste. That is all."

"But we are going to do that anyway." Hardrada stepped closer. At this proximity Hardrada could tell he was a mere fraction taller than the Scythian, but other than that they were almost reverse-images of each other. Where the Scythian was dark-skinned, muscles well defined, the flesh smooth, almost shining, Hardrada's body appeared to be carved from granite, the limbs hairy, rough, scarred and the colour of alabaster. They would make good comrades or, more probably thought Hardrada with grim acceptance, bitter enemies. Well-matched, equals. The Scythian had fought like a demon, and had revealed his skills with frightening, almost nonchalant confidence. A dangerous opponent in every way. He tapped the Scythian on the chest, just once. "Why were you really sent?"

From afar came the sound of raised voices. Crethus snapped his head around, "They are nearer than I thought! We must go." He rushed towards where he had left his own horse and leapt into the saddle.

Hardrada moved quickly, untied Andreas's horse from his own and slapped its rump hard. The animal started, whinnied loudly, and galloped away, back down the path towards the now distant campsite. He needed speed now, and there would be other horses for Andreas. He swung himself into the saddle and spurred his horse on, pounding after the speeding Crethus.

By the time the night had fallen, they had managed to outpace the war band. Although they both knew that the enemy would continue to follow, neither allowed the thought to worry them. Because there, over the rise, lay the camp fires of the Varangian outpost. They reined in their horses and sat there, peering out across the vast plane towards the northernmost limits of the Byzantine empire. Beyond, the unknown. Russians, Normans, perhaps Bulgars. Enemies all, and everyone intent on the destruction of the greatest civilisation on earth. The cradle of knowledge, the receptacle of the collective wisdom of the ancients. A fragile treasure, that required constant defence and maintenance.

"We will make it by morning," said Crethus, repositioning himself in his saddle. "We will make camp down the side of the mountain, find a cave. If those bastards decide to attack us, we can defend ourselves quite well from there. You have the sealed orders?"

Hardrada nodded towards his saddle bags. "Aye. I've kept them safe."

"That's good, because I'll be needing them."

The glint in his eyes seemed accentuated by the night, and it was all the warning Hardrada needed. As the Scythian swung round, the dagger he held cutting through the darkness in a flash of silver, Hardrada struck out, blocking the knife arm whilst striking out powerfully with his other elbow. The blow caught Crethus under the jaw, and lifted him off his saddle with tremendous force. With a guttural expulsion of air, the Scythian pitched backwards and hit the ground with a dreadful, hollow thud. Even as he attempted to raise himself up to a half-sitting position, Hardrada was on him, pulling him to his feet by the throat. The Viking struck him hard across the face and sent him over the lip of the hillside where he disappeared, swallowed up by the blackness.

Hardrada stood and listened. The sound of the body hitting the earth seemed amplified in the still night, and he could hear it sliding all the way down the mountainside. He remained there until he could hear it no more, then, satisfied, he went back to the horses, tied up the Scythian's mount to his own, and continued on along the track that would eventually lead to the Varangian camp. He had no intention of waiting until the morning came. That had been Crethus's plan, but now he was dead and the plans had changed.

Twenty-Six

"General, I need to speak to you, sir."

Maniakes was sitting in his private rooms, relaxing, having finished his early evening meal. The soldier who stood before him looked worried, deep lines of anxiety etched across his face.

Leoni came from around the back of the couch, leaned over the General's shoulder and kissed him lightly on the cheek. "I'll be in the next room," she said quietly and slipped away.

Maniakes smiled to himself. Leoni was an intelligent and resourceful girl. He had made a wise choice there for a bedfellow. He arched an eyebrow towards the soldier, who was studying the girl's retreating body with a look of intense desire. "What is your name, Captain?"

The soldier snapped his head around, "Nikolias, sir."

"Very well, Captain Nikolias. Speak."

The Captain bowed his head and moved closer. "The Lady Zoe is being moved this night, sir. I thought you might wish to know."

Maniakes did not shift his position on the couch. He reached over and picked an olive from one of the many bowls that lay strewn across the low table before him. He studied it carefully before popping it into his mouth. "Captain, I know all about the Lady Zoe being exiled."

"Sir, with all due respect, there is more."

"More?" The General bit on the olive, then washed it down with some wine. "I'm all agog, Captain."

"His Highness, the Emperor Michael has also exiled His Lordship Orphano."

Maniakes almost choked on the last mouthful of his wine, and sat up, coughing hoarsely. Quickly, Nikolias poured him some water and the general gulped it down, took a moment to recover himself, settling his breathing. "Orphano? When did this happen?"

"Within the hour, sir. I thought you should know. His Lordship did send a messenger to you, sir. Unfortunately," Nikolias drew his index finger across his throat, "one of the Emperor's guards got to him first."

Maniakes stood up, and placed a hand against his chest. His heart pounded. This was bad news indeed, and totally unexpected. Michael was moving against them all and for a moment Maniakes was at a loss what to do. His mind raced through a whole string of possibilities, one of which included fleeing the capital and making his way to his troops in Italy. Michael would not dare to move against him with an entire army to come to his aid. He gnawed at his bottom lip, then turned an inquiring eye to the Captain. "Why are you telling me this?"

"Sir?"

"You, a loyal Byzantine officer, are breaking your oath against the Emperor."

"I made no such oath, sir. My loyalty lies with the army. I do as I'm ordered, sir, but sometimes … I had to kill two conspirators, sir. Two boys, barely eighteen, who had come up with some fantasy story concerning Orphano and the Lady Zoe." Maniakes gazed at the officer closely as the chill ran through him. "They told the Emperor that both Orphano and Her Ladyship had planned to poison the Emperor, and had made signed testaments to the fact."

"That's not true. Orphano would have told me. Besides, it would serve no purpose to kill the Emperor, such an act could well plunge the Empire into civil war."

"My thoughts exactly, sir."

"Your thoughts … Captain, you are an interesting man. What else did *your thoughts* tell you?"

"I see the Lady Zoe as a force for good, sir. Bringing solidity and grace to the Empire. I believe her exile to be wrong, sir. The same also could be said for Orphano, sir."

The General, having recovered from his shock, poured himself another goblet of wine. He paused for a moment, considering the Captain, then poured the man a goblet full also. He handed it over. Nikolias eyed it cautiously before taking it from the proffered hand.

"Tell me, Captain. Why are you only a soldier? A man with your insightfulness should be a politician."

"My family were politicians, sir. I preferred to make my own way. But," he raised the goblet, "I fear that the time is close for the army to intervene." He took a sip of the wine.

"Be careful, Captain, that your emerging ambitions don't get the better of you. If the Emperor can remove both the Lady Zoe and Orphano, he would find it a simple matter to destroy you."

"Which is why I came here, sir."

"Oh? And what makes you think that I am not loyal to the Emperor?" Maniakes considered the soldier studiously. Could it truly be the case that the army was on the verge of mutiny? The capital city did not billet many frontline troops, and what Imperial Guard remained had had their ranks depleted by border duties. The City tended to rely on the Varangian guard for defence. The Varangians, however, were in total disarray. The Norse had been violently replaced by Scythians, the most untrustworthy group of curs imaginable. The scene was being set up for a monumental clash of arms, especially if Hardrada returned at the head of the Varangian Norse of Rufus, with Alexius in tow. Perhaps it would be best if Hardrada survived, and Crethus failed in his mission. The pot was well and truly being stirred, and Maniakes had to find some way of watering it all down. In the end, the only thing that mattered was the stability of the Empire; its continuance as a strong, flourishing power was absolutely imperative.

Nikolias tensed. "I believe you are loyal to the Empire, sir."

"You've taken a risk coming here. I could denounce you."

"Yes, you could, sir. But I believe I have not misread the situation. Nor you, sir."

"Don't be so damned impertinent! I'm still your commanding officer, remember."

The soldier lowered his head. "Yes, sir, which is why I believe you will do what is right, sir. You always have."

"Well, on this occasion, you've chosen wisely." Nikolias snapped his head up, and a faint ghost of a smile played at his lips. Maniakes' eyes narrowed. "But don't assume that you know *everything*, Captain."

"No, sir. Absolutely not, sir."

"You've done well." Maniakes drained his goblet. "I have to think about all of this. I won't be able to stop Orphano or the Lady Zoe going into exile, but at least I can do something to lessen the impact." He grinned, an idea beginning to take shape in his mind. "Yes, I think I might just have the answer. Captain, I want you to continue following orders. There must be some reason why the Emperor is sidestepping the Scythian guard. Perhaps he doesn't trust them, who knows. Let him believe he has your loyalty, and do not do or say anything that may alert him to believe otherwise. I will, in the meantime, consider what options I have."

Nikolias swallowed down his wine and placed the goblet carefully on the table. He stood to attention, saluted, and strode out.

Maniakes stood there for a long time. Leoni came up beside him.

"You heard all that?"

"Every word." She lightly drummed her fingers on his shoulder. "What will you do?"

Maniakes smiled down at her. "Time for you to play your part again, my little shrew."

"Do I have to?"

He stroked her cheek with as much tenderness as he had ever shown anyone. "It won't be for long. Trust me."

"You know I do. But I hate it, being with him. He's like a worm." She came around to his front and snuggled into his chest. "I'd much rather have a ram."

He stroked her head. "You will always have that. Just a few more times, that is all. Then, it will all be over."

She closed her eyes and sighed deeply. The general gazed ahead. He had no idea what he could do. Leoni was meant to extract information from the Emperor, information that could ultimately be used against him. But Michael had out-manoeuvred them all and would, no doubt, continue to do so. On the surface a bumbling child, he was in fact an extremely devious and resourceful opponent. Well, Maniakes had underestimated him once, it would not happen again. At least, that is what he hoped. From now on, he would have to consider very carefully each of his moves and try, in some way, to foresee every possible outcome. It wouldn't be an easy task, but he had used superior tactics on the battlefield many times to win through against wily and worthy adversaries. This would be no different. All it would take was planning, and a lot of luck.

Twenty-Seven

The sound from the array of trumpets filled the vast senate house, proclaiming the arrival of the Emperor Michael V, chosen by God as the supreme ruler of the Byzantine Empire. From their stone seats, the senators rose as one, their heads bowed in supplication.

Michael moved in what he thought was regal fashion. His long, heavy robes, inlaid with pure gold and a multitude of precious stones, trailed behind him, making a soft, swishing sound across the polished marble. He looked about him, hoping to catch at least one upturned face. There were none, and he smiled. This was power indeed.

The cacophony of the trumpet blasts rose to a crescendo as he mounted the central dais and settled himself upon the throne. His personal servants stood close by in attendance, and a handful of Scythian Varangians spread either side, helmeted and armed. Michael beamed at the assembly and waited until the trumpets ceased before he began, in a soft and unassuming tone, "Senators. Please, be seated."

As one, the men sat back down, moving robes, nodding to one another, but no mumblings. All of them, the collection of the richest and most powerful aristocracy in the Empire, were hushed by the sight of their new emperor, come amongst them for the first time since his ascension. At his first, inaugural Mass, they had seen him in all his majesty, and the complete and utter ass he had made of himself. But that was on neutral ground. Here, the Senate House was their lair. The emperor had come to them. They waited, in polite, dignified silence, but they were confident of their power and prestige. No emperor could hope to rule without their support and that, above all else, was their ace in the hand. So, although silent, they eyed this young man as nothing more than an interloper who may, or may not, survive for very long.

"The last time we met," began Michael, at ease with himself, leaning back in the throne, one elbow resting on the arm, his fingers rapping against his chin, "I was somewhat … how should I say … distressed." Someone, somewhere, gave a loud guffaw. Senators twisted around, craned necks, began murmuring. "Senators," barked Michael. They all quietened down, turned their faces back to him.

"Senators … I was rash, ignorant, and I must have embarrassed you all. But, a day is a long time in the life of an Emperor of Rome. A long time indeed. I have learned much, and I now freely confess that my outburst was uncalled for, and should never have happened." More murmurings; lots of nodding of heads. Michael allowed it to go on this time and he felt the atmosphere relax. He sat forward, anxious to press home his advantage. "Of course, it was all thanks to the Lady Zoe, who has given me so much guidance over these last few days. Without her," he spread out his hands, "where would I be?"

He waited for a clever, sarcastic remark from somewhere deep within the serried ranks, but none came. Gaining in confidence, he rose to his feet. "It was she who taught me how to conduct myself in future, how to appear and act regally. All of this within a few hours." He laughed. "She is a remarkable woman, so wise, so full of life. Imagine my horror therefore when I discovered it was she who had ordered the carpet pulled up in such a way that it would trip me up! Yes, Senators, that is the simple truth – the Lady Zoe, the very same woman who schooled me so well, before and after the ceremony, was actually responsible for my embarrassment!"

The Senators were stunned. They looked like so many chastised children, withering under a good telling off from an angry tutor. At last, one brave soul shouted out, "That cannot be! The Lady Zoe is a pure and noble defender of our true Church!"

As the voices gathered in agreement, Michael held up both his hands, calming them. "Please, Senators ... I know how much of a shock this must be you, but I have other grievous announcements." He clicked his fingers. At once, one of his servants stepped up and produced a thin piece of parchment, which he unravelled with due reverence and began to read. " 'I swear before God that this is a true and certain testimony. I am in the household service of John the Orphano and saw, upon one evening, my master give to the Lady Zoe a phial of some ointment. He declared it was a poison, to be used against the person of our most glorious Emperor, Michael the Fifth. That such poison would render the Emperor dead within a candle period and that then they could move to re-install Her Ladyship as the true Empress of Rome. I do so swear' " The servant kept his head low as he handed the parchment over to the emperor.

"This witness," continued Michael, holding up the confession as if it were something fragile, to be cosseted, handled with extreme care, "this *saviour*, paid with his life for divulging to me the true depths of the Lady Zoe's ambition."

"Never!" shouted someone else.

"It is a lie," said another.

Michael shook his head, a single tear rolling down his cheek. "No. I thought so myself, until others came forward. All of them told the same story: an assassination plot. To murder me. And the perpetrators – John the Orphano, and the Lady Zoe."

The murmur became louder, turning into a gabble of outrage. Voices became raised, fingers and hands gesticulated this way and that, some senators rose to their feet, shouting, "Shame!" and, "Lies!"

Michael weathered the storm, stayed focused, refused to allow himself to be overwhelmed by this rising tide of indignation. He knew it would be like this, that none of them would accept that Zoe might be capable of such a thing.

He had sat in his private apartments, rehearsed his words, imagined the responses. The reality, however, was much worse than he could have imagined. The vehemence of their denials was, in a way, a denial of him also, and his authority. But how many of them knew, he wondered, that Zoe had been instrumental in the death of her husbands? Surely some of them, and it was to these few that he most directed his words. He didn't know who they were, but he felt certain that once they began to waver in their conviction concerning Zoe's guilt or innocence, he would be able to push home his advantage.

He scanned the mass of senators as they ranted and raved with each other and saw them, those men who had always harboured suspicions about the authenticity of Zoe's righteousness. They were sat there, in two separate huddles a few feet away from one another, all of them chewing their lips furiously, eyes darting around, not sure whether to join in with the cacophony, or simply sit it out. Michael made his move.

General Maniakes marched through the pillared corridor that led up to the throne room of the Emperor. Behind him clattered half a dozen soldiers from the palace guard, adorned in full armour, gripping shields and swords. At the doors, two nervous looking Scythian guards brought themselves to attention.

"Begging your pardon, General," said the first, staring straight ahead. "His Royal Highness has gone to the Senate House."

The news came like a blow. Why hadn't he been informed? Michael had moved fast in a deliberate attempt to out-manoeuvre him. For a moment or two, he didn't know what to do and mulled over the best course. He could, of course, march over to the Senate House and find out what was going on. Or, he could wait. His natural impatience rejected the latter course, and he whirled around and strode down the corridor once again, the soldiers, suppressing weary groans, following him.

If Michael had convened the Senate, he should have been informed. Common courtesy demanded so. Unless, of course, Michael was already distancing himself, creating factions, preparing for another strike. Leoni had her work to do, but maybe that wasn't enough. Perhaps other avenues would have to explored. He had his grand idea, of course, and it had been his wish to use Leoni, allow her to plant the seed. Should he act pre-emptively, get things moving sooner rather than later? He didn't know. Indecision always made him angry. If he suffered from such a trait on the battlefield he would have lost every campaign he had ever conducted. On the battlefield, he was supreme, one of the finest generals the Byzantines had had. In the closed, suffocating world of imperial diplomacy, however, his blunt, rash manner was inappropriate, misplaced and, at times, dangerous. He had to bide his time, let the plans formulate with care, give Michael the impression that it was he who had devised them.

He stepped out into the evening. A cool breeze was playing around the open square and the sky was clear, stars coming out to illuminate the broad expanse before him. Should he burst into the Senate House? He'd come this far, surely it would be best to…

A soldier gave his arm a tentative brush, bringing him out of his contemplations.

"Sir? His Royal Highness approaches."

Maniakes turned and peered to the far end of the square where the royal procession was coming into view. An honour guard at the front and to the sides and within it, Michael himself, accompanied by a gaggle of senators, all of them jabbering away.

As they came closer, Maniakes could see that surly smirk on Michael's face. He was enjoying himself, lapping up the fawning praise of his miserable supporters, supporters whose single aspiration was their own survival and advancement. As Michael drew up to the steps, he raised his hand and at once everyone stopped their talking and all peered towards Maniakes.

"General," beamed the Emperor, coming up the steps alone, leaving the others behind. "This is a pleasant surprise."

Maniakes bowed. "Majesty. I wanted to speak with you, but was told you were with the Senators."

"Yes." Michael rubbed his hands together. "I had to tell them about Zoe, and her plan to poison me."

Maniakes blinked once or twice in disbelief. "Majesty?"

"Shocked, General? You look shocked but then, you ought to be. The Lady Zoe has been arrested and is to be taken away, out of the city. She hasn't resisted because she knows that there is no point. She is guilty."

"Guilty? Guilty of what?"

"Didn't you hear what I said, General? She planned to *poison* me. That is treason, General Maniakes, as well as an affront before God. So, she has been taken to another place, where she can spend time considering the awfulness of what she meant to do."

"I have to say, Majesty, I feel that is a mistake."

"Really? Interesting you should say that, General. Your friend Orphano said much the same thing. And guess who supplied the Lady Zoe with the poison, if you can."

Maniakes had to stop himself from another outburst. He was on treacherous ground now. Behind the emperor, at the foot of the steps, the tiny knot of senators mumbled with one another, the pack waiting for permission to feast on the prey. He let out a long, controlled breath. "So … what has happened to him?"

Michael shrugged, "General, we are not monsters." He smiled, placed his hand on Maniakes's shoulder and patted it, reassuringly. "Suffice to say that he too is considering his actions." He motioned for his entourage to follow and, as one, they began to mount the steps.

"Just one more thing, General, in case you are in any doubt."

"What is that, Majesty?"

"The Senate endorse my actions … to the man."

He swung away, sweeping his luxurious robe around him, servants, senators and soldiers all milling around, desperate to catch a beam of his radiance before he disappeared inside the palace.

For a long time, Maniakes stood there, fuming. Damn his hide, the man was a surly little turd! He would pay for his arrogance, of that there could be no doubt. He snapped his fingers and Nikolias stepped forward. Maniakes pressed a piece of rolled parchment into the captain's hand. "Take this and stop for no one else until you get there. Take your men with you, Captain."

"But that will leave you totally undefended, sir."

Maniakes smiled in genuine kindness. "Bless your loyalty, Captain. I will not forgot it. But, I will be safe." He patted the hilt of his sword. "This isn't just for decoration."

Nikolias saluted and moved away with his men close behind him. The General watched them go and made a quick calculation as to how long it would take them to reach their destination. It was cutting everything very fine. Tomorrow, the games would begin and Michael would open them with a public address. Maniakes prayed that the mob would not rise up at what the Emperor had to say. At least, not just yet.

Twenty-Eight

Hardrada edged his horse along the steep path that led down to the open-plain. It was quite dark now, only a few twinkling stars to lighten up his way, so he had to keep caution uppermost in his mind as he moved across the broken ground. The horse was self-confident, assured of its own ability to negotiate the path, but the track was narrow and littered with shale and rocks. At any moment the horse could stumbled, turn an ankle, or worse might even throw its rider. So Hardrada bent himself over the horse's neck, patted it gently, kept his eyes on to the ground, giving himself whatever warning he could of any danger.

He made the flat of the plain and breathed a sigh of relief. His first instinct was to spur his mount on, but he knew better than that. Coming upon any encampment at night was dangerous; moving towards a Varangian one, more so. Such a sensitive border outpost, established as buffer from those enemies in the north who may feel inclined to range into the Empire, the troops would be naturally nervous and suspicious of anyone. So he kept the pace steady, the distant lights of the camp fires guiding him.

By the time he was within a few hundred paces, he knew he wasn't alone. Noises off to his right, like scampering sounds, made him slow the horse down even more. The animal became skittish and Hardrada thought that the sounds might be that of wolves. They roamed these mountain passes in great packs and no man was safe from their attacks. Should he take the chance and race his mount towards the camp, dodge a few arrows, or a javelin or two, for his pains, or should he stay on his steady course and risk an attack?

He saw the glint of the eyes at that moment. Like tiny, bright shards from a torch, intensely bright, watching him. Then another pair, and another. Over to his left, more noise. They were flanking him, cutting off his escape route. He had to act now. Drawing his sword with great care he threw back his head, gave a mighty roar, brought the flat of the blade down across the horse's rump and charged it forward.

The horse responded and galloped away across the vastness of the open plain. But the hunters were there too, their loping run within just a few paces from him. They would run the horse down, taking it in turns to lead the pack, their boundless reserves of energy allowing them to continue like this for miles.

Hardrada, hearing the closeness of their snarls, the snap of their jaws, forced the horse on, screaming out encouragement, not daring to look back lest that should slow the steed down. Even the slightest deceleration would mean certain death.

One hound, perhaps the pack leader, a great grey ghost looming out of the inky blackness, smashed its bulk into the flank of the horse. It whinnied, almost stumbled, faltered and struggled to recover its speeding run. It was enough to spur the other wolves on, and their baying and yapping grew in intensity as they sensed victory.

Dear God, was this how it was to end, he thought to himself, terrifying images leaping through his mind. Ripped apart on a friendless plain, nothing achieved, no hope of meeting with friends and loved ones, of seeing the journey through to a warrior's end? To be consumed by the foul stinking jaws of dogs? He kicked at the horse's flanks, but this time it didn't respond. Its strength was ebbing; the fear of the wolves forced it to continue, but Hardrada knew that the end was near, and still the camp was a hundred or so paces away.

The first bite must have clamped on the horse's right rear leg. It screamed, kicked out, lost momentum and when the second one came, latching onto its rump, the poor animal wheeled out of control. Hardrada held onto the saddle horn, knowing he was about to be thrown. That in itself could be the end. Gritting his teeth, he managed to hoist himself back into the saddle, tried his best to soothe the hysterical horse, then took a wild swing with his sword. The satisfying penetration of steel into flesh rang up the blade and through his arm. The wolf on the horse's rump howled and fell back into the dirt. But it wasn't enough. The dog had done its work and the horse was rearing and kicking, the pain in its side intense. Hardrada reined her in and was already jumping to the ground as two more wolves came out of the night, their mouths filled with sharp, gleaming teeth, and they slammed into the poor horse, taking her to the ground where she whinnied and struggled to get back onto her feet. Hardrada didn't have time to witness anymore. He ran, head down, beating a track towards the camp, hoping that the wolves would concentrate on the bigger bounty of the horse rather than the meagre pickings of his bones.

Within a few paces, however, the terrifying sound of growling grew louder. He knew they would run him down; wolves overwhelming him, ripping through his flesh. He was damned if he would die like that, and decided he would take at least one of the stinking hounds with him before they fastened their jaws on his throat. Grinding to a halt, he turned in a half-crouch, sword ready, peering into the night.

He heard it. A single animal. Huge. It too had stopped, sniffing the air, judging the distance, readying itself to jump. Hardrada knew this too well. He'd seen wolves before, knew their strength and ferocity, but most of all their courage. He also knew that they were intelligent creatures, ones that could sense weakness or fear. Feet spread, well-balanced, he tensed himself, knowing he would not shirk away. He had his sword. This was not going to be an easy fight, and perhaps the wolf would know this and turn away.

It didn't.

The eyes twinkled like tiny crystals and then came the roar as the beast erupted from the darkness. Caught off-balance by surprise, Hardrada almost tripped over his own feet as he staggered backwards, trying to keep some distance between him and his ferocious attacker.

He brought up the sword, swerved to the left at the last moment, and struck down. This close, he could see the animal clearly now. Curse the low clouds that blanked out the stars. Curse this damnable place, and curse his life for ending like this. The blade sank through the flank of the animal and it yelped and fell to the ground, writhing and squealing.

He had no time to savour his success, for another great beast loomed out of the darkness. This one kept low, its sharp, glinting teeth visible as it came up. Hardrada readied himself.

And then, the clouds parted. Perhaps some forgotten god of the Vikings had been listening, because for a brief moment, the whole plain lit up in a kind of eerie, purple half-light, distant heavenly bodies picking out the shapes of at least ten wolves, more than half of which were feasting on the carcass of the horse. Hardrada's stomach lurched as he saw the four animals before him, fanning out on either side, low, hackles up, teeth bared. They sensed victory, despite their fallen companion cut open and dead at the man's feet.

Another came on, rushing forward. Hardrada barely had time to veer away, lashed out first with his boot, then with a swing of his blade. He gave the animal a glancing blow, but it was enough to deter it whilst the next pressed home, then another. As if struck with blindness, he swiped and cut with the sword in a blur, wild blows raining down on shadowy, heavy shapes that moved and squirmed, dodging blows, lunging, jaws snapping, the growls growing in confidence.

It wouldn't be long before the clouds closed again. A storm was gathering, the temperature falling, the wind growing in strength. What a time to die, what a place to die in. He cried out, hit another wolf, whirled, and then one landed on his back, knocking the air out of him. A mad scramble ensued as he tried to grab its fur and rip it clean from his body. He could feel its hot, stinking breath, knew that the teeth would sink into his flesh, and then he would fall and that would be it. He couldn't get an angle on the dog to stab at it and it was strong and heavy, its paws raking down his jerkin. He twisted himself around and forward, pulling the wolf over his shoulder, but it clung on and he was forced to drop his sword, bring his other hand to bear, and he tore the animal free and hurled it in a wide arc away from him.

He gave a little prayer of thanks that the brute hadn't managed to bite him. If it had, then he would be finished. He knew all about the bites of wild animals, had seen too many companions writhing in agony as the vile poison on their fangs did their grizzly work. Not for him, not yet. He stooped down to sweep up the sword and then caught the other wolf bounding at him, its great mouth gaping open. The leader. The one that had begun the fatal assault on the horse. It was a colossal animal, much bigger than the others of the pack. Hardrada froze, peered into its maniacal eyes and knew, at that very moment, that his life was ended.

The first arrow hit the wolf full in the chest. It howled, rolling over onto its side as another dart thudded into its neck, a third slamming into its open mouth. It writhed, thrashed out with its paws, feeble attempts to rip away the offending arrows. But already its efforts were growing weaker and when two more arrows hit its flank, the light went out of its eyes and it went limp.

All around, the other dogs sensed that they should flee and they did so, as one, tails between their legs, bolting off into the darkness just as the clouds came back together and blanketed the plain once more into impenetrable blackness.

Hardrada's legs went weak, like twigs, and he dropped to his knees, not daring to think who the archers might be. He only knew he was still alive, at least for the moment. Coming this close to death, in such a horrific way, had unnerved him. Fighting with sword and axe against men was one thing, but struggling against wild beasts, with all their inherent unpredictability, was something beyond his experience.

A crushing sensation spread over his chest and he fell forward, his hands pressing down into the ground, preventing his face biting the soil. His breathing grew laboured and he took many moments to bring himself under control. During that time, he was vulnerable to further attacks and, as his mind cleared, he saw his sword. It lay in the dirt, a reach away, but as he found the strength to take it, a boot came down on the hilt.

He looked up to see the outline of a long-haired man staring down at him. Then another and, from somewhere behind him, a third. As he went to move, a sudden rush of wind followed and he knew someone was attempting to strike him. He also knew that they had waited a moment too long.

Strength, born out of anger, terror, frustration or a mix of all three, surged through his limbs and his right arm came up to block the expected blow, but there was none. Hardrada moved anyway, not willing to take a chance. He seized the man's wrist, twisted it and, without a pause, followed through with a clenched fist that dug deep into the attacker's solar-plexus. The man grunted and folded. Gripping him by the throat, Hardrada turned him around, and sent him flying through the air to hit one of his companions. They fell in a heap, both of them a mad mess of thrashing legs. Already Hardrada had found the hilt of the sword and was turning to dispatch the third when a familiar voice cut through the darkness. "Hold fast!" it said.

Hardrada narrowed his eyes and peered through the dimness as the shape came into focus. The voice, much gentler now, calmed him. "Hold fast, Harald. We are your friends."

Hardrada's frown turned into a broad grin and he sheathed his sword and opened his arms to embrace his old friend.

It was Rufus, the leader of the northern mercenary force of Varangians. Hardrada had survived and a tremendous sense of relief overcame him.

"Steady, old friend," said Rufus, holding onto Hardrada as the great man went limp in his arms.

"By Odin's beard, I never thought I'd see your like again," said Hardrada.

"By Odin's beard, you have," replied Rufus, holding him steady. "And all will be well."

Hardrada closed his eyes and for a moment he thought he would cry, the relief was so great. But he didn't and, instead, gave a great bellow, and together with his old friend strode across the vast expanse of open plain towards the ramparts of the Varangian camp.

Twenty-Nine

She lay supine across his bed, a thin satin sheet trailing between her thighs, one leg propped up, breasts exposed. She had the small finger of her left hand resting in the corner of her mouth and her eyes, wide and full of wonder, crinkled with delight as Michael moved over to her and let his mouth fall open.

"I've been waiting, My Lord," Leoni said, a whimsical smile playing at her lips. "I thought you'd never come."

She oozed sexuality and Michael had to hold on to the side of the bed post to stop himself from reeling. His mouth was dry, his loins burned, and his erection pressed against his thin pantaloons as he allowed his eyes to drift over her exquisite body. He had mere moments before dismissed those damned, sycophantic Senators, and now, here she was.

In a flurry, he tore away his robe, stepped out of his pants, and slid across her. She moaned as the weight of him pressed against her, and her arms snaked around his neck.

He pressed his lips against hers, feeling her tongue burst into his mouth, to probe and explore. His heart was slamming against his chest as he held her in the embrace. She smelled divine, a mixture of sweet honey and fresh jasmine, a contrast that surprised and aroused him. He broke free from her mouth, slipped his hands over her firm breasts, marvelling at her young body, how lithe it was, how the muscles spread over her flat belly, the downy hair around her navel golden, shimmering. He trailed his tongue around her nipples, tasting the succulent softness of her flesh and he moaned as her hand clasped his hardness.

"Dear Christ," he said, his voice thick with desire. How this girl captivated him. It was beyond understanding. The need to couple with her, to feel her slim thighs wrapped around him, to sink into the moist warmth of her sex, it was all too much. He was already nearing orgasm, and then her words came and he knew he was lost. "The General had me earlier, I hope you don't mind."

"Oh God."

"That's why I'm so wet. Feel me." She took his hand and pressed it against her sex. It was true. The juices pulsed from between her legs. "He had to hurry away and left me begging for me."

"He was inside you?" He hardly dared believe that in a moment he would be mingling with the remnants of the General's lovemaking, deep within her.

"Oh yes, but I haven't had chance to wash away the remnants of his love-making."

His mind screamed. He had to have her and he pinned down her arms and thrust into her. It was true, he could feel the wetness, how it filled her, and he orgasmed after a single thrust, threw back his head and roared out her name.

Michael collapsed next to her, unable to believe the incredible intensity of feeling he had just experienced. He rolled off her and lay panting on his back. She propped herself up on one elbow and played with the few hairs on his chest. "You were like an animal tonight," she said, voice thick with lust. "I love it when you hold me down like that. So wonderfully dominant."

"Do you?" He looked at her, hardly able to focus on her face. He had never known anything like this before in his life. His secret desires all revealed by this incredible girl, and he wondered if he would always feel like this. Total and utter satisfaction. He stroked her long blonde hair, ran the back of his hand along her cheek, and smiled. There was no guilt, no shame. She understood what to do, how to bring him to the height of ecstasy, and that was how it should be. For his part, he knew that whatever happened between them, in this bed, stayed between them. This was their private, closed world, where fantasy could be given full vent.

"Yes," she said. "You can be very masterful, and I love that."

"That is why you fuck the General?"

She licked her lips. "Well... more to the point, he fucks me. He has always taken charge. I never have much choice, just succumb to his rather ample charms." As she spoke, her hand slid down from his chest and began to toy with his flaccid manhood. "Of course... Mmm... Just the knowledge that he will putting that thing into me, my God, I just can't resist!"

Michael closed his eyes, allowing himself to be taken away again, by her words, the pictures they conjured, and the constant working of her hand. Within a few minutes he would be hard again, and again he would have her.

He lay on his stomach, naked, as she massaged his shoulders and back. She had drizzled aromatic oils across his body and was working it into his muscles, easing away all of the tension of the day. He was shattered, the rigours of the day having taken their toll and now he just needed to relax and sleep. Her lovemaking during the second round had been wild and hectic, and this time prolonged. She had clawed at his chest as she bounced up and down above him, and she had orgasmed harder and stronger than ever before. When she crumpled down next to him, her face glowing, he knew he had given her almost as much pleasure as she had given him. That felt good and afterward she put his arm around her and pulled her close. She, in response, snuggled into him. Such genuine affection gave him a warm glow inside. Now, her fingers worked their magic on the muscles of his shoulders and back.

"Today has been a tiring day?" she asked, her voice soft and husky.

"Yes," he said, close to the edge of sleep, but enjoying the closeness of her. "And tomorrow, you will accompany me to the opening ceremony of the festival. I think you will be a triumph, Leoni. Enough to eclipse the Lady Zoe." He moved, turning over to look up at her. She seemed troubled. A frown on her face. He reached up and stroked her cheek.

She didn't seem convinced, the frown still there, deep. "I could eclipse the Lady Zoe … You think so?"

He laughed at her incredulity. "Of course! You are half her age and twice her beauty. The people will adore you."

She pursed her lips, and rested her head against his chest, but he could tell how she felt, her body still taut. "They love her so much, and when the news is made public …"

"News?" He strained his neck to look down at her, "What news?"

"Of her leaving, My Lord."

He sat up, a stab of panic lancing through his heart. "How the devil do you know about that?"

"My Lord? It is common knowledge – the whole of the court is full of it. And, you forget, I am – *was* Her Ladyship's personal maid."

He relaxed a little. It was true, rumour and gossip circled around the court with alarming speed so he shouldn't be unduly alarmed. However, something niggled away at the corner of his mind, something that made him feel uncomfortable. He hadn't completely forgotten Leoni was Zoe's maid, but now that she had reminded him, he began to feel a little uneasy. She was close not only to Zoe, but also to the General. Could that be the reason why the General seemed to know so much about the workings of the former empress – could it be that Leoni was acting as a sort of spy? And if she were passing information to Maniakes about Zoe, could she not also be passing other things on about *him*? He had to admit that it was a thought that had played around in his mind before, but one he had never given serious attention to. Until now.

Michael stroked the long hair again. She was an innocent child in many ways. Apart from her expertise in the bedroom, she conducted herself everywhere else with coyness and allure. Men gasped when they saw her drift by, just as they had done with the Lady Zoe. However, in their responses to Leoni there was something else. Captivation. Zoe was too powerful for most, an unattainable star, somebody to fantasize about but nothing more. Leoni, however, appeared accessible. Well, all that would change soon. When he presented her as his companion, adorned in rich, sumptuous robes, her head bejewelled with a shimmering crown of gold, sapphires and emeralds, the people would be stunned, enraptured. Into his world she would breeze, bringing with her light and that beguiling innocence that everyone so adored. She would be a triumph, and he would bask in her glow, Zoe forgotten.

"Orphano too has gone."

He held his breath. Very well, she was a conduit of gossip. This could be to his advantage. He could develop intrigues, half-truths, fantasies … Knowing of Zoe's exile was understandable. Unfortunate, but unsurprising. Orphano, however, was another matter. That should have taken everyone by surprise. It was obvious that someone was feeding her, and she was no doubt returning the compliment. He needed to be wary.

He kissed the top of her head. "My child, some things are beyond understanding. You needn't worry or concern yourself with matters of state."

"I understand that, My Lord. I merely repeat what I hear from others. Rumours fly around like bats from a cave, I never know what is truth or lie."

"Most of what you hear is almost certainly a lie."

"Then His Lordship Orphano has not been sent away?"

He paused again before answering. This was not Leoni probing for answers, it was the General. The man played a clever game and Michael would have to move with great caution against him. He did, after all, command most of the army. Although the Byzantine empire was split into districts, or *themas,* each with its own responsibility for defence and the raising of troops, Maniakes had control of the Imperial Guard and oversaw the equipping and maintenance of the Varangian mercenaries. That made him powerful, and dangerous. "Orphano had transgressed," began Michael, imagining he was speaking to the General. "He betrayed me and the Empire by conspiring with Her Ladyship to poison me."

Leoni sat up, a look of abject horror on her face. "The Lady Zoe planned to kill you?"

He almost laughed at her wide-eyed amazement. Could it be that she was actually unaware of what had happened, the reason why Zoe had been sent away? Perhaps the General didn't confide in her totally. Michael waved away her seeming surprise. "Child, the details are of no matter. The Lady has gone, and so too has Orphano. Trust me, we're better off without either of them."

"But, Highness... Orphano? What will you do without him and his skills at administration and diplomacy?"

He held back his rising anger. None of this had anything to do with her, and her tone and high-handed manner set his teeth on edge. He struggled to remember that this was all subterfuge, all playacting. All for the General's sake. "I shall just have to find someone else. He shouldn't be that difficult to replace."

"My Lord," she swung her leg over his body and straddled him. He gazed up at her nakedness, the young breasts firm and so well developed, the slim waist, the swell of her hips. He stirred beneath her, looked up into her beaming face. "I think I know someone."

So, Michael thought, this is how the game is to be played. Entrapment, clever manoeuvring, lulling him into her soft, open arms... My God, what a minx! "You know someone? What do you mean, you *know someone*? How can you?"

"It's obvious, My Lord." She smiled and bent down to nibble at his ear. He squirmed, feeling an icy thrill running across the nape of his neck. "His own brother. The cleverest man in the whole empire, the man Orphano himself had exiled!" She sat up, placing the flat of her hands on his chest. "If you reinstated him..."

Michael gaped at her. Dear Christ, if this was her idea then he had seriously underestimated her intelligence and political acumen! If it was the General's... either way, it was something that he had never considered, and should have. It was patently obvious, the most natural solution to the problem of who should control the Empire's administration. Why hadn't he thought of it himself? The girl was a marvel.

He reached up with both hands and cupped her face. "Leoni," he said, beaming, "You are quite brilliant!"

And then, before he could say another word, her hands slipped down to his crotch and at once everything else became a blur and was forgotten as her fingers went to work on his blood engorged flesh.

Thirty

The little boat cut through the mirror-like surface of the water, oars muffled, as silent as an owl skimming across the night sky, prey spotted, death close. She felt like that. A prey. Michael had struck, his talons seizing her and she had no way to escape. It had been pointless to resist. What could she do, a single woman against the most powerful man in the world? All of her scheming, her plans, all of it gone adrift. Not so this boat, the men pulling it towards the island, the outline of the monastery barely visible in the moonless night. How cold it was out here in the middle of the sea. How cold, and how lonely. She huddled down inside her thick, fur lined robe and gazed out across the black water. Nothing to look back on, accept a string of futile marriages, lovers, escapades, a mountain of fine clothes, jewels, all the trappings of royalty. None of it mattered now. Everything had passed; now all she possessed was her wits and a few trinkets. No more visits to the halls of distant kings, feasting, cavorting, dancing to wild, untamed music. No strong arms to hold her, lips to caress her. All of it gone.

 She thought back to Crethus, her latest lover. If she tried hard enough she could still taste his scent. Yes, taste it. So strong, so manly. His superb body moulding into hers, taking her to heights unknown. He had told her not to worry, that he would return. Could that be true, could that be the one hope that would sustain her? That the mighty Scythian would return and free her from bondage? It would be enough

Varangian

for her to cling on to, to get her through the next days, weeks, even months.

The pilot gave a sharp command and the oarsmen raised their oars as one and allowed the boat to drift. Other men rushed to the bow and a shadow fell over her. Zoe looked up.

"Lady. We have arrived."

* * *

Andreas stretched his arms and sat up. He rubbed his chin, felt the stubble and pondered on what had happened. Looking around, it was clear he was in no immediate danger. The tent was large, the leather sides offering good protection from the elements. Around him were the trappings of a simple life, but a clean and ordered one. Whoever had saved him was well organized and knew what they were doing. That had to be the case. He was alive.

He flexed his legs, rubbed his arms vigorously, and stood up. A sudden wave of faintness ran through him and he had to wait a moment to recover. The sudden rush of getting to his feet made him light-headed. He took a few breaths and reached down to pull on a thick, linen jerkin. He noted that his lower body was covered in a simple loincloth and he wondered where his breeches might be, and who it was that had stripped away his original clothes.

Standing there, tying up his jerkin, snippets of memory came back to him, fragmented, jumbled. He remembered going to the river, of reaching over to scoop up water, how the tide had carried away the pot and he had made a grab for it. How cold the water was, how his breath was taken away and with what frightening speed he was dragged under. Hands, he remembered big, strong hands, taking him somewhere, and voices. Gentle voices, full of concern. But that was it. Nothing else.

Hardrada. He remembered Hardrada, remaining behind to start the fire. The horses, their things. Their quest. It came to him in a rush; his orders, what he had to do.

"Christ!" Anxious to be on his way, Andreas threw back the flap and went outside.

It was early morning, the sun not yet risen above the horizon, the sky a dull, metal-grey hue. Rain was in the air and he could smell the dampness clinging to everything. He shivered as he tried in vain to spot his equipment, his armour and weapons.

"How are you?" The voice came from somewhere beyond the trees.

He whirled around, hands instinctively coming up in a defensive attitude. The camp sat amongst a natural ring of large boulders, punctuated with thick bramble and gorse. Beyond, a hillock gave protection from the elements, and the trees added to this, at once a barrier and a veil, difficult to see beyond. From what direction the voice had come he couldn't tell. A woman's voice, not threatening, but kind. Nevertheless, he remained tense, ready to act if the need demanded.

She seemed to materialize from between the trees. Her dress was green, speckled with brown, a perfect disguise for when she stood amongst the foliage. She glided towards him, her face split by an open, welcoming grin. Andreas stood mesmerized, her face so lovely, like something from a dream. He did not think he had ever set eyes on anyone so divine. Unable to look away, her spell cast, all he could do was tremble and bask in her loveliness.

Andreas stood transfixed as she came up to him, looked deep into his eyes, then stroked his chin. At the touch of her fingers, he almost swooned, thinking himself transported to a mystic glade, the enclave of some Elvin princess. The sounds of nature all around him seemed to increase, the beauty of the birdsong mirroring the loveliness of her face; calmness overcame him, not unlike how he used to feel as a child when his mother folded her arms around him and rocked him gently to sleep.

She took him by the arm and helped him down to an overturned tree trunk, which served as a seat. He watched her, bedazzled as she prepared some gruel from the pot suspended over the camp fire. Carefully, she brought over the steaming bowl. "Eat," she said, stroking his face again. "You have been asleep for a long time, and your body will need nourishment."

It was true; the smell of the soup wafted into his nostrils and he suddenly realized how hungry he was. Taking the bowl and the wooden spoon she held out to him, he plunged straight in, filling his mouth without ceremony.

She stood and watched him, a look of quiet amusement on her face, until he had finished and he smacked his lips, running the back of his hand across his mouth. She took away the bowl and spoon and lay them down on the ground, then she sat down next to him and took his hand in hers. "Good. You want some more?"

Andreas shook his head, "Maybe later."

The girl nodded. "There is plenty in the pot. And later I will make you a stew of rabbit and herbs. That should sustain you for a while."

He could hold it back no longer and blurted, "Who are you?"

"No one really. A forest dweller, nothing more."

"Nothing more? You saved my life!"

She squeezed his hand and he looked down and realized that he liked the feel of her skin, so warm, so soft. "I did what I believed was right." As her face came up, he saw the wetness gathering in her eyes. "I suppose you will be leaving soon?"

"I'm not sure ... My companion, the big man. Have you seen him?"

She nodded. "What happened to him?"

"The Viking? Yes, he left, going to the north, or so he said."

"North? So, he was well?"

"Well? Of course, I tended to him also. He took you from out of the water, wrapped himself against you and kept you warm. Without him, you would have died. I merely continued what he had already done."

Andreas looked away. Hardrada had saved him, pulled him out of the water? Why would he do such a thing? And now he had continued on his journey to the north, to the Patriarch and now Andreas would have no chance to carry out his secret orders. He eased his hand from between her fingers and stood up. "I must go after him."

"You cannot."

He felt a sudden surge of anger. "Cannot? I will do as I please – I am a soldier of Rome and my orders are clear."

The girl held onto his arm. "Please. I meant no offence. You cannot, because he took your horse."

Andreas reeled as if struck. Damn the man. After coming this far, without a horse he may as well have been left for dead in the river. He fell back onto the tree trunk. "Then I am undone."

"He will return. He said as much."

"No. There is no reason. I know him."

"Obviously not well enough. He saved your life. He had no need to do that if he meant to abandon you. I believe him to be a man of honour, a true warrior. If he said he will return for you, then he will."

Andreas let her words simmer in his mind. It could be true, although why Hardrada would choose to return for him he couldn't begin to understand. If the situation were reversed, he doubted if he would do so. He doubted he would have saved the man from certain drowning either. He knew little about Hardrada, save that he had once been the commander of the Varangian guard before shown to be a philanderer and thief, ferreting away hordes of stolen cash to fuel his licentious lifestyle. As far as he was concerned, the man was an abomination, a nothing. His one value on the quest was that he held sway over the Varangians encamped on the northern border. They would trust him and follow him. As for anything else, Andreas doubted that the man had little real value for the new emperor, His Royal Highness Michael.

But Hardrada had saved his life. How could he ever forget that. It was a debt that had to be repaid.

"You seem troubled by all of this," she said. "I am sure that when he returns, everything will become much clearer."

"You seem to set great store in this man. What else do you know about him?"

"Nothing. My natural instincts to guide me. They have done well enough to help me in this life of isolation I have chosen. There is something very different about him. A strength, not only physical, but mental. He bears himself like a king and I foresee great things for him."

"Really? And what do you foresee for me?"

She titled her head, frowned, and then pressed the flat of her hand against his brow. He felt coolness spread through him, soothing him, quietening his concerns, his anxieties. He closed his eyes and allowed himself to drift.

"Your path is clouded," she said softly. "You grapple with conflicting emotions, torn between carrying out your duty and what you know to be right. I see you riding on a white horse, regaled in the fine clothes of a great officer, or nobleman. You ride at the head of many troops and people cheer for you. I believe that in the end you will win through, conquer your fears and emerge triumphant, at peace with your god."

He snapped his eyes wide open. "Are you a witch?" he gasped.

She smiled then, shook her head, and let her hand fall away from his face. "No, not a witch. I have a gift of prophesy, that is all."

"Some might call that witchcraft."

"Then they would be wrong. I cast no spells, but I do mix potions that heal and soothe. Often, my own people visit me, seeking out remedies for agues and other ills. They did it with my mother, and they continue to do so with me."

He didn't like the sound of this. Potions – wasn't that just another word for poisons? The beauty of her face belied a deeper, much more dangerous personality lurking within. She had cared for him, but for what reason? What was it she wanted from him? He sucked in his breath. "Why did you save me?"

"Why?" She frowned again, as if the question was not only unnecessary but also a little offensive. "Because you were sick, close to death."

"But you said Hardrada saved me. Why did you take it upon yourself to keep me here, to give me potions that would make me sleep."

"My one thought was for your welfare." She reached out to touch his face again, but this time Andreas knocked her hand away. "Please," she said, her eyes brimming up with tears. "Your mind is upset, rest for a while, gather your thoughts."

"I've rested enough," he said. "Where are my things? My armour, my sword?"

"But you have nowhere to go. You have no horse, no means to travel."

She was right, of course, and that thought brought yet another wave of anger to the fore. Damn that bastard Viking for getting him into this mix in the first place! It would have been better if death had come. An eternity beneath the water would be more preferable than living another moment in this God forsaken place. He squeezed his hand into a tight fist. "By Christ, I'll not be tempted by a witch!"

She recoiled, her hand flying to her mouth. "Please believe me, I have done nothing wrong! All I did I did for your welfare. I have never *tempted* you nor even thought to do so."

"You live here alone, in this wild and desolate place, with no man to guard you. You say your people come here for potions and the like. And you save my life, that of Hardrada's too ... No, there is something more to all of this than what you say. Are you a spy, perhaps?"

"A spy?"

"Aye. Perhaps you have been sent here, by someone, to wait for us, to lure us into some sort of a trap." He rubbed his forehead. God, how his head hurt now. All of this thinking, the confusion. He had slept too long, his mind becoming addled. None of it made sense, no one was this good, this kind. There were always ulterior motives for why people did what they did. Mankind was sinful and wicked, no goodness in any of them.

His thoughts were wheeling around inside him, everything become groggy and mixed up, as though someone was stirring his brain around and around. "Oh, Jesus," he said, lurching forward, his hands grasping out before him, the ground beneath him feeling like mud, or water. No solidity to it. "Oh, Jesus Christ, the soup." It was true, he knew it now. He stared, saw her body moving in and out, as if it were liquid, of no substance. A heaviness enveloped him, thick, all consuming, pressing him down, down to the ground. The liquid earth, opening up to embrace him. He could taste the earth in his mouth. He knew he had collapsed, the strength gone from his limbs. That was why he had these conflicting thoughts, these apparitions. She had drugged him. The bitch had drugged him.

"Secure him."

A voice, coarse and distant. Rough hands on his shoulders, hoisting him up. A bright sun invading his senses, more voices, becoming more distant now. Greek voices. He understood some of it, but not much. He no longer cared. A wonderful warmth was seeping through him, so seductive. All he need do was close his eyes and surrender to it, then all would be well.

So he did.

Thirty-One

Alexius, the Patriarch of the great city of Constantinople, came striding through the camp, his arms open in greeting, a beaming smile across his face.

"Welcome, Harald!"

He took the huge Viking in his arms and clapped him on the back, stepping back to look at him admiringly. "Thank the Lord you have come! What news do you bring, my friend?"

"News?" Hardrada shuffled his feet, turned a cautious face to Rufus, who stood there, not giving anything away. "I was sent to bring you and the Varangians back to the city, sir. I have little in the way of news."

"But when I left, there was chaos! Michael had sent men to arrest me and the Lady Zoe. Zoe begged me to come here, to bring these men to the city and help her overcome the tyranny that was threatening to overwhelm everything and everyone." He nodded towards Rufus. "Allow me a few moments."

Rufus bowed slightly, clapped Hardrada on the shoulder and went off towards his troops. Alexius took Hardrada by the arm and led him over to his tent. He didn't speak to the Viking until they were inside.

"We were attacked," he began, pouring some wine for them both. He handed a goblet to Hardrada, who drank the liquid down in one. Alexius charged the cup, then took a sip from his own before sitting down on his camp bed. "It was dreadful. I have never seen such ferocity. It has delayed our departure, a fact for which I am forever grateful."

He closed his eyes and made the sign of the cross. "The Lord is with me, that much is certain. I came close to death, in a manner that I do not wish to dwell on for too long." He gave a rueful smile and took another drink. "I think they were Normans, or perhaps Russians, I know not what."

"If they were Normans, that is serious news indeed. If they have managed to come this far east ..." Hardrada stared at his wine. "Russians would be better ... but not by much."

"Well, that's as maybe. However, any news you can give me about what is happening in Constantinople is far more pressing. There must be something you can tell me, some development?" He looked with wide, pleading eyes but Hardrada shook his head. "But what did My Lady tell you to do?"

"Who, Zoe? It was not Zoe who ordered me here – it was Orphano."

"Orphano." Alexius stood up, his face pained, losing what little colour it already had. "Then, it is beginning, as I knew it must."

"You've lost me, sir. The beginning of what?"

"Civil war, of course! Orphano is moving against Michael. He wants these Varangians to aid him in his designs, and that is why he sent you. He doesn't care about Zoe, or me. All he wants is power for himself – he always has. He has waited for Michael to strike, which would bring chaos to the institutions of Rome, and now he moves to counter." He rubbed at his face, looking tired. "But he's underestimated you, my friend. With you leading the Varangians, we can outmanoeuvre him, reinstall Zoe to her rightful place as Empress, and I will bless the ceremony. The people will be ecstatic."

Hardrada pressed his lips together. The man's words made sense, of course they did. Michael was incompetent and Orphano was a weasel who wanted power for its own sake. The best for everybody would be for Zoe to ascend the throne once more. However, Orphano had Hardrada where he wanted him, and there was no getting away from that. "He told me if I didn't do as I was told, he would kill my friends."

"Your friends? What do you mean, 'friends'? We cannot allow personal attachments to cloud our judgments, Hardrada. Rome is greater than any one man."

"Or woman?"

Alexius stopped, arched an eyebrow. "What?"

"He also threatened to kill Zoe."

Andreas woke. The sunlight hurt his eyes, even though he hadn't opened them yet. He waited, gauging the numbers of those around him. They moved about, some spoke, others laughed. All the while, Andreas remained motionless, maintaining his playacting despite the terror that gripped him.

The worst of it all, was the girl. An enigma in every sense. He couldn't work out why she would at first help him, nurse him back to health, only to then drug him. For the life of him he couldn't understand why that would be, unless she was involved in some perverse means of psychological torture. All that talk about foretelling the future, the image she brought up about riding a white charger; it all seemed so unreal, almost forced, lulling him into believing her whilst preparing that damnable concoction that pitched him into nothingness. What was in store for him, he couldn't tell, but he would have to give himself some time, so he pretended to sleep, and waited for the right moment.

When the cool hand touched his brow, however, he couldn't help but open his eyes. It was the girl, staring down at him, smiling. For a moment he almost believed it had been a dream, but then the other face loomed towards him and he knew then that the reality was just as terrible as he had imagined.

The man, a wild looking beast with a dirt-streaked face, black eyes and a mouth full of chipped and yellowed teeth, reached down and seized Andreas by the throat. "The bastard awakes!" Then he pulled the young officer up to a sitting position and struck him once, a backhanded slap across the face.

"Stefano!" The girl shrieked, clawed at the brute's arm as he readied himself for another blow. The man shrugged her off, pushing her backwards with a hard shove in her chest.

Andreas, still smarting from the slap, came to his feet, and swung up his knee into the man's groin. Before the man had even fallen, Andreas was already turning to receive the next attacker.

As a captain in the Imperial Guard, Andreas was no mere journeyman. He was a trained fighter, well able to defend himself against any attacker, large or small, armed or unarmed. The man rushing towards him didn't understand this or, if he did, chose to ignore it. Sensing an easy victory, the man came on, drawing out his blade. Whatever these people had in store for Andreas, death certainly seemed one of the main options. As the man closed and swung, Andreas neatly dodged, hitting his opponent hard in the guts, then swinging round for a second strike against the man's temple. He grunted, pitched forward, and Andreas caught his falling sword and made a grab for the girl.

"Come on," he snapped, picking her up and pulling her away.

He could see it was too late. Even with two of their number down, this did nothing to cause the others to reconsider their actions. There were at least five of them, dressed in animal skins, cloaks flapping in the breeze, curved, evil looking swords in their hands. They had noted Andreas's fighting prowess, were cautious now, circling him, preparing for an onslaught.

He readied himself. If he were die, then so be it, but he would take as many of them with him as he could. He had no idea who they were, or what they intended, but neither did he wish to share niceties with them. They seemed primitive people, unwashed, bent over, eking out an existence in the foothills and mountains of this unforgiving land. How they managed to survive was beyond him. The simple pleasures were alien to them. Born in the chill air of the mountains, this was how they lived their lives until they met their ends, no doubt cruelly, bodies aged before their time, a mad scramble into oblivion. Dear God, to be like that. He gritted his death, hefted the blade and prepared himself.

"You cannot win," the girl said, releasing herself from his grip. She stumbled, fell over again, and looked up at him in despair. "Please, put down your sword."

"What, and die like a dog by these animals? No, I'll not yield." He went into a half crouch, "Come on, you shit shovellers, come and find out what it's like to fight a Roman!"

Three of them rushed him, moving as one, swords aloft, their battle cries piercing the air and freezing his very soul. He roared himself, to dispel his inertia, moved, parried and countered, but it was hopeless and he knew it. They were too many and the remnants of the drugs in his blood made him sluggish, his muscles like lead weights. It would not be long before he succumbed, and this thought, perversely, spurred him on a little, and he struck with success, the edge of his blade slicing through one of the men, the jugular vein spewing out a crimson ribbon.

He backed away, parrying, slashing and cutting, trying his best to keep them at bay, but then the other two, who had until now held back, joined the fray and, beyond them, the others that he had struck were recovering. The girl scrambled away to safety, pressed herself against a nearby tree and set up a dismal wailing that did nothing but add to the ensuing horror.

There was something else too. From out of the trees, a huge shape. It seemed to dominate everything, a great bear-like thing, a guttural roar erupting from its open mouth. The man who had slapped Andreas turned too late, a blade flashed and his head arced through the air, the body gouting blood, felled like a tree. Andreas tore his startled eyes away, concentrated on his own fight, finding the strength from somewhere to parry, turn his opponent's blade, and cut him across the flank. The man screamed, writhed and stumbled into one of the others. Andreas pressed forward his advantage and ran another wild man through.

To the rear, it was clear who the mysterious assailant was. A huge man, arms bristling with muscle, his black face lit with a wide grin, hacking down Andreas's captors with ease, like one would sheaves of wheat. When the last of them lay sprawled upon the blood-spattered ground, the stranger drew in great gulps of air and turned to beam at Andreas. "By Allah, you are hard to find."

The girl yelped, scampering backwards, eyes wide with terror. Andreas grinned, tossed the curved sword away and lifted his voice, "Crethus! God bless you man." Then he took the huge Scythian's hand and pumped it furiously.

Crethus looked past Andreas and nodded. "Who's that?"

Bending round, Andreas scowled towards the girl. "She almost killed me. Poison."

"Harlot!" Crethus went to move towards her, the sword, still dripping with blood, gripped in his hand so tightly the knuckles showed white beneath the skin.

"No, wait, Crethus." Andreas held the massive Scythian back. "I think she was forced to do it. By these animals, whoever they are."

"Thracians."

Andreas frowned. The girl had spoken, her voice a low, trembling. "Thracians? Why would Thracians want to murder me, a soldier of Rome?"

"Not murder you. Hold you for ransom."

Andreas looked at Crethus, then back again at the girl. "But no one would pay anything for me!"

"I told them you were a prince."

Andreas blinked, and Crethus let out a loud guffaw. "Dear God," he bellowed, "Andreas, the Prince! You'll be an emperor next."

Despite himself, Andreas couldn't help but join in with his friend's laughter and soon, more out of relief than amusement, he laughed so much that the tears rolled down his cheeks.

"I had to," she shouted, climbing to her feet, dragging a hand across her face, a face red with anger. "If I hadn't, they would have slit your throat." The two men stopped laughing, although Crethus could not contain his sniggering. Andreas, for his part, stood and gazed at her, as if seeing her anew. He stepped towards her, wringing his hands, ashamed for thinking that this girl had betrayed him. "They came when you were sleeping and wanted to kill you then. I persuaded them that you were a man of importance in Byzantium, that I had found you washed up on the bank of the river, the current having taken you under."

"Almost the truth."

"Yes. Almost. They believed me, the cretins. Their leader," she pointed a finger vaguely into the distance, beyond Crethus. "The one without his head, he was the one who came up with the idea of taking you for ransom. When they discovered your armour and your sword, they knew you were a warrior, that you would be dangerous. So they forced me to make a concoction, to subdue you."

"Perhaps it wasn't strong enough."

"That was meant to be the idea. I think perhaps I got the mixture a little wrong. They watched over me, never let me out of their sight. I am sorry. I never meant to hurt you."

"You didn't." Andreas ran his fingers down her arm, and she gave a little shiver. He could tell it was not in loathing and when she looked away, somewhat coy, he took the chance and placed his hands on her shoulders, turning her back again to face him. "You never did tell me your name."

"Analise."

"Beautiful," he said, eyes locked on hers, smouldering as they were, drawing him in. He knew he couldn't resist, that his desire to possess every inch of her was too strong. Her lips parted and he leaned in towards her.

"Andreas!"

He stopped, closed his eyes for a moment in frustration, and looked back at the Scythian. "What?"

The huge guardsman was beaming again. "We need to talk," he bowed, giving a wide flourish of his right arm, "oh Prince!"

"Bastard," breathed Andreas, gave the girl a smile and stomped towards his friend. "This had better be good."

Crethus steered him away, out of earshot of the girl which meant tip-toeing through the heap of dead that lay all around. Close to the tent in which Andreas had spent most of his recovery time, Crethus lowered his voice to a whisper. "I have orders."

"Orders? Who from?"

"The Emperor himself. We are to kill Hardrada."

Andreas stiffened. For a moment he didn't know what to say and his mind spiralled in a hundred different directions. Kill Hardrada, the man who had saved his life – how could he justify such a thing? And yet, he was an officer of the Imperial Guard, a *Dekarchos* in charge of ten men. Not a high office, he knew, but an important first step. He had sworn loyalty to the Emperor, to obey him on pain of death.

"I have tried already," said Crethus, cutting into Andreas's thoughts. He touched his chin and Andreas could see the nasty looking smudge of purple and red that followed the line of the man's jaw. "I got this for my trouble. The man is a monster. I almost died, caught up amongst some bramble. By the time I had managed to get out, he had gone, away to the Varangian camp."

"But, I don't understand. I was meant to ensure he followed through his own orders, to bring the Varangians back, to force Alexius to return and support His Royal Highness. It was all arranged." He patted his clothing, looking for his orders, but they were no longer there. No matter, he had aired them to Crethus. And now, despite it all, they had been superseded.

Slowly, the Scythian's eyes turned into black beads, "Plans change. Times change. Michael is flexing his muscles and wants no obstacles in his way." Crethus squeezed the young man's arm. "Orphano has had his time, Andreas. There is a new order now. And the order is simple. Hardrada must die."

Thirty-Two

The camp was filled with the sound of an army preparing to march. The Varangians had loaded up their carts until they groaned under the weight of baggage; drovers screamed and pulled at obstinate mules and donkeys, and officers roared at men to move into column. From the entrance to Alexius's tent, Hardrada hefted the great battleaxe in his hands. It felt good to have it back. For too long he had been without the comforting weight of the huscarle's favoured weapon. Swords were prized, handed down from father to son, runes inscribed upon blades to lend some of them mystical powers. Treasured possessions, not to be lost or broken in the heat of battle. At such times, it was the axe that reigned supreme and holding it now, Hardrada felt the heat of his blood pulse through him, filling him with the urgent desire to lock horns and deal death blows with his opponents.

But before this happened, however, he would have to make his detour.

He had already hinted as much to the Patriarch, who did not seem best pleased when Hardrada told him of his plans to go and find Andreas.

"You will lose vital time," the Patriarch had said as he packed away his few belongings. "It is a meaningless deviation, Hardrada. You duty lies in returning with us."

"My duty lies in doing what my heart decrees, My Lord. I will not be so long that I will not be able to overtake you on the road. The Varangians march, whilst I ride."

"Nevertheless, I feel it is a waste of time and energy, best employed by leading these men."

"Rufus is more than capable. You must trust me."

Alexius had looked up from his packing, his eyes meeting that of the giant Norseman. "Of course I trust you! Your loyalty and bravery are beyond question. It's just that I have a bad feeling about all of this. I can't explain it, and I don't even know this man of whom you speak, this Andreas, but..." He shook his head. "I can see you are determined. Leave before us then, ride hard, then rendezvous with us farther down the road. As you say, the Varangians march."

Hardrada bowed. He was glad the Patriarch had given him a sort of blessing, but he knew that he would have gone to find Andreas without it. Why Alexius should have a 'bad feeling' about anything was curious, but Hardrada didn't dwell on such superstitious nonsense. Now, standing there watching the Varangian mercenaries preparing to leave camp, he felt a sudden pride at how well they looked with hauberks scrubbed, round shields strapped to backs, axes sloped on shoulders. The men looked hard and mean, just as Vikings should, their ranks swelled by other regiments coming in from the west.

By Odin's beard, they would make those Scythians wish that they had never betrayed the Varangian Guard, and done such vile things to such great men. At the thought of it, Hardrada squeezed the handle of his own axe, and made a silent promise that he would cleave as many Scythian heads as he could, and relished the thought of doing so.

Without another thought he went over to where his horse stood, tethered to a post. He unhitched it, threw his bedroll over its back and swung himself into the saddle. Rufus came up, patted the horse's neck, "Don't tarry."

"Never fear, old friend," grinned Hardrada, "when you and I are back in the city, it will be like old times."

"Better, I hope."

Hardrada nodded. "Aye. Better." Then he flicked the reins and guided the horse through the camp towards the entrance. As soon as he was through the gates, he spurred the animal on and broke into a steady canter, putting distance between him and the Varangians. He didn't look back; there was no need. They were on the move and soon the whole of Byzantium would quake at the sound of their marching feet.

Many miles to the south, Nikolias stepped off the small rowing boat onto the shingle beach and signalled to his men to wait. He made his way up the slight incline that led away from the sea and soon he had crossed into the coarse grass and found the path that would lead inland. He knew the villa was not far. Maniakes's instructions had so far proved sound.

It was quiet here, the early morning bringing little warmth, nevertheless, the close proximity of so much undergrowth made the air feel close and humid. Within a few moments, the sweat ran down from his brow into his eyes and he paused to take off his helmet, and dragged his forearm across his face. He sighed, repositioned his headgear, and pushed on.

After a short distance, the grass gave way to an open space with harsh, hard, compacted earth sapped dry by the summer sun. Even now, with the weather colder, it remained arid and the soles of his hobnailed boots crunched loudly as he crossed towards the villa, which revealed itself some fifty or so paces away.

It was luxurious; brilliant white walls smiled from under a red-tiled roof. Acacia and orange trees gave shade, dappled patterns spreading out across the front and a little veranda shielded the house still further from the sun. Arranged around the terrace, were various couches and seats where one could relax in the evening air, drink wine, and ponder all of life's little idiosyncrasies. Nikolias longed for such a life, to sit back, not worry about anything except whether the next bottle of wine tasted as good as the present one. To idle time away doing nothing: that was what he yearned for. His life as a soldier had been dangerous and taxing, and he didn't know for how much longer he

Varangian

could do it. The chance of a good pension was still many years off, and the General would be arbiter over the amount Nikolias would receive. Faithful service often enjoyed rewards, if one lived long enough. That was his concern. He knew of the rumours, of warriors from Russia in the north, Normans in the West, Saracens in the East. All of them pressing on Byzantine borders, stretching the limited resources of the empire to breaking point. For how much longer could the great empire keep out the barbarians? It had happened to Rome. Over-stretched, its defences cracked, the hordes came in. He may well be called upon many times to fight. Rome had fought, and lost. He had listened to the stories, envisaged the great city in its heyday. Now, so the stories went, it was a rotten place, its once splendid buildings decayed and broken, the people living like rats, no order, no control. Only the mighty church of St Peter and its surrounding area, where the Pope resided. He knew nothing about the Pope, who he was or what he stood for; all he did know was that the religion he headed was close to his own. Close, but not the same. For one thing, they didn't have an emperor, who was God's representative on earth. Perhaps the Pope was a sort of emperor, but not one that had anything to do with God. Nikolias shrugged. Such thoughts were for men far more intelligent than he. For now, he should concentrate on carrying out the General's orders. That way, Byzantium could win back its proper ruler, its proper representative of God – the Empress Zoe.

The place was very quiet. It was early, so perhaps the occupants were asleep. There were no guards, but then again the General had told him there would be none. Drawing his blade, Nikolias positioned himself in front of the main door, and pounded the wood with the pommel of his sword.

He waited. When no sound came from within, he attacked the door again, this time much with far more intent and for a longer period.

A disgruntled voice bellowed, "Who in the name of the Holy mother is that?"

The door was torn open, and there stood a short, squat looking man, hair standing on end, eyes full of sleep, a thin cotton robe barely covering his swollen, round body. Nikolias couldn't help but smile. Shave his head and he would be identical.

Standing there was one of the great officials of state, a man who had served previous emperors with distinction, before banishment by Zoe. Constantine, the brother of John Orphano, and the man General Maniakes believed could help the Empire to survive.

The girl stood, watching. Andreas was aware but paid her no heed as she stood in silence, studying him, as he packed his few belongings. His sword he had cleaned meticulously, oiled the blade, moved it in and out of the sheath a few times. The rest of his panoply was ruined, the iron bands of his body armour rusted, the rivets broken, the leather straps frayed and brittle. He would have a lot of explaining to do when he finally got back to the great city. More than that, he would have to try and conjure up a believable story about why he hadn't killed Hardrada. That was a certainty, and there was nothing he could do, or would want to do, to change it. The man had saved his life, risked his own to drag him from the water. How now was he expected to turn on his saviour and murder him? So, he had come to the decision that Crethus would have to do it on his own, whilst Andreas made his way back to Byzantium. When Crethus had finished the deed, he could catch up with him on the road. But as far as the killing of Hardrada was concerned, he wanted nothing to do with it.

"You seemed troubled."

He started at her voice. "What? Oh, no, nothing."

"Something I think."

Andreas closed his knapsack. She had prepared them things; dried fruit, a few vegetables, flour and salt to make *Paximadion*, the hardtack bread that was the soldiers' staple during campaign. Her kindness had been exceptional and he wondered what she would do now, with the wild war band dispatched. No longer would she need live in fear, forever worrying about when they might appear from out of the forest. She was free now and he took a breath, summing up the courage to ask her the one thing that had been formulating in his mind since the moment he had reached forward to kiss her. "I wonder if I might …" His voice trailed away. This was harder than any battle against barbarian tribes! He rubbed at his face and straightened up. "Listen, why don't you come back with me, to Byzantium? There is nothing for you here now. Come back with me."

She blinked, taken aback, her face draining of colour with the shock. It took her some moments to recover and when she spoke, her voice sounded unsure, as if her thoughts were jumbled, confused. "I …What? To the city, *me*? With you?"

"Why not? You could live a comfortable life. I have ambitions, and this quest, once it is fulfilled, will stand me in good stead for promotion. I could be the commander of a *bandon*. That would mean more pay, a chance to save for the future. Our future."

Her eyes grew wide and she turned away. "I don't know, Andreas. I have lived all my life here, amongst the trees and the animals. To begin a new life, in the city …" She shook her head. "I don't know."

"Listen," he stepped closer, placed his hands tenderly on her slim shoulders. "Say you'll consider it. Please."

Lost in thought for some moments, her features revealing the struggles going on inside, she finally smiled. "Yes. I will consider it. Maybe you are right. Maybe there is nothing here for me now."

He felt such a sense of relief then, and he held her to him and his heart leapt as she responded, slipping her arms around him, holding him tight. He spoke into the nape of her neck. "I'll go to the city with Crethus, then I shall return. A week, ten days perhaps. That will be time enough for you to consider my proposal."

"I will consider it."

He lifted his head, turned her face to him and kissed her. Her lips opened and soon he was lost as their embrace grew more powerful, her soft mouth melding with his. His knees weakened as he sampled the sweetness of her, breathed in her perfume, felt his loins yearning.

Breathlessly, she pulled away, grinning, all previous coyness gone. "You promise you will return?"

"With all my heart," he said, his voice a mere whisper, consumed by the need for her.

"And when you return," she said, an index finger tracing itself across his lip. "You can tell me all about your adventures, your city, your hopes and dreams?"

He blinked, felt his cheeks reddening as the heat swelled up from deep within. "I think you already know what they might be."

"No, I might guess, but I do not know." She smiled, closing her eyes as their lips pressed together once more.

He felt the air grow hot as all of his being centred on her mouth. Soon, their passion was escalating, soaring off into any number of different directions. He was lost in a whirlwind of desire and passion, his hands roaming over her slim, taut body. She responded, her hands clamping over his hard back and he groaned as they fell to the floor. Time and thought lost as they embraced, lips everywhere, both of them moaning in their shared need, urgent now, no thoughts for anything else.

Sometime later, Andreas became aware of Crethus. They were both still on the ground, a simple blanket covering their bodies. As the Scythian stood in the entrance to the tent, Andreas sat up and began to pull on his jerkin. He gave Analise an awkward grin, and stood up, reaching for his knapsack. "It seems we must leave."

Crethus loomed there, his great size filling the confined space. He was grinning. "Sorry to interrupt," he said, his voice laced with sarcasm, "but I wonder if I might beg your pardon, sir, and ask you to come and inspect your horse."

Andreas shook his head, ran his hand down Analise's arm, and then followed the giant Scythian outside to where the two animals were saddled and waiting.

"I put the bodies in a pit," Crethus said, gesturing to a small earthen mound a few paces away. "I covered them well. There shouldn't be any danger of plague."

"Well done. And these animals," Andreas patted the neck of the closest, "how did you find them?"

Crethus shrugged. "My people have always been good trackers, Andreas. It is not something you can easily forget. I will use the same skill to find Hardrada. He won't even know I'm there, until he feels my blade across his throat."

Andreas winced, threw his knapsack over the back of his horse and put his foot in the stirrup. "I don't want to know, Crethus. You understand?" The Scythian nodded. "Never. Not a word. The next time I see you will be in Constantinople." He turned to move back to the tent, but Crethus held up a hand.

"Best if you move swiftly," said the Scythian. "We have tarried too long as it is."

Andreas made a face, but realized that the Scythian's words were wise. There would be time enough to spend a whole lifetime with Analise. "Tell her I shall return as fast as I can." He swung himself up into the saddle, sat there for a moment, then moved off, following the track that would take him to the ford, then eventually to the old road down towards the great city.

Analise busied herself with cleaning the few pots she had used for preparing Andreas's meagre rations. She wished she could have done more. He seemed like a little boy at times, desperate for someone to care for him, look after him. Yet, at the same time, he was strong, virile, would truck no nonsense from anyone. She had seen him fighting, and it had frightened her but at the same time thrilled her. His body was lean and hard.

She recalled his body, lean and hard, when she had laid him down on the camp bed, and slipped off his soaking wet breeches. She had not been with a man for so long that she had begun to believe she never would again enjoy the feeling of hard muscle, of being taken completely. Then, they had joined, and it was like nothing she had ever known. He was so caring, so mindful of her needs, and his eyes, the way they blazed, never leaving hers.

When he had asked her to go with him, to Constantinople, it was as if she had slipped into a dream world. Such an idea! To live with him, in that wondrous place. The place of fantasies. Golden streets, happy, smiling people, food and drink in abundance. To never go hungry again, to lie on soft mattresses, be clothed the finest satins and silks, to be loved by a man like Andreas. Successful, charming, kind and generous. She would be a fool not to take him up on his offer.

A shadow fell over her and she flinched as the huge Scythian dropped down on his haunches. "He's a good man, Andreas."

She frowned. Something glowered in the man's tone, not friendly, almost accusing, but accusing her of what? "Yes, yes he is."

"Not rich, but he could be. One day. He's got quite a thing for you."

Those eyes, like burning coals, piercing her. She wanted to turn away, but she had neither the strength nor the courage to do so. "Has he?"

"Oh, yes, and you know it. Asked you to go back to Constantinople, did he?"

He already knew the answer. He'd obviously been listening, so was this some sort of test, to gauge her honesty? "He did. And I will think about it."

"Gracious of you."

She felt a stab of fear at that point. His voice had hardened even more and before she could react he had her by the throat, pushing her down onto the ground. She struggled to wriggle out of his hold, but he was too strong, stronger than anyone she had ever known. His hand was so big it almost encircled her entire neck. His black face came close to hers, his breath wafting over her. "Mark this, woman. If he does return, you will refuse him. A harlot like you doesn't belong in the great city. Andreas has a future, a future based on fidelity and loyalty. He does not need any distractions, and certainly none from the likes of you." He came even closer and she closed her eyes as spittle sprayed from his mouth as he rasped, "Do *not* return with him. If you do, I will cut your throat. We understand one another?"

Varangian

Her bowels loosened as fear overcame her. His words, so vehement, so horrible, struck her like blows and even if he hadn't held her by the throat she would have found it difficult to reply. She managed to whimper, "Yes," and then he released her and moved away.

She lay there, gasping for air, clutching at her bruised throat. Dear Christ, what an animal! And why was he so determined for her not to go with Andreas? What was it he had in store for him, what was it that he was so afraid of? She didn't know, nor did she want to know. His words had shaken her to her very core and now all she longed for was his departure, to allow her some time to think. Already, however, one thing had been decided. A new life in Constantinople would be what it had always been: a dream and nothing more than a dream, now more distant than ever.

Thirty-Three

The procession wound its way through the Royal Gates towards the imposing sight of the Hippodrome. All of the extended royal family had gathered, in their very finest robes of state, to wend their way towards the place where the games would begin. It seemed that the entire population of the city had come out onto the streets to witness the slow, deliberate march. The Royal bodyguard, in their lamellar armour, kite shields and *rhomphaia* slung over their backs, looked resplendent, everything finely polished, horses with manes and tails decorated and inlaid with precious and semi-precious jewels. Rarely were ordinary people given the chance to see the Imperial guard, but now they trotted file after file, the *Scholae* being the most senior, and oldest of all the regiments, leading. General Maniakes rode at their head and many people bowed to him, knowing him to be their greatest defender against the incursions of so many enemies. They were not many, no more than two hundred, the rump of what was once a formidable force. Border duties, the constant threat from enemies made the billeting of troops in the city itself a luxury now. Nevertheless, they were an impressive sight.

Trumpets blasted out and musicians marched, giving out the steady beat, as golden carriages rumbled by, the state coach gleaming, with Michael standing in its centre, waving to the people as he passed by. Alongside, on either side of the carriage, danced a host of white clad maidens, throwing up bunches of white camellia petals. An air of festivity and happiness pervaded everything and Michael felt relaxed and confident. He had arranged for Leoni to greet him in the royal Box in the Hippodrome, from where he would address the people. An underground tunnel ran from the palace complex to the royal box but on this occasion, the emperor had decided that the procession should be in full view of everyone, and it was proving a triumph.

This was to be the start of five days of feasting and entertainment, meant to herald the beginning of a new era. Not for a generation had so much been lavished on free games for the people, and Michael had banked on their gratitude and goodwill. Since the debacle of his inauguration, he was determined that nothing should go wrong. To cement this, the Scythian Varangians lined the main street to the Hippodrome, placed strategically amongst the people, eyes alert, searching for any would-be saboteurs. Whoever had rucked up that carpet would not be allowed a similar chance to disrupt the proceedings and bring more shame to the Emperor.

The procession entered under the main archway of the hippodrome, splitting into two, one arm going to the left, the other to the right. Here too the *Numeri,* the permanent guard of the city, stood to attention, shields glistening in the brilliant sunshine. Michael had prayed for good weather. He had already promised himself that he would attend a special mass that very evening to give thanks to God for blessing him with such superb weather.

Michael was dressed in his purple robes and had, on this day, adorned himself with a breastplate of pure gold. From his waist hung a ceremonial sword, sheathed in a scabbard of scarlet coloured leather, which matched his greaves and cloak. He wore a simple band of gold around his head, not wishing to appear too opulent; one of his most publicized reforms was that money should not be wasted on the fineries of the royal household, but on the continuing security of the empire. He believed he had chosen wisely and when he stepped down from his carriage and the mob pressed inwards, their faces were full of awe, wide smiles abounding. He waved to them constantly as he mounted the steps. The trumpets blared out and all around the sound within the Hippodrome swelled, bathing him in the awe and wonder he had always longed for. This was the gift of being Emperor, the chosen ambassador to God. Giddiness washed over him when he stood in the royal box and looked out at the sea of people who clambered into the tiers on either side to get the best possible seat.

The opening races were a throwback of the ancient games of Rome. Chariots, shimmering with fitments of silver and ivory, clattered out onto the sand floor, horses prancing, drivers struggling to keep them in line. Michael had wanted to stage some old gladiatorial games, but Maniakes had persuaded him that such a spectacle would be too much for the more refined Greek taste. "Some things are best left in the history books, sire," the general had said, and Michael had to acquiesce, although he did insist on the re-enactment of a battle or two, without the bloodshed of course. The mainstay, as always, would be the horse races, punctuated with various other entertainments, from tumbling acrobats to streams of semi-naked dancers performing to newly composed music. Michael was looking forward to it and stepped forward to address the multitude. The trumpets blasted out to warn those within earshot that the Emperor was about to speak, and the assembly settled down. Courtiers were placed throughout the Hippodrome ready to repeat the Emperor's words to those who were too far away to hear him themselves.

The trumpets ceased and an expectant hush settled down over the crowd.

Michael drew in a deep breath. He had never seen so many people in one place before, and every single one of them had their faces turned to him. He tried to settle his stomach, which was beginning to turn over quite alarmingly, and spread out his trembling hands to give himself a few moments to ready himself.

"People of Rome," he roared. "I bid you welcome!"

The crowd erupted, cheering and screaming, throwing their caps and anything else they had to hand, into the air. How they loved to be addressed as Romans, and how Michael milked it, beaming at them, nodding his head in arrogant acceptance of their praise. This was better than he expected.

Haldor jumped down from the barred window and grunted, "It's no good, I can't see or hear a damn thing."

Ulf pulled a face, "Well, it's not normal. No noise at all?" He went over to the door and tried to peer through the tiny grill to the corridor beyond. His stomach rumbled loudly. "No one. When did they last feed us?"

"I can't remember." Haldor sat down.

Ulf tugged on the grill, lifting his voice, "Hey! Anyone out there? We need food, damn your black hearts – *food!*"

"You think that will do the trick?"

"Well, it's better than sitting here starving to death."

Haldor shook his head, a little sadly. "You always think of your stomach ..." He cocked his head. "Hear that?"

Ulf listened to a very slight roar from the far distance. "Sounds like a crowd."

"It is a crowd, damn it!" Haldor jumped up and went over to the barred window again. "Maybe it's some sort of celebration ... a festival."

Ulf didn't like the sound of that. Festivals or religious holidays always meant everyone had to attend – including guards. He gripped the grill again, "Anyone? Come on, you lazy, idle good-for-nothings! I want my dinner!"

From down the corridor they heard a small, throaty cough, followed by a forceful spit. Ulf tried to squint down the corridor so he could catch a glimpse of whoever it was, but the angle was too acute. He let his shoulders drop and stepped back from the door. "There is someone out there." He pounded on the door, angry, roaring, "*Come on, you idle shit!*"

"Pipe down, you noisy sod!"

Ulf turned to Haldor and winked. "Leave this to me. You, get yourself in a heap on the ground – now!" Haldor frowned, but with some reluctance did as asked. "Now, groan a little, like you're in pain."

Ulf returned to the door, hammering it with both fists, "Hurry! My friend is sick." He saw a small squat figure approaching.

"What the hell's the matter with you?" Only the top of his head could be seen through the grill.

Ulf pressed his face up against the grill. "He's sick. We haven't eaten for hours, and I don't think it's done him any good."

"Well, there's nothing I can do. The Scythians are all at the Hippodrome."

"The Hippodrome? What the hell's going on?"

"Games," said the voice, and Ulf could hear the man turn to move away.

"*Wait!*" Ulf clung onto the grill. "For pity's sake, my friend needs food! He has a fever and he cannot stand."

"I don't think there is anything," said the man.

"Please," said Ulf, putting as much authenticity into his voice as he could muster, "anything will do – some bread even."

A long silence settled, then finally the man muttered, "I'll see what I can do." The sound of his feet, shuffling down the corridor, soon faded.

"So much for your plan," said Haldor, sitting up again.

"He'll be back," said Ulf, still trying to peer down the corridor. "I know it. And when he does, you get back down on the ground, really roll around, make out as if you are in terrible pain."

"And if he comes back, you think he'll open the door?"

"Once he sees you and I tell him what will happen if he doesn't help you – remember, we're prisoners of the Emperor! We're valuable to him and he wants us alive."

"You've become something of a strategist all of a sudden, old friend. I'm impressed."

"You'll be more than impressed when that fellow comes back – you'll be free!"

Varangian

George Maniakes stood some distance from the Royal box. He had never been wholey comfortable with the trappings of privilege, even when he had marched through the Golden Gates at the head of his victorious troops. The mob had gone wild that day, showering him with flower petals, chanting his name. The defender of the Empire, the crusher of souls. True, it had filled him with a sense of pride that so many should come out to greet him, but he never felt at ease with any of it. He was a soldier at heart, gruff and hard. When he cast his thoughts back to battle, the dead and the dying, all of this pomp filled him with revulsion. He surveyed the assembly of royal hangers-on, the so-called *extended* family of the Macedonian Dynasty, and his mouth turned down in disgust. They were soft, pampered and indolent. The Senators were the same, especially the fawning ones, the ones who would gladly kiss Michael's arse if he asked them to. He longed for a return to the days of the great Emperor Basil, who tamed his enemies with hard fought battles, not mealy-mouthed words. In Sicily it had been like that, when he and Hardrada had fought the Normans to a standstill. It could be like that again, perhaps. He had no understanding of John Orphano's great plan, why Hardrada posed such a threat to everyone. The man was controllable so long as he had something to do. Killing and fighting in battle were the things he did best. To control Hardrada, you put him to work, not murder him.

Orphano had got that part wrong. And now, the Royal eunuch, once so proud and so powerful had been ferreted away by Michael. Just like the Empress Zoe. The whole edifice was coming down. At first, Maniakes had been wrong-footed, but now he had recovered. With Orphano's brother returning to the scene, Maniakes could manipulate the entire situation to his own liking, restore Zoe to the throne, and go back to doing what he did best – war.

He caught a movement over to his left and turned to see a dust-covered soldier standing there, kicking his heels, looking a little sheepish. He bowed his head to the General, who beckoned him over. The man scurried forward and, keeping his face averted, spluttered, "He is here, sir."

Maniakes filled out his chest, dismissed the soldier with a flick of a hand, then beamed at the throng. Sometimes it felt good to be alive.

* * *

The key rattled in the lock and Ulf stepped away from the door as it opened.

The squat, little man stood there, eying the writhing Haldor with distinct unease. "What's the matter with him?"

"I don't know," said Ulf, trying his best to sound concerned. "His guts probably – he hasn't eaten for days. I think he's poisoned."

"Poisoned?" The man's face blanched. "By those Scythians?"

"More than likely. If the Emperor hears about it, he'll have a fit. Demand a few heads be struck off."

The man's mouth fell open. He stood a little way back, in the corridor, and the curved blade in his hand looked sharp. His shoulders were wide, bunched with muscle and Ulf took him as quite a dangerous adversary. "There's no one here except me – they're all on guard duty." He rubbed his face. "I'll go and fetch him some water."

He turned and Ulf took his chance, deftly slipping through the door, catching the man around the throat with one arm, clutching the hand that held the sword with the other. But the man was indeed no walkover. He yelped, threw back his head and connected with Ulf's nose with an evil sounding crack. As Ulf staggered back, blood gushing from his face, the man turned, and screeched, "Bastard!"

From nowhere Haldor stepped forward and kicked him, a perfect blow, right between the man's legs. He squealed, bent double and vomited on the ground as Haldor neatly picked up the fallen sword and sliced through the man's throat in one, swift move.

Ulf staggered backwards, holding his face as Haldor cleaned the blade on the dead man's jerkin. Haldor looked around at his old friend. "Bloody stupid thing to do. Why didn't you just hit him?"

"I tried, didn't I?" His voice was muffled beneath his hands. The blood seeped between the fingers. "I don't think you should have killed him. When they find him, those Scythians, they'll want our balls on a plate."

"Fuck them," spat Haldor. He weighted the sword in his hand, studying the curved Scythian blade with something akin to admiration. "Bloody sharp this. I'll take great pleasure in slicing up some of them bastards before they get me. Come on." He thrust out his hand and pulled Ulf to his feet.

Ulf said, "Let's put him in the cell. That'll give us some time."

"Time for what?"

"To get away." Ulf sniffed and took his hand away, stared at the blood and sniffed again. "Bastard broke my nose, I think."

"You should be used to that – besides, it'll improve your looks."

Ulf dragged the back of his sleeve across his face. The blood had almost stopped. "We need to get into the streets, perhaps make it to the outer limits of the city. We might be able to steal a couple of horses and get away."

"And Harald?"

"Well, we'll have to try and find him, won't we?"

"That'll be hard, seeing as we don't know where he is, and this is the biggest city in the world!"

"What the fuck do you want us to do, then? I don't hear any great ideas coming out of your gob."

Haldor grinned. "No, you're the brains of the outfit, I'll just follow your lead. Sir."

"Fuck off!"

Haldor bowed. "Gracious majesty!"

Ulf groaned and kicked at the dead jailer. "He's going to be a heavy bastard to shift. It's not going to be easy."

"Yes. You'd better get to it then, hadn't you?"

Thirty-Four

Hardrada doubted it had been Normans who had attacked the Varangian camp. The idea that those bastards could have come this far east was too terrible to contemplate. His suspicions centred on Russians, or even those accursed Patzinaks.

Spread out across the northern shores of the river Danube, they had been constantly encroaching south for years. Some time ago, reports came through of a mass of them descending almost as far as the city of Adrianople. Nearly a million strong scouts had said, great trails of them winding their way as far as the eye could see. They were a redoubtable foe and Hardrada felt certain that not so very many years away, Byzantium would have to face them in pitched battle to halt their advance.

For this current incursion, in his mind he was sure it had to be Russians. From the descriptions Rufus had given him, the way the men were dressed, their form of attack, the pallor of their skin, they surely must have come from the armies of the Russian leader, Great Prince Iaroslav, known as 'The Wise', a mantle he had assumed because of his cautious diplomacy with his enemies. This included the Emperors of Rome. Perhaps he too was feeling the threat from Normans and wanted to extend his borders.

The more he thought about it, the more Hardrada convinced himself that his tenure with the Varangian Guard was coming to its natural end. He had the urge to return home, to fulfil his destiny as king, not to serve others. His pockets had been well lined, and when he returned to the Great city, the first thing on his list would be to track down that cur, Orphano, and demand his money back, the money that the detestable eunuch had hidden away. If that didn't happen, then the man would die and Hardrada would take whatever he could find anyway. He had had enough of others telling him what he could and could not do. At the head of his Varangian troops, he would make all of them pay.

* * *

The track snaked through the forest, gently descending down to the river. He recognized certain features of the landscape and felt reassured. It would not be long now before he came to the crossing-place, and the little camp. He wondered in what condition he would find Andreas. There was something about the lad that Hardrada admired. Initially he had seemed sullen, almost as if the great weight of his responsibilities had sucked away his humanity, his personality. As the journey developed, however, Hardrada came to grudgingly like him. His sense of duty was admirable and Hardrada felt that if he ever did have a son, he would wish him to be like the young Greek officer.

Heavy rain must have fallen in the distant mountains, because the speed of the river had changed, now becoming much stronger, and considerably more swollen. Hardrada repeatedly glanced across to the far side, searching for signs of movement, smoke, or anything that would indicate he was close to the camp. By the time he reached the ford, he questioned whether this crossing place was safe to negotiate. The current was swift here, the water rushing by, angry and dangerous. However, he had little choice and he tentatively urged his horse down the slight incline towards where the water became a little shallower.

The horse whinnied as they balked, reluctant to plunge into the icy depths. Hardrada urged it on, kicking hard into its flanks and then it was in, head held high, nostrils flaring as it forced its way across. The water almost came to the top of Hardrada's thigh, causing him further alarm. He was a big man, and his mount was equally huge. It had to be, to supports its rider's weight. Even so, the sheer power of the water forced them both further downstream. Soon, they would be in the river proper, with unfathomable depths. The fear of being swept away seemed to spur the horse on and it strained and sweated as it struggled across, all the time Hardrada encouraging it with soothing words.

At last, the horse scrambled up the opposite bank, slipping in the mud but managing to maintain its footing. Soaked up to his waist, Hardrada leapt off the horse's back and shook himself, the horse copying him, sending out a fine spray of water in all directions. It whinnied again, stamping its feet in a mixture of anger and relief. Hardrada patted its trembling neck, nuzzled his face into its skin, soothing it with more, calming words.

He checked his sword and battleaxe, wiping off the surplus water with a cloth. His bedroll was wringing and he would need to lay it out in the sun in order to dry it before night came. He estimated it was past noon, but not much. He had been on the road a good four hours or more and had made excellent progress so far. However, he couldn't expect the horse to face the river again that day, so, as soon as he found Andreas and told him about the Varangian advance, he would spend the night there, in the camp. The journey towards the Great City would continue on the morrow and he would probably still be ahead of Rufus and the patriarch Alexius.

Leading the horse by the reins, Hardrada now set to tramping through the thick undergrowth of the opposite bank. Here the land was much more thickly wooded and again, his eyes kept turning to the forest, squinting to see if anyone or anything lurked there. He did not want to repeat his earlier encounter with the wolves, even with his axe in his hands.

He was close now, just a few more paces. He considered calling out; coming upon a camp, any camp unannounced was always a dangerous thing to do. But the girl was no threat and Andreas would soon recognize him, so he moved on, unconcerned about any noise he made.

The first thing he saw was a large mound, newly filled in. Beside it, a collection of arms. He stopped, frowning. It hadn't been there before. He glanced up, peering through the thinning trees at the little camp whose outline he could just make out. It was quiet, no movement, no camp fire. He kicked away at the mound gently, knocking away some of the earth with his foot. He gave a start when a stark white hand fell out from beneath the earth. His horse shivered, stamping its feet again, yanking at the reins. Hardrada calmed it and tied it to a nearby tree. Taking his axe from around his shoulder, he moved on towards the camp, much more surreptitiously now, sensing that something was wrong, very wrong.

He crept forward in a half-crouch, making sure each footfall was as light as possible. Every now and again he would stop, cock his head to one side and listen. Nothing. Not even bird song to interrupt the stillness. This in itself was strange. A forest such as this, teeming with wildlife ... He set his jaw and moved on.

Using one arm, he parted some branches that barred his pathway forward and almost cried out in alarm. For a moment he had to refocus, because what he saw was beyond belief.

The tent was there, its flaps pulled back, revealing the empty interior. In front, the camp fire, dead, the pots and pans still lined up ready for use. But the wood beneath the homemade hanging bar upon which the pots would be suspended was nothing but a pile of cold ashes. No need for fire, no need for anything else.

She lay there, spread out upon the ground, her legs wide open, the thin cotton shift rented, exposing her naked body beneath. Her eyes stared sightlessly towards the sky, and the gaping wound across her throat was black with congealed blood. Hardrada went forward without another thought, dropping his axe to the side, and stooped down to her. He knew she was dead even before he took her in his arms and felt the ice coldness of her limbs, stiff as boards. He gasped at that and gently laid her back down to the ground. A slight breeze whistled through the camp, disturbing the girl's hair, and he brushed it away from her face, and then closed her eyes, not wishing to gaze upon her death any longer.

Who could have done this, and why? He knelt there, pressing his fist into his mouth. By Odin's beard, he would find out who the culprit was and flay them alive. Or worse.

He buried her next to the tent, lining the little pit with some furs he found, and covering her with an old blanket so that the soil would not smother her lovely features directly. When he had finished, he sat down on an upturned tree trunk and gazed into nothingness. He sat like that for a very long time.

Thirty-Five

"Why am I here, and for how long are you going to keep me waiting?"

Nikolias shifted his weight uncomfortably, seething at the man's arrogance. It had taken a lot of persuading to get him to come along, to scramble into the boat and take the short crossing to the city. Even then he had mumbled and groaned the entire way. On entering the Palace complex, the man hadn't even paused to take in the marvel of the surrounding offices of State. His indifferent air riled Nikolias more than anything else about this surly, pompous man. Now, as they sat outside the private apartment of General Maniakes, Nikolias wished with all his heart that he could leave this snivelling in-bred to whatever fate Maniakes had in store for him. He only hoped it would be nasty one.

"I want some wine," the man said at length. Well accustomed to giving out orders, he looked down his nose at Nikolias and sniffed loudly. "Now."

As Nikolias rose, a great roar could be heard in the distance.

The man frowned. "What is that?"

"It's the opening of the games."

"Pah! Games indeed. What is the point of that?"

"I haven't a single clue."

"What did you say your name was?"

"I didn't."

The man pressed his lips together as his cheeks reddened, "Let me put it another way – what is your name?"

"Nikolias. I am a *Dekarchos* of the *Tagimata*."

The man sniffed. "Am I supposed to be impressed by that?"

"I don't care what you are, it's what I am. You asked me, I've told you."

"You could do with lessons on servility, young man. I don't care if you are lowly officer in the Imperial Guard, you will give me the respect I am due."

Nikolias held his breath for a moment. He had a sudden urge to strike the man across the face, but he knew better than to do that. Instead, he stood rock still, controlling his temper. The arrogance of the man sickened him. "I'll go and find you some wine."

The man nodded his head then folded his arms across his generous torso and closed his eyes. As Nikolias strode off, he could hear the man already snoring.

Outside, Nikolias found a servant and sent him to fetch some wine. Another roar rang out. He sighed, wishing he could be there, at the Hippodrome, to watch the races. He'd never seen them, not in all his years of service. Campaigning had dominated his life, ever since his early years when he first became a soldier. His father had been a soldier, after serving for a short time as a secretary to a Senator. He became a *Drakonarios* – standard-bearer in the Imperial Guard. It was a position that afforded him great privilege, both on the battlefield, and in the city. Now Nikolias was following in his footsteps and he felt sure his father would be proud. His father had died fighting the Normans in Sicily, beating them back, defending the standard until some coward shot him from behind with an arrow. Typical Norman treachery.

"Nikolias!"

The young man swung round and brought himself to attention. General Maniakes strode resolutely towards him, his face stern, and a little concerned. "Where is Constantine?"

"I've just left him, to fetch some wine, sir."

Varangian

Maniakes scowled, placed an index finger on the soldier's chest. "Don't ever leave him again."

Nikolias stiffened. "No sir. Sorry, sir."

"He should be all right, though. Everyone is at the games. Come on, take me to him."

Nikolias marched off, down the corridor to the private apartment anteroom. He eased open the door and stood aside for Maniakes to step through.

Constantine still dozed, exactly as Nikolias had left him. The general gave a short laugh. "Dear Christ, that is one fat bastard."

"Not just a fat one, sir."

Maniakes shot him an inquiring glance. "What does that mean?"

Nikolias shrugged, "Permission to speak freely, sir?"

"Go on."

"He is a surly, arrogant pig, sir. Likes giving orders, expects things to be handed to him on a plate with no questions asked."

Maniakes laughed again. "Nikolias, the man is part of the Royal Family. Well, he likes to *think* he is. He is used to respect."

Nikolias gulped, taking the guarded reprimand on the chin. "Yes, but he's surely not still thinking he has any influence, sir?"

"Oh yes. Our dear, sweet friend, Constantine, brother of the illustrious eunuch John Orphano, has a great deal of influence. Or, should I say – he will have, if things work out the way I hope they do. Listen, Nikolias, I want you to hang around His Royal Highness's throne room. I have a feeling you will be asked to go and fetch our dear friend Constantine very soon."

"Fetch him, sir? What, from your office, sir?"

"No, from his island villa."

Nikolias was at a loss to fathom this. "Er … I'm not quite sure I understand you, sir. I *have* just fetched him from his island villa."

"Yes, you have. But Michael doesn't know that, does he. And I don't want him to. Neither do I want anyone else to know it either. It must be Michael's idea, you see. Whilst you pretend to go and get him, I will have a little chat. Make sure that he is well aware of the situation."

Nikolias still wasn't too sure of the General's thought-processes, but decided it best not to pursue the matter.

The sound of approaching footsteps caused Maniakes to tense grip Nikolias by the arm. "No one must see him, not yet!"

"Don't worry, sir." Nikolias drew his sword as the servant appeared, carrying a small tray with a jug of wine and two goblets.

"Your wine, sir." The man smiled, bowed his head and settled the tray on a nearby table."Will there be anything else, sir?"

Nikolias nodded, turned to the general and said, "Shan't be a moment, sir." Then took the servant by the arm and led him outside.

Again, from the distance came a loud roar. Maniakes blew out his breath before crossing the room to the table where he poured himself a goblet of wine. He tasted it, made a face, and tipped it back into the jug. He turned as Nikolias returned.

"All done?"

Nikolias nodded. "All done, sir."

Even Maniakes gave a little shudder at just how nonchalant Nikolias appeared after dealing out death so passionlessly. "Remind me to always have you on my side, Nikolias."

"Yes sir. You can rely on that, sir."

"I hope so, my friend. I hope so."

Thirty-Six

As was his want, Michael changed his mind. He was enjoying himself, sitting back in his throne, watching the various games, basking in the delight of the crowd as they drank in the spectacle. He signalled to one of his servants to pass the message on. He would introduce Leoni tomorrow. By then, the crowd would be so drunk with happiness that they would be bound to welcome her with tumultuous appreciation. Then, he settled back, sipped at his umpteenth goblet of wine, and continued to be entertained.

He had another idea a little later, but he needed to talk to Maniakes about it. Now that neither Zoe nor Orphano were around, the General was the only real person he could ask advice. Unless, of course, he pursued Leoni's brilliant idea. Contact Orphano's brother, bring him back to court and reinstate him in a high office of state. Renowned as the most brilliant mind in the entire Empire, he could help Michael re-establish authority. Yes, it was a majestic idea and he was anxious to put the plan into operation.

By the late afternoon, stuffed with quail eggs, chicken breasts and various spiced dishes, Michael told his immediate retinue that the time had come for him to leave. He rose to his feet, threw out his arms to the baying crowd, and bade them farewell until the next day. "I will have some surprises for you, my beloved people," he told them and as they cheered and waved, he made his way out of the Royal Box to the main gates of the Hippodrome. He nodded to a couple of brutish looking

Scythian guards. "I am walking through the streets. The tunnel can wait until tomorrow."

The return to the Royal Palace was a much more conservative affair. The streets were quiet, everyone either being at the games, or pressing in around the side walls for a glimpse of the proceedings. All around lay the detritus of the earlier procession and Michael, choosing to leave the royal coach behind, took his time, ambling along the main thoroughfare, glancing around this way and that. He had a curious feeling of depression overtaking him. The opening ceremony had been a triumph. He had expected the crowd to demand Zoe to appear, but nothing had happened. The chariot races had proved their worth, and tomorrow he would give them something else. He had thought about it before, mentioned to one or two people, but everyone had seemed reluctant to agree. Well, not any more; emboldened by his success, Michael believed he could do nothing wrong. The people loved him, and he would reward them with a spectacle from the glorious past. Gladiatorial combat.

He meandered through the Lion Gate, his bodyguard shuffling all around him, but no one else. He had waved them away, wishing to be alone. As he mounted the steps of the Palace, he reflected on how fortunate he had been. His plans had fallen neatly into place, the mob were happy, the future seemed bright. And yet, despite all of this, he still felt empty somehow. Stepping into the main corridor of the palace, he looked around him at the fine statues and paintings adorning the walkway. He stood and took in the treasures of the ages, the finest artists and craftsmen producing decorative items which would grace even the most hallowed halls of the Emperor Augustus. Along this avenue of riches, the most powerful men in the world would pass, to pay allegiance. Michael had sent messengers out to all corners of the Empire. It was time the world knew that the Empire had come under the tenure of a reforming and proactive leader. They would come and they would kowtow to him. He should feel elation. Instead, all he could think about were his cold, empty apartments; no companions, close friends, confidants to while away the hours. Another lonely night.

Except for Leoni.

He gave a little smile. Yes, there was always her. When he had first laid eyes on her, he had felt the rush of desire erupt through his loins. The curve of her young breasts, the swell of her buttocks under the thin cotton shift. She dripped sex and he had wanted her there and then. She had succumbed to his charms, despite the fact that she was the general's lover, a fact that made the entire ménage so much more exciting, delicious even.

The thought of her now, those slim, long limbs, the flatness of her belly which contrasted so gloriously with the fullness of her buttocks brought his erection to full bloom. He quickened his pace and almost broke into a run to get to his inner rooms of his private apartments.

He reached the great double doors and pushed them open with a mighty shove. He stood there, a hand on each door, gasping.

There she was, lying on the bed, a thin satin sheet covering one leg, the rest of her exposed. She smiled when she saw him and turned, barked at his guards, "Leave us!" Then he slammed the doors shut and leaned back on them. "My God, but you are beautiful."

"I missed you today, My Lord."

"Did you? By Christ, I missed you!" He virtually ran towards her, pulling off the heavy ceremonial robes as he did so, leaving them to drop to the floor in unruly heaps. He ripped away his blouson and struggled with his scarlet pantaloons. He was already hard and ready and Leoni reached out and guided him towards her, throwing away the sheet and opening her legs to receive him.

Michael proved a passionate lover and she felt alive under him, at his attention, his desire. She had struggled against it, not allowing herself to accept that she might have feelings for this man. She had told Maniakes many times that she loathed coupling with the Emperor, but somehow none of that seemed to matter now. Her heart was warming towards him. So attentive, so urgent. She clasped at his buttocks, urging him on; he responded, his thrusts becoming faster and she gave herself up to the wonderful sense of wanton openness that engulfed her. She felt him tense, his breathing coming in sharp gasps as he drove to further heights, then gave a great roar as his hips ground into her, holding tight, fingers digging into the flesh of her upper arms, and then he collapsed beside her, gulping in the air.

Leoni lay there, staring up at the ceiling, aware of the glow enveloping her. She could never have believed it possible, but her feelings for this man were real, and growing stronger. She turned to him, gazing at his face. His eyes were shut, and she studied him without interruption. The sharp, aquiline nose, high cheekbones, full lips. Some might call him effeminate, others had already labelled him a parody of the former emperors of Rome, the way he deliberately curled his hair into ringlets, the rouge he rubbed into his cheeks, the black liner he applied to his eyes. The suspicion was that he preferred boys, but Leoni knew that this could not be the case. True, the idea of the general fucking her seemed to give him a surge of uncontrolled desire, but she believed that had more to do with the thrill of being humiliated than any physical desire the Emperor might have for another man. The idea that she should be ravished by such a powerful lover turned him on. It was that simple. And, if she were to be honest, she quite liked the idea of having two men feasting on her flesh. What more could anyone want … unless, of course, one sought love.

Love. She let out her breath in a long, slow stream. She doubted if Michael was capable of such an emotion. The General certainly wasn't. He used her and, when she grew fat, he would dispense with her. She had no illusions. So, she had decided to make the best of her time with her lovers. Her herbalist always gave the correct concoctions for preventing pregnancy – so far they had worked. Perhaps, if she were to stop, allow herself to be impregnated by the Emperor, that might give a degree of power and privilege she had never dreamed. She suppressed a giggle. What would the General say to that, she wondered.

Michael stirred and turned to face her. He smiled, his hand snaking out to brush against her cheeks. "Tomorrow, I will introduce you to the world. I want you to dress in the finest robes. Have your hair made up and prepare yourself for the greatest day of your life."

"Oh, My Lord," she snuggled into him and he put his arm around her. "You are so generous."

"You think so?"

"Oh yes, most definitely, My Lord. Generous and kind."

He gave a slight guffaw, "I doubt if many would agree with that!"

"That is because they do not know the true nature of your heart."

"Is that true?" He arched an eyebrow. "And you do?"

"I know of your kindness, your selflessness, your thoughtfulness."

"Again, I doubt if the majority would hold with your opinion, however well-intentioned it may be." He looked up at the ceiling. "I've been thinking about what you mentioned last time, about Orphano's brother."

"Oh?" She propped herself up on her elbow. "You think it is a good idea?"

"I think it is a wonderful idea." He looked at her. "Of mine."

"Of course!" Her fingers traced a line over his chest, settled on his right nipple and circled it. He gave a little moan.

"I want you to go and tell my guards to fetch Constantine and bring him to court. And then, go and inform Maniakes of my intention."

"The General? Why, My Lord?"

"Oh, I think he will be suitably surprised." He laughed again. "I can't wait to see the look on his face!"

Leoni smiled herself and placed her head on the Emperor's chest. "You are so wise, My Lord." She closed her eyes, longing to add, "But not as wise as the General!" How wonderful it was to have the ear of two such important men, and how decidedly wicked to watch them as they sparred.

* * *

Nikolias looked up as the girl came padding down the hallway. He could see right through her thin dress and he sucked in his breath as he took in her lithe figure, the roundness of her hips. She smiled as she approached. He had made no secret of his lustful gaze and now, with her standing so close, her full breasts a mere arm's reach away, he found it difficult to conceal his desire.

"Hello, Captain," she said, that mocking tone creeping into her voice. She gave him an admiring glance, her eyes lingering on the obvious bulge in his pants. "Been waiting long?"

"No, mistress," he replied, giving a little bow. My God, to be this close to her. His heart hammered against his chest as he looked at her once more under his brows. He had heard the rumours of her sensuality, but until now he had dismissed it all as barrack room invention. Having her here, the smell of her, the long blonde hair sweeping down over her face, those lips … He wiped a hand over his face, a face that had broken out with sweat. "You have instructions."

"Yes. Tell the General, it is done. You have to go and fetch Constantine."

She swung around and glided away. He stood and watched her voluptuous buttocks swaying first this way, then that. She relished displaying herself in this way, he thought. She must love all the attention, the obvious effect she had on men. God, how he would love to tame her, to tie her arms back against the bed, to ravish her. He closed his eyes, his whole body trembling at the thought. Such a woman could make a man lose his mind with desire. He would have to be careful. Both the Emperor and the General enjoyed her soft, giving flesh. If they even suspected that he might harbour desires for her, then his head would be on a platter.

What he needed was a woman of his own; difficult in his position, a rough, hardened soldier. Meeting women wasn't the difficult part, finding women of quality was. Someone with a body like Leoni's and the mind of a talented, educated maiden. As unreachable as the stars. He grimaced to himself. It would never happen, and all he would ever have were his fantasies.

Reluctantly, he forced his mind to dwell on much more mundane things and hurried away. However, his erection still pressed against his leggings and he knew that before he did anything else, copious amounts of cold water were required to quench the raging fire tormenting him..

* * *

Sitting at his desk, Maniakes had already put into place a whole raft of measures that would help bring his schemes to their natural conclusion. Constantine now lay at the heart of them, but the man must not know. He was dangerous, unpredictable. There were still factions at court who supported him, who could not understand the previous emperor, Michael the Paphlagonian, not giving him the rewards he so justly deserved. Instead, Constantine had been exiled, forced to live as a recluse whilst his other brother, Orphano, ladled success and riches upon his own head. What a family they were; a nest of vipers to a man.

There came a tentative knock on the door and Nikolias put his head in. "Sir?"

Maniakes waved the Captain inside. "It is done?"

"Yes, sir. The Emperor believes that even now I am arranging the journey to Constantine's home. How long should we wait?"

The General shrugged. "We'll give it till this evening. When the games finish for the day and the people are wending their way home, we will bring Constantine to the palace. The Emperor's entourage will be there to welcome him by then, if they are still sober enough to stand."

Nikolias had to smile at that. "Perfect timing, sir."

"Then, I want you to deliver these orders to the various guard units." He pushed a collection of rolled up parchments towards the Captain.

"Sir?"

"New orders." He stood up and crossed over to his open veranda and breathed in a deep lungful of late afternoon air. "It won't be long now, Nikolias. The Empire is passing into a new phase and the future is bright."

"And what then, sir?"

Maniakes frowned, and turned to look back at the soldier who still stood to attention, eyes straight ahead. "What do you mean?"

"I mean ... What will happen when the Lady Zoe is returned? To the Empire, sir."

"What are you getting at, soldier?"

"Well, it's no secret sir. Our enemies are gathering, on all sides. Turks, Russians, Normans. The *Themas* are all hard pressed to keep up their contingents. Individual generals and noblemen jostle for position. If they think they have an opportunity to further their ambitions, they will take it. Then, the dangers will come from within, as well as without."

Maniakes listened without comment, then returned to gazing out across the quiet city. In the distance, the roars of the crowd were becoming more erratic. The wine was taking grip, as he knew it would. Free drink and bread, in abundance. What Nikolias had spoken of lay at the heart of his deepest fears. The Empire needed strength, not just adoration for its leader. Zoe reinstated had to be good, but direction and security were uppermost. Constantine could be the man to deliver it all, or perhaps there were other avenues to explore, just in case...

"You speak wisely, Captain. For a man of your humble standing, you seem to have a wealth of knowledge inside you. Where did you come by your wisdom?"

"My father, sir. Standard-bearer for the Royal Bodyguard. You fought with him, sir."

"I did?" Maniakes studied Nikolias once more. "Yes, so I did. Dear God, where do the years go?" He shook his head. "That was a dreadful day. Troina. How we fought – how we died. That was the day Hardrada received his accolade, *Bolgara Brennir* – Devastator of the Bulgarians. He was a mad dog that day, swinging that great axe of his. But your father ..." Maniakes returned his gaze to the city rooftops. "I had forgotten, Nikolias. Forgive me."

"No need, sir. My father was a great man, sir. Destined for greater things. But he died as he would have wanted, cleaving the heads of the empire's enemies. He taught me much in his life. How to read situations, how to respond. Lessons that have stood me well. Like now, sir. Many dangers lie ahead, dangers that we have to face down, sir."

"Together, Nikolias?"

"Sir?"

"You said your father was destined for greatness. What about you?" Maniakes turned around to consider the Captain, folded his arms across his chest and gave a tiny smile. "Are you also destined for greatness?"

"I am here to serve, sir, for the greater good of the Empire. If, in the end, I should profit by my service, then that is all to the good. But it is not something I seek for its own sake."

"So, you're an honest man, Nikolias? Is that it?"

"I like to think so, sir. Do you doubt me?" He turned his face to the general, a slight frown creasing his face.

Maniakes held the man's gaze for a moment, resisting the urge to admonish Nikolias for his insolence. Best to keep him on board. Honest men were few and far between these days. If Nikolias was to remain faithful, then he should be given a certain degree of freedom, just so long as that didn't afford him ideas above his station. "I don't doubt it, Nikolias. If I did," he came forward, patted the Captain on the shoulder, "your head would already be displayed on the City gates." He grinned as he sat down again behind his desk, "Go and bring Constantine to me. I have much to discuss with him."

Nikolias saluted stiffly, gathered up the pieces of parchment, and turned to go.

"You *will* be rewarded, Nikolias. Have no fear."

He watched the man's back, and hoped that he was smiling.

As soon as Nikolias stepped outside and closed the door, he let out a long sigh of relief and gave up a silent prayer of thanks to God that Maniakes had not grilled him further. To even intimate that his loyalty might be in question was an insult that he would have responded to violently if anyone else but the general had voiced it. The man held the entire future of the Empire in his grip, and the Emperor Michael didn't know what was going to hit him.

When all of this was over, and the dust had settled, then Nikolias would have look deep into his heart to find out where his true loyalties lay; for although he knew for certain that Michael was not what the Empire needed, he wasn't at all sure of the General's choice either. Zoe was too used to fine clothes and fine living. How was she supposed to run an empire on her own? Of course, the general had it all worked out. Zoe would be the figurehead, Constantine would see to the governing of the whole of Byzantium, and Maniakes would be the real power behind the throne.

Where would that leave Nikolias? He would have to play his part with great care, ally himself to the right factions, keep his opinions to himself. In time, he may well be given the call to help the Empire in great endeavours, just as his father had done. When that call came, he would have to be ready.

He opened his eyes. Ready. He looked at the bundle of parchment rolls, containing Maniakes's orders for the Guard. Was that call about to be made, he wondered.

Deep in thought, he walked down the corridor, his heart heavy with uncertainty about what was to come.

Thirty-Seven

Reining in his horse in at the top of the rise, Andreas looked out across the vast plain towards the glittering city of Constantinople. Already the sun was setting behind the mountains and he could clearly see the many lights that signalled it as the greatest city on earth, huge, solid, eternal. He shifted his weight in the saddle and cast his mind back. His orders had been explicit – ensure Hardrada convinced the Patriarch to return to the city, lead the Varangians in triumph through the city gates. Reinstate Zoe to the throne. With the arrival of Crethus, it had all changed. Hardrada was to die. The Varangians had to remain in the fortified camp. Alexius was to be escorted back to the city, alone.

As far as success was concerned, he had none. Except for the hoped-for death of Hardrada. What of Alexius and the Varangians? How was Crethus to prevent them coming back to the City?

And then there was Analise. He had never experienced anything like this, a smouldering fire deep within him, inextinguishable. Her face came into his head, her eyes drinking him in. How could this happen, out there, in the middle of nowhere? Such a woman as that, living a life of solitude, danger. God knows he had fought against it, tried in vain to quench the fire. She wouldn't go away, no matter what he did. He was sick, with no cure. And he knew, if he knew nothing else, that he did not wish to be cured. He had found her, that elusive lover who clings to your heart and refuses to let go. He was consumed, and he loved it. Loved her.

He pressed his fingers into his eyes. He had to stop, make camp somewhere. The ride back had been lonely and cold. In the morning, things might seem better. He sat up and looked around for a patch of ground that might afford him some shelter , where he could think about what to do, how best to continue. By the morning, he reminded himself, the man who had saved his life, Harald Hardrada, would be dead.

For all he knew, Hardrada was dead already.

Hardrada had decided to settle down a little way off from the girl's devastated camp. A deep depression had settled over him. The girl had been kind, had saved both himself and Andreas and had asked for nothing in return. A soothsayer she may have been, but kind and generous nevertheless.

Munching through the hard tack that he took from one of the saddlebags, he lay back on the hard earth and stared up into the swiftly darkening sky. He would make an early start, perhaps even before the birds began to sing. He might even double back and rendezvous with the Varangian column. Andreas may be dead himself and at this thought a little stab of grief pierced his heart. It must have been the war band that the girl had mentioned. Perhaps they had come to the camp, found her with the Byzantine officer and dispatched them both. If that were so, however, then where was Andreas's body? Why leave the girl exposed, and not Andreas? And what of that mound, with the dead body lying beneath? He bit his lip. He should have dug down into it, to check if Andreas lay there, cold. He cursed and promised himself to carry out an investigation in the morning.

He turned onto his side, still nibbling at the bread. Of course, it probably wasn't Andreas. Who would have buried him there? The girl? That would mean he had died first. Perhaps the prolonged effects of his near-drowning in the river. He had heard of people dying days, sometimes weeks after such trauma. Had that happened to Andreas? Had he died, unexpectedly, the girl had then buried him and then...

Allowing his mind to wander away, he felt the heaviness of his limbs and the gnawing cold in his bones. He pulled his cloak around his shoulders for protection from the rapidly lowering temperature. He closed his eyes.

The sounds of the forest were changing. The birds had not sung all through the afternoon and early evening. Now, other animals were emerging. The hunters of the night. He considered making a small fire, in case any wolves ventured into the camp.

Something certainly seemed to be moving out there.

He lay rock still. Something big was moving around, but wolves always moved in packs. This was a single animal and it was trying very hard to remain quiet.

Taking his time, Hardrada closed his hand around the hilt of his sword. His axe lay propped up against a nearby tree. He had never considered he might need it.

When his horse whinnied and stamped its feet in alarm, Hardrada threw back his cloak and rose up, sword ringing from its scabbard. He was in a half crouch, left hand stretched out, palm forward, right hand gripping the sword.

Within a breath, a man erupted from the trees, sword held high above his head, two-handed, preparing to deliver the killing blow. He screamed as he charged and any lesser man would have frozen in terror. Not so Hardrada, who waited, perfectly balanced and, at the very last moment, swerved, taking the downward, swinging strike with him, his blade deflecting the blow, using the attacker's forward momentum to help him on his way, sending him staggering like a drunkard.

Hardrada countered, his own blade slashing through the air, catching the man across the shoulder. He screamed again, but this time through pain. Recovering, he attempted to bring another blow to bear, but Hardrada was in complete control, his mastery of the sword beyond limits. He parried, thrust, countered, slashed and stabbed, driving the attacker back, towards the trees. The man's face was covered by some sort of scarf, his eyes alone showing. Eyes which flashed white in the darkness. However, his sheer size gave away his identity. It could be no one else.

Moving with light-footed grace, Hardrada feinted to the right, the man followed, but suddenly Hardrada was not there. His foot came round, connected with the man's groin and, as he folded, another blow, this time from the Viking's sword pommel, hit the man square on the side of the head and he fell forward with a loud grunt, his sword clattering to the ground.

Backing away, Hardrada waited whilst the man picked himself up, staggering under uncertain legs. He retched, holding out a hand to steady himself, found a tree and stood there, bent forward, breathing hard. Hardrada moved closer, the point of his sword hovering a hand's width from the man's throat.

"Take away your disguise," said Hardrada.

Crethus relented without a pause, pulled away the scarf and let it fall to the ground. He glanced askance at the Viking. Hardrada could see, despite the dark, that the man's expression was one of pain, anguish. And defeat.

"I thought you were dead."

Crethus hawked and spat on the ground, "Then you thought wrong."

"Before you die," said Hardrada easily, "tell me who sent you to kill me? Whose orders do you follow?"

"Damn your eyes, Viking. I'll not tell you anything."

"Then I'll hang you from that tree, castrate you, and watch the ravens feast on your evil flesh." He grinned. "I'll take your cock as a trophy and present it to the Lady Zoe."

Crethus shuddered. He closed his eyes for a moment, and winced when he straightened himself. "Michael."

"The Emperor ordered you to follow me and kill me?"

"Yes. He countermanded Orphano's orders to you and Andreas."

"And Andreas?" He brought the blade up and pressed the point into the big man's throat. "What orders were you given about him?"

"None." Crethus grinned, "You're the threat, Hardrada, not him. Andreas has returned to the city."

"I see." He twisted the blade, causing the big man to wince, and asked the question he needed the answer to. The identity of the murderer. "So where is the girl?"

Crethus frowned. "Girl? What girl?"

Hardrada snarled, pushed the sword point forward, breaking the skin. "The girl who looked after me and Andreas. You know who I mean."

Wincing again, Crethus swallowed hard, "I don't know what you mean. I left her, together with Andreas. As far as I know she is still there … unless she has returned to the city with him."

Hardrada thought about that. The Scythian had a black heart, as they all did, but could it be that he told the truth? He must know that any doubts in Hardrada's mind would bring quick, painful death. "So, Andreas was still there, in the camp?"

"He had still not fully recovered his strength. There was a fight, with some wild looking men. I came upon the camp, helped Andreas to overcome them."

"Convenient."

"I told you, I was sent to kill you, Hardrada. There is no point me lying about anything else."

It sounded plausible, but something didn't fit right in the puzzle. "So, you fought these men, killed them … all of them?"

"There was a band of perhaps five or six. But yes, we killed them."

"But you said Andreas had not yet recovered his strength. How could he fight?" To give added emphasis, he jabbed the blade forward again, this time drawing blood from the man's throat. Crethus stiffened, his eyes widening in panic. "What did you do with the bodies?"

"Buried them."

"And Andreas was unhurt, and the girl also?"

"They were both unharmed. Do you know differently?"

"She's dead."

Crethus' eyes grew wide, sweat breaking out across his brow. "Dead? But what of Andreas?"

"No sign. I assume that the mound I discovered holds the bodies of the war band dead." Hardrada considered the Scythian's words, words that must be true unless he was an actor of consummate skill. The terrible thought took hold in his mind. "Andreas must have killed her." He allowed the sword to drop and noted the Scythian relaxing as the pressure was released from his throat. "Why would he do that?"

Crethus shook his head once or twice, his mouth turning down. "Perhaps they quarrelled, or maybe she tried to rob him. Who knows?"

That didn't make sense to Hardrada. "Why save his life if only to rob him? And rob him of what?"

"Like I said, who knows? Women are strange, flighty creatures. Perhaps she was a sorceress. Strange that she should live alone, miles from anywhere. Perhaps she tried to put a spell on Andreas, and he fought against it."

That sounded more reasonable. Hardrada stepped back, sheathing his sword, and regarded the Scythian closely. "I should kill you, but something tells me that you might still be useful."

"Useful? In what way?"

"I want you to return to the city. Tell the Emperor that you have succeeded in your plans, that you have killed me and that the Varangians are not on their way."

"But he will want to know about Alexius. What should I yell him about the Patriarch?"

"Say he is following. Do not give him any reason to suspect."

"But if he does, he will kill me in a blink of an eye!"

"Crethus, if you don't do this, I will personally see to it that the Varangians hoist you up on the highest wall of Byzantium and flay you alive for everyone to see." He leaned forward, using his great height and size to intimidate even this large warrior. "Once the Varangians have entered the city, Michael's time on the throne will be ended. Choose, Crethus. Choose whether to live, or die."

Thirty-Eight

The thought had been building in his mind for some time. As he sat with his back to a nearby tree, the little camp fire giving off barely enough heat to warm his fingertips, Andreas considered his options once more.

To continue, or wait – if he continued, would the guards even let him through the great Lion Gates of the City? He no longer possessed all the trapping of his officer status; his armour, helmet, greaves, they had all been lost, or stolen. His sword alone remained. The guards could quite easily mistake him as some sort a bandit, or indeed the very thief that had relieved him of all his belongings, the sword especially. He looked down at the scabbard, scarlet coloured with bronze fittings. The sign of his rank. And then, with a growing sense of despair, he let his eyes roam over the rest; the filthy shirt, the torn leggings, the sandals that were held together by frayed leather straps.

No, the guards would take one look and haul him to the city dungeons. He would probably never see daylight again.

Andreas put his head back against the trunk of the tree and closed his eyes. Best for him to wait for Crethus to come down the road, then he could join the Scythian and let him explain the situation to his compatriots on the gate. He should be here within a few hours, then they could wait until morning to continue on the short distance that remained before reaching the city.

He closed his eyes and tried to sleep.

Maniakes had much to do. He had prepared Constantine well. The man had listened to the story with growing alarm, but had told the general everything. During the last administration, Constantine had been happy to let his brother John take the reins. Being at court, with all of its intrigues and factions, was not something Constantine had ever relished. When Michael the Paphlagonian had moved against him, Constantine had not tried to defend himself. The idea of living out his life quietly, in seclusion or not, was something to be savoured.

Now, with all that the general had promised him, the idea of returning didn't seem quite as bad as he had first thought. With Michael gone, Zoe reinstated, John banished, he could begin to do things the way he wanted. And there would always be the possibility, so Maniakes had suggested, that Zoe would want to seek out another husband.

Above all things the General had talked about, this was the most beguiling. Constantine's face told its own story, as he gazed into the distance, his lips wet, the tongue running over them, a snake on the hunt. "To find myself in the arms of that glorious woman, sample the delights of her firm, rounded body," he said aloud, not caring who heard. "Even the thought of it brings such a fire to my loins, I doubt I will be able to maintain control once I see her!" Maniakes seemed amused by the very obvious bulge in the man's pants and walked off, chuckling to himself.

He was chuckling again now. Constantine had weaknesses. Already a plan was formulating in the General's mind, something that might cause Michael such distress, such confusion that he would feel that his entire world was crumbling. And when those Varangians returned…

If they returned.

They should be here by now, with Alexius. Crethus should have carried out his orders, tied up all the loose ends, removed Hardrada from the scene.

So why weren't they here?

Tomorrow was the second day of the games. The people would want to see Zoe. Michael would have to make his announcements and the crowd's reactions may not be what he hoped.

That was the hope. In the meantime, there was much to be done. The Guard had their orders. There would be no repeat of their presence the following day. By the early hours, they would have decamped and moved out of the inner city, away from the Royal enclave, and taken up their positions well away from any serious trouble. It might even be the case that Maniakes would lead them further north, well away from the city itself. If the Varangians did not return, then the results might be a little difficult to gauge. The Scythians were formidable; many citizens would die if they reacted angrily. With the Varangians, the outcome would be very different; not certain, but almost.

So many variables, so much to consider. What if things went disastrously wrong? Another avenue to consider. Maniakes buckled up his sword belt, repositioned his helmet, and strode out of his office.

He had a rendezvous.

Leoni was in the antechamber, readjusting herself whilst Michael slept. She took a moment to peer at herself in the steel mirror, pulled down her bottom eyelid to reveal the slightly bloodshot sclera, and sighed.

Michael.

What had begun as one of the General's many schemes had developed into something meaningful. She had seen the Emperor's vulnerability, his weaknesses, experienced his needs and desires and though disgusted by him at first, gradually her feelings had altered. Sometimes he spoke so gently, so openly that she felt a growing warmth towards him. Michael had opened up a new door of opportunity. Allowing herself to step inside, she also allowed him to enter into her heart.

She put her face in her hand, tried to think things through. It was nonsense, of course it was. Michael, the Emperor, just another man. A liar, cheat, scoundrel. All the things men are. She had known many men, all of them users. He wasn't any different. In many ways, he was worse. He would use her, he had said as much. Tomorrow he would introduce her as his 'companion', whatever that meant. She had the dress to wear, the tiara, the jewels. It was all so wonderful to be pampered in this way, to have everything anyone could ever wish. So why did she have the doubts? Was it because she was supposed to be detached, uncaring, had only to follow the General's instructions and lure Michael into the net? Emotions were involved, and Leoni knew how dangerous that could be.

Emotions. Danger. A heady mix.

The door eased open and she span around to see Maniakes standing there. She gasped and he stepped forward without warning, pressing his hand around her mouth.

"Quiet, my pet." He looked around furtively. "The Emperor sleeps?" She nodded. "Good. Now, I want you to listen to me very carefully, Leoni. I have a little task for you to perform." He let his hand slip from her mouth and she gazed at him in bewilderment as he began to outline his next scheme.

* * *

Hardrada decided to double back, now that he had convinced the giant Scythian to go on to the city. Gently leading his horse along the river edge, he made good time, camping on the far side from where his chosen vantage point would give him a perfect view of the advancing Varangians.

It was a view he didn't need; the tramping of their feet could be heard for miles as the cast, rolling plain spread out before him. In the darkness this was better signal than any dust swirl he might see in the day. Although still distant, he estimated they were a handful of hours away, so he settled himself down for some well-earned rest. As the new day dawned, he would intercept them, tell Alexius and Rufus what he had discovered, and then march on to the City itself. The reckoning was close. A reckoning for the Empire, for Michael, and Andreas.

For his own part, Crethus was pushing his horse hard. He had never liked riding at night. Too many encounters with some of the most dangerous people on the planet had taught him the safety of numbers, of encampments, of being prepared. At this pace, with his head down and his horse thundering across the plain, he felt exposed, despite the night. The clouds were much thinner and his way well illuminated. Soon, the city lights would direct him, and his goal would draw close. So he kept moving, an arrow targeted to the horizon. Perhaps what Hardrada had said was true. The lots had been drawn, and he had to make his own choice. There could be no second chances. The Lady Zoe would offer him some protection, he felt sure. As soon as he made the city, he would visit her, throw himself into her arms and then, after he had partaken of her delights, he would go to Michael and tell him Hardrada was dead and that the Patriarch Alexius travelled by carriage and would be there by the mid afternoon. He prayed that Michael would believe him.

If the Emperor didn't, then Crethus always had his sword.

Thirty-Nine

Maniakes stood on the parapet, staring out into the vastness of the open plain that swept across this part of the city approaches. Nikolias stood next to him, desperate not to shiver. The night was bitterly cold, the absence of clouds making the chill air so much more keenly felt.

"We have to try and put our plan in place as soon as Michael wakes," said the general, face straight ahead. "I want you close by. Nothing must happen to Constantine, you understand?"

"Of course, sir."

"If Michael goes berserk, which he might, you have to prevent any unnecessary violence."

"As you wish. Sir, I have some other news to report."

Maniakes barely glanced. "What? Not bad, I hope."

"That depends. On returning to their duties after the games had ended for the day, a couple of the Scythian guards discovered that the two Norsemen had escaped."

"What two Norsemen?"

"Compatriots of Hardrada. They were held in a tower, close to their old barracks. They killed their jailer and have escaped."

Maniakes arched an eyebrow. "I don't think we have to concern ourselves with such a trifling thing, Nikolias. Put out an alert, find them, and put their heads on the Lion Gate." He looked out across the plain again. "I have much more important things to worry about. Now, go to Leoni's bedchamber and make sure nothing happens."

Nikolias brought himself up to attention, saluted and marched off.

He closed the door to the apartment and let out a long breath. Maniakes didn't seem to appreciate the dangers of having two such men as Ulf and Haldor loose in the back streets of Constantinople. They were commanders of the Varangian bodyguard, sworn to defend the Emperor with their lives. Not mere mercenaries, like those Scythian dogs, but men of honour, courage and tenacity. They would not be easy to find, nor subdue.

More dangerous would be their ability to muster up men. Nikolias had no idea what schemes and machinations were running through the General's head, but on this count he had miscalculated. It might all turn out for the best; the men might be found. Nikolias, however, thought it highly unlikely.

Something moved close by. Andreas woke with a start, but before he could close his hands around the hilt of his sword, someone else's hand closed around his mouth, followed by a razor-sharp blade pressing against his throat. He froze, feeling his bowels loosen. Was this it, the end? He offered up a small prayer and waited for his life's blood to spill down his front.

The voice breathed down his ear, "See how easy it is?"

The hand relaxed and so did Andreas as the huge Scythian, Crethus, moved round to face him. The young Greek officer put his head back against the tree and blew out a sigh. "Dear Christ, please don't ever do that again."

"I have news. Grave news. News which I don't think you are going to want to know."

"What are you talking about?"

"I did not find Hardrada. The man is like some sort of phantom. I followed his trail though, which led back to the camp."

Andreas sat up, gripped by a cold, biting terror. "The camp? Analise? Was she there."

Crethus let his heads hang down. "My friend, you must be brave."

"*Brave?*" He leaned forward and gripped the other's arm. "What has happened?"

"There could be no mistake. It was the Viking."

Andreas felt the world press in around his ears; the pressure increased, becoming almost too much to bare. His voice was a croaking whisper when he spoke, "Please. Tell me."

Crethus brought up his head and held Andreas with a long stare. "He killed her. I found her there, her throat cut. It must have been Hardrada, there were no other signs."

For a moment, a huge great black cloud descended over Andreas, consuming him. He couldn't think, let alone breathe. Analise, *dead*? Murdered by Hardrada? "Why would he do such a thing?"

"I don't know. You must ask him when you next see him."

"See him?" Andreas brought his teeth together with a snap, snarling. "The next time I see him will be his last! I will kill the bastard myself." He stood up, clutching his sword in his hand. He glared out across the plain. Dawn lit the distant horizon. A new day. For Hardrada, his last. Andreas swore it, there and then, to God, and to himself. He glanced towards Crethus, "I am going to find him."

"That won't be difficult. He is with the Varangians. They march to the city."

"Dear Christ." Andreas slid his sword into his scabbard, gathered up his things and strode over to his horse. "I'll find him nevertheless, slit his accursed throat." He threw his bedroll over the back of his horse, which snorted at the thought of starting out so early. "Thank you Crethus. I won't forget you, or your kindness."

"Be wary of the Viking, Andreas. He is a formidable opponent. Perhaps the most formidable you have ever encountered."

"I won't underestimate him – but I suspect he will underestimate me."

Crethus nodded. "I remember how you fought against those wild men. You could be right. But, nevertheless, take care."

"I will." He put out his hand and the great Scythian took it and held it warmly. "I hope we will meet again." Then he swung himself up into the saddle and took the horse away from the makeshift camp.

As soon as he was out of earshot, he reined in his horse and sat for a moment. Her face, that lovely face, those eyes … he would never again see her loveliness. He dropped his chin onto his chest and the first time in his adult life, and for the last time ever, he allowed the tears to roll, unchecked, down from his cheeks.

Soon Andreas was out of sight, the plodding of his horse become more faint until, at last, there was nothing to disturb the quiet of the morning. Crethus stood, hands on his hips and grinned.

Damn them all, fools that they were, each and every one.

In his newly made bed, Constantine rolled over onto his back and let his eyes open. It was cold and he was thankful that the blankets were many and thick. If he were honest, he would have to say that this bed and its fittings were more comfortable even than his own. Whatever happened over the course of the nest few days, he was going to enjoy himself as much as possible.

The general was a rude fellow, but a clever one. Ambitious too. Constantine wondered if that ambition was limited to returning Zoe to the throne, as he had said, or whether he had wider goals to achieve. He would have to be wary and play the game with guile and care. If he could become essential to Zoe's reinstatement as empress, then he would go and visit his brother, Orphano, make it clear to him that there would be no hope of any reconciliation. The bastard had not given Constantine a single thought in all the time he had been banished. Not even as note to ask him if he were well. Or even alive. Now, the tables had turned, and it would be Constantine's chance to rub salt into the wounds, and make the little shit pay.

Leoni caught hold of the young maid and took her over to their old mistress's bed. They sat. The girl was young, hair pulled back in a tight bun, accentuating the high cheekbones, the oval eyes, the soft, olive skin. Slim, young limbs exposed, long and supple. Perfection.

"We have a task, you and I," Leoni began.

The girl, whose name was Cristina, frowned slightly. "What sort of a task? We are all packing away our possessions now that our mistress has gone." She stopped, the memory bringing the tears to her eyes once more.

Leoni squeezed the young girl's hand. "No, it has nothing to do with our mistress. It is the general."

"The general?" Cristina's frown grew deeper. Leoni saw in that look that the girl knew all about her coupling with Maniakes.

"He has given us a task. It is not … *unpleasant* … and the rewards will be great."

"Not unpleasant … I don't fully understand, Leoni."

Leoni pressed her tongue between her teeth, trying to hide her feelings, her disgust. The general had been so insistent. Leoni was to make her way to Constantine's bed, seduce him, bring him to the height of ecstasy in the way that only she knew how. But Leoni could not do it. She had had enough. Her disturbing thoughts about the emperor had planted a seed. A seed that was rapidly growing. For how much longer was she going to allow herself to be used as a harlot for these men? To couple with the emperor was one thing, but that fat slug Constantine. She shuddered at the thought.

So, she had come up with her own idea. Another would play the seductress. Cristina. She had mentioned rewards, and she would have to honour that. She had, over the years, secreted away bits and pieces of the Lady Zoe's vast wealth. She had a sizeable fortune now, one that could ensure her a comfortable life, well away from the intrigues of the city. Part of that she would give to Cristina. It would be well worth it. She smiled at the girl, drew her close and told her of the plan.

Constantine turned to his side, pulling the covers over his head, snuggling down into the wonderful warmth of the bed. This was heaven indeed, such comfort, such luxury. He moaned and then instantly froze.

The door opened and the sound of bare feet slapping across the cold marble floor drew closer. His heartbeat pounded in his ears. An assassin, come to murder him. My God, that was what the general had in store. Well, damn it all to hell, he would not go easily. He threw back his bedclothes and was about to cry out when the words caught in his throat and he gaped into the dim light of the room.

A young, slim girl, her limbs wonderfully long, the dark brown hair tumbling down in ringlets to her shoulders, stood before him. Her pert breasts were well proportioned, her hips full and rounded, the buttocks jutting out, contrasting sharply with the slimness of her waist. His erection was instant.

When the girl slipped in between the sheets and ran her fingers over his stomach, he knew that the general had sent her as a bribe, a gift, a piece of security to ensure his compliance with the plan … it could be any of those things, but at that moment he couldn't give a damn which it was. He turned into the young girl's arms, felt her muscular thighs drape themselves over him, and he ran his fingers over the swell of her buttocks. She moaned, her hand guiding his cock into her and he grunted as he pushed it inside, her warmth flowing over his engorged member. Soon he was pounding into her, aware only of her soft, yielding flesh against his, and her tiny moans as he relentlessly plied into her.

If this was what working for the Empire meant, then he would have very little to complain about.

He felt cold and reached out to pull the cover over him. But his fingers found nothing and, anger building, he sat up and groped around for it. It had gone. Puzzled, Michael rubbed his eyes and, yawning loudly, got up out of bed and looked across the room. The candles were still burning, but the dawn was now streaking through from his balcony. The door to his room was wide open and there, just on the threshold was the bed cover.

Frowning, he crossed the room to pick it up. Leoni must have taken it, perhaps wrapping herself in it to keep warm. But why had she left it here, on the floor, forgotten? Even more puzzling was the sight of her thin cotton shift, lying another ten paces or so at the end of the antechamber. There too the door was open. Without a pause, curiosity now getting the better of him, he went over to this second door, wrapping the bed cover around him to shut out the cold, and peered into the corridor beyond.

There was a guard there, one he had never seen before. An officer, resplendent in the full uniform and panoply of a Royal Bodyguard. Michael snapped his fingers and the officer came forward.

"Where is the lady Leoni?"

The man shifted his gaze, looking around as if struggling with something of enormous import.

"Damn it man, I command you to speak!"

"Highness!" The man brought himself up to attention with a snap of his heals. "Sorry to report, sire, but the lady has gone, sire."

"Gone? What the devil do you mean, gone? Gone where?"

Again, that uncertainty to continue. The man grew more uncomfortable and Michael's tempered snapped. He seized the officer by the top of his breastplate and pulled him closer. "Where the fuck is she?"

The officer gulped. "I will escort your royal Highness … with your permission, of course, sire."

Michael pushed him away and the soldier swirled around and strode off. Michael followed.

It was not long before the officer stopped outside a door and beckoned with his hand. "She is here, sire."

Michael stared at the man, then at the door. It was the official chamber of John Orphano, never used by him, but always prepared just in case he did not, for whatever reason, wish to use his private apartments in their own, separate building. "What is she doing in there?"

The man ran his tongue along his lip and closed his eyes. "Perhaps, Majesty …"

The words drifted away and Michael felt that sudden surge of anger washing over him. He threw away the bed cover and burst through the door without waiting another second.

He stood there, transfixed, unable to fully register what he saw, or even begin to understand it.

Leoni, naked, sat on the edge of the bed, breathing hard, head down. She looked up quickly when she saw the Emperor, gasped, and stepped away.

There, on the bed, another girl, with her back to him, bounced up and down on a man of enormous proportions. She had her held thrown back, crying out in obvious pleasure. The man gripped her hips with podgy fingers as he grunted like a horse, thrusting upwards to match her downward strokes.

Leoni came forward, pulling her dress around her. She was trembling, "My dear Lord," she said, giving a fleeting glance to the soldier in the doorway. "This is not what you think, please believe me."

Michael, eyes bulging, looked from the girl on the bed to Leoni, then back again. He blinked a few times, lips moving, but making no sound.

"My Lord," cooed Leoni, stroking his cheek. "The man is masterful. He had us both. I am sorry, but neither of us could resist."

In one sickening moment, Michael felt his knees go weak and the floor swung upwards to meet him. Everything spun around him and he knew he was sinking, sinking into an unfathomable void. He became vaguely aware of strong hands grabbing him before total blackness engulfed him.

Forty

He stood, feet planted slightly apart, leaning on his great battleaxe, the wind whipping across his face, hair like a mask. His gaze was fixed, his jaw set hard. The army had decamped and was moving in a long, snaking column. The scouts had spotted him and were already approaching on their ragged, sturdy steeds. Hardrada waited.

The first scout reined in. In his hand was a javelin, arm cocked, ready to hurl the dart if necessary. Hardrada watched him and grinned, "You've made good time."

The scout relaxed and lowered his arm, "Forgive me, sir. I didn't recognize you."

Hardrada nodded, swept some of his hair from his face. "It's this damned wind. I'll come with you, speak to Rufus."

At that moment, a second scout came up, struggling to control his pony. It whinnied loudly, blowing out a great stream of hot air from its flared nostrils. "Well met, sir!"

Hardrada went over to his own tethered horse and pulled himself up onto its back. He kicked its flanks and the three of them wended their way down the slight incline towards the marching column.

Rufus, riding next to the covered wagon inside which the Patriarch Alexius sheltered, saw the riders and kicked his horse to join them He raised his hand in greeting as he saw the giant Hardrada, his sheer size making him instantly recognizable.

"Damn your eyes, Harald! I thought I wouldn't see you for at least another day."

Hardrada brought his horse under control and settled in next to his old friend, whilst the scouts pounded away to return to their duties ahead of the column. "It didn't take as long as I first thought – to find Andreas."

"So where is he?"

"I have no idea. All I do know is that the man is a murderer."

"Eh?" Rufus pulled up his horse, which stamped at the ground angrily.

"That's what I said." Hardrada reined in his mount also. "And I intend to bring him to justice, when I find him."

"I thought you said something about him being honourable – didn't you save his life?"

"Aye, and a damned bloody stupid mistake that turned out to be. He murdered the woman who tended to his wounds, who saved me. I'll cut out his heart when I catch him."

At that point, a stern voice rang out, "Of whom is it that you speak, Hardrada?" It was the Patriarch Alexius, who had pulled back the flap of his covered wagon and was peering out as it trundled beside the two mounted men.

"Andreas, sir," Hardrada replied, bowing his head in respect. "The man who accompanied me on this journey," Hardrada flicked at the reins and his horse moved in alongside the wagon. Rufus fell in behind.

"He murdered a woman?" Alexius asked.

"Aye, sir. The one who saved both our lives."

"Are you sure? I know a little of Andreas, know his family. It came to me after you had mentioned him. His family is of noble birth. Murder is not in his blood."

"Well, something must have happened, sir. Betrayal I shouldn't wonder. There had been some sort of fight, and the Scythian Crethus told me—"

"Crethus?" Rufus came up, his face livid. "That black-hearted dog? Whatever he told you was a dammed lie, Harald."

"You know him?"

"I know *of* him, which is almost the same thing. He is a callous and brutal man, who hates us, Harald. Hates us all." He turned a meaningful gaze to Alexius. "Christians, Greeks and Romans ... Vikings. All." Rufus twisted in his saddle, hacked and spat into the dirt below. "Damn his hide, they are all the same. We know what they did, Harald, to your men – our kindred. News travels fast, especially bad news."

"I also have told Rufus of the dark crimes that were committed against the Varangian Guard, Harald." Alexius turned his mouth down. "There are many mercenaries here who will gladly cut down the Scythians without taking a single penny in payment."

Hardrada smiled in gratitude. But his mind was confused. He knew himself that the idea of Andreas murdering that girl was difficult to accept. If she had betrayed him, it would not have been something she would have done freely. Those wild men, the war band as she called them, they would have forced her. So why would Andreas murder her? Perhaps it wasn't him at all, perhaps it was one of her own kinsmen. If that were so, why would Crethus lie? Unless...

"Come on, old friend," said Rufus, and he clapped Hardrada across the shoulder. "Let's get these miles out of the way, and wash our axes with Scythian blood. The time for brooding is over, the time for killing is here!"

Hardrada knew it was so, and the thought of the killing to come filled his heart with joy.

Two things woke Michael. The first was the incessant shaking; the second was the noise. From his deep slumber he managed to rouse himself, groggy, disorientated, he lashed out with his hand to knock away whoever it was that was shaking him. Then he sat up, running both hands through his hair. "I feel awful," he groaned.

A goblet of something was thrust into his hand and he stared at it, then looked up. The young soldier was there, face very serious.

"Majesty," he said.

"What? What is it? What's all that noise?"

"It's the people, sire. Thousands of them."

"People? What do you mean?" He made to stand up, but his legs gave way underneath him and the young army officer had to stop him from collapsing onto the floor. "What is happening?"

"Sire," the officer tilted his head, looking worried. "Sire, they are calling for the Lady Zoe, sire."

Michael's eyes bulged wide. He looked from the soldier to his balcony. He listened. It was quite clear now, the constant chanting, the noise of the mob, "*Where is Zoe? We want the Lady Zoe!*"

He put his face in his hands. He tried to think, to try and come up with something, anything that would make it all go away. But as he thought, something came into his mind. A memory. The vision of what he had seen, of Leoni, and that girl bouncing up and down on the fat man. Michael sucked in a large, loud breath and let his hands slide from his face."What is your name again?"

"Nikolias, sire."

"Nikolias, who was with her?"

"Sire?"

"Damn it man, the lady Leoni! Who was she with when I collapsed? You were there, you showed me the room."

"A young serving maid, by the name of Cristina I believe."

"Not the girl, damn your eyes! The man – who the hell was he?"

"I'm not sure if it would profit you, or anyone else to know his identity, sire."

"Profit *me*? Who in the name of Christ do you think you are talking to? I could have you castrated, you insolent dog!"

Nikolias frowned and stepped back, bristling with indignation. Michael could see it and for a moment his heart froze. No soldier, Guard or otherwise, would ever have the audacity to talk like that to an emperor, unless … Michael rubbed his face and stood up. He pushed Nikolias away and strode over to the balcony.

From here he could look out across the royal enclave to the great Forum of Constantine. It was some way off, but not so far that he couldn't hear their cries, and see them, that great swell of humanity, like some huge, bloated beast. And like a beast, it had to be tamed. Michael swung around. "Summon the Guard, I will go and present myself to the people. I will need protecting, however, for I get the distinct impression that they are not happy."

"Sire, there is no Guard."

Michael blinked and took a moment for that news to filter through. "No Guard? I don't ... what do you mean, of course there is the Guard! They escorted me to the games only yesterday!"

"Aye, sire. But that was before the news came of the incursions. The General has ordered all available men to march to meet them."

"The General ... " He swung round and looked out again at the forum. The General. So that was it. Dear God, here he was trying to outfox everyone and all the time, that bastard Maniakes had been scheming himself! Michael squeezed his hand into a fist and brought it down on top of his balcony balustrade. Damn him! "Have the Scythians gone also?"

"No, sire. Not them."

"And their number?"

"Around five hundred, sire."

Michael closed his eyes. Five hundred? Not enough, not by a long chalk, not to quell the mob. "Send word to the General. Go yourself, on the fastest horse. Order him to return five hundred of the Guard, and have them return to the city."

"Their number is little above that, sire. Almost all of the Royal Guard have been away on the frontiers, guarding your Empire, sire. I doubt if the General will now—"

"Damn it, man!" Michael whirled around, teeth set in a grimace, "Do as I command!"

Nikolias saluted, turned and left the room without another word.

It was only after he had gone that Michael realized that he still didn't know the identity of the fat man who was so enjoying himself under the firm, young thighs of the girl Cristina. No matter, there would be enough time. First, he would have to deal with the mob. In a rush he went back to his bed and began to pull on his robes.

Leoni tried but couldn't open the door. It was bolted, from the outside. She pounded on the door, but it made no difference, no one was coming. She turned and leaned back against it, closed her eyes and reminded herself of what an idiot she was. Cristina lay on the bed, her body naked. Leoni quickly crossed over to her and peered down at her face. Her cheeks were glowing, lips slightly parted. She had been well pleasured, that was for sure. She laid a hand on the girl's shoulder and gently shook her awake.

Cristina blinked open her eyes, smiled, and stretched. She sat up, yawning. "Mmm ... Leoni. As you said, not unpleasant!"

Leoni curled her mouth in disgust. She had chosen the girl well, perhaps too well. "The door is bolted. Something is going on."

Cristina shook her head. "Going on?" She swung her legs over the bed and stood up, stretching again, like a cat, arms high above her head. Leoni stared at her lithe body then stopped and whirled as the door to the antechamber opened and the awfulness of her plight became more sharply etched in her brain as the man came out from the bedroom, pulling a thin, satin robe around his ample frame.

She trembled at the sight of him, the memories of him grunting like a pig as he thrust relentlessly into Cristina causing a curious tingling to ripple across her belly. The general, he had ordered this. That gorgeous man, Nikolias, he had brought the demand, that she should seduce this, over-fed bull of a human being. Why couldn't it have been Nikolias, that might have been more preferable. His dark good looks, granite-chiseled chin, the way his muscles rippled over his lightly burnished arms. She wondered why she had never noticed him before now. Had the general, perchance, kept him purposefully hidden away, she wondered.

The man came towards her, assured, confidant and she felt her legs give way a little as he ran the back of his index finger over her cheek. "Mmm, I haven't had *you* yet."

Leoni gaped at him, felt a thrill of expectation ripple through her. What did that make her, she considered. A whore. Of course it did. She knew that this was what she was, and the thought disgusted her. She had believed she may have been developing some feelings for Michael, but that was not the case. She had no morals, no self-worth. She allowed herself to used, and abused. Cristina had been an attempt to outmanoeuvre the general and his despicable plans, but now it was all falling apart and she was returning to her natural role.

Damn it all. Did she have no common decency, no strength left to stand up, reject this squalid, hopeless existence? The general had this power over her, and she was slave to it. Any hint of her disobeying, even questioning, and her life would be snuffed out. How much longer could she live like this? How much longer could she live with herself? Feelings. What a joke that was. She didn't have feelings for anyone or anything. Not Michael, the general, not even herself. It was all so utterly pointless.

The man wheezed over to Cristina, smiled, his lips like wet worms, bloodless, cold. He was a powerfully built brute, but his face, that was repulsive. Florid, slack, not like his great bulk at all. His body bulged with muscle and sinew, and his breathing sounded laboured, almost as if his body was too big for his heart to support. "How are you, my dear?" He leered, ran a hand across the young girl's body. She shivered, and he took it for a sign of her pleasure because he now moved closer, wrapping his arms around her.

Leoni watched, transfixed. Christina closed her eyes. It was going to happen again, just as it had before. The man was an animal, ramming into the girl's flesh without any gentleness or care, rutting on and on, like no one else Leoni had ever known.

Poor Cristina. Leoni backed away as she saw the man run his hands over her flesh, "My God, what a treasure you are," he hissed, nuzzled into her neck, his wet lips running over her taut skin whilst his fingers found the nub of her sex and played with her. His other hand snaked around to her backside and was now seeking out her anus, the thumb plunging inside. Cristina yelped, her knees buckling, a movement which allowed him further access.

"Divine," he whispered into her neck, letting his tongue run over her throat and down to her breasts. He giggled as her body grew limp and he looked across to Leoni and winked. "You'll be next, my dear."

A shudder ran through Leoni and she took a another step backwards and looked around for any means to escape.

Cristina gasped and Leoni turned again to see the girl caving in, all the strength draining from her, and then both of his hands clasped her buttocks and lifted her off her feet, slamming her against the door. His cock, rearing up from between the folds of his robe, pushed forward, finding her, filling her. Cristina held on, gripping his shoulders as he slammed into her. She threw her head from side to side. There was no mistaking this man was an expert lover, the way he varied his speed, his direction. And all the while, his hands, folding over her buttocks, fingers pressing into her from behind. Leoni closed her eyes, envisaging what it must be like, that wonderful feeling of being totally filled. Her lips ran wet with spittle and she opened her eyes to gaze upon them, coupling so fervently. The strength of him. My God, the way he held her so easily, pinning her. It was as he had said, divine.

He thrashed into her, a blur of movement, grunting again as he rushed towards his end. Cristina held onto him, shuddering, crying out, begging him to come. But he wouldn't, not yet. He held her there, on the precipice, all the while letting her know that he was in charge, that he would set the pace and that he would come when he wanted, when she was totally spent.

When he withdrew, Leoni thought that was it, that he would turn to her, but she was wrong. He roughly turned Cristina around, pulling back her head by the hair, pushing himself into her, an act Leoni believed would split the poor girl open with the violence of it. "Relax," he said, his voice so caring, so comforting. It made Leoni's stomach turn to liquid, and saw his words had the same effect on Cristina as she relaxed, allowing him entry. Any pain gave way to undoubted ecstasy, that exquisite feeling of being totally taken, of submitting to the power, the man's mastery. Slowly he slid in and out and the sight of it caused Leoni to at last place her fingers to probe deep inside her, bringing herself to the peak of her own pleasure.

Grunting loudly, he pushed into Cristina so deeply her eyes looked as if they would explode out of her head. He kept himself inside for a moment after he had stopped, then his face fell into her neck, his breath coming in great gulps, and he slipped out of her, moaning. Cristina straightened and turned, wiping her mouth with the back of her hand. Her face was flushed, and she was about to say something when all of a sudden, the man tottered backwards a few steps. Leoni screamed as he fell to the ground.

Both girls exchanged wild looks then dropped down to his side. He was convulsing, going into some sort of a fit. Leoni gaped at him, a sudden fear gripping her, and she gasped at Cristina, "Get some wine," then cradled his head in her arms.

His face was twisted into a mask of pain, teeth clamped together, his entire body in seizure. She didn't know what to do, so she hung onto him as he went into spasm, his great spade-like hands clasping her forearms, and she offered up silent prayers. What had happened, why was he like this?

Cristina returned with the wine and Leoni took it, dabbed some of it on the man's lips. Nothing changed and Leoni experienced the complete and total horror of watching the man the general had committed to her care slip away towards death.

The door behind her opened and without turning she heard the intruder shouting, "Holy Christ!" All at once, Nikolias was there beside her, pressing his palm against the man's barrel chest. "What have you done?"

His voice was sharp, almost a squeal. She glared at him, "Me? I haven't done anything – he collapsed."

Nikolias looked around at Christina, then motioned to the man's sleeping member. "I'd say you've done something – you bloody bitches!" He took the wine from Leoni's hand and threw the goblet across the room. "Go and get some water, quick!"

Varangian

Leoni ran off without another word, whilst Cristina stood shivering, hands clamped to her mouth. She set up a low, continuous groan as if she too were in some sort of pain.

"Shut the fuck up," spat Niklolias.

Leoni fetched the basin from the bedroom, and trotted back in. Nikolias looked up to take the bowl and paused, drinking in the sight of her lithe, naked body. He swallowed hard, then seemed to recover. "Get some clothes on," he said softly, "the pair of you!" He settled the bowl next to the man and began to dab his pale lips with the water.

By the time Leoni and Cristina came back with their thin cotton dresses tied at the waist, came back, Constantine was sitting up, but with his skin still the colour of chalk. Nikolias was easing him to his feet. He gave Leoni a withering glance. "What have you done, poisoned him? Is that it, another of the general's schemes?"

"I swear to you, Nikolias, I haven't done anything. We were … you know … and when he had finished, he collapsed."

"Too much for him were you?"

His words stung like a slap and she winced, looking away. She so much wanted to tell him the truth, but she knew it would be fruitless. "No. The other way round I think."

Nikolias nodded, "Aye, by the size of him, I would say that was true enough! Help me get him back to bed."

So, the three of them struggled with the man, taking him step by step back to his bed, all gasping with the effort. It was a slow task, and Constantine, although recovering somewhat, seemed almost like a dead weight, and offered very little in the way of help. Eventually, they made it to the bed where they gently laid him down and covered him with a blanket. At once, he fell into a deep slumber. Nikolias moved away from the bed, breathing hard. "He's like a bloody elephant! I want you to go and fetch a doctor whilst I stay with him and make sure he remains well." His eyes blazed, " Hurry up!"

Leoni left the room at a run.

Nikolias flopped down on the edge of the bed after he had sent Cristina away and ran his hand through his hair. "Damn it man, you'd make a bloody good actor."

Constantine laughed and sat up. "By God, that girl is a good fuck!"

Nikolias winced. The thought of Leoni with a man such as this, it made his skin creep. "And you are an uncouth bastard."

"Watch your tongue, soldier! Once I'm established in power, you would do best to remember who I am."

"Oh, I know who you are all right. A word to the wise, Constantine. Great men fall. Look at your brother, and what is going to happen to Michael."

"And Maniakes, what of him?"

"Don't underestimate him, Constantine. He is a man of great intelligence and supreme cunning."

"That he may be, but why all this pretence with the girls? Why force me to become like some pathetic, shambling invalid?"

"Leoni will go and tell Michael of your condition – it all adds to the intrigue. He will think he has some chance to end your life before you even start in your new position. When he comes to finish you off, my task is to kidnap him and take him to the outskirts of the city, where he will meet his end."

"Dear God. Is this the general's plan?"

"It is."

"But why not just kill him anyway."

"Michael has become nervous again and is surrounded by the Scythians every moment. Even now he is planning to meet the people, surrounded by a *bandon* of heavily armoured Scythian Varangians. He is not taking any chances. But once he has recovered from the slur you have made on him by taking his concubine, he will want to slit your throat. That will give me my chance."

"And if it doesn't work?"

Nikolias shrugged. "Then, we will just have to think of something else."

"And me? What about me. What if Michael decides to send his Scythians to finish me off?"

Nikolias's smile grew broad. "Well, that will be something we will all have to live with. Or, in your case, die with."

Forty-One

Nikolias found Michael putting the finishing touches to his royal robes. His dresser, a weedy little man, worked dexterously, his fingers moving in a blur, repositioning, adjusting, ensuring that Michael looked his resplendent best. The Scythian guards brought their spears together to bar Nikolias's entrance.

"Sire, I must speak with you."

Michael gave him a cursory glance. "*Must*, Nikolias? I have to admit, I am becoming tired of your insolence. What do you want?"

Nikolias gave the guards a look. They didn't move until Michael snapped his fingers. Bristling with indignation, Nikolias strode forward and saluted. "It is Constantine, sire. He has had some sort of attack. I think it has something to do with his heart, sire. Perhaps he has been overexerting himself, and for a man of his size, that is never a good thing to do."

Michael's face came up, a dark cloud settling over it. His lips were drawn back over his teeth, and he snarled, "Is he dying?"

"Er ... I'm not sure, sire. He is very ill, I know that."

"Bastard!" Michael pushed his dresser away and brought his right fist into his left palm with a smack. "I'll roast him alive for what he did! Is he still in his room?"

"Yes, sire. He is too ill to be moved. His face is like alabaster, and he shakes constantly."

Michael smiled. "Wonderful. Listen, I am going to the Forum to speak with the people. When I return, I will go and see him. Remind him of just who I am." He chewed at his lip for a moment and Nikolias waited, holding his breath, wondering what outburst was to follow. "Leoni ... you will find her, and send her to me." And with that, he flicked his hand in a dismissive gesture towards Nikolias, and turned once again to his dresser. "Hurry up man, I need to get moving!"

Nikolias bowed, turned and went out, the guards closing the double doors behind him. He let out a long breath. The man was starting to crack, the pressure of the past few days becoming too much. The general's various plots were beginning to come together nicely. Nikolias did not wish to know the outcome. He had made his decisions, settled for what he thought was the winning side, but he had to admit that the whole situation made him feel uneasy.

This latest complication, with Leoni, Constantine, and that other girl, he didn't like that at all. Leoni was being used, and abused, by the general. Usually Nikolias couldn't give two figs for any such woman, but she seemed different somehow. A waif of a thing, young, innocent looking, but so worldly-wise when it came to the ways of the flesh. An intoxicating mix.

He moved on; he had his orders to carry out. The Guards had all been moved away from the city, leaving only the Scythians in control. He had sent out mounted scouts, as the general had insisted, to seek out the Varangian mercenaries and gauge how far away they were. He had ensured that agents had been deposited amongst the mob, to stir them up, instigating the rioting that had now begun. Everything the general had planned was happening. The only doubt, the only tiny little fissure: was Hardrada dead?

Maniakes knew that the Viking would have the loyalty of the Varangians on his side, and that would make him dangerous. He would be seeking his revenge and now his two compatriots were loose somewhere in the city. Tiny fissures which could become cataclysmic. Nikolias would have to watch his step and perhaps it would be sensible if he made some contingency plans for himself if things turned nasty. And in those plans, perhaps there could be a place for Leoni.

He experienced a little thrill of anticipation running through him as he quickly made his way along the corridor towards the rooms where Constantine was staying.

* * *

Michael decided to walk, with his Scythian bodyguard pressing in all around him. As he strode through the palace grounds towards the royal Gate, the sound of the crowd grew louder. His heart was already racing and now he felt the first tendrils of fear curl around his stomach.

What was it about Zoe that made these people love her so much? She squandered money, spent her life surrounded by luxury, hardly ever did anything for anyone else, and yet the people idolized her. Was it her supposed beauty, the way her skin looked as fresh and as sparkling as it did when she was a girl? Did people perhaps believe she was in some way immortal, and that by smiling upon them, she might give them a gift of eternal life? He didn't know, and he didn't care. All he did care about was the fact that he had to convince them that she was of no importance anymore to Byzantium. Her time had gone, finished.

Now was the time of Michael V, a new dawn, the beginning of an age of expansion and glory. He would have to discuss the finer points with Maniakes, but already Michael had pored over maps, looked with envy at the lands of the Persians, the Arabs and the Russians. So many opportunities to reach out, crush them. Just as his predecessor Basil had done, with such success. Now, it was his time, his moment. And the people must embrace that, follow him and begin to write new chapters in the annals of history. He would be known as Michael the Great; all he needed was the opportunity.

The Scythians were restless, he could see their eyes darting this way and that and their hands clutched at the hilts of their great, curved swords, knuckles showing white beneath the skin. Michael frowned. What was causing them such distress? He looked up and saw what it was. They had now reached the Gate and were just beginning to move through it. Citizens were gathering even here and the murmuring amongst them sounded angry, impatient. One or two threw insults, but Michael kept his eyes ahead. He would not speak until he had mounted the steps of the forum, made his presence felt, shown the people that he was strong, determined.

"Majesty." An officer came striding forward, his face a perfect mask of concern, deep lines etched around his eyes and mouth, eyes wide and deeply troubled. "Majesty, the crowd is becoming increasingly restless. I fear for your Majesty's life."

"Nonsense," said Michael with a smile, not breaking his stride. "Once they see me, they will become calm and accept my authority."

The officer stepped in beside him. "Majesty. I must insist."

At this Michael did finally stop, and turned himself to face the Scythian officer, and he could feel the heat rising from deep within. "Why am I surrounded by imbeciles who never show me the slightest respect! *Damn your eyes, man – insist?*"

The man baulked under the onslaught, and backed away, looking sheepish and confused. "Forgive me, sire," he stooped low, realizing he had over-stepped the mark.

"No matter," said Michael, looking past the man to the great buildings of the city, and the huge open area known as the Forum of Constantine. Beyond, and to the right, the magnificent Hippodrome where, only yesterday, the people had been so responsive, so thankful for his gift of games. Now, like a herd of baying dogs, all they wanted was Zoe. "Call out the rest of the Scythians, and order them to assemble here. Every last man of them. And have them fully armoured."

"Sire?"

"I mean to teach this swaggering mob a lesson it won't forget!"

* * *

Hardrada watched as the scouts came pounding down from the hills, their horses blowing out their breath. Rufus had to control his own horse before it became spooked and galloped off.

"What is it?"

"Riders sir. From the city."

"Did they speak, give any clue as to who or what they were?"

"No, sir. They saw us and sped back. They were not Norse though, sire."

"Scythians. Damn their eyes!"

"Difficult to say, sir. The distance." The man shook his head. "They could have been, or they could have been Greek. Either way, they were from the City, and they saw our number. They must have been able to estimate our distance, sir."

Rufus looked at Hardrada, who shrugged. "It can't be helped. We were bound to be spotted sooner, rather than later. All we have to worry about is the Royal Guard. We could do with their support, and if they side with Michael…"

Rufus nodded his head, looked again at the scouts. "Range as far as you are able, skirting the city as far to the West as is possible. Look for any signs, any signs at all. The last thing we need is an ambush."

"Sir!" The man kicked into the flanks of his horse and sped off, signalling to the other scouts to follow.

"Well, Harald. It looks as though the sand is running out."

"It does that. We fight and die this day, perhaps, old friend."

"It is a good day to die."

"As is any."

Rufus grinned. "Aye, as is any. If I don't see you in the fight, Harald, I'll sup wine with you this night, either in the city walls, or in Valhalla. Either way, we'll sing songs and remember how well we died!"

Harald noticed the Patriarch glaring at them both, squeezed Rufus's arm and moved over to Alexius. "Do not be too angry at our ways, sir. Christian our world may be, but the old ways are hard to forget, especially when death is so close."

"You think we will lose, then? Dear God, have I come so close as to be denied now, within sight of the gates of my glorious city?"

"It is not our intention to lose, sir. But if the City Guard are mustered, it will be a hard fought fight. We are just over two and a half thousand men, but if they join with the Scythians, then it will be a close run thing."

"Surely they will not side against us."

Hardrada looked out across the plain and his eyes grew heavy. He squeezed his finger tips into them, "I am so tired," he said. "Sometimes I think that perhaps I have run out my span of years." He shook his head and let his hand drop to his side. "If they do side against us, we will be hard-pressed. No one can say what the outcome will be." He looked at the Patriarch and kept his jaw firm. "Pray for us, sir. With all your heart."

The two young men who entered into the church were not the same brutes who had brought her here so roughly, and without ceremony. These men – officers, adorned in ceremonial armour, burnished with gold and bronze – were reverential, bowing low, helmets tucked under their arms. They had even left their swords outside the church door.

Zoe lifted her head from her morning prayers and waited. The Mother Superior was with them, wringing her hands, and it was she who came forward initially, and spoke in that soft, kindly way of hers, "Your Royal Highness, these two men have come from the city. They have news."

Zoe smiled slightly, but did not allow any other emotion to show. Inside, her stomach was turning. She had been here for such a short time, had barely unpacked her bags, but already a message? Something cataclysmic must have happened, whether good or bad. Of the two, she knew which travelled the fastest. "Yes, gentlemen?"

The first man stepped forward, went down on one knee, with his head lowered. "Majesty, I am commanded by his eminence, General Maniakes, to escort you back to the City of Constantinople. I beg your indulgence, and gracefully request that you prepare yourself for the journey, for we will be departing for the city before evening."

"So," Zoe brought her hands together, squeezing them tight shut. She looked across at the Mother Superior who stood there, eyes wide and expectant. "This is where it ends. Michael and his cronies have decided to remove me completely. I should have guessed it, but I never knew it would come so quickly."

"Majesty," it was the second officer, younger than the first. He stepped forward now, arms spread out, for a moment forgetting the protocol. "Majesty – the general wishes you no harm."

The other, still on his knees, shot his younger companion a sharp glance, then returned to Zoe. "It is true, your Majesty. The general wishes to make it plain to you that you are under no threat or danger. You are to be returned to your previous office of Empress, your Majesty. The ceremony will be conducted in a matter of days."

Zoe was truly staggered. Her hand came up to her mouth as she struggled to find some sort of response that would convey her total and complete bewilderment. What could have happened to bring about such a change? She had to clear her throat, allow herself a little pause to gather what wits remained. "Michael? What of the Emperor?"

The two soldiers exchanged nervous looks. It was the younger who spoke, head lowered this time, "Majesty, the Emperor Michael V is facing …"

"He is to be overthrown, Majesty," finished the other. "The Varangian Guard are to be reinstated, and your Majesty is to be returned to your former office of state."

"Michael overthrown?" She could no longer keep the incredulity out of her voice. She came forward, right up to the two men, and looked from one to the other. "When did this happen?"

"It is in the process of happening, Majesty."

She recoiled, stepping back, hand to her mouth once again. She felt her eyes beginning to fill. Michael, overthrown? What could have happened to bring about such a sudden and violent change? And the Varangians, reinstated? What of Crethus? Crethus… She spun round, "The Scythians. What has befallen them?"

"There will be fighting, Majesty. When we left, it had barely begun."

The young one brought his face up. "I doubt if any will remain alive, Majesty."

He had a look on his face, one of curiosity, somewhat severe, as if he were testing her. She ignored him. There would be time enough for explanations, but not to these two, however well connected they might be. Zoe took hold of the Mother Superior's arm and led her away to a far corner, out of earshot of the soldiers. Even so, she kept her voice low, "This is monumental news. I am not sure if I believe them."

"You feel it is a trick?"

"It might be, yes. I will make as if I am preparing myself for departure, but will do it slowly, give myself time to think. Come up with some sort of plan."

The Mother Superior pressed her lips together. "We have a small boat, the one Paulus uses to bring us supplies from the mainland. There could be a chance that we could secrete you on board that, but Zoe," the older woman forced a smile, "if these men force you, there will be nothing we can do."

"I know that. And so do they. For now, I will go along with their instructions, bide my time, and hope that the opportunity for escape will come."

"But where would you go?"

Zoe closed her eyes. If events had now already spiralled out of control, she knew exactly where she would go. The one problem was how to get a message to him. To Crethus. If, of course, he still lived.

Forty-Two

Crethus came up to the gates of *Charisus*, the huge walls towering thirty feet above him. The guards had already recognized him and the great doors were pulled open. He steered his horse through the gap and immediately the men pushed the door closed again.

"What is happening?" he asked, struggling to keep his horse under control. He could hear the clamour of the crowd within the inner city. "Where is everyone?"

One of the Scythian guards took hold of the reins. "Sir, you have returned at just the right moment."

Crethus watched as the other soldiers mounted the parapets again. "What is it?"

"Scouts have returned, sir. They have seen a large army moving towards the city." The man swallowed hard. "From their banners and standards, it is clear they are Varangians."

"I must go to the Emperor. Tell him what I know."

"The Emperor has gone to the forum sir, to address the crowds."

"And the Royal Body Guards, where are they?"

"They have left the city, sir. To face the threat of Russian incursions to the far northwest."

Crethus felt as if he had been hit by a mallet, full in the chest. For a moment he thought the entire world was about to collapse all around him and his mouth hung open, dry, sick. "But... but that cannot be..."

"It is, sir. We are the only soldiers left."

Crethus squeezed his eyes shut. The Scythians, the only soldiers left to defend the entire city? To leave it like this, open to attack from any number of directions, through any one of the many gates that punctuated the Walls of Theodosius, it was pure madness. The one good thing was that the Varangians had no siege equipment, and would not have the necessary means to break through the massive doors. But they would *all* have to closed and barred. "Get your men to man all the gates, make sure they are secured. We cannot hope to man the entire length of the wall, so send signalmen along—"

"Sir, forgive me. There is no one here but us."

Crethus shook his head, at a loss at what to think. He looked up. There were half a dozen Scythian archers here, no more. To secure all the gates along the wall, it would take hours with only these men available. Crethus felt crushed. There was no way to stop the Varangians moving through the city. Their one hope now, as far as he could see, was to leave the outer wall undefended and retreat towards the inner city, leaving the Constantine Wall also undefended, to make their stand inside the confines of the royal palace itself. "Very well, abandon your post here, move down to the Severan Wall and secure the gate there. It's clear we cannot prevent the Varangians from gaining the outer limits of the city, but we might stop them near to the forum. I will ride ahead, gather whatever men I can."

"But the Emperor, sir? He is at the forum!"

"Then I shall have to extract him, won't I?"

Crethus spurred his horse and galloped off down the long straight thoroughfare that would take him into the very heart of the majestic city.

The crowd was ugly, twisted faces, open mouths, grimaces. Many shook fists, threw out insults. As Michael stood on the steps and looked out across the vast assembly of baying citizens, he felt his stomach tip over. This was worse than he could ever have imagined. They roared their insults, demanded to see Zoe, to have her presented to them. What could he do, how could he make it right? He was at a loss. He needed Orphano, he needed Maniakes. And where were they … dear God, how could it have come to this.

From somewhere a rock, or something struck him on the side. He staggered, one of his guards rushing to his side. Michael brought up his arm, "*I command you,*" he screamed, "*I command you in the name of Christ!*" No one listened, no one cared. He could see that. The great throng roared as one, "Zoe!" He fell to his knees, pressing his hands over his ears as the sea of noise grew ever greater, drowning him. He fought against it, floundered, arms striking out this way and that, but the surge was irresistible. "Zoe!" Irresistible, over-powering. He succumbed and fell back. Those parts of the crowd that were closest saw him, yelled in triumph and rushed forward.

Michael rolled over, getting up on his hands and knees as the Scythian raced past him. He heard the cries and the screams, wild, uncontrolled now. He turned and looked back to see his troops striking against the crowd, swords flashing in the light, blood spurting, people dying. His people, citizens of Rome.

He looked up to the nearest guard. "Get me out of here," he said, his voice hardly above a whisper.

The man immediately pulled the Emperor to his feet. Another came and took his other arm and they quickly escorted him away from the forum. He allowed himself one more, brief glance, saw the tide of people beginning to scatter and break as the Scythians hacked through them, undefended people running for their lives in the face of such ferocity.

"Dear Christ," he muttered, and allowed himself to be taken away.

Within a few paces, the soldiers drew themselves up to attention and Michael, breath ragged, hair dripping with sweat, saw the giant Scythian commander standing there, as strong as an ox. "Crethus! By the love of God, you have returned!" He shrugged his escort away and, without thinking, threw himself at the giant and embraced him. "Oh thank Christ! It's all unravelling. The people, Crethus, the people want Zoe."

"But, sire." Crethus carefully pushed the Emperor away from him, attached as he was like some great, slavering limpet. "Sire, simply show them Her Ladyship, and all will be well."

"I can't, Crethus. I have sent her away. Banished her."

A feeling of utter hopelessness fell over him then, the black clouds closing in, his chest becoming tight, breathing difficult. He looked up to the sky but could find no solace there. He knew, more than ever before, that everything was coming to a close.

Forty-Three

There was no one on the walls, and the Fifth Military Gate was wide open. Scouts had reported that the Gates of Charisius were closed, so the army had diverted itself, a short deviation in actual fact, most of it uphill, and now they were crossing the city towards the main avenue which led into the centre of the city. It was deathly quiet, no one about, streets and buildings deserted. As they tramped along, with Hardrada and Rufus now at the lead, everyone was on their guard. Rufus shifted his weight in his saddle. "I can hear something, a long way off. Fighting maybe?"

Hardrada strained to hear. Ahead, the second great defensive wall of the city, the Constantinian Wall rose up before them, although in places the wall had been allowed to fall into disrepair. Again, it appeared undefended. Hardrada could just about hear some cries beyond the walls. "Seems like it could be fighting. It is not the sound of merrymaking, that's for sure. Have those other scouts returned from the north yet?"

"I doubt it," said Rufus. "Don't worry, it is as was first reported – the garrison troops have all left. The city is open. Once we get into the Royal Enclosure, we will have those Scythians once and for all."

They passed through the great wall, and around them spread the many fine buildings and churches that made up this part of the City. Over on their left, the Valens aqueduct that brought water into the inner city, traversing the open area between the Fourth and Third Hills.

Varangian

It was a glorious sight, a testament to the past artistry and craftsmanship of the Eastern Romans. Hardrada wished he had the gift to appreciate such monuments, but he did not. When he looked back at his own childhood, a simple village life, harsh and cruel, such luxuries, and achievements, left him cold. As far as he knew, Byzantium had always existed and, given the size of this great city, it always would. Could the same be said for his own land, with its small villages and homesteads? The Halls of the Norse Kings were as nothing compared with the glory that was Rome. The Eternal City. And yet, here he was, marching towards an uncertain fight, hell-bent on destruction. The destruction of glory.

"You are deep in thought, my old friend," Rufus clapped him on the shoulder. "Why so morose?"

"Thoughts of home, Rufus. Nothing more."

"Aye, well, when battle awaits, thoughts often return to loved ones, family and distant friends."

"I have no family and few friends, distant or otherwise. No, my thoughts are of more what will happen afterwards. To remain here, in this fabulous place, or to return to what is rightfully mine. Kingship."

"Well, this may be a fabulous place, but it is alive with worms and weevils, all burrowing away at its underbelly. At least back home you can meet your enemies face to face, and never have to worry about your back!"

"Aye, that is true enough. And, if I am none too mistaken," he reached behind him and pulled out his great battleaxe, "our enemy presents itself!"

Rufus followed his line of sight and saw that it was true.

Scythians, dozens of them, fanning out from the sides of the great forum. Behind them, the walls of the inner city, the Royal Enclosure. The Hippodrome, that most magnificent of all structures, loomed huge. People, citizens, ran in every direction, many of them screaming, some clutching at their children, dragging them away from the Scythians.

Hardrada turned in his saddle, roaring, "Captains, to your positions!"

Immediately, the column began to spread out; well-drilled, the men responded to the barks of their officers, and horns blasted out the signal to form up in line.

Rufus tugged at his beard as he pulled his sword from its scabbard. "It'll be difficult fighting in close order amongst all these streets, and with so many people."

"It will, but what choice do we have?" As Hardrada spoke, a woman ran by and he caught sight of the blood streaming from her head. More followed, gasping for breath, some stumbling, others too frightened to even care about their wounds. Children wailed. One young boy, no more than twelve, stopped by Hardrada's horse and looked up. "They are killing everyone. I've lost my mother. Please, please help us."

It was the only spurt Hardrada needed, and he leaped off his horse and hefted the axe in his hands. "For our friends then, our dead friends. Heroes all."

Rufus fell in next to him. "We'll remember them with Scythian blood!"

Hardrada turned to his own friend, clenched his teeth in a maniacal grin, and lifted his axe high above his head as the young boy stumbled away, crying out in alarm, eyes wide with terror. Hardrada took a breath and bellowed, "Onward, lads! *To victory!*"

Crethus pushed past the jumble of mad, desperate people all running around, screaming, hands clawing at their heads, many of them staggering, all of them terrified. As he emerged through the mob, he could already see his Scythians reforming, notching their arrows. He looked past them and gasped. The Varangians, stretched out in a ragged line, some of them between buildings, coming forward, horns blaring, standards held aloft, axes slamming against shields, chanting, "*Out, out, out!*" Crethus paled. He had never seen anything so terrifying and he knew that this day could well be his last. He drew his curved sword and examined the blade. His hand was shaking. He closed his eyes, gave up a silent prayer, and pushed on, joining his men as they prepared to lose the first shower of arrows.

Varangian

***

Hardrada dropped his hand in a signal, the horns changed note, and the Varangians broke into a wild dash, clumps of men moving around buildings and through streets as the arrows came down, black smudges across the sky. But their effect was mitigated by the Varangians opening up their line. In the squeeze of the streets, all advantage the Scythians might have had was nullified and soon, the two forces smashed into each other, fearful hand-to-hand fighting breaking out all along the line.

It was cramped and difficult and the Scythians were ferocious warriors, their evil blades slicing through flesh, severing limps, cutting vein and sinew. But the Varangians were their match. All around men fell screaming, razor sharp swords causing horrific, debilitating wounds, axes cleaved through skulls, hacking off limbs. The Scythians were quick on their feet, adept to this sort of warfare. They could skip away from the swung axes, counter with wicked swipes. The Varangians were solid, dependable and imperious. Men speared, parried, ducked and dived. The noise of battle ran through the tightly packed streets, desperate struggles in every direction. Guts spewed out on the ground, throats opened up, death seeped all across the paving stones.

Hardrada was in the thick of it, towering over everyone. His sheer size served as a beacon. Individual Scythian warriors, anxious for fame and glory, would press towards him. All met the same fate, his great axe cutting deep into the bone, parting skulls, great gouts of hot blood erupting from opened bodies.

He swung the huge axe, the lust flooding through his body, relishing the screams of his enemies. He strode out, cutting a swathe through them, moving like a wild animal, always alert, eyes searching, knowing full well the penchant the Scythians had for the cowardly attack from the rear.

As the dead lay in heaps, he caught sight of his main quarry. Crethus.

Both men stood some twelve paces apart, neither moving, both looking into each other's souls. Hardrada flexed his muscles, held the axe across his body in both hands. The blood dripped from the blade.

For a moment, a hush descended upon the furious fight as if everyone knew that here was something special, something to remember. Crethus, glancing around, ran the back of his hand across his mouth.

"Our paths cross again."

"Aye, and this time you die."

"I thought we had a bargain?"

"For what you did, to my men?" Hardrada laughed. "All bargains are null and void." He quickly went into a half-crouch and bellowed his battle-cry. Then he rushed forward, the great axe swinging through the air.

The city appeared empty. No guards, no people. Andreas slipped down from his horse and looked all around, not for the first time taken aback by the grandeur of his beloved city, his home. However, in all his years, he had never experienced anything like this. Empty streets and houses, gleaming buildings, grand statues, avenues and highways. Nothing but stone. No sign of human life. He shuddered as he led his horse along the main thoroughfare.

By the time he passed through the Constantinian Wall, he could hear the sound of fighting. Drawing his sword, he moved on, more cautiously now, checking each street and building as he went.

He came across the first bodies not long after that.

A woman, eyes staring sightlessly, propped up against a fountain, its water running down over her face, mixing with the blood, causing tiny rivulets to trail away into the dust. Across her lap, a boy, no more than twelve, his throat open, the blood dried across his chest.

Andreas moved up to them, dipped his hand in the water and washed his face. He looked along the street and saw other bodies. Citizens and soldiers. The numbers increased as he continued on his way.

He came across the first frantic struggle not long afterwards. A group of screaming citizens came running down the street and, beyond, two Scythians, swords raised, mouths fixed in maniacal grins. He steadied himself.

The people veered away from him. Too late the Scythians saw him, tried to react and halt their run, but already Andreas was moving, cutting through the midriff of the first, then swivelling to deliver a second cut across the rear shoulder of the second. Both men fell, hitting the ground with a loud, solid thump. Neither moved.

"Please help us," came a voice and Andreas straightened to find a young woman, holding onto a much younger girl, both of them obviously terrified. They kept looking back, as if expecting more Scythians to emerge down the street like dogs from hell. For all he knew, they might be right. Andreas took them by the hand and led them over to the nearest building. It was one of the many tenement blocks dotted along the main thoroughfare. He put his shoulder against the main door, but it wouldn't budge. He took a step back, readied himself, then thrust his foot against the wood. Another blow, and it splintered and broke, bursting inwards.

"Come on," he said, and pulled them both inside.

Like so many of these buildings, it was dark and damp inside, the gloom making it virtually impossible to pick out details, despite it being daytime. Andreas edged forward. There were stairs, leading up to the upper floors and he stopped and peered up into the darkness. The Romans had these buildings, in the heyday of the empire. Rotten, stinking places they were, people crammed together, living like rats, and amongst rats too. To emphasize the fact, Andreas heard the all too familiar scurrying of tiny feet and he baulked and turned away.

The two females stood, huddled together, the little girl crying unabated.

"I am an officer," he said, trying to keep his voice low and steady. "In the Royal Guard. Do you know what is happening here?"

"Monsters," the woman hissed. "We…" Her voice broke and for a moment she couldn't continue and she dropped her head as the girl buried herself into the woman's robe and cried even more.

"Just take your time," said Andreas, every now and then turning his gaze to the broken door and the street beyond.

"We were at the forum, waiting for the Emperor." Andreas locked his gaze upon the woman and held his breath. "He tried to speak, but no one would let him. We wanted Her Majesty, Princess Zoe, you see. But she was not there. Then someone threw a rock and that was when his guards attacked us."

"The Scythians?"

"Yes."

Andreas slid his sword into its scabbard. "But where are the other soldiers? The Royal Guard? The *Scholae,* and the *Anitolikon?* Where have they all gone?"

"There is a rumour of Russians breaking through along the northern borders, so the great general, Maniakes, has led the men to face this threat."

Andreas grunted. The great general ... "And who fights the Scythians? I have seen their dead."

"Norsemen. We saw them."

"A giant." The little girl looked up from the other's robes. Her eyes were red with tears, and her lips trembled as she spoke. "A giant fought with them. Goliath."

Andreas felt his jaw go slack and he gripped the hilt of his sword. So, Hardrada was here, leading his men as he had always said he would. He pulled in a ragged breath, "Then we have come to it. The reckoning."

The woman frowned. "Reckoning?"

"No matter. Come, I will find somewhere safe for you to hide, then I will return."

"After this reckoning?"

"Yes. After this reckoning."

Forty-Four

Standing by the quayside, Nikolias and his armed guard stared out across the Sea of Marmara, waiting for the boat to arrive. He didn't know when it would come, he only knew that this was the most important mission he had ever been entrusted with. To return the Lady Zoe to her Royal apartments and guard her whilst she readied herself to be once again presented to the people.

The day was drawing on. He had no idea what was happening around the inner city. All he knew was that people were running, coming onto the quay, telling stories of fighting. Dying. This had to be the Varangians and the Scythians. Locked in a life and death struggle, it could go either way. He pressed his fingers into his temples and massaged away the blinding headache that had been with him for the past few hours. Stress. He looked across at his men and smiled. They too looked grim. One of them noted his look, coughed, and came to attention.

"How much longer do we wait, sir?"

"Until she comes."

"And if the Scythians come this way?"

Nikolias made a face. "We fight."

The soldier stuck his tongue against his cheek and blew out a breath. "Might be difficult, sir."

"Nothing is too difficult for soldiers of Rome."

The soldier stood up straight again, jawline set. "No sir! Didn't mean it like that, sir."

"I know you didn't, Marios. Relax. You're right, if the Scythians prevail..." He let his words hang unfinished. There was no need for anything further. They all knew what the outcome would be.

* * *

Alexius sat inside his covered wagon, a ring of well armed Norsemen outside. This was the worst time, the waiting. He sat in an attitude of prayer, hands clasped, eyes closed. With God watching over them, the righteous would win through. And they were the righteous, there could be no doubt. He had never believed it could come to this, fighting within the city, Byzantine soldiers struggling against each other, no matter what their race or background. All were citizens of Rome.

He looked up at the beautiful, illuminated icon that he had managed to fasten on the inside of the wagon. It showed Christ, giving his blessing, the radiance of the work clearly portraying the artist's devotion to his Lord. How beautiful it was, how sacred. Alexius stared deeply into the face of Christ, felt the stirring inside him as the Holy Spirit moved, strengthened his faith, quietened his beating heart. He made the sign of the cross, and turned to pull back the covered opening to the wagon.

"Any sign?" he asked to no one in particular.

"Not yet," grumbled a nearby Norseman.

Alexius sighed and dipped back inside. How surly they were, how utterly unchristian. Not for the first time he wondered if he had fallen in with the wrong side, but then he looked again at the icon and reminded himself that the Lord Himself had guided him unerringly so far. He smiled. And so it would continue.

As he sat down, drawing his robes closer, he hoped it was indeed the case.

The two Scythians took Michael away from the fighting, and led him to the Chapel of the Saviour. Its open terrace, next to the huge Banqueting Hall, was hyphenated with statues, the most exquisite in all of the City. The faces of past emperors and heroes looked down, and Michael stopped, holding up his hand. "Give me a moment."

"We haven't a moment, sire," said the one known as Stracchus, a burly brute who had manhandled Michael as if he were nothing more than a lowly peasant. Michael had chosen to ignore it; in the face of so many threats, these men were the one thing between him and assassination.

"I just want to rest." He put his palm against the side of his head, where the rock had struck him. It throbbed beneath his hand. "I feel dizzy."

It was an ordered, tranquil place with laburnum and jasmine scattered in abundance around the statues. Honeysuckle added to the aroma, the air thick with an abundance of various perfumes, at once heady and relaxing. A place where worries could be put to the back of the mind, where the present could become suspended.

Today, however, the atmosphere was somewhat different as the distant sound of fighting broke through the usual air of calm and quiet contemplation.

"We must get you inside the church," said the other guard urgently. "No one will dare to attack you there."

"Attack me? You think anyone will?"

Stracchus shrugged. "Possibly."

The second guard tensed, and he took a step backwards. "Oh, fuck!"

Michael looked up at the other Scythians's outburst. He looked towards the throne room and saw the reason and he quaked at the sight, his stomach tipping right over.

Two men. Only two. They were racing towards them.

Only two.

The Scythians went white, faces drained of colour. Stracchus groaned and the other didn't wait, he simply turned on his heels and sprinted away. "*You bastard!*" roared Stracchus at his comrade's retreating back. Then he glanced to Michael. "You're on your own."

Michael stared, open-mouth in total disbelief, as Stracchus turned to go as well. But before he could take a step a javelin came out of the air and hit him between the shoulders. He grunted and pitched forward onto his face.

Losing control, the strength drained out of Michael's limbs and he crumpled to his knees, mouth quivering , all rational thought gone. He watched as the two men strode up to him.

"Well, if it isn't His royal Highness."

"Steady, Ulf. Don't insult him. He might order you to be executed."

Ulf laughed, then hacked and spat into the dirt. "You don't half talk some crap when you want to, Hal."

Haldor put his sword back into its scabbard and crouched down and peered at the quivering emperor. "What shall we do with him? Kill him?" Michael blanched, made a little squeaking sound and fell back onto his backside, legs splayed out, hands coming up in supplication.

"Nah," said Ulf. "Best leave him to Harald. He'll know what to do for the best."

"Yeah," said Haldor, grinning, his eyes never leaving Michael's. "Probably castrate him."

"In public," added Ulf.

And at that point, Michael blacked out.

* * *

They bundled him inside the church and secured him to the altar there. When they were satisfied that he couldn't escape, Ulf and Haldor went back outside. It was late afternoon, the sounds of fighting less now. The two Vikings breathed deeply, looked at each other, and then strode back across the open area that ran along the side of the Royal Bodyguard quarters. Neither spoke, both of them tensed and ready to draw their weapons. By the time they reached the Royal Gate, they could see that such an action might not be required.

The dead lay strewn all around the huge area between the Hippodrome and the Palace of the Patriarch and the Senate house. Men groaned and moaned, some dragging themselves across the ground, blood leaking from the many wounds they had suffered. Most were dead. Limbs – arms, legs, heads – decorated the area in a grizzly parody of the calm and serene enclosure beside the Chapel of the Saviour. There, statues of glorious leaders offered hope, provided inspiration. Here, glory was dead and inspiration no longer had any place. All was carnage and horror.

Varangian Norse picked their way through the bodies, dispatching those still alive with a single knife cut across the throat. As they did so, in the distance, one more fight raged. Perhaps the final one.

Ulf gripped Haldor's arm, and motioned with his head. "Harald."

Haldor looked and saw it was true.

Hardrada, unmistakable due to his enormous size, swung the great axe, and the massive Crethus blocked and parried with his scimitar. Forced back, the Scythian was putting up a spirited defence, but the relentless surge of Hardrada's attacks were becoming too much. Slamming up against a wall, he tried to dodge a blow, but as he did, Hardrada kicked him full between the legs, and the man toppled forward, his sword clattering to the ground next to him.

Bringing up the battle axe, Hardrada prepared to strike the final blow and cleave the Scythians' head from his shoulders.

At that point, came the sound of another.

"*Hardrada!*"

Everyone froze, even the men carrying out their gruesome work on the dying.

For a moment, time seemed to hang in the air, everything having stopped.

Everything except for Andreas. He strode through the twisted, mangled bodies, his sword at his side. He fixed the giant Hardrada with a look of sheer hatred, and waited.

Hardrada slowly lowered the axe and turned to face the young soldier. "I was hoping to find you alive, Andreas."

"Then you and I have the same wish."

"Aye. And your death will follow this bastard's." He toed Crethus in the side. The Scythian groaned, looked up, his face screwed up with the pain. Hardrada ignored him and glared again at Andreas. "Come here, boy, and embrace your doom."

Ulf and Haldor saw it all then. Everything happened so quickly and yet, looking back, it was if everything had become slowed down. They saw Andreas charging forward, and Hardrada preparing himself. But then the Scythian, recovering himself a little, reached out for his sword, brought up his blade and readied himself to strike.

"We have to help him," roared Ulf, and ran forward, Haldor close behind. Ulf swerved away to the left and tackled Andreas, whilst at the same time Haldor raced across to intercept Crethus.

Hardrada whirled, not knowing which attack to defend himself from first. His friends emerged from nowhere, friends he had virtually forgotten in the sweat and heat of battle. Friends to whom, he owed everything. He stepped back, as Haldor grappled with Crethus and then, across to his right, he saw Ulf hitting Andreas hard in the midriff. He had launched himself full length at the boy, and now they both crashed to the ground in a mad tangle of arms and legs, wrestling with each other, scrambling around in the dirt.

He should have known that it would end this way. To be denied the pleasure of killing the two most hated men in his world. He cursed everyone and everything in general, gripped the haft of his axe as the frustration overwhelmed him, and then saw that he still might have the chance to fulfill his wishes, and he smiled.

Crethus was enormously strong, Hardrada knew this and had already felt it. Haldor was a great warrior, but the giant Scythian shrugged him off as if he were nothing more than a small child. As Haldor fell to ground, sprawled out on his back, Hardrada moved in.

At that moment, a cry. Hardrada turned for a fraction of a minute, but it was enough. Crethus hit him square on the chin with the butt of his sword hilt. The Norwegian's head rattled and he flayed around, all senses gone. He could not even think how to reply as blue and red lights flashed across his eyes.

As if drunk, he could see the Scythian, knew that the end was close. Then Ulf, or someone like Ulf, stepping up to him, then nothing, nothing at all.

The Scythian ran through the streets, not knowing which direction to go, his single thought to get away. He bolted through the main doors of the Imperial Palace, stopping for a moment to look around him. He remembered the layout fairly well. The last time he had been here it had been with Stracchus, discussing how they would partake of the flesh of Zoe's hand-maidens. That seemed like a lifetime ago but could it really have been the previous day? He ran a quivering hand through his hair. Stracchus ... dead. Now he, Bathar, the only one to survive, knew he might still find a way out of his predicament. If he could get to the tunnel that ran from the throne room to the Hippodrome royal box, he could still find an escape route. He clenched his jaw and edged forward.

It was like a vast tomb, deathly quiet. Usually the place teemed with people – servants, courtiers, soldiers. Not now. Now everything and everyone was gone.

The stillness of the place was accentuated by the harsh, biting cold that seemed to emanate from every stone. Bathar shivered and then flattened himself behind a nearby pillar as a single laugh cut through the huge interior.

He stopped, hardly daring to breathe. Bathar knew he hadn't imagined it. A man's laugh, a guffaw. He waited and then, as if by reward, another, followed by the raised giggling of a woman.

Using extreme caution, aware of every tiny sound, Bathar crept towards the sound. A door was straight ahead. He kept close to the wall, in the dark shadows behind the pillars.

It came again, quieter this time, but the sound of laughter nevertheless. He slid his curved scimitar from its sheath, and steadied himself in front of the door. He waited, took a few breaths, then slammed his shoulder against the entrance.

The girls screamed and someone moved, but Bathar had stumbled to the floor, letting out a cry as he cracked his knees on the hard marble. Desperate now, he tried to bring his sword around, to ward off any attack.

He saw the man. Huge he was, a massive belly hanging over his tightly drawn pantaloons. Behind him, a girl, cowering. Naked. Bathar gaped at her, distantly aware that there was someone else in there. Too late, he turned and screamed.

Leoni stood panting, the large, heavy candelabra in her hands, the blood dripping, single splats falling to the marble floor, sounding loud. And terrible.

She looked up her eyes locking with those of Constantine who stood there, quivering.

"Is he dead?" asked Christina, stepping forward.

Leoni looked down again at the spread-eagled Scythian. She had reacted without thought, swinging the candelabra with all of her might, smashing it down onto the man's skull. It had cracked open like an egg and now he lay there, his eyes wide and the blood blossoming around his broken head like a huge rose. "Yes," she said, surprised at how tiny her voice sounded.

Constantine took the candelabra from her and nodded. "I shan't forget this, child."

"Shan't you?" Leoni glared at him, then turned her glare to Cristina. Sickness rose up into her throat. She groped forward towards the bed and flopped down on the edge.

"We must go," said Constantine, jabbing his chin towards Cristina. "Get dressed. There could be more of them."

Leoni watched them as they scrambled into their clothes, panic engulfing them.

"Come on, Leoni," said Cristina. "We have to try and get away."

"You do what you want," said Leoni. "I'm staying here."

"What? But you can't!"

"Can't I?" She shook her head. This was the end. She had done many things, despicable things, things she could no longer come to terms with. Now, she could add killing another human being to the list. Enough was enough. "I'm staying."

"Leave her," snapped Constantine, and took hold of Cristina's wrist. "We shall think of you, child."

Leoni turned her face away. Only when the door had been closed did she allow herself to cry.

"Harald!" Ulf held onto his old friend's shoulders as the giant Viking crumpled to the ground. He was too heavy, too big and he hit the dirt with a sickening thud. Ulf whirled. He had struck the Scythian across the jaw, sending him crashing backwards. He now lay unconscious. Both of the giants felled. Ulf took a moment and looked across to Andreas, who still knelt there, the blood running from his nose and mouth, battered into submission, but not yet subdued. He decided that his other friend, Haldor, needed tending to most. So he crossed the ground and stooped down, cradled his companion's head. He needed water, and there was none to be had, not anywhere close at least. So, clutching his sword, Ulf marched off, back towards the Royal Gates, certain that somewhere, amongst the dead, he might find an old animal skin with enough water to wash away the blood from Haldor's face, revive him a little. As Ulf moved passed Andreas, he aimed a hefty kick at the young warrior's head, and smiled with relish as he heard the satisfying crunch of bone. Andreas grunted, fell sideways, and lay still. Ulf broke into a jog, making his way towards the Royal Gate as quickly as he could.

Crethus stirred and rolled over. His head banged as if it were being struck like a drum. That man could hit hard! Tentatively, he ran his hand across his jaw, shook his head and got to his feet. Hardrada, as he could see, was also stirring. Crethus knew that it would take some moments for both of them to regain their strength and join in battle once more. And soon, that other damned Viking would be back. So, a little reluctantly, Crethus turned and made his way, swaying this way and that, away from the area and headed for the closest building he could see, The Chapel of the Saviour.

Forty-Five

In and around the forum of Constantine, the last few skirmishes were fought out. Rufus, drenched in sweat and blood, summoned up one last effort and brought his axe down across the shoulder of the Scythian in front of him. The blade cut into the body, slicing through the clavicle, bisecting the heart, and the man tried to scream, but already the life had gone from him and he folded and fell, the two halves of his split carcass rolling down the steps. Rufus half stood, hands on knees, unable to believe that the fight had ended. The Scythians had fought like demons, had killed many, but now the bloodletting had ended and he allowed himself a moment to relax, falling to his knees, breathing hard.

"I need water!"

Rufus looked up, frowned. It was Ulf. Barely recognisable, his eyes were like moths arcing around a candle flame. Possessed, maddened, Rufus didn't know which, but his old friend was in a desperate state. "Water?"

Ulf ran on, twisting and turning to avoid the bodies that lay in obscene attitudes all over the ground. Rufus watched him, without understanding, saw him grab at a small water bottle, and run off again towards the Royal Gate. Rufus stood up.

"They're dead," said another warrior, coming up, his tread heavy. "By Odin's beard, they fought well. I don't think I've ever closed with men so strong, so fierce. But, for all their strength, they are dead. Every one."

"All of them?"

"Aye. All. But we have lost many, Rufus. Too many, I think."

Rufus turned his eyes to the vast open area and saw that the warrior's words were painfully true. Between the Forum and the entrance to the giant Hippodrome, the ground was littered with the dead. Warriors mingled with citizens – women, children, men. And everywhere, blood. Rufus had fought many times, but he had never witnessed such wholesale slaughter of the innocent. The Scythians may have been indomitable foes, but their hearts were twisted. Rufus would shed no tears over their end, but these people…

He slumped down on the steps and let his axe clatter to the stone. Life, death, so transitory, changing in the blink of an eye. He had prevailed, but at what cost. He had a family, he could see them in his mind's eye if he tried hard enough, memories stirring from deep within. Where would they be right this moment, he wondered, what would they be doing. To return home, to the calm serenity of the Norse, to look out across the fjord, stroll through the great forests, feast in the great hall. Would any of that ever happen again and, even if he could go back, would those of his own blood even remember him? The years had come, and they had gone. Too many to know.

"Rufus?"

The warrior's voice cut through the Varangian commander's thoughts. He glanced up. "What is it?"

"Reports are coming in."

Rufus felt his stomach lurch. "What sort of reports?"

The warrior stooped down, his hand gripping his commander's knee. "It is the Byzantine Guard. They are approaching the city."

Rufus swallowed, the weight across his shoulders becoming unbearable. "How many?"

" Around a thousand."

* * *

Hardrada spluttered as the water splashed across his face. He gagged, sat up, and went to get to his feet. Ulf held him back, "Relax," he said. "Your friend has run off."

"Friend? What the hell—"

"Your Scythian buddy, the one who smacked you on the chin with his sword. He could have killed you."

Hardrada knew it and he stared past Ulf into the distance. "So why didn't he?"

"Don't know. Maybe he thought your destiny lay elsewhere."

"Don't be so bloody..." Hardrada blinked and looked at his friend as if for the first time. "Ulf? Where the hell did you come from?"

"We escaped, old Haldor and me. Which reminds me..." He stood up and went over to his other companion, turned him over and poured more water over his face.

Hardrada looked beyond them at the prone figure of Andreas. He felt the anger returning, surging through him. "That little shit," he muttered to himself and got to his feet. He felt his chin and winced. That was some blow Crethus delivered. Perfect. Why the hell hadn't he finished him off. Was it all down to Ulf and his timely intervention?

"Is he dead?"

Ulf brought his old friend up to a sitting position and laughed. "Take more than a Scythian the size of a barn-door to put paid to this old fart."

"I meant the Byzantine."

"Oh, him. Nah, just resting. I beat the shit out of him. I didn't think you wanted me to kill him. Thought you might want to do that. Doesn't like you very much, does he? I suppose you're going to tell me some tale of valour and heroism, how you and he fought over some poor, imprisoned maiden and when you won her heart, he swore revenge. Am I close?"

"Not by a thousand leagues."

"Mmm. Not sure I know how far that is, but something has gone on. Care to tell me?"

"I'd rather not. Suffice to say he murdered a good friend of mine, a young woman who saved my life. And his."

"Saved his life? Why did he kill her then?"

"I don't know, but I tend to find out. Throw some of that water over him will you, I'm going to beat a confession out of him."

"I'll string him up first. Then, if he doesn't talk, we'll castrate him."

"Good idea. Why didn't I think of that?"

"Because you're not an evil bastard like me, that's why. Come on, give me a hand, Haldor will be all right."

So together, the two companions dragged the unconscious Andreas over to a nearby tree, lashed him there with some leather thongs they found, and then ripped off his breeches, exposing him to the elements. He didn't stir until Ulf threw water over him, and after he had taken a moment or two and regained some of his senses, he realized what was about to happen, and screamed.

Rufus mustered his men. They stood in a ragged line, shields interlocked, occupying the space between the forum steps and the hippodrome. There were about eighteen hundred or so men able to stand. A further two hundred, give or take a few tens, were in the rear, nursing their wounds. They would fight if they needed to, but Rufus hoped that he wouldn't have to rely on them. If it was to be their last stand, then it would be this first line which would take the full brunt of the Byzantine guard. Then ... well, then it would be up to the gods. Christian or pagan, it didn't matter which. When the day was done, Rufus would be in another realm and all of his worries and concerns would be as nothing. Nothing. He squeezed his eyes shut. All those thoughts of home, they had made him weak. He was a warrior, a Viking. If he were to die, then this was the way he should do it. Not growing old in some farmstead in his homeland.

"They are here."

He looked across at the warrior again, the one who had spoken to him earlier. "What is your name, soldier?"

"Aelred."

"Aelred? You're a Saxon?"

"Aye. And proud of it."

Rufus thrust out his hand. "Well met, friend." Aelred took the proffered hand and clasped it hard. "We'll stand, side by side, and live and die here, together."

"That we shall." He hefted his axe. "That we shall."

Rufus let his gaze turn to the front. He thought he knew what he would see, but even he quailed at the sight before him.

Serried ranks of bronze-clad soldiers, a thousand or more, spearmen, but mostly archers, spread out across the huge plaza. They were in the process of positioning themselves, various regiments of imperial guardsmen, many mounted, pendants fluttering in the breeze, horsetail plumes stirring. Supreme confidence, perhaps even arrogance seemed to ooze from every part of the array of armed men. It was enough to send even the bravest heart into an immediate seizure. Rufus gasped and for a moment had to hold onto his new-found friend, Aelred.

"Steady boys," rasped Aelred.

Rufus gritted his teeth. To die, like this. Aye, better than anything else. His men were weary, too weary. They had fought so hard and now exhaustion rather than the blades of the Byzantines could be their undoing. Rufus steadied himself, took a deep breath before raising up his axe high above his head. "Varangians!" he screamed. "Let your blood write the saga of this day!"

Even before his voice had drifted away, the Varangians began to smash their axe handles against their shields, chanting, "*Out, out, out!*"

The deep, rumbling Viking battle-cry came from beyond the Royal Gate. Hardrada shot a glance towards Ulf. "What the fuck?"

"Battle," spat Ulf and brought up his sword. "More Scythian dogs to slaughter."

"Get Haldor comfortable, and ensure that Andreas is well secured. Then meet me at the forum." Hardrada moved away. His chin was still tender, but he pushed the pain to the back of his mind. Perhaps there were more Scythians than anyone knew. A hidden contingent, lying in wait. Who knew what other tricks they would stoop to in order to survive?

He could almost taste the blood in his mouth as he broke into a run, looking forward to the cleaving of more skulls.

Tearing through the Royal Gate he almost stumbled and fell as he pulled up sharply.

Byzantines, over a thousand, stretching back towards the centre of the city, in steady, disciplined ranks.

Hardrada gaped, knowing that here was something not even he and the valiant Varangians had expected. The well trained, experienced Byzantine Royal Guard. Perhaps the most formidable troops on earth. And their number matched the Varangians, battle weary and bloodied as they were. This was going to be the fight of their lives. Tearing his eyes from the vision of invincibility, he tried to pick out his old friend Rufus. Instead, what he saw brought the gall to his throat.

General Maniakes, resplendent in gold panoply, his helmet topped with a large white horsetail plume, cantered forward on his majestic warhorse and reined in not ten paces from the Viking.

"Hardrada. I thought you were dead."

"Not yet, General. Not for want of your assassins trying."

"*My* assassins? Harald, it was never my intention to have you killed, I'm just surprised to see you, that's all. My orders were for you to bring the Varangian Guard back to the city, overcome the Scythians. This they have done, and your orders are fulfilled." He frowned. "But I know nothing of any assassination attempts. Alexius told me that when you arrived, you spoke something about Andreas ... about him murdering some peasant girl. A sorceress. Andreas would never do anything like that."

"No? Well, he's certainly intent on murdering me."

Maniakes shifted his weight in the saddle. "So where is he?"

"I have him tied to a tree, ready for castration."

The General blinked, taking I moment to allow Hardrada's words to sink in. "I see. You haven't changed much."

"No. Nor you. Where is Michael?"

Varangian

"I was hoping you would tell me."

Hardrada shrugged. "Sorry."

He turned as Ulf came up next to him. He was smiling. "What's it worth?"

"Huh?"

Ulf chuckled. "You heard, General. What's it worth – me telling you where Michael is?"

For a moment, it looked as if Maniakes was going into apoplexy. He spluttered, "You insolent cur, how dare you barter with me!"

Ulf laughed again, clapping Hardrada on the shoulder. "He doesn't get it, does he? Tell you what, General. We'll do a deal with you. We'll give you Michael, *and* Andreas, if you give us our lives."

A hush fell upon everyone. The Byzantine soldiers stood ramrod still, their banners flapping in the slight breeze the only sound. Even the horses took their cue and held their breath. Maniakes grasped the pommel of his saddle and looked back at his men. He raised his arm and a slight gap broke through the ranks. Through it strode Alexius, the Patriarch of Byzantium. Soldiers close by lowered their heads. Some fell to their knees. Still no one spoke.

The Patriarch smiled broadly as he came up beside the general's horse. "Well met, Harald."

Hardrada smiled in return, tipped his head. "My Lord."

"It seems that your men have done what was expected. They have removed the Scythians."

Hardrada almost had to grin at the choice of words. "Aye, that we have. One thing puzzles me, however. Why couldn't the General do it?"

Maniakes tilted his head. "A General of Rome, butchering the personal bodyguard of the Emperor? What would that make me, Harald?"

"So, all of this … all so you could what – look good for the history books?"

"Harald," Alexius raised his hand. "The General has done what he had to. The Scythians are gone, the Lady Zoe is about to return and…"

Hardrada let his mouth fall open and he looked across at his friend Ulf. "The Lady Zoe? She still lives?"

"Yes," said Maniakes. "Exiled. However, she is about to return and, as soon as she does, she will present herself to the people and peace shall be restored."

"Peace, and order," added Alexius.

"So, Harald," Maniakes smiled, the glint in his eye betrayed the machinations working away in his mind, "We have no time to lose. Here is the deal – with your compliance, your companions here, your Varangians, and yourself … you will all be spared."

"Compliance?" Hardrada arched an eyebrow. "Compliance about what?"

"You will find Michael, and assassinate him."

It was Ulf who stepped in again, his hand still resting on Hardrada's. "In so doing, it will be us who are condemned by history, not you. Clever, General. Seems like you have everything you want."

"What *I* want," said Hardrada evenly before anyone else could speak, "is my treasure – the money I have saved during my time in service here. I mean to take it, and return to my native land."

Maniakes pushed himself up from his saddle, pressed his lips together, then finally nodded, just once.

Alexius breathed a deep sigh. "Harald, I am not convinced that killing Michael is what we should do. We are not of the old world. Caligula, Nero, Commodus, they murdered. We have moved on since then." He glanced across at the General, who, tellingly, did not meet the Patriarch's gaze. "You shall have your treasure, as well as your life. In return, you shall not kill Michael, Harald." The general went to speak, but Alexius held up his hand, stilling him instantly. "No, this is my judgement. Find him, Harald, And when you do, you will blind him."

Forty-Six

They pushed open the heavy double doors of the Chapel and stepped inside. It was murky within, the majestic chandeliers hanging from the ceiling not having been lit for days. There was some relief however – shafts of light speared out from the high windows, cutting through the gloom, picking out various details. At the far end, they could see the large altar, draped with a cloth of scarlet, interlaced with gold thread, and on it three large, impressive chalices, shimmering with ornate gold and jewel decorations. From here the priests would offer up the mass, spoken in Greek, giving hope and the promise of salvation to the faithful. Today, there was no such hope. Not for Michael at least. He sat there, slumped against the side of the altar, his legs and arms lashed together. As the two Vikings strode forward, he looked up and the fear broke out across his features. He tried to scramble backwards, but of course he could not; his tethers were too tight. He whimpered, like a small child.

"Ulf, watch the door."

"Aye, Harald." He eased a long, slim looking knife from its scabbard around his waist and handed it hilt first to his friend. "You'll need this."

Hardrada looked down at the blade and shook his head. "No. This is personal, my friend."

Ulf frowned and went to move away. As he did so, a shadow moved out of the far corner and a man of enormous size revealed himself.

Hardrada sucked in his breath and gently pulled Ulf aside. "I thought you'd fled, you evil bastard."

Crethus chuckled, stepping closer. His curved scimitar oddly small in his enormous fist. "Not without killing you first."

Ulf touched his friend's arm. "Harald, I can—"

"No, old friend. This will take but a moment."

As if this remark were a trigger of some sort, Crethus screamed and charged, the sword raised two-handed above his head. Hardrada barely had time to shoulder Ulf out the way before the great blade swept down, its razor sharp edge slicing through the sleeve of Hardrada's tunic. He swore, and managed to swerve out of the way as a second blow whistled through the close, thick air of the chapel. He retreated a couple of steps, dodging this way and that, as the Scythian brought down blow after blow in quick succession. With his back against the far wall, Hardrada had to hurl himself over to his right as the sword struck against the masonry, great chunks of stone flying out like tiny projectiles.

Hardrada rolled over, coming up to his feet ready, coiled like a panther. His axe was outside, lying next to Haldor, but he had his sword, and that would suffice. With controlled menace, he drew the blade and prepared himself.

At once, the Scythian rushed forward again, grunting and roaring as each swinging blow from his scimitar streaked through the air. Hardrada parried. The clash of steel on steel rang out through the church, the clattering of the metal echoing through the various naves and vaults, soaring up into the vaulted ceiling, amplifying the sound to an unnatural level as the two men thrust, blocked, and countered.

It was as if the Scythian was possessed. He had learned from his previous mistakes, that was obvious. The knowledge that Hardrada could be damaged by a well delivered blow seemed to have given him new reserves of strength and skill. Hardrada had to work hard to keep the man at bay, but he was relentless, face set, teeth clenched, grunting and growling as he drove on. Hardrada struggled to maintain his defences. And that was all he had, his counters were not penetrating;

desperation began to gnaw away at him. He fought to keep himself under control as he moved backwards, his sword growing ever heavier in his hand.

The Scythian had to tire soon. No one could maintain this ferocity of attack. But with each blow, the man seemed to become even stronger, and Hardrada quailed under the onslaught. Was this the day he would finally fall, cut down under the evil blade of this foreign devil?

A violent swipe pierced his defences and sliced through his bicep. Hardrada yelped, fell backwards, his arm ringing with the pain. It was not a deep cut, but it drew blood, caught him unawares and that was all the encouragement Crethus needed. He moved in, under Hardrada's guard, sensing victory, and struck home towards the Viking's midriff.

Through a cloud of disbelief that he was about to be defeated, Hardrada managed to turn at the last moment, caught the blade in his free hand and brought his right fist, still holding the sword, to smash into the Scythian's nose with a tremendous crack.

Crethus screamed, blood erupting from his face in a great spurt, and he tipped backwards, the hold on his blade lost. Hardrada moved on, lifted his boot into the man's groin with tremendous force, then brought his own blade around in both hands and swung it mightily across the man's neck and severed the head.

The Scythian's body stood there, swaying, the blood spurting like fountains from the open neck, whilst the head rolled across the marble floor, sightless eyes staring towards the ceiling.

Hardrada, breathing like some great bull, had neither the strength nor the inclination to even look at it. He fell onto his knees, the sword clattering from his hands, and remained there, staring into the distance, the sweat pouring down his face, mouth open. He had come so close, closer than ever before, but now ... now it was done.

Ulf loomed next to him, arm around his shoulder. "Sweet Christ, Harald, I thought he had you there."

The great Viking managed a smile at his old friend then, as if remembering, he clutched at the wound on his arm and winced. "By God, this hurts. Get me some water, would you."

Ulf grunted and pulled round the water bottle he had found earlier, pulled out the cork, and splashed some of the luke-warm liquid over the cut on his friend's arm.

Hardrada clamped a hand over the wound, pressing hard. He clenched his teeth. "He was a hard bastard." He jutted his chin towards Crethus and Ulf turned to look, the headless corpse lying on the floor, a great plume of blood spreading out around where the head should have been.

"Well, he won't be bothering any of us now." Ulf laughed, put his hands under Hardrada's armpits and helped his friend back onto his feet. "Do you want me to look after Michael?"

Hardrada thought for a moment, took another glance at the wound, then returned his hand to it. Ulf was already ripping apart a strip from an old, sweat-stained bandana. Harald watched him, thinking again at how close he had come to death, how the world had, for a moment, moved away from him, as if he were no longer of any consequence. Perhaps it was some sort of warning, a signal that his days were numbered, that soon there would come one last battle, one final dance with death.

"When this is done," he said as Ulf soaked the strip of cloth and began to wrap it around Hardrada's arm, "I am returning to the Norse."

"That was always the plan." Ulf grunted as he pulled the cloth tight.

"I feel that this place holds nothing for us anymore. You, Haldor, me … we have come close to death this day."

"That's the nature of things, isn't it?" Ulf tied off the strip and stepped back to admire his handiwork. "When you flirt with death, Harald, sometimes it gets the better of you."

"I don't want to flirt around with it anymore, old friend. I want to take back what is mine, by right. I have lived under the control of others for too long. It is time I fulfilled my true destiny, and claim my birthright. To be king of the Norse, to rebuild our past glories, instil fear into the world once more at the very mention of our name." He flexed his arm once or twice and smiled. "Good job, old friend. Now, let me attend to the simple matter of Michael."

Varangian

The boat clattered against the side of the quay, and the crew rushed to secure it, the soldiers lending a hand to draw in the thick, heavy ropes. Nikolias was already jumping on board. He gave a cursory nod to the captain and went over to the small covered area, a sort of rectangular tent, that was situated towards the aft of the boat. To the side, two soldiers stood, ramrod straight at attention.

Nikolias coughed nervously. "My Lady, I am an officer of the *Tagimata,* come to escort you to the royal Palace where you shall—"

The entrance flap was abruptly pulled back and the Lady Zoe stepped out into the sunlight.

Nikolias gasped.

The woman, her face stunningly beautiful with high cheekbones, eyes so big you could dive into and disappear... lips... Nikolias found it difficult to breathe. He had heard the stories, of course, even seen her once or twice, but never like this, so close. Her head was covered in a gold bedecked headdress that fell down the sides of her face, gems of ruby, emerald and amethyst studded in between the precious metal plates. Her dress, which hung down to her feet, was the same, a richly embroidered robe of exquisite artistry, designed to accentuate her figure, and declare her as the royal personage that she was.

"Thank you," she said, reaching out her hand.

Nikolias took it, unable to tear his eyes from that face, and he gently led her from the boat. Other soldiers came to her aid, lifting her onto the quayside.

"My Lady," said Nikolias, at last finding the strength to speak, "It was the General's desire that you return to the Palace, to await him there."

"There is no need," she said unabashed. "I am prepared. I shall make my way to the Forum, present myself to the people."

"My Lady, there has been fighting. The dead litter the streets. It is too dreadful for you to look upon."

"Dead?" Zoe let the words slip away into the air. Her eyes became moist, "Is that what it has led to, Michael's misrule, the deaths of my people?" For a moment, her eyes clouded over with some distant thought, perhaps images playing out in her head of citizens butchered, bloated bodies rotting in the sunlight.

Nikolias stood, as if in a trance, gazing. Waiting. She blinked once or twice and pulled herself up straight, regaining her regal composure. "So be it. Better for the people to see me amidst their suffering. Lead me to the Forum, Captain."

"My Lady, I must ask you to—"

She held up her hand, cut him off mid-sentence. "I have spoken, Captain. Escort me, now please."

Nikolias bowed, giving way to her authority. He stepped back, gave a signal for the soldiers to fall in behind, and slowly the small entourage moved away and began its journey towards the inner city.

* * *

Harald stepped outside, Ulf beside him. In Ulf's grasp was Michael, wailing like some stricken banshee. Disgusted, Ulf flung the broken and shattered former emperor to the dirt, where he writhed and floundered, a drowning man, great trails of black blood running down each cheek, holes like coals where his eyes had once been.

Maniakes stood a little way off, flanked by thirty or more armoured foot soldiers, spears readied. He was grinning as he pulled off his richly decorated helmet, blew out a breath, and came forward. "Ah, Michael." He looked down at the wounded man, squirming in the ground, hands pressed against the horrific wounds in his face, pain and terror now his masters. Maniakes looked up at Hardrada. "You have fulfilled your part of the deal. Therefore," he turned and signalled to the soldiers close by. They parted and two slaves struggled forward, carrying between them a chest. Bringing up the rear was Haldor, looking a little sheepish as he eyed the soldiers arrayed all around.

The slaves settled the chest at Hardrada's feet then scurried off.

"Is that all of it?" asked the Viking.

"As far as I am aware. That was what Orphano had hidden away. You can take it, and leave. You understand? Leave."

"My intention anyway."

Maniakes bowed his head, "We always were of the same mind, old friend. I discovered that back in Sicilia."

"Aye, and I discovered much about you." Hardrada looked down at Michael, whose cries had now become nothing more than a constant, rumbling groan. "What will happen to him?"

Maniakes shrugged. "I shall leave that to the Lady Zoe. She will be here soon, restored as Empress. We shall wipe away Michael's pathetic attempt to reign, and begin the rebuilding of our empire."

"With you at the helm?"

"Not at all. I'm sick of politics, never had the stomach for it. No, I shall go back to what I do best – soldiering. I shall leave all the intrigue of government to those who know it best. Orphano, and his brother." He wiped the back of his hand across his brow and settled his helmet back over his head. "I have a few loose ends to tie up, but nothing that need concern you. " He frowned. "What happened to your arm?"

"I had to deal with someone, before I saw to Michael."

"Who was it?"

"The Scythian commander, Crethus."

Maniakes paused in tightening up his chin strap. "Ah. Well, if I were you, I would best make haste your departure – the Lady Zoe was particularly fond of that gentleman. I wouldn't like to vouch for your safety once she finds out what you've done."

"Which, of course, you will take great pleasure in informing her."

The General screwed up his eyes. "Like you said, you have discovered much about me."

Hardrada shook his head, no longer possessing the strength to converse any more. He nodded to Ulf who, in turn, waved Haldor over. Together, the two men lifted up the chest and Hardrada led them away, across the open area towards the Lion Gate. None of them looked back, but all of them could feel the General's eyes boring into them as they went.

Past the gates, Hardrada saw the many soldiers piling up the dead into heaps, Scythians in one pile, Varangians and citizens in another.

Over on the steps of the Forum, Rufus. The seasoned Viking caught sight of him and came across at a run.

"All is well?"

"Aye," answered Hardrada, clapping his old friend on the arm. "We have their promise, given by Alexius, that you will remain unharmed. Reinstated, I would hope."

Rufus nodded. "I will offer these mercenaries the chance to enter into the Royal Varangian bodyguard." His smile faded. "But what of you? Will you not stay and lead us, as you have always done?"

"No, old friend." He nodded at his two companions, who had put the heavy chest down whilst he spoke. Both of them appeared slightly annoyed. No doubt they felt somewhat put upon, having fought and saved Hardrada, only to be rewarded by becoming pack-mules. "Don't look so pissed off, lads. We'll soon be gone from this place."

Rufus sighed. "So, you mean to leave?"

"Aye. We are going home. Why not join us? I could use a good man like you. Someone I can trust."

"Ungrateful bastard," spat Ulf.

Hardrada laughed, slapped Rufus's arm again. "Good luck, Rufus. Stay well."

Rufus nodded, but didn't speak. Instead, he merely placed his own hand over Hardrada's and squeezed it before turning away to return to his men.

Hardrada looked askance at Ulf. "Don't be so churlish, you old fart. We'll make our way over to the port, find a ship, and get the hell out of here."

Ulf shook his head, raised his eyes, then said to Haldor, "Come on, seems like his majesty doesn't want to get his hands dirty." Together they lifted up the chest and continued on their way.

Hardrada however, remained where he was. The tension knotted his stomach and his hand closed around the hilt of his sword.

Andreas stood there, some way off, his face blank, eyes like beads, staring without blinking. "I shall find you, Hardrada. And when I do, I will kill you."

"Many have tried," said Hardrada. "Many that did now lie cold in the earth."

A smile, thin and without humour, spread across the young soldier's face. "You can say hello to them, when you join them. For I will not fail, Hardrada. I promise you that."

The air turned chill and Hardrada started as a raven flew out from the rafters of a nearby building and veered off across the sky. He watched it as it disappeared into the blue, then turned his eyes back to face Andreas.

Except that Andreas was no longer there.

Hardrada caught his breath, throat becoming dry. He allowed the grip on his sword hilt to weaken and when he turned to go, he looked at his hands and noticed that they were shaking.

Words, he said to himself, mere words. Nothing to be afraid of, not when he had faced so many dangers, so many threats, conquering them all, prevailing.

And yet, coming from Andreas, those words held more truth and more promise than any Hardrada had ever know, All that remained, was when they would be fulfilled.

Some Twenty-Four Years Later

Near the River Ouse in what is now Yorkshire, England.

They had put a great distance between themselves and the Viking force back at Fulford. Now, rolling fields had given way to cultivated farmland and soon they came across a lonely homestead; a few buildings scattered haphazardly about an uneven square of rutted, broken earth. The buildings were poor, dilapidated and as the warriors moved cautiously forward, men appeared, grasping pitchforks and scythes. Their eyes were wide with fear, their bodies trembling, but it was obvious that they were prepared to fight, and die if need be, to defend their home.

Hereward held up his hand, "Hold, friends. We are Saxons, as yourselves. All we ask is some water, perhaps a little bread."

"Where have you come from?" asked a gnarled, snow-haired little man, stepping half-a-pace forward.

"Fulford," said Morcar. He shook himself at the mention of the name, as if already its resonance rekindled the horrors of what had occurred there.

"I have to go back," said a voice.

They all looked up as the foreigner amongst them turned his face back the way they had come.

"That way leads only to death," said Hereward. "You will have your chance, once we get word to Lord Harold. He will gather an army, the like of which has never been seen, and we will crush those Viking scum once and for all."

The foreigner looked again at Hereward. "I have vowed to kill him, and I will not fail."

"No, I don't think you will," grinned Hereward. "But for now, you must have just a little more patience."

The foreigner pressed his lips together and thought for a moment. Then, at last, he let his shoulders relax. "Very well. I will do as you say, but when next we meet…" He gripped his sword. "I have waited over twenty years, I can wait just a little longer."

"By God, you breathe fire, that is for sure," said one of the other housecarles. "What did Hardrada ever do to you?"

"Enough," the man replied. "Soon, I will draw a blind over it all."

"What is your name, friend?" asked Hereward.

The foreigner looked across at the strapping Saxon earl, and pulled in a breath. "My name," he said, "is Andreas."

Dear reader,

We hope you enjoyed reading *Varangian*. Please take a moment to leave a review, even if it's a short one. Your opinion is important to us.

Discover more books by Stuart G. Yates at
https://www.nextchapter.pub/authors/stuart-g-yates

Want to know when one of our books is free or discounted? Join the newsletter at
http://eepurl.com/bqqB3H

Best regards,
Stuart G. Yates and the Next Chapter Team

The story continues in:

King of the Norse

To read the first chapter for free, please head to:
https://www.nextchapter.pub/books/king-of-the-norse

About the Author

Stuart G Yates is the author of a eclectic mix of books, ranging from historical fiction through to contemporary thrillers. Hailing from Merseyside, he now lives in southern Spain, where he teaches history, but dreams of living on a narrowboat in Shropshire.

Books by the Author

- Varangian
- King of the Norse (Varangian Book 2)
- Origins (Varangian Book 3)
- Unflinching
- In the Blood (Unflinching 2)
- To Die in Glory (Unflinching 3)
- A Reckoning (Unflinching 4)
- Blood Rise (Unflinching 5)
- Bloody Reasons (To Kill A Man 1)
- Pursuers Unto Death (To Kill A Man 2)

- A Man Dead (To Kill A Man 3)
- Lament for Darley Dene
- Minus Life
- Ogre's Lament
- The Pawnbroker
- Sallowed Blood
- The Sandman Cometh
- Splintered Ice
- Tears In The Fabric of Time
- The Tide of Terror

Printed in Great Britain
by Amazon